| DATE DUE | | | |
|---|---|---|---|
| | | | |
| | | | |
| | | | |
| | | | |
| | | | |
| | | | |
| | | | |
| | | | |
| | | | |
| | | | |
| | | | |
| | | | |

# THE VELVET DOUBLET

# Books by James Street

JAMES STREET

# The
# Velvet Doublet

GARDEN CITY, NEW YORK

DOUBLEDAY & COMPANY, INC.

1953

813.52
St8v

With the exception of actual historical personages identified as such, the characters are entirely the product of the
author's imagination and have no relation to any person
in real life.

30727

aug. 1953

*For* D. A. ELLIOTT

THE POSTHUMOUS PAPERS of *Juan Rodrigo Bermejo* of *Triana*, a Voyager with *Christopher Columbus* to the New Lands beyond the *Ocean Sea* anno Domini MCCCCLXXXXII and cunningly misused by the *Great Explorer*; this *Bermejo* being the avenger who, under duress, changed his name to *Mudarra* and suffered the calumny of bastardry to vindicate himself and punish his Oppressors; and his singular Adventure being entitled *The Velvet Doublet*, inasmuch as an historic raiment entangled his Destiny and thereby altered the Lives and Fortunes of divers *Notable Persons*.

THE VELVET DOUBLET

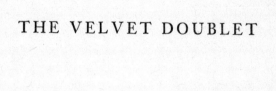

THE VELVET DOUBLET

*I*N THE NAME OF GOD, THE CLEMENT, THE MERCIFUL!

I, an Andalusian, born Juan Rodrigo Bermejo of Triana, now known as Mudarra the bastard Moor, was the first Christian to sight the New World, although my own captain, the niggardly Christopher Columbus, tried to cheat me of that honor and did cheat me of his promised rewards: the Queen's pension and a velvet doublet.

Thus my vengeance was foretold, as no glib Genoese dreamer can trod Andalusian pride without payment for his transgression.

And now, if my vengeance is an abomination to any man, brother or stranger, I caution him that I alone must be held to account and that no censure will be passed to Mita, for I will avenge her against any mocking tongue or accusing finger, and may God witness this vow.

Mita's temptation was the sin of Eden, which was sweet Paradise, and of Eve, who was Earth's own mother; and Mita loved me as only a woman of stature can love a prodigal, as pure gold clings to vile dross.

Therefore, to share my story, these indivisible truths you will remember: that Mita bargained her heart for her soul, and that I saw it first—the white cliffs of San Salvador, the moon waning behind the lonely isle and the night dying pale. That voice that called "Land! Land!" was my voice, and no man born of woman will rob my life of that rapturous moment, even though he be Grand Admiral of the Ocean Sea, heavy-laden with honors, who stooped to cheat one of his own sailors because I dared demand my crumb at the feast of the mighty.

He, Christopher Columbus (Colombo, Colomo, Colom, Colonna,

Colon, or whatever his true name may be), Viceroy of all strange lands he found, to have and to hold in perpetuity, bargainer with Crowns, breaker of vows—he cost me my name, my country, and my faith, and yet his deceit brought Mita to me and bound us together with chains of oppression.

Oh, Mita, my beloved. Forget the years and remember the minutes. Forgive my vanity and pride, for these are the burdens of men. Forgive my lust, my faithlessness, and pray for me in Paradise.

In the name of God, the Compassionate, the Merciful!

Say: *He is God alone:*

*God the eternal,*

*He begetteth not, and He is not begotten,*

*And there is none like unto Him.*


I was born in Triana in 1469, the year Isabel of Castile, the Catholic, was married to Ferdinand of Aragon, the perfidious trickster who was not worthy to tend the twelve white mules that Andalusia sent to them as a wedding gift.

This marriage ended seven hundred years of separation between Castile and Aragon and united most of Spain under the brotherhood banner of the holy Cross and the unholy Sword, as though Cross and Sword can be brothers.

Andalusia, naturally by choice, long had been loyal to Castile and thereby Isabel was our Queen and a fie for all the royal diddlings. Our lives and our sacred honor belonged to her, but Ferdinand was never our King, only her consort, the jack to stand for the filly and produce a line to rule from the Pillars of Hercules, in our own Andalusia, to the Pyrenees.

The struggle in Spain between Christendom and Islam was coming to a close after seven hundred years of bloodletting in the name of God and of Allah, who are one and the same in Fatherhood. Only Granada remained in the hands of the Moors and was the one kingdom in the west of Europe where the muezzins still called the Faithful to face Mecca five times each day and prayerfully submit to the will of God.

However, the scimitar of Islam was on guard in all of North Africa and around to Asia's shores of the Mediterranean, Mare Nostrum, which was Our Sea because Andalusia stood sentry at Gibraltar, where the Pillars of Hercules held back the wrath and mystery of the Ocean Sea, stretching westward to the Unknown.

...man Empire had been dead sixteen years, rasping its last ... fall of Constantinople to the Turks. And now all of ...urtain and there was no trade with Cathay or ...oble backs, no spices for pickling onions, ... the usurers' coffers, and no aloes[1] to purge me... ...sweeten the humors that determine our temperaments.

Thus ...as when I was born; Islam's sword between Christendom and the riches of the East, the roadstead of Palos empty, and brave Andalusian sails furled and moulding. Europe's belly wailed for bread while the Holy Orders harangued for souls and fought and schemed among themselves for power. Faggots lit manifold stakes for the trials by fire, and trumpets of hungry kings blared for armies to march again, and the soldiers died like maggots in the dung heap of a summer drought. The long, bleak night was upon us and Europe held out her bony arms to the East, waiting for the grace of God to open the treasure chest once more.

But a few men—only a few—turned their backs to the East and stared westward toward the Ocean Sea and the Unknown; and wondered. The sun came six hours out of the east and went six hours into the west. What lay where the sun sank? How big was the world? Round, to be sure. No man even of meager learning questioned the shape of the earth. It was round like a ball or a pear. Then if India were to the east, it also was to the west. But what lay between here and there? And how far?

The living lights in all Spain were not the holy fires of the zealots who burned flesh to purify souls into heaven, but the feeble candles of the despised visionaries who traced lines on their maps, rubbed them out, and traced again, resting their eyes by looking up at the stars, and always west. Impractical dreamers who had never sailed a ship and yet they dared counsel sailors. Scorned by the multitude that thought yesterday was better than today because they had lived through yesterday, these few watched the cold Polar Star due north and the sun going down warm in the west, and asked questions, and wondered.

Such a man was my father, Vicente Bermejo, a dealer in pottery and sundries and a confidant of sailors. He was a hidalgo, the son of a

---

[1] In the Middle Ages, the term "aloes" was applied to many of the succulent plants, including cacti, which were sources for cathartics, poisons, and emetics.

Goth, and that deserving title testified to his gentry. He had never been to sea, but his ears were longer than his tongue and his fancy was larger than his purse. He taught me early that a lie can grow on truth like a barren limb on a fruitful olive tree, and that dreams and reality come from the same mind. A great man was my father. Peace to his tortured soul.

My mother was Sereni Betancour, also gently born and very pious, a frail saint who died soon after my advent, thereby being spared, through the clemency of God, the travail of her loved ones.

Our home in Triana was in the poorer section, I confess, but my father's shop was across the Guadalquivir River in Seville and, as is known to all except the most ignorant, Seville is the queen city of Andalusia, and Andalusia is the brightest gem in the Spanish crown.

With the passing of my mother, my care was given into the hands of my Aunt Ronda Bermejo, a woman of excellence and judgment, although a spinster whose betrothed was lost at sea while in Portuguese service on a voyage of exploration down the coast of Africa. Her home was in Lepe, down near the sea, where were bred the sailors who took Andalusia's caravels out of the roadstead of Palos and hired their skill to any ship's master who met their demands of 5000 maravedis[2] a month, onions once daily, and salted flour for their bread.

A woman of mettle was my Aunt Ronda, but with a clapping tongue and an idolatry of orderliness that vexed my father, who was one to leave a candle burning while he napped, or a window open at night. She held to her grandmother's ways, that a boy should be bathed all over four times a year, at the beginning of each season, and that a reddened bottom was evidence of discipline. I splashed almost every day in the river during the warm months, but that was not tallied in her ledger of ablutions. She scolded me often that I was spoiled and scolded my father that he was responsible.

She tyrannized the tutors my father hired to help him and her teach me my letters in Latin and Spanish, and the sums of figures, and went into a veritable tizzy on my Saint's Day when my father gave me a blue doublet of Italian velvet. No stripling of my acquaintance had such a prize and it set me apart from the others and made me feel

[2]One copper maravedi roughly was equivalent to one seventh of a cent in pre-1934 American currency. Hence an ordinary seaman's pay was about seven dollars a month in pre-1934 American money.

14

pleased with my lot, and of kindly disposition toward my fellow seedlings who were not as fortunate as I.

Of course, blinded by my own splendor, I did not notice that my father's doublet, tight-fitting from his shoulders to his waist and with loose sleeves, was frayed at the collar and patched at the cuffs. Aunt Ronda complained that my beautiful doublet was a waste, and that waste is sinful. I pouted my dejection, and it was not that I felt sad but because I knew my behavior would arouse my father's sympathy and thus protect my own interest.

"He will outgrow it in a year," Aunt Ronda lectured. "It is vanity, and vanity in men brings more tears to our sweet Savior's eyes than the lust in men." She tossed her head in annoyance. "A velvet doublet for a boy not long from his wet straw; and this family with only goose grease for our chick-peas, like the Jews."

I resented her forthrightness for I was in my fifteenth year and long past the habits of my childhood, and the doublet was a gift from my father and of no concern to her.

"We will discuss it later," my father told her.

They sent me to bed immediately after we said our Pater Noster in unison and sang our nightly Salve Regina, and they adjourned themselves to the first room of our house, where a Crucifix hung on the wall by my father's couch to ward off the Death Angel.

I tiptoed from my pallet, a childish transgression and unseeming curiosity for a youth of my years and dignity, and stood behind the Moorish drapes in the alcove and heard all they said. I hoped my father would box her ears, as she often did mine in witless offense to my personal esteem, or at least raise his voice in anger at her and in praise of me. But he was mild.

"Now, Ronda, sister of mine." He put his hand tenderly on her shoulder. "My seed has sprouted and I will tend my sapling in my own way."

She shook off his hand and pulled her shawl high on her shoulders. "You will send him to the galleys or the stake, and mind my words, Vicente Bermejo. That imp needs a strong hand. Every colt needs a halter."

"Now, Ronda——"

"Did he not stare impudently into my face when I talked to him this morning, instead of lowering his eyes in shame as a boy should?

Did he not? Answer me *that*." She flounced across the room and sat on a bench.

"Now, now——" My father was scratching his head, a superior head of tar-black hair that he oiled once a week.

"And did he not say his prayers to the Blessed Virgin so rapidly last night that even She could not understand him, though She be the sweet Queen of Heaven?" Aunt Ronda made a quick sign of the Cross and bowed her head as though asking mercy for me. I itched to call out that she had fallen asleep the week before while saying the twenty-five Hail Marys that were her bedtime prayers.

"Do you want him to be a Friar Minor?" My father's gentle patience was on trial. "A Franciscan zealot to prattle Latin he does not understand and cry for the blood of heretics?"

Aunt Ronda was shocked and her wits were stunned momentarily. To utter criticism of the Franciscans was sinful in her eyes because she held that order the most noble of all. "Blasphemy!" She hissed the accusation. "I shall pray for your soul."

"Never fret yourself about my soul." His words came harsh, as she had touched him where the quick was raw. "It is time for a decision about my son. I will send him to the Dominicans."

She drew back as though a spider had lunged at her, as though an evil djinni had swirled out of the night. "Black Friars!" The words slipped out and she clamped her hands over her mouth, her eyes wide as she stared at her brother. Aunt Ronda held the Dominicans in dread, for they, even more than the Franciscans, were masters of the Inquisition. Also, her loyalty to the Gray Friars of St. Francis made her suspect of the rival order. "Ah-h-h, brother of mine——" She found her voice and began wheedling. "You are amusing yourself at cost to me. Your wit was ever sharp, with two edges."

"I am serious." He sat down on his couch and tugged at his short, billowing breeches, which were gathered high above his knees in the manner of the French. "The boy goes to the Dominicans."

I was neither elated nor dejected. If I was to go to school, I would as leave the Black Friars pound my skull as the Gray Friars. Remember I had tasted of the cup of knowledge from the hands of tutors and my own family and if I was to drink deeply from the goblet, then so be it. Remember, too, that this is being recounted through the intelligence of my manhood, but as I saw it as a youth.

She crossed the room and sat by my father and, having sensed the futility of temper, she ventured upon persuasion. "The Friars Preachers——" She was dignifying the Dominicans by their lofty mission, and rested her hand on her brother's arm as she talked. "They are more zealous than the Franciscans."

"And better teachers," he said.

"They are not as strong in the Faith and they mumble the devil's words."

"Careful, sister of mine. The windows are ears and the wind has tongue."

"No one can hear us, Vicente. Do not send him to the Dominicans. I will meddle no more. He is a good boy. They will stuff his head."

"With knowledge," my father said.

"With wild ideas and heresy." Her tone was tremulous and she was frightened, not for herself but for me. "They wrangle over the size of the world as though God had not already set the limits of His firmaments. They talk of new lands and new seas, and waste candles over maps instead of burning the holy wax to the sainted motherhood of the sweet Virgin."

"Now—now, Ronda." My father patted her hand. "He goes to the Dominicans."

"No, Vicente. Not Rodrigo. I took him from his mother's breast and held him here." She put her hands on her own breast and looked up at the Crucifix. "School is not good for God's creatures unless they take Holy Orders. But if he must study, then let him go back to Lepe with me. To the Franciscans. They are very learned."

He would not be moved. "The Dominicans, Ronda. Benjamin Marino is coming here to lecture to them."

That was the first time I heard his name. Benjamin Marino. It sounded strange and piqued my interest even then.

My aunt's face paled and twisted as though she was to be seized or stricken. "He is a Jew." She said it and crossed herself at the same moment.

"He is the best map maker in the world," my father said.

"But he is a Jew, Vicente. My confessor has told me of him. He practices all the rites and sips Christian blood at Atonement."

"Nonsense!" He smiled for the first time that evening and his strong face became gentle. "Benjamin Marino has been heard at the University of Salamanca and he is coming to Seville to impart his knowledge to the Dominicans. He often has lectured to the Franciscans. He

17

is no ogre, sweet sister. Only a man of learning and I want my son to hear him."

"But he is a Jew." She clung to the indictment.

"So was our Savior," my father said and got up, thereby giving notice that his part of the conversation was closed. He lit a candle and put it on the table and began reading his precious books, the fanciful tales of Sir John Mandeville and Pierre d'Ailly's *Imago Mundi*.

Aunt Ronda watched him, the candlelight on his face, and then walked to him and rested her hands on his shoulders. "A father knows best for his son," she said in grievous resignation. "I will return to Lepe."

My father pushed aside his books and stroked her hands. "You are welcome here. This is your home."

"Lepe is my home. From there sailed the love for whom I might have borne a son of my own. I will go back to Lepe."

A sadness came over me, and I was lonely for the first time in my memory, and slipped back to my pallet. My beautiful doublet was on a bench near by and I felt it, the soft velvet sensuous and pleasing to my fingers. I did not hurry my prayers this time but whispered each word distinctly so the blessed Queen of Heaven could understand them, and I said them for Aunt Ronda—ten Hail Marys and five Our Fathers.

Down on the river that flowed behind our house and on to the Ocean Sea the bared masts of the caravels were naked to the moon, swaying like the tall salt grass in the marshes of the Guadalquivir; and the sailors, riotous in wine, bellowed the chantey that was my lullaby:

> From the far region of Calcutta
> With toil and strick attention to business
> We have brought here many sorts of spices.

It was drunken mockery, for Calcutta was behind Islam's barred gate.

I heard Aunt Ronda go to her couch, sighing her bulk into comfort, and soon the house was still and the water front too, save for the ships' lookouts, who called the watch and the hour as the sandglasses were turned.

> One glass is gone and another flows;
> It all shall run down if God so wills.

I pulled my cherished doublet to my pillow and sank into troubled

18

sleep, haunted by lean ghosts of Black Friars and sailless masts on the Unknown Sea, where the sun hissed down into the West, and nothing.

My father waked me by tugging at my ear and tousing my hair, and Aunt Ronda came in smiling the morning's greetings, and I wondered if all the events of the night had been a dream. She sent my father out for honey and paced me through five Hail Marys, then waited for me to dress.

I was embarrassed by her presence, for my manliness was obliterating the last traces of my childhood and gave evidence of my puberty. I reached for my old jacket, intending not to flaunt my doublet, but she chuckled her disapproval.

"Put it on," she commanded. "Your teeth grind your own food now and the seeds of your maturity gather in your loins."

She laughed and slipped the doublet over my head and tugged it tight across my chest and middle, herself feeling the lovely velvet. Then she wet the tip of her forefinger and rubbed behind my ears. "You have our family's ears, Rodrigo. Not quite as large as a mule's." Again she laughed and kissed my cheek. "But you have your mother's hair. Thick and brown. And her bright blue eyes. Ah-h-h. They are not the black eyes of Andalusia. Your mother's family came from Leon and there were wild Irish in Leon; blue eyes and strong backs and no brains. I have seen Irish sailors in Lepe. I am going back to Lepe."

"Back to Lepe?" I pretended surprise. "You must not leave us."

"A doublet and your last teeth." She put her hand under my chin and looked at me. "You know your prayers and already a goat fuzz is springing from your chin. You do not need me longer. I will go back home."

I am glad I cried. Women like tears, as I was to learn, and mine overflowed and she was pleased and hugged me, and we both cried. I wiped her tears on the soft cuff of my doublet.

We had honey cakes for breakfast, and she stayed close to me all that day and the next, and on the third she boarded a barge for the trip down-river to Cadiz, then up the coast and across the sand bar that made Palos a port, and to Lepe. The very names stirred me: Playa de Castilla, Rio Tinto, Huelva, Palos, and the Ocean Sea.

The pilot of her barge was Martin Alonso Pinzon, whose eyes were red-rimmed from the night's wine and whose straight black hair hung close over his ears and almost to his shoulders. This Pinzon knew my father and called to him as we approached his berth. "Your saint's blessing, Vicente. I will see to your sister's well-being and deliver her in Lepe."

My father hurried forward and embraced him. "Pinzon! You on barges! A caravel master on a floating pig? You are a deep-water man——"

"You take what you get these days," Pinzon replied. "Palos is as quiet as my bridal chamber. The East is blocked and the West unknown, and no man dares sail full into the Ocean Sea. Our ships rot for need of salt in our guts."

They talked casually of trade and voyages, and at mention of new routes Pinzon scowled and scratched himself, a most unseeming gesture in the presence of my aunt. "It takes money, Vicente. I have some, but not enough for an expedition. And the Queen is as stingy with ducats as she is liberal with prayers."

"Mind you." My father held up his long finger. "Portugal will steal Spanish wind. They will not wait forever, not the Portuguese——"

"Mind yourself, merchant!" Pinzon's dark face clouded. "I know all you say, and more. Even today a mysterious pilot is at Portugal's court, asking ships for a voyage westward to the Indies. He says he has God's ear and good maps."

"Who is he? Andalusian?"

"God knows." Pinzon turned to his duties and two lines were cast off. "Some say an adventurer from Genoa. Others a stargazer from Galicia. God knows." He leaped onto his barge and waved farewell, and Aunt Ronda was beside him.

We watched the barge float out into the river, the sailors at poles, and then the channel took it. The helmsman clung to the great tiller and Pinzon waved again.

My father and I were alone. The year was 1484 in the temporal reign of Isabel and Ferdinand, and the eternal reign of God.

*In saecula saeculorum!*

# CHAPTER 2

THE LITTLE DOG ROSE OF ANDALUSIA WAS FADING AND BIRDS were winging from the reeds along the Guadalquivir River that autumn morning when my father and I walked from Triana across the bridge into Seville for my submission to the Friars Preachers of St. Dominic, the learned and grim order of the midnight office, of perpetual abstinence from meat, of poverty, and long fasts.

I gave all appearance of befitting passiveness and pious meditation, but, and may God forgive me, my mind was on worldly things: the ships in port, the smell of hemp and tar, an orange peel floating down the river, and the heat prickling under my doublet.

The streets were well-nigh deserted, for it was Faggot Day and two heretics were being burned in the first meadow beyond the city. The populace was there and that wisp of smoke to the south was the heraldry of old Quemadero, as the stake was called. I did not know the names of the doomed and, the truth pulls like the deep roots of a rotten tooth, I did not care.

Triana, squirming in squalor and stench, was my home but Seville was my city, and my heart rejoiced my pride as we walked her streets; my father tall and of long strides and I in the manly elegance of my velvet doublet. The court of the saintly Isabel and the rapacious Ferdinand was in Seville that season, she to pester her mind with details of the latest Inquisition while he studied the Moorish defenses over in Granada and schemed against his turbulent nobles for the autocratic centralization of his realm.

But royalty meant nothing to me that day. The city was my queen, her age reckoned in centuries and her strength in her rivers, the Guadalquivir that tides that far inland, fifty-four miles from Cadiz and the sea,

21

and the tributaries that feed her and send her flooding almost every year.

My city was guarding her rivers in the days of the prophets and long before the Miracle of Jesus. Here came Phoenicians for pottery clay, then Greeks for cork, and Caesar with his legions. We gave the Emperors Hadrian and Trajan to Rome, and Rome gave us the Cross; and Seville unsheathed the sword that drove the Moors from Andalusia more than two hundred years ago.

The Alcazar brooded its memories that morning as my father and I walked near the wall that had enclosed it until Christian iron breached the rampart to the glory of Spain's own St. James and the renown of Seville's patron saints, Justa and Rufiana, who were potters like my father. The minaret of San Marcos needled into the sky and workmen mortised the cathedral to Santa Maria de la Sede. They had been working on it for eighty years and the nave was not yet complete. Already, however, it was the most beautiful cathedral in the world. Perhaps not as large as St. Peter's, but unquestionably superior.

The monastery where the friars met in college was between the cathedral and the river and was under the priorate of Alphonso de Hojeda, who bravely had opposed Isabel's Inquisition on the issue of whether Rome, whom he supported, or the Spanish Crown would name the Inquisitors. Isabel had won, as usual, and now Alphonso de Hojeda was daring have Benjamin Marino, an orthodox Jew, lecture to the college on geography and map making. There was talk that the prior himself was a converso, a Jew converted to the Cross.

My father turned down an alley where sewage drained into the cobblestones and tugged a bell rope at the side door of the monastery. There was no answer and my father yanked the rope impatiently, for nothing daunted my father.

The friar who opened the door, in his own good time, was as gaunt as a caravel's mainmast with bonnets and course furled tight, and his breath reeked of his breakfast onions and wine. Over his greasy white habit was the black mantle that gave his order the name of Black Friars, and his right hand was full of dried beans that he tossed into his mouth, one at a time, and chewed with a revolving motion of his long jaw.

My father presented himself and said with firm pride, "This is my son Rodrigo about whom I spake to the prior, my esteemed friend Alphonso de Hojeda of holy works and envious intellect."

22

The friar turned his face to me and I saw that his gray eyes were flecked with yellow and that the veins coursed blue under his poxed skin. For a long time he looked at me and I stood straight and resolute. Then he returned his melancholy gaze to my father and mumbled, "I am Juan Ruiz de Medina."

My courage wavered for an instant and there was a quick nauseous surge in my stomach. Juan Ruiz de Medina! This specter was one of the Queen's Inquisitors, as powerful in Seville as the inscrutable Torquemada and even more punctilious.

He gave us his back and led the way into the monastery, his bare feet trudging the worn stones of the cloister. My father patted my shoulder in reassurance and we followed him to a chamber that was bare except for a bench, a table, and a Crucifix. Friar Juan sat down and indicated that my father was to sit beside him. I remained standing and gulped my heart back into place, and folded my arms behind me, my nails biting into the sweaty palms of my hands.

"Who is your patron saint?" They were his first words and my astonishment seized my tongue and bound it, for his tone was as soft as the velvet of my doublet, as melodious as vesper bells.

"St. Christopher," I stammered, and the words brought back my composure.

Friar Juan stroked his chin and the stubble rasped under his fingers. "What of this St. Christopher?"

"A martyr," I said with alacrity and was proud of my knowledge. "He bore the Babe across a bridgeless river and is the patron of ferrymen."

"Naturally you know your saint's breviary." He tossed a bean into his mouth, crunching the morsel as he looked up at the ceiling where the damp oozed from the stones.

I was filled with trepidation and my pride melted, but I found comfort that my father was near. "Not yet," I confessed.

The friar's tone changed into stringent austerity and his face was hard. "Then speak not his name for mortal ears until you have informed yourself. See to it!"

My father's head came up quickly as though he would speak out, but he did not and the Dominican gave him no heed whatsoever. Instead he peered at me and demanded, "Your Latin?"

"It is no credit to my father's efforts." A rebellious urge was upon

23

me and there was no humility in my demeanor. "Or to the prayerful endeavor of my Aunt Ronda Bermejo of Lepe."

Father Juan grunted and spat out the hull of a bean, and he began speaking Latin with diction so simple and distinct that, to my happy relief, I understood every word. "How long is a league?"

"Four Italian nautical miles." I answered in kind, stumbling through the sentence.

Again he grunted and I knew it not for disdain or pleasure, but my father was smiling and thereby nourished my confidence.

"Name the North Star." Friar Juan glared at me like a hungry falcon.

"Polaris." I did not hesitate.

"And the guards?"

"The Little Bear, Father. Kochab is the brightest."

He stopped chewing and his lips were thin and were wrinkled at the corners. Then he closed his hand into a gnarled fist and asked, "How many beans have I in my hand?"

"I do not know, for I cannot see."

His stare was as penetrating as the needle of conscience, as sharp as the briers of remorse. "Take off the doublet."

My father forsook his silence at that moment and spoke out clearly. "The doublet is a gift from me."

"Now it will be a gift to God." Friar Juan Ruiz de Medina delivered his will, nodding his head in confirmation of his judgment. "It will be sold and the money will be given to the Crown for the wars against the infidels in Granada."

Slowly my father got to his feet and addressed his protest to the Inquisitor without fear or trembling. "Are the orders of the gentle Dominic so harsh that a boy is forbidden a gift from his own father? May not a father express his pride in his only son by clothing him in raiment of merit?" He stood tall and valiant as behooves an Andalusian. "Am I a lesser breed than Abraham who loved Isaac?"

The friar arose also and was taller even than my father. "Vicente Bermejo! You have brought your son to us from breast and bed. Our knowledge we will share with him, *Dei gratia*, but we will not moderate our discipline one cedilla." He looked down at me like a vulture from a lofty limb, his long neck stretched and his repellent eyes smoldering the fire of his zeal. "*Vincit qui se vincit!* Your doublet is vanity. Take it off!"

24

I looked to my father for guidance and he turned his face from me, and mortification and loneliness tugged my heart. I jerked the doublet over my head to hide the tears that betrayed my manliness, and when the anguish had seeped from my eyes into my soul I removed the doublet and handed it to my tormentor. My shoulders were naked and I shivered in the damp gloom of my prison.

Friar Juan hurled my proudest possession into a corner as though it were filth and gave himself to bitter eloquence. "Raiment of pride and arrogance! Scourge your soul, Christian seed, instead of pampering your flesh with soft garments. Seek not to exalt yourself above your fellows." He rested his hands on the table and enjoined me to contrition. "Never again, Rodrigo of Triana, will you wear a velvet doublet until you have earned it by homage to God or charity to your brothers. This day your back will be bare. Now come with me."

I embraced my father and yearned to dry his tears on the fulfillment of his hopes for me, and then I followed my mentor down a long passage to my chamber, a musty cubicle of one tiny window, a straw pile in a corner, and a bench.

The friar nudged the straw with his foot and examined it for lice and other vermin. It was clean and he nodded approval. "Hereafter you will see to your own straw," he said. "And now your shoes, little brother."

I took off my sandals and gave them to him. "Meditation is my first instruction." His voice was gentle, even soothing. "You will close your door when I am gone, for never will I close a door to any man." He looked at me as though he might speak further, and then a scowl passed his face and he turned and went away.

The door closed easily and I sat on the bench, and the chill damp of the floor seeped into my bare feet. I slipped to my knees in prayer, but the words were hollow and surely not pleasing to the Mistress of Heaven, whose intervention I implored, or to my own St. Christopher, whose advocacy I beseeched.

Soon my knees were raw and the blue cold pimpled my flesh, driving all moods of prayer from my mind. No one could see me, so I got to my feet and walked to the window, and looked at the sunlight. The smoke of old Quemadero had vanished and the triumph of the faggots was done. The river below was in bloom with ships. I know not how long I stood at the window, telling my misery in doleful count. There was no food and I was hungry; and no warmth and I was cold.

25

The day passed and my belly was gnawing when Friar Juan opened the door and found me at the window. I expected a rebuke, but he looked at me and then at the window and said, "There are men who meditate by watching the sky. Others the ground. Always lift up thine eyes, little brother."

He had two books under his arm, and one he laid on the bench and the other he handed to me. Its thin parchment was bound in soft leather and the feel was like the velvet of my lost doublet. "My breviary," he said. "I copied the words while a student in Rome. This jewel will open to you the truths of St. Christopher."

I thanked him, forcing the amenities into utterance.

"That one, now——" He pointed to the book on the bench. "That one is a ladder of jewels by which man can reach the stars. It is the written wisdom of Isidore of Seville, who lived more than eight hundred years ago." He stooped and stroked the treasure as a shepherd strokes the lamb whose seed will build a new flock. "Guard it well, Rodrigo."

The mystery of things hoped for filled me to abundance and there was no fear in me; only awe. "Thank you, Father," I said and knew that my patron saint was rejoicing in my humility.

Friar Juan felt under his habit and brought forth a leather jacket and put it around my shoulders. Then he strode to the window and gazed down at the river as though his fancy, like mine, could soar out of this place and into the world of temptation. He shook his head and rubbed his long fingers over his eyes. "The river is filled with ships today," he said. "There is a caravel. The first in many weeks."

I wondered if I had the prerogative of disagreement, and then took it. "It is a nao, if my assertion is pardonable. Not a caravel."

"And what is the difference?" He barked at me like a mastiff that has found a new hole to explore.

His tone dismayed me, but I dared venture farther. "A nao is a ship, Father. A true ship. High fore and aft in the manner of the carracks of Venice." I stood close to him by the window and shared his view. "A caravel is lighter and the bow broader."

"So-o-o." His bold forehead was creased by wrinkles. "Are all the sprouts of Triana so learned in these matters?"

"I spent every hour along the river that I could steal from my Aunt Ronda's lessons." The truth, I knew, was better than subterfuge.

The darting twinkle in his eyes softened them and some of the

26

furrows left his brow. "Know you that ship?" He pointed toward the nao.

"Yes, Father. She is *La Gallega*. Built in Galicia and owned by Juan de la Cosa of Santoña. A heavy ship to come up-river except at flood stage."

"Her saint?"

"Santa Maria." The talk of ships had alleviated some of my misery and had dissipated much of my loneliness. "The sailors who know her capricious ways have nicknamed her *Marigalante*."

"Frivolous Mary." The jest brought a quick smile to his lips, but just as quickly he erased it and his demeanor was as stern as before. "The tall mast in the center is the mainmast? Eh?"

"Yes, Father." I glanced at him, suspicious that he was making sport with me by his doltish questions. However, his face was as bland as an infant's. "That mast carries a topsail up above the crow's-nest. Also the main course, the biggest sail, and two bonnet sails."

He rubbed his chin again, a gesture that indicated contemplation. "And that slanting mast at the back?"

"The mizzen. You will perceive that it is over the quarter-deck—that high structure at the stern." It came to me that I, a mere boy, was lecturing the learned Juan Ruiz de Medina and the role was eminently satisfactory. "The mizzen sail is lateen, that is, triangular, and is the helmsman's sweetheart, for she handles easily and fast on a break to the wind."

"H-m-m-m." He seemed to be enjoying the discourse as much as I and was unashamed of his ignorance. "Now the mast up front."

"Fore." I presumed even to correct him. "That is the foremast and carries one course."

"The pole that sticks out in front. What is that?"

"The bowsprit. It carries the spritsail and is the pilot's sweetheart, for it keeps her nose clean and sharp in rough weather."

He turned from the window and sat on the bench. "Thank you, Rodrigo. Now tonight I can tell my brothers that *my* student is alert as to things nautical."

The accent of the possessive surprised me because it indicated that, instead of being put into the care of a lesser tutor, I was to study with him. The intimation rekindled dire premonitions within me, and left me distraught.

I pretended not to discern his monkish subtlety and gave my attention to the leather jacket he had fetched me, pulling it into fit around my shoulders and testing the wooden buttons. I sensed that he was observing me closely, and then he picked up the book of Isidore's wisdom and opened it at random.

The gloom of my stall defeated even his sharp eyes, and he moved back to the window and held the book in the brilliant ray of Andalusian sun that pierced into the shadows around us.

Then he read.

The sonority of his words filled the room, and the prison could not contain them and they floated free on wings of Lydian measures. The light touched his face and reflected a serene radiance, as a burning taper brightens the face of the saint it glorifies. Was this the Queen's Inquisitor? Was that the voice that had doomed men to the faggots' feast, into the charred embrace of old Quemadero?

I was fascinated into languor and was drawn to him as the compass needle seeks the lodestone of Polaris.

He finished a page and closed his eyes, then closed the book and handed it to me. "It is heavy going, little brother. But the brightest pearl is the one hidden deepest. The best olives are on the highest branches."

The sun was down behind the masts of *Marigalante* and the sailors were gathering on the foredeck for Salve Regina. Friar Juan breathed deeply of the sweet air at the window, and stepped, perhaps reluctantly, to the door that opened on the dank corridor. "Tonight you will choose your confessor," he said.

"May I choose you?" It was an impulsive plunge, but in my youth I was given to impulsive behavior.

He looked at me with a poignancy that wrenched my heart, and his face was contorted by an emotional intensity that passed through him like a rigor. "No student ever before has chosen me as his confessor. A queen once. Even a cardinal. But never a youth. You will attend vespers in the chapel, Rodrigo of Triana, lover of ships. Now good night, little brother, and may the blessings of heaven attend you."

"The grace of God upon you, Father Juan, that you may dispense His mercies." I, too, was capable of subtlety, even in my menial years.

His bare feet sounded down the passage and for the first time in my life I was alone at eventide. My only companions were two books and a little window, beyond which swayed the ships. I gave myself to deep

28

meditation, not on things sacred, and may God forgive me, but on my own discomforts, for I was very hungry. Then the vesper bell summoned us to chapel and I dashed out of my stall and along the corridor, my impetuous haste being most unbecoming to a penitent neophyte in the ancient College of Seville.

The other students trod decorously and ignored me as though I were a flyspeck and, in the chapel, the blemished face of Friar Juan was an agreeable solace, for, at least, I knew him. I felt his gaze in the murky shadows and seemingly surrendered myself to the hour, beating my breast in contrition while my gnawing belly mocked me.

After vespers we supped on bean soup and watered wine, and the prior himself, the illustrious Alphonso de Hojeda, allowed me a second bowl after a whispered word from Friar Juan. Our prior was a red-faced Colossus, given to corpulence and a rumbling mirth that was most un-Dominican.

There was an hour of twilight between supper and darkness and it belonged to us, and we gathered in the yard. Still the other students shunned me and I was lonely and yearned to join one of the groups. They were all older than I and bestowed only disdain and suspicion on me as I walked about the yard, my head high as befits an Andalusian. I heard one say to another, "He is the chick of Monster Juan Ruiz, a page for Lucifer himself."

I parried their insolence with hauteur, and properly so, being a Sevillano, and strolled to the center of the court and took my ease on a stone bench. Their prattling tittle-tattle plainly was audible and they talked of Benjamin Marino, whose lecture they had heard that day.

One of the students, obviously a swine herder of magnificent ignorance and no breeding, expressed himself most coarsely. "That I should come all the way from Cartagena for instruction only to find myself at the feet of a gluttonous Jew."

"Hammer on!" His comrades encouraged him. "The stake and faggots are the proper remedies for Judaizing. And this Marino boldly proclaims himself a Talmudist."

Their intemperate words convicted them of gross benightment, for orthodox Jews were not sent to the stake in Queen Isabel's Inquisition. The fire was for the purification of Christians, not for Jews and Moors. This circumstance is the origin of so many false ideas, even in my lifetime, that I must pause here and expound the realities, inasmuch as the Inquisition changed my hopeful course of life into a twisted and grotesque path. Therefore, mind the roots of this narration if you will pluck the fruit, if you care to know my story of Christopher Columbus, of the Unknown Sea, of the fate that transformed Rodrigo of Triana into Mudarra the bastard Moor.

Now we begin with this true premise: the Inquisition, as a judicial instrument, had existed in Spain for many years, flaring spasmodically into terrifying fervor. The Church assumed the right to judge her children on matters of faith, but the punishment for heresy was the duty of the State. Hence, the Church judged and the Crown punished. Of course, if the Crown was remiss there always was the retaliatory weapon of excommunication.

The Jewish segment of Spanish culture and wisdom, particularly in finances and the sciences, was the seasoning in the potpourri of the New Kingdom. As powerful as this segment was, however, restrictions had been placed upon the children of Moses for centuries, and occasionally the rabble of Spain followed Christian agitators into pogroms.

These restrictions included the ghetto and had locked the door to many trades and arts and sciences. Jews could not levy taxes on their own communities or settle their internal disputes in their own courts. They could not carry arms or be Dons or trim their hair and beards. They could not leave the country or travel without permit and were compelled to wear mantles of coarse cloth. A breach of these regulations brought one hundred lashes and heavy fines, one third of which went to the informer.

To circumvent these shackles, many Jews accepted the Cross, some in holy conversion, but others as a ruse for survival. The Semitic Christians were conversos, or, more often, marranos. This word has come into polite acceptance within the past few years, but when I was a boy it meant "swine."

Now all the conversos were suspect and thus to save their skins, and thereby prosper, the faithful converts were the best informers and often were the first to point trembling fingers at their brothers, and some wailed for the privilege of lighting the faggots. The most merciless Inquisitors of the Church were conversos.

The prey were those who accepted Jesus by day and then Judaized at night behind the heavy curtains of their homes. These were the ones who, hidden from prying eyes, covered their heads with the prayer cloth and intoned the Kol Nidre, the plea which begged God to forgive them for embracing Christian ways and to release them from the vows of their people. The forbidden prayer, in effect, said to the God of Abraham, "I did not mean it, Lord. I am still a Jew."

Hence, the Judaizing conversos were old Quemadero's fodder, while the orthodox, or public Jews, were spared legal punishment as long as they subscribed to the restrictions. These Talmudists, alas! were quarries for the depraved rabble, which, in fetid ignorance, hated them to abhorrence. The common herd of Spain, starving in mind and belly, called them pigs and filth and stench pots because they cooked their food in oil.

The basis for this hatred lay in the fact that the Jews were *different* and stubbornly insisted upon remaining so. And they were clannishly aggressive and argumentative, eternally espousing strange causes. Also, they were the usurers, and debtors fear creditors. Then to make bad matters infinitely worse they were the publicans who collected taxes on a structure of fees and favors.

Spain's educated classes befriended the Jews and even leaned on them, feeling for their purses and picking their brains of knowledge and ideas. Isabel herself often sought their counsel in matters of statecraft and finance until the grinding pressure of her reign trapped her between the nether stones of Church and State, and that came to be in this manner:

Isabel and her noxious consort were in struggle against the nobles; the Crown for the unification of Spain, and the nobility for division that they might retain their power. The loyalty of the people was indispensable if they were to follow her house and the house of Ferdinand's Aragon into a war against Moorish Granada and, if necessary, against the nobles themselves. And the people, the ragged horde, demanded an Inquisition in the hopes that God would be pleased and thereby alleviate their misery.

Reluctantly, and under compulsion of the times, Isabel released an inquisitorial spark early in her reign, and it fell on the dry grass of the rabble's woe and burst into flames. The people even threatened pogroms against the public Jews, and Isabel, possibly to divert their savagery, turned the full force of the Inquisition on the Judaizing conversos. She spread the honey and the flies feasted, and armies came to her standard to take the Cross into Granada and smite the Moors.

Old Quemadero and his handmaidens of faggots had been back in Spanish service for three years when I came to the College of Seville,

31

and perhaps a hundred men and women had embraced his charnal mania and three hundred more were awaiting his summons.

Thus it was that night-coming when I sat in the monastery's yard and listened to the students grumbling their contempt for Benjamin Marino, a public Jew who refused to compromise his heritage for rewards here; or hereafter.

The darkness, once it breached the sky, closed in fast, and I went back to my dungeon and surrendered myself to doleful laments, then to my straw, and tears.

# CHAPTER 3

*I*WAS AROUSED THE NEXT MORNING AT THE THIRD HOUR BY A STU-
dent nudging his dirty foot in my face, and soon thereafter Fray
Juan came with a candle and confessed me, and I took the Wafer in
chapel with my fellows. We broke our fast on stale bread and a sop of
wild honey, and some of the students ventured fraternal overtures but
naturally I scorned this presumptuous familiarity.

It took only a few minutes to tidy my quarters and then dawn had
brushed through the night and was caressing the meadows of my
Andalusia into life. The sounds of creaking tackle and the chant of
sailors called me to my window and *Santa Maria* was in the channel
and standing down-river for Cadiz and Palos, and perhaps even the
Canary Isles in the Ocean Sea or the *terra incognita* of Guinea, as the
West Coast of Africa is called.

I whispered her name. *Santa Maria*. She was so free, so gallant and
alone, that I honored her with the name of her saint, and never again
was I to call her Frivolous Mary in smirking derision or staid *La
Gallega*, under which she was registered.

I watched her out of sight, then gave myself to meditation, knowing
that, as a neophyte, I faced several days of solitude. I read the breviary and found it dull, and for lack of else to do I plunged into the
depths of Isidore's wisdom. It was worse than dull; it was drab and
ponderous.

All that day I was in seclusion, except for chapel and meals, and the
next, and even the next, and on Friday Fray Juan came to confess
me again. My only sins were those of the mind. How could it have
been otherwise? I received my absolution and penance with bowed

33

head, but when the sacred rites had passed I presumed a jest, for I was one for mischief in my youth.

"My most grievous sin, Father, was boredom and it was accentuated by the sluggish words of the great Isidore."

He dropped his chin to his chest and stared his concern for me. "Do the sprouts of Triana also judge genius?"

"Even an infant's nose can smell bad meat." I was quoting my father. "And if that be arrogance, I am sorry." But I was not sorry at all.

His eyes rolled upward as though he were seeking the witness of heaven. "Rodrigo." He held out his hands in a gesture of futility and emptiness. "If arrogance were a mortal sin, then every Andalusian would voyage down the Stygian rivers forever. Without sail or tiller. Arrogance is as natural to an Andalusian as is hauteur to a Biscayan, melancholy to a Galician, and impetuousness to a Catalan. As is patriotism to an Aragonese, pride to a Castilian, and insolence to an Estremaduran. It is the way of Spain. Our breath and our bread, and it will be our doom."

"Doom?" I suddenly was serious.

"Yes. Spain kindles sparks and France nourishes them into fires, but it is England that gets the warmth while Spain's obtrusive individualism kindles more sparks for French fires to warm the mean and avaricious spirit of Albion's ghouls. We husband the world and then glean the fields."

"But they are barbarians, Father."

"Aye. So were the Vandals that gave us the Vandalusia that we call Andalusia. The barbarian of today is the prince of tomorrow. The peasant of the morning is the patrician at twilight. We will talk further of these things. You have done well, little brother, and you may attend lectures next week."

"Your bounty and my gratitude fill my cup," I said and bowed my thanks.

"And you may spend two hours this afternoon with your father."

"In Triana?" I asked eagerly, thinking of a peppery soup, a spread of sardines, and perhaps a chicken smeared with garlic.

"No. That will only make you more homesick. At his shop here in Seville." He reached for his breviary but left Isidore on my bench, and swung open the door. "You will remember, Rodrigo, that you are a member of this college and will conduct yourself to its credit. You will return for vespers."

34

He was gone before I finished my profuse and eloquent acknowledgment, and, with hours on my hands and nothing else to occupy me, I returned to the volume that was trying my patience. Such was the method of the Dominicans. They placed an unsavory feast before a boy, then starved his mind until he gobbled up the knowledge and digested it.

After a noontime respite for bean soup and dried fruit, one for our bellies and the other for our bowels, Fray Juan brought my sandals to my quarters and picked off the few bed straws that were clinging to the back of my jacket. He fetched a basin of water and directed me to wash my neck and ears and then, O *tempora!* O *mores!* He himself washed my feet and dried them on his habit. He escorted me to the entrance of the monastery and stood watching as I walked away, decorously as befit a student of the College of Seville.

However, the minute I turned a corner of the old wall I began running, and scudded through the streets until I reached the Torre del Oro, where my father kept shop in an alley of merchants. The salesroom and bargaining counters of the mart were empty, and for the first time I noticed how bare the shelves were. No Eastern merchandise at all and no jars of African aloes and other purgatives and poisons. Only pottery gathering dust.

The rumbling and profane voice from the shop's rear enclosure brought a surge of anticipation to my heart.

"*Amir el bahr!*" He was calling me admiral as always. "Rodrigo! By the holy well of Zemzem and the flow of Halima who wet-nursed The Messenger!"

And now you meet old Mudarra, my father's potter, and now you know whence came the name with which I have bowed the stiff necks and proud backs of my enemies.

I hastened into his shop, flinging aside the heavy draperies that hid it from the salesroom, and he greeted me in Arabic:

"There is no God but Allah! Mohammed is His Messenger!"

I struggled through a reply, faltering shamefully over the Arabic words he had taught me:

"Praise be to God, the Origin of all good. And may the blessing of God be on Mohammed, the Prince of Prophets."

Old Mudarra glowered at me and his sunken eyes judged me wanting. "There are fetters on your brain, Rodrigo. Your gloomy Dominicans have stuffed you with the Latin of Caesar and neglected the sweet

35

Arabic of the Prophet Jesus." His teeth were few and were broken and yellow, and hung loosely to his wrinkled gums. "Speak forthrightly, you colt of Dominican trickery and chewed pap."

I tried again, quoting the words of Mohammed himself. "Say unto the Christians, their God and my God are one."

"Now that is better." Old Mudarra held out his arms and I ran to him and embraced the bony shoulders under his coarse brown cloak, then kissed his forehead at the edge of his turban.

"Where is my father?" I asked, and looked around at the rumpled couch where Mudarra slept, at his potter's wheel, and the little trough that brought water from a cask. A supply of damp Andalusian clay, cleaned and kneaded, was by his bench and rows of jugs and bowls were on shelves by the window, taking the sun and hardening before their first turn in the oven outside.

"Your father stepped out for a minute." The old man did not look at me as he spake, but reached for an oil jug and began rubbing a blue compound into its surface, readying it for baking and glazing. His brushes and paints were in orderly array, and they and his wheel were the only things he kept in order.

"I have only two hours," I explained. "How long has he been gone?"

Mudarra set the oil jug on the bench and the sun caught the blue, turning it deep and seeping it into the clay. Again he glowered at me. "Already the Black Friars have whetted your wits on curiosity and suspicion. Curiosity killed Lot's wife."

I laughed and took no offense inasmuch as I long since had grown accustomed to the old despot's petulant temper and garrulous tongue. He had helped rear me, squabbling always with my Aunt Ronda, and had been my father's potter for more than twenty years, having come from God knows where, his paints and wheel in a creaking handcart that day he presented himself at the shop. I had heard the story a dozen times, how my father had asked him whence he came, only to be told, "From the womb of Eve, you Gothic punchinello."

No man ever had talked in such manner to my father, but old Mudarra moved in and, pumping his wheel, had not thrown his first Bermejo bowl for a second time before my father succumbed to his autocratic affection.

Mudarro was a Morisco, which is to say a Moor who has accepted Christianity usually under duress and particularly the threat of expulsion. To him, however, Christianity merely was a protective garment over a heart as loyal to The Messenger as any Moslem seed of Ishmael, as the guardians of the Kaaba, which is the only known handiwork of Adam himself.

The authorities, especially the Inquisitors, counted old Mudarra as a harmless dote, a bit unbalanced in his mind and therefore possessed of devils. It was forbidden, and ill luck, too, to lay hands on one so possessed of the malady of the blessed Magadan, called Mary of Magdala.

I had learned through frequent cuffings never to question him too closely about anything and never at all about his frequent disappearances, when he obstensibly was digging his own clay in the far places of Andalusia, and so on this day of my visit I was most discreet as to inquiries even about my father.

Therefore, with proper patience, I sat down near the water cask and answered his demands about the monastery, concealing my amusement at his obscene denunciation of the Dominicans. His Spanish was more lucid, perhaps, than Friar Juan's, but without warning he often slipped into Arabic and I had to be alert to reply in the same tongue.

The room was stuffy in the autumn warmth and I was becoming drowsy when the putrid odor suddenly offended my nostrils and then assailed them in nauseating repugnance. I tilted my nose and sniffed and for the first time I noticed the little patches of goat's hair and chicken feathers in the corner under the cask. There were splotches of dried blood, too, and bits of flesh. These were the offending agents.

Mudarra shifted his eyes from me to the corner and, obviously anticipating my rightful query, he hastened to make explanation. "A fresh chicken for this servant of The Messenger," he said and touched his chest. "I prepared it myself and cooked it over coals from the oven."

I knew he never ate meat, that he lived on bean soup, curds, and honey.

However, I gave it only passing thought, assuming he had used a fat hen to lure one of the alley's chicks to his couch, for Mudarra, although very old and unwashed, was a man of majestic and successful licentiousness.

I moved to a far corner and the first hour of my visit passed without my father's appearance. I grew restless and then Mudarra, mouthing his contempt for impatience, sought to lessen my anxiety. "Your father is very busy," he said. "Times are hard."

"I know. But it is not like my father to leave his shop for so long."

37

The old man picked up the oil pot and gently rubbed the smooth surface, squinting at his handicraft. "Your father has taken an associate into the business."

"A partner!" I was astonished. The shop had been in my family since my great-grandfather founded the enterprise, and only a Bermejo had ever supervised its affairs.

"I did not say a partner," Mudarra barked at me. "I said associate. He is Luis Harana, a traveler and a gentleman of extraordinary perception."

Luis Harana? I tasted the name and did not know it.

Old Mudarra gave his hands to his work and his eyes avoided mine. "Luis Harana is a trader of rare acumen." He mumbled the words and chewed them as though in distaste. "He has aloes and no shop. Your father has a shop and no aloes. It is as simple as that." His stooped shoulders shrugged the timeless gesture of the East.

"I have never heard of this man," I said.

"He has taken expensive residence on the Street of Felicity. A widower he is, and with one daughter."

"A Sevillano? An Andalusian?"

"Mother of man, Rodrigo!" His irascible temper seethed into disapproval. "Already the Dominicans have shaped your tongue only for questions." He turned his gimlety eyes to me and volleyed an oath in Arabic that spent his anger, and then he said, "Luis Harana is of Catalonia, I think. A converso."

"Marrano?" The accusing epithet came without deliberation or malice.

"Enough!" Old Mudarra shook his finger in my direction. "I will have no vindictive locution from a foal I warmed with my own breath. Luis Harana is your father's friend, and do you cry swine to such a man in driveling insolence?"

I was chastened and the shame of my effrontery left me distraught and penitent, and I adroitly shifted the subject to the potter's art and thereby, through flattery, embellished his vanity and sweetened his spleen. He was expounding volubly the minute differences in the golden pottery of Aragon and the golden luster of Malaga when I heard my father enter the front doorway of the shop, scraping his feet on the threshold.

Mudarra, too, cocked his ears and listened and I bowed my leave of him and darted into the salesroom.

38

My father was arranging new jars of aloes on the shelves and beside him was a haggard man with a hawkish nose, and there by the window was a girl of my own years; a flower bud from the Gardens of the Moon.

Her hair was primrose yellow, almost molten amber, and the sun through the window framed her into a portrait of celestial radiance. She smiled at me, demurely of course, then lowered her head in maidenly shame for her boldness. I was transfixed to the spot, impaled by a thrust of Astarte's lance, and I gawked like a dotard on Faggot Day.

My father laughed at my derangement and threw his arm around my shoulders and presented me to Luis Harana, who, in turn, presented me to his daughter, calling her Maraela.

Maraela Harana. The very name sang like the sweet innocent voices of the children's choir, like reeds swishing along the river in twilight breezes, the call of birds at nesting time, the silver bells for Salve Regina.

And I, blessed with fluency since my tender years, was as mute and as clumsy as a foal dropped in a mire and struggling for the dignity of equilibrium. Again she smiled and I wished for my lost velvet doublet and was bitter toward the Dominicans who had robbed me.

"Your father told me he had a son." Her voice was softer music even than her name. "But I did not expect one so stalwart."

My manhood, itself in bud, swelled to rapturous torture and I found my senses and spoke with a confidence that my feelings mocked. "This is an honor that should come only to one more worthy than I." My bow was proper, but I was terrified lest I bow too low or press the grace of my gesture.

Harana and my father glanced at each other and gave their attentions to the aloes, and I stepped closer to her and saw that her eyes were the blue of my Andalusian noons. And this flower the seed of a converso? There was nothing Eastern about her at all, none of the heritage of Sarah or Hagar, none of the vein of Ur.

I was sagacious enough, albeit in my youth, to know that Jews and other Semites had been in Andalusia since Phoenician days and that time had erased all the vestiges of Shem from many of his descendants. But Maraela was as fair as the Gaels about whom my Aunt Ronda so often spoke, as the Rhine maidens whose legends the Goths whispered. Her father, on the other hand, had the cast of Abraham, the black hair of Judah, the piercing eyes of the Desert of Edom.

She did not move from the window, from the sun in her hair, and we talked first of the day and the shop, the aloes and the pottery. She had met old Mudarra, and smiled when she spoke his name and nodded toward his quarters, where he had secluded himself. Then she told me they had come to Seville from Cordova, but originally from Catalonia. "My mother has been with the saints for many years," she said. "And my father and I have traveled much."

Our parents, at mention of Catalonia, looked our way and they both joined us, and my father explained to me that he and Harana were associating themselves together for sale of aloes. I congratulated them and expressed my pleasure, meaning every word I spake, for such was the hold of Maraela upon me from the beginning.

My father eradiated good cheer as he talked of plans for the business, but Harana was morosely taciturn, his sharp vigilance appraising every sound and every sight. His doublet of Milanese silk was richer than my father's, although the carriage of the two men weighed the balance of elegance in my father's favor. Harana also wore an ample skirt to his knees and his long stockings bore testimony of the Italian influence. For all that, however, his legs were shapeless, with none of the sinewy strength of my father's, a blessing, incidentally, that he had passed to me.

The luxurious silk of Maraela's raiment shone of the fine looms of Tours and her billowing skirt was caught up in front and attached to a golden chain that encircled her waist. Her braided hair was wound loosely around her head and was held in place by a silk cap, richly embroidered and studded with opulent stones.

My own jacket and coarse stockings were pitifully mean and to draw her attention from them and to me, I began discoursing lucidly on the wisdom of Isidore and pretended surprise that she had never heard of him. My father was proud of me and it showed in his eyes and on his face, banishing for a minute the careworn lines that troubled me.

The time, as with all pleasures, sped so fast that it was falling twilight before I was aware of such prosaic things as hours, and then, remembering Friar Juan's injunction that I return for vespers, I was seized with a panic and begged their leave to depart in haste, and this I did, racing for the monastery and frothing myself into a most noxious sweat.

I crept into the chapel and felt my tutor's eyes upon me, even in the gloom, and after benediction I slipped to my stall and lit my stubby candle and buried myself in Isidore's morass.

The shadows moved and my candlelight flickered on the sallow cheeks of Friar Juan Ruiz de Medina, touching his yellow eyes into luster. He pushed the candle to a far end of the bench and sat by me and I began my excuses for my tardiness to vespers.

He nodded his head slowly, then spoke without rancor. "Tomorrow you will fast, Rodrigo. No food. No water."

"Yes, Father." I wished I had eaten at the shop, but the thought of food reminded me of the fetor in Mudarra's room and I choked back a surge of warm bile.

"The next day you may have bread and water."

"Yes, Father."

He wet his finger and toyed with the dripping wax from the candle, and broke off a portion and rubbed it into a ball. "Did you meet Luis Harana?"

It caught me unaware and I jerked upright. But of course he would know my father's associate. Luis Harana was a man of obvious wealth and a converso, and the Queen's Inquisitors knew everything. "I had that honor," I said, recalling my wits for an instant use. "Harana and my father are joining business hands for the sale of aloes."

"Yes, I know." He put the bit of wax in his mouth and chewed thoughtfully, his jaw revolving in that relentless motion that I detested. "Aloes are rare now that the Moslems have closed our African trade."

"Harana is a trader of merit and acumen," I suggested.

"Yes, I know."

"I also met his daughter——" I would hide nothing from him, knowing he would find it out anyway. "Maraela Harana. Her refinement and maidenly virtues do honor to her father."

Friar Juan lifted the candle and sat it between us, the better to see me, and our shadows danced high on the walls, and he looked at me, his eyes more piercing than Luis Harana's. I returned his gaze without flinching and he put his hand on my arm and said, "Rodrigo, know you the story of the jar of water and the drop of oil?"

"No, Father."

"Well, it was thus——" He folded his hands in his lap and his chin dropped low. "A drop of oil asked sanction to mingle with the water in a jar and the water said, 'No! For you can only rise to the top of the jar and spread, and even if the jar be washed, yea, scoured, it will remain oily forever.' "

The parable saddened me, for I had heard my Aunt Ronda speak in such manner of Jews and Gentiles, of oil and water. Then I resented his insinuation and spoke out. "The Haranas are conversos, but firm in the faith of our blessed Savior. Or else, Father Juan, my own father would not associate himself with Luis Harana. Remembrance of this truth will do me honor, and I request it."

"Yes, I know." He arose and his shadow darkened to the ceiling of my prison. "I am a Dominican friar, Rodrigo. Remembrance of this truth will do me honor, and I request it. Therefore, I am your brother and am to be called Fray Juan, and not Father Juan. And now blow out the candle, little brother. Wax is precious and all treasures we have must go to the realm for the crusade against Granada." He rested his hand on the door latch. "You will attend the lecture of Benjamin Marino on Monday."

Then he was gone, but his pronouncement rang in my ears.

Fray Juan Ruiz de Medina, and I his brother? I the brother of the Queen's Inquisitor, the eunuch of old Quemadero's shrieking harem? Never! So I swore and called upon St. Christopher to witness.

And in my loneliness, the fancy of my desires cried out for the beauty of Maraela to comfort me, and then her image was before me, banishing the gloom of that hateful place, of that hateful hour.

## CHAPTER 4

BENJAMIN MARINO WAS THE GREATEST MAN EVER TO CROSS my path, and this encompassing declaration includes Christopher Columbus, whose standard I followed into the Unknown, and Martin Alonso Pinzon, whose caravel I helped sail on the voyage that ended the Age of Darkness.

O God, the Clement, the Merciful: how well I remember! O Mita, my beloved, that hour I can never forget.

The college assembled at six o'clock on Monday morning for the Marino lecture and, after prayers, the friars counseled their students to attention and we sat erect on the benches until the sun brushed the last shadows from the room, and then Benjamin Marino entered.

He had no books, no charts, but only himself; a slight man of infinite patience, and proudly wearing the beard of David and a brown doublet loosely woven of goat hair. One of the students snickered and Fray Juan cuffed his cheek with an open palm.

Teacher Marino went straight to the podium and there, to the witness of all, he bowed his head in the supplication of Judah, then lifted his eyes to us, and his eyes were brighter than the flames of old Quemadero. "Friars Preachers and young Sirs." His voice rang the salutation. "By your gracious leave, I will borrow your minds and the interest thereon will be knowledge of things mundane and not godly, if any man can separate the world from the God who willed it. Seek ye the truth!"

The words sang like the wind in sails full-blown and my heart swelled with a new yearning, and suddenly nothing else was important; not my father, neither Maraela, but only this man whose eyes burned bright.

"*Mundi formam omnes fere consentiunt rotundam esse.*" His Latin was immaculate and he was quoting the pronouncement of Sylvius Piccolomini, who, as a writer, had given us *The Story of Two Lovers*, but who, as Pope Pius II, had given us the dictum: "Virtually everyone is agreed that the world is round."

Teacher Marino gave the words free flight, watching our faces, and seemingly mine more than all the others, and then he gripped the edges of the podium and spoke again.

"Yes! The world is round. The Prophet Esdras was right. God's earth is a sphere. And, yet, Esdras was wrong."

It was a bold thing to say to the Dominicans, who espoused the teachings of that ancient messenger. I glanced at Fray Juan and his jaw was still and his eyes were fastened on Benjamin Marino, the meek Jewish schoolmaster who was daring to contradict Esdras, the Jewish prophet.

"This great man of my people, this Esdras of your sacred books, held that the world is only one-seventh water. That is his error. The world is larger than you believe, for the sin of this age is man's conviction that he alone is master and that the stars revolve around his head. It is worse than sin. It is stupidity."

Here again was dangerous ground, but he trod it underfoot, undaunted and unafraid, and the college was as hushed as the blue distance of Andalusia's sky.

"We are gnats and the earth is larger than you think. The seas are deeper. The seas are wider. The skies are higher. The world is older than you say and will live longer than you teach.

"We journey east to India. Then is India also west?" He leaned forward and his ardor held us transfixed. "Yes. India is east, and India is west. But how far?" Teacher Marino straightened and smiled for the first time. "Answer that conundrum and Spain will hold the world in her palm."

He rubbed the back of his neck, staring up at the arched ceiling as though awaiting the Word, and then resumed his lecture, speaking slowly in Latin and only rarely in Spanish to strengthen a point. "The cartographers and astronomers of the College of San Esteban, University of Salamanca, now hold that land is only 700 leagues to the west of the Canary Isles. They dispute among themselves as to whether that land is India. I say it is not." He stressed the negative, rapping the stand to emphasize his point.

"The illustrious Florentine, Paolo del Pozzo Toscanelli, has prepared a map for the Portuguese Crown. Colleague Toscanelli is an excellent physicist, but a naïve cartographer. He places Asia 8,000 miles to the west." His smile was wan and he covered it quickly by rubbing his chin and his mouth. "The earth is larger than Toscanelli thinks.

"Hence, we have two schools. Salamanca says unknown land is 700 leagues west, or roughly 3,000 miles. Toscanelli says Asia is due west." He lowered his voice and prepared us for the calculated thrust that we knew was coming.

*"They both are right!*

"There is land in the Ocean Sea. *Terra incognita*. Perhaps the Atlantis of Plato's vision. Or——" And he hurled the words at us. "Or Antilia and her Seven Cities."

I heard Fray Juan gasp his incredulity and the other Dominicans scowled their disapproval of myth-teaching, but Benjamin Marino was not perturbed. "Do not scorn the stubborn tradition that, more than seven hundred years ago when the Moors expelled Spaniards from Spain, your breed followed seven bishops into the West of mist and mystery. Scorn nothing. And never tradition. As a Jew, I counsel this."

He was so sure of himself that our college, mostly Andalusians and therefore men of abundant confidence, gave him our most meticulous heed although he already had strained our credibility. If he sensed the skepticism, he nevertheless chose to hammer on.

"We know that strange trees have washed to the shores of Ireland and Scotia. That strange birds have been seen. Whence came they? Cathay? Never! For Marco Polo discovered, and we have confirmed, that Cathay is a place of seafarers. Assuredly then"—he smiled at the simplicity of his own logic—"if winds and channels of the Ocean Sea can move huge trees to Europe's shores they would have moved Cathay's ships, or the wreckage thereof: *if Cathay were so near.*" The point impressed even the Dominicans and they stole glances, each at the next.

Teacher Marino clasped his hands behind him and hunched his shoulders for one more thrust. "It is not Cathay. Of this I am convinced. It is not India or even Asia. It is unknown land of a sedentary people, if there are people there at all." His voice rose in the passion of his scholarly vision. "New Land! New flora! New fauna! A virgin world, a treasure chest, awaiting the touch of Jason."

I was enthralled and my heart beat a cadence to the drumming of his words and then he closed his formal lecture with a quotation from the ancient *Medea* of Seneca:

" 'There will come a time in the long years of the world when the ocean sea will loosen the shackles that bind things together and a great part of the earth will be opened up and a new sailor such as the one who was Jason's guide, whose name was Thyphis, shall discover a new world, and then shall Thule be no longer the last of lands.' "

The prophecy echoed against the high ceiling and the stone walls and he bowed his gratitude for our attention, and the college, led by Fray Juan, arose and bowed its tribute to his wisdom.

Then Marino relaxed at the podium and scratched his beard and neck, and flexed his muscles in a luxurious stretch, until his audience was still again. "We have arrived at the hour of discussion," he said, and the college no longer was stiff and formal. He reached into his doublet and lifted forth an orange and sucked it noisily, and spat out the pips. Fray Juan took a handful of beans from his habit and soon his jaw was revolving again.

"From the court of Portugal, there has come to the town of Palos de la Frontera——" Teacher Marino laid the wrinkled orange on the stand. "Rather to the Franciscan monastery of La Rabida, which is near Palos—a most extraordinary adventurer who gives the name of Christopher Columbus——"

It was the first time I heard his name and it impressed itself upon me only because it was the name of my saint, the sturdy Christopher who braved bridgeless waters in the service of mankind.

"One report is that this Columbus is a Genoese explorer, a cosmographer of envious repute." The learned Marino was discoursing as matter-of-factly as a merchant discussing accounts. "Another report is that he is a Galician astronomer. Neither of these is true as no Christopher Columbus is counted among the scholars of Spain or Genoa."

It came to me then that this was the strange pilot mentioned by Alonso Pinzon to my father that day on the barge. Obviously Columbus had arrived from Portugal and had gone to Palos while Pinzon was yet in Seville.

Here was a suggestion of mystery, possibly of deception, and my interest, nettled by his name, increased with each observation propounded by our teacher. "I am concerned only with the scholarly pretensions of this stranger and with a most singular fact: he has a copy of Toscanelli's map of the Ocean Sea, a work prepared exclusively for

46

the King of Portugal. And, most interesting of all, he seeks support for an expedition westward and glibly prattles knowledge of India that we do not have. Therefore, it might behoove this college to invite this alien to our counsels. And now I surrender this podium to Juan Ruiz de Medina who"—a quick smile lighted his face—"as the Queen's Inquisitor is in position to extract facts that are denied to me."

He stepped back to a bench near the wall and Fray Juan arose slowly, gouging his teeth with a long fingernail to dislodge the bean hulls, and moved to the station of authority. There he unrolled the scroll he had prepared and began reading, his Latin being as proper as that of Teacher Marino's.

"In the name of God, the Clement:

"Firstly." My fray wet his lips as though to oil the words. "Christopher Columbus will not attend this college to share his wisdom, feigned or genuine, with us. He seeks audience with our blessed Queen here in Seville and is concerned only with money and grants, and not with impoverished Friars Preachers of the sweet St. Dominic. Also——" A grimace twisted his lips. "He wears the girdle of the Third Order of St. Francis and, regretfully, Franciscans do not willingly share their benefits with Dominicans.

"Secondly. This Columbus is most secretive as to his origin. He has left the impression that he is a native of Genoa, or at least of the province of Liguria, but never so declaring forthrightly. Moreover, he neither speaks nor writes Italian, but rather Spanish with a Catalan accent, and idioms of an earlier age.

"Thirdly." Fray Juan paused and motioned to one of his fellow Dominicans, who looked around and rapped the nodding heads of two students, extracting a howl from them that brought titters from the other students and a raucous guffaw from our portly prior.

Then Fray Juan resumed. "Thirdly. Our subject of inquiry once was in the employ of Di Negro and Spinola, the renowned Genoese exporters, in the capacity of a traveling agent, or salesman. As such, he traveled possibly to England. He pretends to have visited Ultima Thule[1] and Ireland. The first we challenge categorically; the second we accept suspiciously."

Already, looking back at it now, the Fates had cast my lot with Christopher Columbus, for as my Dominican mentor indicted the

[1]Iceland.

adventurer I found myself leaning his way in spirit. At least he was in activity and accomplishment, at least he was daring attempt things while his critics canted scholarly judgment.

Fray Juan cleared his throat and held the scroll closer to his eyes. "Fourthly. This Columbus has turned his hand at seamanship in many ways and is a proved captain, a man of masterly persuasion. He has sailed as a corsair in the service of France's René Anjou and under the standard of a French admiral also named Columbus, or, more properly, Coullon, which is to say Colon in Spanish."

My ears burned for more and my spine tingled in anticipation, for here indeed was mystery and a hint of devious plots and plans, with fame and fortune as the prize; a New Land as the booty.

"Fifthly. As a raider under French colors, he attacked Genoese shipping; a most remarkable incident. For if he be Genoese, would he fight his own state? In a battle off Cape St. Vincent, eight years ago, his ship was sunk by the Genoese and he was cast upon the Portuguese shore. The firm of Di Negro and Spinola has, as you know, offices in Lisbon, and the adventurer, a man of rare guile and laudable patience, ingratiated himself into their service and made the voyages of which he boasts, or, more truthfully, some of them. The lure of the open sea gripped him in Portugal, for, as is well known, the fever of exploration is epidemic in that kingdom and Lisbon is in ferment with schemes for expeditions down the coast of Guinea and also west into the Unknown Sea."

Fray Juan laid his scroll on the podium and rested his eyes while his colleagues yawned and stretched, a luxury they denied the students. Benjamin Marino was staring at the ceiling in obvious contemplation of all he had heard, and I was eager for resumption of the session; my fancy churning my mind into images of gallant caravels in boiling seas.

The college settled again into silence and Fray Juan picked up his scroll and continued. "Sixthly. At Lisbon's convent of the Military Order of St. James, where maidens are trained in virtuous endeavor, Christopher Columbus met Felipa Moniz Perestrello, a lady of noble birth, and, most important, the sister of Bartholomew Perestrello, governor of the Isle of Porto Santo, which is a steppingstone to the Ocean Sea. This lady became his wife and bore him a son, christened Diego, and then this Columbus took residence on the said island of Porto Santo and there had frequent opportunities to engage in nautical enterprises and thus improve his knowledge of navigation. He entertained and succored mariners who called at that outpost and examined them shrewdly on their adventures and observations.

"Seventhly. One Martin Vicente, pilot, showed him a utility found floating some two thousand miles *west* of Portugal and made of a wood unknown in Europe. One Pedro Correa, pilot, showed him a cane tree, also found floating, each section of which would hold a gallon of wine. A persistent report, although wisely suspect, asserts that Columbus talked with the valiant Alonso Sanchez soon after that navigator was washed ashore on Porto Santo and a few days before the redoubtable Sanchez expired from the ordeals of his adventure, and, as we all know, Sanchez insisted he had seen the shores of Antilia beyond the Ocean Sea."

Even the dunderheads among the students were alert at this juncture of the report and I, enthralled by the unfolding narrative, was annoyed that Fray Juan should hesitate long enough to clear his throat and mop his brow on the hem of his mantle.

"Eighthly. It is possible, albeit far from confirmation, that Christopher Columbus also knew on Porto Santo the Unknown Pilot whose exploits, fanciful or real, have sharpened the imaginations of all men concerned with exploration. My investigation of this story has foundered on the rocks of myth and rumors, but the Unknown Pilot swore that, blown from his course, he sailed about seven hundred leagues west and there came upon a floating meadow——"

A gasp went up from the college and even the unperturbable Benjamin Marino arched his black eyebrows, and Fray Juan hammered on:

"Yes, a floating meadow. A sea of grass. And through this he sailed and saw an island, but so frightened were his sailors that they forced him to turn back. This corresponds, in position and description, to the Newly Discovered Island that appeared so mysteriously on Bedaire's map of sixty years ago and subsequently on Bianco's map with the legend: *Questo he mar di Spagna.* Here is Spain's sea."

My fray moistened his lips and thrust out his chin and I envisioned how he looked and how he performed before the Queen's Court of the Inquisition, thorough and relentless as he recruited for old Quemadero and the faggots of purification.

"Ninthly. From Porto Santo, this Columbus returned to Portugal and eked out an existence by drawing charts and tracing maps and then, abetted by the influence of his wife's family, projected himself into the councils of his betters. Let us assume that this is the point where he came into knowledge of Toscanelli's map, although that document was prepared under the patronage of King John of Portugal and was a state paper, supposedly safe from the prying eyes of schemers."

The constant disdain and frequent flares of contempt were so flagrant, and the bias so obvious, that I was puzzled as to why Fray Juan was so scathing of a man he did not know except through channels open only to an Inquisitor. Was it because the stranger seemingly preferred Franciscans to Dominicans? Nonsense. Juan Ruiz de Medina was as loyal to his order as any friar, but he was not a blinded partisan in matters of letters.

"Meanwhile——" Fray Juan's voice grew stronger as the report lengthened. "His wife died and left their son, Diego, only a year or so out of swaddling clothes. This blow did not deter Christopher Columbus one whit from a dream he was nourishing into an obsession. Eventually he reached King John himself and brazenly proposed a voyage to India, advocating with more fervor than reason that Asia is 700 leagues across the Ocean Sea. It is astounding but true, the King of Portugal was swayed by the indomitable audacity of this interloper who offered not one item of nautical lore or wisdom that was new to Portuguese mariners. When pressed for facts, or even theory, he wrapped himself in a cloak of omnipotence like a prophet from the wilderness, argued that he was anointed of God to find the Holy City of the Mysteries, and prattled parables about the rivers of Paradise and pretended knowledge for himself that is known to no other man. So eloquent was his plea that King John actually asked his terms——" Here my fray paused and smiled, and it was one of the few times I ever saw him smile.

"Without one gold ducat in his purse, without one sail at his command, this namesake of our stalwart St. Christopher did propose to voyage west or south and discover happy lands, islands, and *terra firma* most rich in gold, silver, aloes, pearls, and precious stones and infinite peoples; and to come upon the lands of India and the kingdoms of the Grand Khan, the same having been previously dicovered to the east by Marco Polo."

Several students snickered and a few of the friars themselves smiled their amusement at such fancy, at such wild dreaming. Benjamin Marino, however, did not smile. His brow was furrowed in thought and his eyes never left the countenance of Juan Ruiz de Medina, Inquisitor for the Queen and judge of conversos.

"In payment for this fantastic enterprise——" Fray Juan's face was solemn again. "This said Christopher Columbus, known as Christovam Colom in Portugal, demanded immediate knighthood and golden spurs. Next he demanded heraldry and titles perpetually, including Admiral of the Ocean Sea." All the college laughed, save only Benjamin Marino, and even I smiled at the temerity of an itinerant entrepreneur, a pauperized wayfarer and promotor, presuming such demands of the King of Portugal.

"Hold! And hear you!" My Dominican mentor held up his hand for silence. "Furthermore, he demanded one tenth of all income accruing to the King within limits of the Admiralty. One pearl of every ten pearls! One ounce of gold of every ten ounces! In addition to all this, he also demanded the right to contribute one eighth of the expenses of every expedition to any lands he discovered and to derive one-eighth profit."

A gale of laughter swept the college and even Benjamin Marino smiled.

Fray Juan waited until the merriment subsided and then added: "The King of Portugal declined."

The Inquisitor rolled the scroll and tied it and put it away, and a fellow Dominican handed him another, which he opened carefully and resumed his array. "Tenthly. Rebuffed in Portugal, this unspurred knight-errant of ludicrous imagination considered offering himself to England or France, but aware that those kingdoms are remiss in knowledge of cosmography and astronomy, he decided that Queen Isabel should be his patron and that our Spain should launch his expedition to India. His retreat from Portugal was most furtive, possibly due to debt but more likely because he had seen the Toscanelli map and had noted its secrets.

"Lastly. In a manner we have not solved, he secured passage for himself and his son, Diego, now of five years, and left Lisbon for the Condado de Niebla,[2] that territory that includes Andalusia's Palos, Huelva, and other ports. He landed at Palos, wearing the garb of

[2]Condado de Niebla, hereafter called the Niebla, was a small area on the Atlantic, facing North Africa, and included the towns of Palos, Huelva, and Moguer, and the lower reaches of the rivers Tinto and Odiel, which flow into the Saltes River and thence to the Atlantic.

the lay order of the Friars Minor, and, his son by his side, walked the three miles to the Franciscan monastery at La Rabida; well aware of the hospitality of the Minorites and surely also aware that the prior of La Rabida has confessed the Queen and is among her favorites.

"Fray Juan Perez welcomed the stranger and offered sanctuary and schooling for Diego, and Christopher Columbus tarried there until the return of Fray Antonio de Marchena, the astronomer of the monastery and a man of quizzical mind and boundless curiosity. Fray Antonio himself saw to it that our new luminary was in communication with the Duke of Medina-Sidonia——"

The words quickened my brain and awakened sleeping intelligence. Fray Juan Ruiz de Medina was of the same lineage as the Duke of Medina-Sidonia. Was this then the source of my mentor's information? But why the antagonism? The bias and contempt? Why a hundred things?

"And, as is known to every Spaniard——" Fray Juan was reciting without a glance at his scroll. "The Duke of Medina-Sidonia is the richest man in the kingdom and a confidant of our gracious Queen. He has seen a map based on Toscanelli's theories but prepared by this gross upstart who calls himself Christopher. This map——" His voice crackled ridicule. "This devilish hoax has the Cipango[3] of Marco Polo's journey only 700 leagues west of the Canary Isles and in the position of Antilia.[4]

"This is his secret; that Cipango and Antilia are the same. This is the lodestone with which he intrigues to lure our Queen into a reckless venture for his own profit."

Fray Juan dropped the scroll on the stand and it rolled into shape and he tied it and put it under his arm, then faced us all. "In conclusion, a few observations. This Columbus, this charlatan in matters mundane, is, nevertheless, firm in the Faith, a man of much piety and frequent prayers. However——" His tone hardened to a rasp. "This shipless mariner, this impostor, seeks the company, the solace, and the wisdom of conversos at every opportunity."

So that was it. That explained the prejudice, the cynical denunciation by the Inquisitor. Christopher Columbus trafficked with the peculiar people, the Hebrews who had turned Christian. This charge

[3]Japan.

[4]Cuba?

52

demanded an immediate explanation and Fray Juan was quick to give it.

"Let it be said, in justice to truth, that the conversos of his circle all are true Christians, staunch in the Faith and high in the graces of our Queen. They are men of wealth and influence, which may explain his affinity. I submit to this college, as I will submit to the Queen, that Christopher Columbus, if that be his true name, is a man to be watched."

He bowed his head and mumbled a *Pax vobiscum* and we mumbled the same words in echo, and the morning session was over. All the students crowded around Benjamin Marino and none gave attention or praise to my fray, and he, in majestic solitude, walked slowly out of the hall.

I, too, preferred a minute of chitchat with Teacher Marino, but I renounced that privilege and caught up with Fray Juan and fell in step with him. He was the one who could give me liberty to visit my father, and thus, incidentally, see Maraela Harana, and so it was his favors I curried.

"A masterly presentation," I volunteered, seeking to flatter him. "This Columbus is a trickster."

He turned his cold, yellow eyes on me and grunted. "The same was said of Marco Polo, who gave us more knowledge of the East than any man, before or since." Then he looked into the blue distance, the sky free and unbounded. "At least this wandering and homeless Christopher dares dream of a new world and dares scheme its conquest while we peck at his flesh like starving ravens."

I did not comprehend. He had condemned in public and now he defended in private, and I was turning the riddle in my mind when he said:

"It is not necessary, Rodrigo, to pamper my vanity. A visit to your father will depend on your knowledge of Isidore. I will examine you Friday morning."

"Thank you, Fray Juan."

"Your father is well and busy. So is Luis Harana and his daughter. Your friend Mudarra, the wise old fool, is making her a vase with a glaze of azure and gold."

I thanked him again and went to my stall and there waded into the morass of Isidore until boredom subdued my ambition, and then I stepped to my window and watched that small portion of the city that

53

was visible to me. First the ships, and no new ones were in, and next the streets, along which sauntered groups of soldiers in convivial abandon. Seville was accustomed to soldiers and these were the King's own guard, stationed in Seville because the court was here, and awaiting his command which would send them, and all the army, against the Moors in Granada.

Ships and soldiers, and the Andalusian sun in golden glory behind the Castle of Triana, where the Inquisitors met. The dying splendor of Moorish grandeur in western Europe; old Quemadero and his crackling wrath; and now Christopher Columbus. These days were to shake the earth and reshape it, maybe for a thousand years, maybe forever. What an age was my youth.

However, I had no thoughts for such things, for in the sun's golden warmth I saw only the radiance of Maraela's hair. There was a surging in my heart and a yearning in my loins and for this I was ashamed of my manliness and sought to banish my lustful hunger; but it had seized me and I surrendered my mind to my enraptured fancy, kindling an image of Maraela in sweet and joyous submission, and knowing this was one sin I would never confess to Juan Ruiz de Medina.

# CHAPTER 5

*M*Y NEXT MARINO LECTURE CAME ON WEDNESDAY AND I
remember the event most vividly because on that occasion I first heard
mention of the Marino map, which was another thread the Fates
wove into the tapestry of my life. I am positive of the day inasmuch
as Fray Juan was not present, and it was his custom to give Wednes-
days to his duties at the Court of the Inquisition.

Death's warrant on Wednesday; Death's fire on Friday.

I sat next to our capacious prior, whose belly frequently rumbled
his morning chick-peas and onions, and these finding vent in gaseous
detonations which disturbed the other friars and amused the students.
Benjamin Marino seemingly was impervious to such physiological
phenomena, and gave his attention to his involved discourse on Cardinal d'Ailly, chancellor of the Sorbonne and author of *Imago Mundi*,
a Gallic Prince of the Church and ludicrously ignorant of Spain's
geography.

Regretfully I record that the learned Marino gave more attention
than he received, as most of us already were versed in D'Ailly's flummery, and this including his thesis on the Phoenix bird and Asbestos
stones that burned forever, and on griffins, on blackbirds of dazzling
whiteness, trees of golden fruit, and gems in the skulls of dragons. This
nonsense, I suppose, was acceptable to France's Sorbonne, but Spanish
colleges scorned such drivel and, as is well known, our institutions
were infinitely superior to all others in the world.

(The foregoing is noted only to explain my surprise years later
when I discovered that D'Ailly's *Imago Mundi* was one of Columbus'
guidebooks and that he had underscored all references to gold and

55

pearls, and *Jews* and *jewelry*, the conjugation of which, even in my youth, had given rise to many witty maxims and arrant puns.)

As Teacher Marino droned on and on, my mind wandered first to my immediate surroundings and then to food and then, inevitably and without struggle on my part, to Maraela. I was drowsing in my sensual contemplations when Benjamin Marino said:

"I have been requested by Don Luis de la Cerda, the fifth Count and first Duke of Medinaceli, to prepare a map of the Ocean Sea. This commission I have accepted."

(Yes, a hundred times yes! And hear me, Mita, and believe me, my beloved, my bewitching flame of a thousand nights. By the bones' of Abraham, by the True Cross, by the Black Stone of the holy Kaaba— I heard him say it. The sun was touching the leaded windows of our *sanctum sanctorum* and he was hunched over the podium, his eyes blazing his visions and his voice strong and unafraid.)

The mention of Cerda brought my mind quickly from its reverie, and my head snapped up, as did our prior's, his pudgy face suddenly hard and his stare cold. For Don Luis de la Cerda was of Spain's most noble lineage and whereas not as rich as the Duke of Medina-Sidonia, who had shown interest in Christopher Columbus, he was, nevertheless, more influential at court; and like the Duke, and like Columbus also, Cerda was an advocate of Franciscan pre-eminence in affairs of state, learning, and ecclesiastical jurisprudence.

Was this, then, a devious machination of Franciscan conception to entice Benjamin Marino from the Dominicans? That is why our college instantly was alert and why I gave my unstinted attention to the words of our geographer. We did not connect the events with Christopher Columbus at all. Not then. We were concerned only with our lecturer's association with Cerda and the possibility of Franciscan chicanery.

The guileless Marino warmed to the subject of his map and made no pretenses of secrecy. "For this work," he said, "I will use the theorem of El Fargani, who, more than seven hundred years ago, used 56⅔ miles to the degree as the proper measurement of the earth. Now——" He held up his hands and touched his fingers to emphasize his point. "El Fargani's miles were Arabic miles, each of 1,973.50 meters. Our modern cosmographers have based their calculations on El Fargani's dictum, but have broken his degrees into Italian miles, which are much shorter than Arabic miles. Hence a great error."

A twinkle of mirth came to his eyes and he said:

"It is possible that Christopher Columbus, a subject of discussion here the day before yesterday, is a victim of this delusion. I shall strive to avoid it.

"I will presume to fix the meridian on Gomera, that western point of the Canary Islands. Seven hundred leagues west I shall place Antilia and behind that island will be a mass of *terra incognita*, land of which we know naught. But it is not India! The world is larger than you think. Over and over I say to you: the world is larger than you think."

His lecture was given over then to facts and tables and again my mind wandered and remained on its wool-gathering journey until Benjamin Marino concluded his discourse and turned the session over to our prior for discussion.

The prior, dripping sweat, expediently was concerned with things closer than India and exhorted us to patriotic endeavor. The infidels were still in Granada and it was the duty of every Andalusian to support the Crown and drive the Moors in the sea. Oh, that he were young enough to lift lance and sword himself. And this from the Dominican who once had supported Rome against his Queen. Yes, he had heard that indulgences were being sold and the money given for the Granada campaign.

This was justified; so he said.

Yes, he was aware that some convicted heretics were being fined instead of burned, the money going to the war against the Moors.

This, too, was proper, we were told, inasmuch as the end justified the means.

Then our prior, using a scroll that bore the royal ribbons, read the new mule law and praised it as an example of the Crown's astute statecraft, and urged rigid adherence to its provisions. Of course, the prior himself was exempt from the regulation by royal sanction.

The mule law? Your smile is forgiven and I take no umbrage, being aware that few men have connected King Ferdinand's mule ban to discovery of the New Lands, although it is a strand in the rope that Christopher Columbus swung from Palos to San Salvador, as important, surely, as the broken tiller that bedeviled us, as Alonso Pinzon's deaf ear, as the bits of tarred rope that almost caused a mutiny.

Now this mule law was a war measure. The Andalusian mule, as is well known, is the best in the world and is prized highly for purposes

57

of saddle as well as husbandry. The Arabian horses of Andalusia, superior though they be, are too expensive for common use. Therefore, in those days mules were plentiful and horses were rather scarce, and King Ferdinand needed horses for his cavalry.

Hence, he simply banned mules as saddle beasts, except by royal permit, and thereby gave impetus to horse breeding. To deny an Andalusian his saddle mule was to shorten his legs and the law brought howls from the people, and many violations with subsequent punishment. It was this punishment that helped launch our expedition across the Ocean Sea. It was a mule and not a miracle. It was the hybrid foal of a jack and a mare and not the heavenly anointment of Christopher Columbus' broad forehead.

After the morning session and a lesson on mulery to season Benjamin Marino's lecture, I returned to my quarters and gave all that day to Isidore, and then Fray Juan examined me. I am sure he was pleased with my progress, although he gave no hint thereof, for he tarried with me and talked of ships and geography. This brought our conversation to Teacher Marino and I presumed to ask about Cerda's commission for the map.

"It is true," my fray said. "Benjamin Marino will enter the employ of Don Luis de la Cerda."

"Then the Friars Minor are taking him away from us." I was indignant and assumed the Dominicans would protest this Franciscan outrage.

"Benjamin Marino belongs to the world, Rodrigo." Fray Juan stroked his chin and if he felt any bitterness he concealed it. "I have sought a commission for a Marino map, but our prior and King Ferdinand think the Moorish War is more important than the Ocean Sea. So Don Luis de la Cerda opened his own purse, and if the Franciscans profit then so will the world." He sighed his resignation to events he could not master. "Aye, little brother, Benjamin Marino belongs to all."

"But he is our teacher." I was dismayed and angry, for defeat is a thing I have never taken lightly and the Franciscans had bested us.

Fray Juan paced the floor a time or so and then smiled, apparently seeking to allay my anger. "There are other teachers. We should be grateful for the knowledge Marino has given us. He will be leaving soon."

"To eat the rich viands of Don Luis de la Cerda and slake his thirst on the distilled metaphysics of the Minorites?"

A short, quick laugh, a lean expression of mirth, escaped my fray. "No Christian lance will ever pierce the Jewish armor of Benjamin Marino. He is not going to Don Luis at all. He is going home to do his work."

"Catalonia?"

"Yes. To his wife and children; a son, I am sure, and a daughter, I think." He yawned the drowsiness of autumn's somnolence. "I will send you the writings of El Fargani. You read Arabic?"

"Why, no, Father." I was so surprised that I forgot to call him brother.

"But you speak it." His eyes fastened on me. "Old Mudarra has taught you."

"Not much, Fray Juan." I corrected my error. "Only some conversational Arabic and a few proverbs."

"Including praise of Mohammed." The Inquisitor lifted the latch on my door. "I, for one, think we should teach Arabic in our college, but I am alone in this idea. Therefore, learn all that Mudarra offers. He is wiser than most men think." Fray Juan stepped back to my bench and picked up the book of Isidore to take it away, thank the Mercy of God, and laid his hand on my shoulder. "But do not repeat the praises of Mohammed, Rodrigo. These are times when men are indicted by innuendo and judged by rumors and hysteria."

He was gone and a cold terror gnawed in my breast, for I knew by his warning that Mudarra had been discussed in the Court of the Inquisition, and if Mudarra the Morisco, then what of Luis Harana the converso? Or Maraela, his daughter.

All that day I was troubled by misgivings and that night I dreamed of djinn and other evil spirits, and of old Quemadero; his molten lust embracing Maraela and her shining face wreathed by flames, like the saintly countenance of Jeanne, The Maid, dead at Rouen for fifty-three years while her ashes kindled fires of protest in all Europe.

Then the next morning I heard Benjamin Marino's last lecture to the College of Seville. It was only my third and yet it seems now that I knew him well, but that, I know, is my old age exaggerating the distinction of my youth, a failing common to most men after forty. Actually I saw the great Marino three times and never spoke one word to him, but he is engraved on my memory like the wind etchings on the Pillars of Hercules.

Fray Juan, in reward for work well done, gave me permission to visit my father's shop again on Friday afternoon, and I drew a jar of water from the well in the patio and washed myself all over and beat my dusty clothes with the flat of my hand, brushing them as best I could.

I walked jauntily out of the monastery and among a muddle of soldiers on leave, and rapidly to the store in the hope that Harana was there and perhaps Maraela, and I was determined to see her even by ruse if necessary.

My father was at his desk, examining accounts with a clerk from the Seville agency of the House of the Medici, the powerful Italian bankers and merchants; this clerk being one Amerigo Vespucci who was well known to us as a Florentine braggart, a liar of indefatigable practice, and a counting-room sailor.

Harana was not present, neither Maraela; Amerigo Vespucci and my father greeted me, Vespucci with a familiarity I did not reciprocate. Their conference was business and so I turned from them, after the proper amenities, and walked into Mudarra's shop.

The old man was napping at his wheel and, awakened by my entrance, cocked one eye at me and muttered, "*Assalamu alaik*"—the greeting and peace of his people. I answered in the same tongue and glanced around, conscious that something was different.

All the putrid odors, so offensive on my last visit, were gone and the room was spotlessly clean, although sand and water had failed to remove the blood spots under the cask.

"Maraela," the old potter explained, anticipating my question. "She had my stable scoured and sees that it is kept that way." He mouthed the words, chewing them into mangled Spanish as though contemptuous of the realm's language.

I sat on his bench and, after a lapse that should have concealed my curiosity, I said, "I thought perhaps she might be here."

Mudarra yawned and scratched and actually was civil in his reply. "She comes twice a week. And her father is here only in the mornings. Business is flourishing again, Rodrigo, which explains the presence of that Florentine toadeater in the showroom."

I was turning in my mind an excuse to visit the Harana home when Mudarra, squinting at me, demanded with an officious show of authority: "Is mooning also a lesson from your Dominican masters? What other drivel have they seeped through your armored skull?"

"Isidore," I answered and none too politely.

"That madman! That eater of meat with his fouled hand!" He spat his disgust. "That dabbler in mysteries too deep for his puny mind——"

"And El Fargani." I interrupted his tirade.

His eyes popped wide and his clapping tongue suddenly was stilled, and then he nodded approval. "Well, now, that is better. Peace to the bones of El Fargani."

"And I learned of a most extraordinary man." I was saving the choice morsel until last. "One Christopher Columbus, mariner."

"The Redhead of La Rabida?" He began pedaling his wheel and cleaning its surface with a rag that he dipped in water.

"Redhead?" My surprise abused my composure. "Do you know him?"

He laughed his derision and pumped his wheel furiously, slinging water and bits of clay around the room. "Did not your Dominican hinnies tell you he is of rusty countenance and red hair? A most singular appearance for one of Genoese extraction."

"I did not know that." All the wind was out of my sails. "I know only his Portuguese story and that he is at La Rabida and seeking patronage of the Duke of Medina-Sidonia."

Old Mudarra broke into a cackling laugh and he slapped his knee in visible approval of himself. "Tell Juan Ruiz de Medina that his Inquisition has lost its eyes and ears. Tell him it is a tiding from Mudarra the Morisco." His mirth wrinkled his face into dry parchment. "Christopher Columbus is not at La Rabida. The Duke of Medina-Sidonia has washed his hands of the matter. Columbus demanded the moon in his lap and a silver spoon with which to eat it."

Here was good news, an indication that the Franciscans had failed to ally their protégé with the richest house in Spain. This would please my fellows at the college and give me stature as a man capable of sifting for facts in matters of pertinence. I was jaunty again and the wind was back in my sails, and then Mudarra snapped the mast.

"Christopher Columbus is in the home of Don Luis de la Cerda at El Puerto and under the patronage of that bilious lackey of Isabel's court."

Cerda! Columbus with Cerda, and this the Queen's favorite and

Franciscan partisan who had commissioned our Marino to map the Ocean Sea. The news agitated me and left me most distraught, so much so that for a minute I forgot even Maraela and the real purpose of my visit. "Where did you learn this, Mudarra——"

"More questions." He jeered my inquiry and raised his finger to point in my face and I pushed it aside, gently, to be sure, but firmly.

"Where did you learn this, Mudarra?" Slowly I repeated my request.

He blinked at me and looked into my face, then at my shoulders, most broad for my age, and at my hands. "The kid," he said almost sadly, "has grown into a ram. The head high and proud and the horns curving strong, and seed in his groin." He stopped his wheel by pressing his knee against its edge, and nodded toward the front room. "The Medici have more fingers than the Inquisition, Rodrigo. That is why they are the most powerful house in Europe. And Amerigo Vespucci is a chattering jay."

So Vespucci was the source. Then I must know more and walked resolutely into the salesroom to question him on this matter of concern to my college and to my Dominican brothers. The Florentine was gone and my father was frowning over his ledgers.

"I was going to call you in a minute." My father pushed the books aside. "Sit on the bench there and tell me of yourself."

The bench was under a shelf of aloes and I sat down and crossed my legs. "I was hoping Amerigo Vespucci was still here," I said. "There are some questions I would ask concerning one Christopher Columbus, mariner. Know you of him?"

My father nodded. "Every merchant in Andalusia knows that he has arrived in Spain to finagle a westward voyage of exploration. A most secretive stranger, however. And cagey."

"He is under the stewardship of Don Luis de la Cerda." I felt most important discussing current affairs with my father.

"Yes, I know."

"And Cerda has enticed Benjamin Marino from our college."

My father flipped his hand upward in a gesture of impatience. "Monastical politics. I care not a tittle for the feuds of friars over their accursed inquisitorial powers." His face was reddening and his tone was stern. "If the Franciscans use Cerda to wheedle the Queen's sanction for a westward expedition, we all are their debtors."

He was right and, sitting in his presence, the schisms and schemes

62

of the orders seemed abstract and mean, for above us was the sky and there was the river flowing to the Ocean Sea, and the world was larger than we believed. I changed the subject, approaching a matter closer to my heart. "Mudarra tells me business is better since you accepted the association of Harana."

The flush left his cheeks and his eyes twinkled his geniality and this was his nature inasmuch as he was blessed with adequate bile and hence favorable humors. He arose from his desk and reached to the shelf above my head and took down a most hideous object of wrinkled tentacles and mushy substance. I drew away instinctively and asked, "What is it?"

"The Medusa," he said proudly. "Also called the devil's fig tree. Properly it is a euphorbia, named for Euphorbus, King Juba's physician."

"An aloe!" I exclaimed and touched the thing gingerly. It was the size of my two fists and with tendrils, or fingers, squirming out in vulgar abundance.

My father put it on his desk as carefully as though it were the Cup itself. "It is more valuable than any pearl," he said. "It is the Medusa of Mauretania, found in the Atlas Mountains, and the world's best source of emetic drugs." He leaned over and smelled it and wrinkled his nose. "It also is a specific for the stomach maladies that will follow the army into Granada."

"Can you get more?" I dared smell the thing, too, and its odor was wet and succulent. Inasmuch as it came from North Africa, where the Moorish ban was drum-tight, I knew its rarity.

My father smiled, somewhat wryly I thought, and shrugged. "Luis Harana furnished this one and I did not pry into his source. If he can supply aloes, I can sell them."

I asked of Harana's health and of Maraela's, hoping to swing the conversation to her, and my father assured me they were well and, in mentioning them, his tone assumed a bland flavor that was not like my father at all. Then he shoved one of his ledgers closer to me and I glanced at the figures.

Pepper was selling for 7000 maravedis a hundredweight in India and 210,000 a hundredweight in Seville, for so taut was Islam's curtain over the East. The profit on ginger was even more and England was begging for ginger at any price. Aloes, between Africa and the apothecary's jar, fetched a margin of 15,000 maravedis a pound, even at smugglers' costs.

I whistled my surprise at the figures and my father closed the book and handed it to me. "It is Luis Harana's custom to check the accounts each afternoon about sundown."

"Does he come here?" I asked hopefully.

"No." My father turned his face and looked out upon the alley, at the soldiers jostling by. "I take the books to him."

I felt the flush mounting my cheeks and clamped my lips to hold back the protest that burned my tongue. My father an errand boy for a rich converso? Luis Harana's presumption needed a quick sting of Andalusian dignity. However, my judgment mastered my pride, and I realized on proper contemplation that my father had his reasons.

He drummed his fingers on the ledger and the twinkle was back in his eyes. "I was thinking perhaps you could deliver the record this afternoon, Rodrigo. It would save me a trip and, as you can see, I am busy."

Now that was different. At my age it was quite fitting for me to wait upon an elderly gentleman, especially my father's own associate. Besides, I was willing to crawl from the shop to the residence of Maraela. "If I can be of service to you, sir——" I bowed to my father and reached for the book.

He laughed and then I laughed, and he told me which was the Harana house on the Street of Felicity. I put the ledger under my arm and walked to the door, and old Mudarra called from the back room. "*In sha Allah, Amir el bahr.*" He was calling me admiral again. "And remember that from the seed of a young ram came the flocks of The Messenger."

My face tingled my mortification and embarrassment and I bolted through the doorway before he said more.

The Harana residence was near the river, at the end of the street and through a sheltered passageway, lonely in its location and almost concealed from the casual eye. The door was bolted and I swung the clapper against the bronze cymbal, on which was engraved: "Luis Harana, Merchant."

Harana himself cracked the door and peered at me, then nodded for me to enter. I stepped inside a hallway heavily draped and leading directly to the dining room, where candles burned on a table set with

64

many bowls and plates. I was motioned into a large room off the hall and Harana held out his hand and I gave him the ledger.

Maraela was nowhere in sight.

"Thank you, Rodrigo," her father said and bowed quite gracefully for a Catalan, but did not offer the hospitality of his home, or even a bench for a minute's visit.

I had come to see her. Of this I had dreamed all week and, even in those days, I was never one to accept defeat without a thrust in my own behalf. So I glanced around the room in a manner most gauche, caring not one whit if Luis Harana thought me untrained in the graces. I was resolved upon any artifice to delay my departure and thus compel him, if he had manners at all, to offer me a seat and the vintage of his table.

A poniard in a leather case was hanging by the window and I pretended immediate interest in the dagger and extracted it from its shield, exclaiming my delight although, truthfully, I knew nothing of such weapons except that they were the favorites of sailors.

"Ah! Damascus," I said and ran my thumb along the triangular blade.

"Toledo," he replied flatly.

I was flustered and, hoping my chagrin was not evident, I balanced the knife on my palm and examined it closely, thus bowing my head to conceal the tinge on my cheeks. The hilt was wrapped in fine wire and the bar was the same metal as the blade and across it was engraved the ancient cry of Andalusia: "Trust God and hammer on!"

Harana was fidgety and I returned the poniard to its sheath and gave my attention to a tapestry by the door. "Ah, beautiful," I said, dawdling my admiration in the manner of a critic. "Obviously Florentine."

He smiled in spite of himself and his face was gentle. "No, Rodrigo. My daughter wove it."

It was the opening I wanted, and I bore in. "I had hoped, sir, for the honor of seeing your daughter."

He looked at me without disapproval, I must say; the smile softening his long countenance. "Your wish is my command, sir."

Luis Harana was the first man ever to call me "sir."

I bowed my gratitude and he stepped into the hallway and promptly was back with Maraela, and this indicating she had been near all the while. A lace cap covered the crown of her head and a meshed chain of silver encircled her waist like a girdle. Her reception was courtly and

65

exquisitely refined although perhaps a bit too cordial for an Andalusian maiden, but, then, she was Catalan, and manners differ in Spain.

Naturally, the warmth of her greeting pleased me exceedingly and she sat on a couch near her own tapestry. I remained standing until Harana left us, explaining that he would be in the next room, checking the ledger I had brought. I took no offense that he did not close the door between us and him.

For a minute or so, as becomes good breeding, I walked around the room and commented on the pictures and congratulated Maraela on her family's excellent taste. Her gaze followed me and that was the reason for my demonstration; to give her an opportunity to see and judge me without our eyes meeting.

I stood before her own tapestry and said, "It is magnificent."

"It is nothing, Rodrigo."

The liberty of my first name was a boldness that brought a tingle to my manliness and I sat on the couch and was near enough to detect the anise of her perfume. She folded her hands in her lap and her eyes were downcast in maidenly propriety. "Your father says you are doing well at the college."

It was an invitation for me to pursue that subject and this I did, launching into a discourse on Benjamin Marino, whose name evicted no interest from her, and then on Fray Juan, the mention of whom brought her eyes up to mine.

"Juan Ruiz de Medina?" she asked. "The Inquisitor?"

"Only in Seville," I explained.

"Yes, I know. Torquemada—Fray Tomas de Torquemada—is being made Inquisitor-General for all of Spain."

Here was intelligence of which I had no knowledge and I was displeased that she, a girl, should have information about which I was ignorant. Apparently she sensed my embarrassment, for she said quickly, "We hear things outside the monastery that do not penetrate the Dominican walls. Torquemada is of a converso family, even as I."

This was ground I did not like, miry and mussy. "I am aware of the lineage of Tomas de Torquemada, prior of Santa Cruz," I said. "He is a Dominican in the Queen's graces and favored of the Pope himself. A scourge of heresy." Then skillfully I shifted the subject to my father's business, elaborating at length on the aloe her father had furnished, the Medusa of Mauretania. "It was discovered by King Juba," I said in airy assurance.

66

"King Juba II," she replied demurely. "He wed Cleopatra Selene, the daughter of Anthony and Cleopatra. Do you know his lineage too?" Her blue eyes bespoke sweet innocence, but the delicate smile indicated a wit and talent that is rare in her sex.

I laughed at my own confutation and congratulated her on her nimbleness and was bold enough to praise her raiment. She held up her hand to halt my flattery and for an ecstatic moment I thought she was going to touch me, but slowly she dropped her hand to the sanctuary of her lap and lowered her eyes again.

I might have spoken the urge of my heart even then, being a victim of my own rash impulses, but Harana came into our presence and laid the ledger beside me. "I thank you, Rodrigo," he said. "And tell your father all is well and in order."

Maraela arose and excused herself and I spoke hastily. "Next week, to help my father, I will bring the records again."

I wanted her to hear me, and she did; her eyes telling me so.

There were no clouds that afternoon and yet I walked on clouds back to the shop and returned the accounts to my father. "That was a pleasant chore," I said.

"The ledger will be here next Friday." He indicated the corner of the desk where it would be. "The errand is a service for which I am grateful." Then he embraced me and counseled me to diligence and piety, and I shouted good-by to Mudarra and took my departure. This time I was determined to be back at the college for vespers.

The streets were swarming with soldiers and I gave them no thought. The river was swarming with ships and I saw them not. Only the blue of the sky, like her eyes, and the sun golden on the horizon, like her hair, and red in its farewell, like her lips.

The joy of my youth took hold of me and budded into ambition and noble resolve. I would study hard and soon would enter my father's business to honor the name of Bermejo. A merchant of Seville. Ah-h-h, worthy endeavor. And Maraela shared my dreams, the abode I would purchase by the river, my doublets and silk stockings in the alcove of my chamber, and an open passage between my couch and her boudoir.

Where is the bridle for youth's fancy? The stone of reason to balance the hazy illusions? The quickening from the slumber of things unreal? The awakening from the dream of Alnaschar.

How the Fates must have jeered as they measured the days of my

67

years; Clotho spinning my destiny, Lachesis disposing the lots, Atropos cutting the threads.

Stygian sluts of the inner darkness, their river seven times around the world. They let me dream on.

CHAPTER 6

*A*ND THUS IT WAS WITH ME.

I applied myself zealously to my studies and other monasterial duties and conducted myself in a most exemplary manner to win favors from Fray Juan, particularly the fleeting surcease and liberty of Friday afternoons.

Then always I hastened to my father's shop and always the ledger was on a corner of his desk, and I tarried only long enough to exchange pleasantries with him and old Mudarra, and was away for my hour of Paradise with my lovely Maraela.

It was always the same. I swung the clapper and Harana unbolted the door and peered at me and took the accounts, and I followed him into the hall and thence to the big room, and there she came to me and he went away, always bowing his leave.

Maraela and I sat on the couch under the poniard and near her tapestry, but her father was always nigh, either in the adjoining room, the room of the open door, or padding about the house in his velvet slippers. We talked, she and I, of things as they were and sometimes, in the desperation of my ardor, I dared whisper of things as I dreamed they could be. And always she listened and lowered her eyes, and said naught.

Once, to stem the flow of my fervor, she touched my hand and her fingers were cold and I seized them and held them until the fire of my blood warmed them, and then slowly she pulled her hand away and raised her face to me and drank deeply of the desire in my eyes and murmured tenderly, "We are young, Rodrigo mine."

"I am almost sixteen," I said. "A man's age in Andalusia."

"I, too, will soon be sixteen," she said. A woman's age in any land."

69

I felt for her hand and she moved it away, and I, calling on words I could not create, sought expression in an old Moorish poem that Mudarra had taught me, and whispered the sentiment:

> "I come from fields of death, and in its sheath
> My good sword rests; but thou, O glaive of Love,
> Giv'st no repose; still thou dost wound my heart
> With torments ever new. Afar, methought,
> Were pain and woe that could not well increase,
> Yet fiercer glow the fires within my breast
> As I draw near thee, Love . . ."

Impulsively she snatched my hand and held it hard in her lap, her fingernails biting into my flesh, and she closed her eyes and breathed the ode of Alhakem, the ancient elegy of the East:

> "From thy sweet eyes, in that sad hour of parting,
> There fell hot tears; but thine, they bathed thy cheek,
> And lay upon thy loveliest neck, a circlet
> Of pearls beyond all price. My tears were rubies
> Of purple glow, and now, e'en now, sweet Love,
> I marvel that the heart within me break not,
> For fain would then my soul have ta'en her flight.
> The tears that drowned my eyes were not from them,
> But from my heart; and they betrayed their source,
> By that deep tint which never comes but thence!"

Through my tears of love's sweet torment her golden hair shimmered like the horizon halo of sun embracing sea and I leaned close to entreat her lips, but she drew away in fright as Harana moved in the next room and then joined us.

He returned the ledger to me and said, "Tell your father all is well and in order."

Always he said that and then, after Maraela had excused herself, he always opened the door for me and bade me good day, and always it was before sundown.

At another time, a Friday soon after the New Year of 1485, Maraela's restraint relaxed again for a brief minute and her thigh touched mine as we sat on the couch and heard her father's footsteps move from the room of the open door into the rear of the long hallway. She made no effort to loosen the seal between her loin and my loin and I felt the warmth through her garment and, most tenderly, I stroked her cheek.

Again she seized my hand and buried it deep in her lap and, aroused by her transformation from maiden into nymph, I fumbled for her breasts and she tilted her head to the back of the couch and breathed rapidly in a spasm of elation. Then the footfalls again and she jerked erect, biting her lower lip into white pain as Harana came into our presence, the ledger in his hand and the bid of good day in his demeanor.

Thus it was in the bloom of my first love, the sap strong from the roots and the flower sensitive and tipped with gold, and then pink in its maidenly blush, and then deep scarlet in its Sybaritic glory.

The Andalusian winter lay calm on the land, and Christopher Columbus was at El Puerto in the home of Cerda, his patron, and together they planned an audience with Isabel and Ferdinand at the court here in Seville. Aye. *Vincit qui patitur*. Christopher Columbus, with the patience of Job and the dream of Jason, kept one eye on the court of Isabel, awaiting her call, and one eye on the Ocean Sea, awaiting its call, too.

But I had eyes only for Maraela.

The captains and the soldiers had departed Seville and were thrusting into Granada against the battlements of Boabdil the Moor, shouting the ancient cry of Andalusia, "Trust God and hammer on!" The bombards and now the lance! The crossbow and now the sword! And they died screaming fealty to Santiago and all the saints of Spain, and a salute for the Royal Banner of Isabel's Castile, a prayer for the Golden Cross of Ferdinand's Aragon.

My emblem was golden, too; gold and blue and red, her hair, her eyes, her lips.

The court had moved to Cordova, eighty miles up the Guadalquivir River, for the emblazoned retinue of monarchy had feasted too long on the pimpish largesse of Seville's nobles and the earthen floors of the castles were strewn with bones from the royal board.

But I feasted on the beauty of Maraela Harana.

Torquemada had become Inquisitor-General for all of Spain and old Quemadero burned from the Pyrenees to the Ocean Sea, purifying the souls of conversos by roasting their flesh.

My soul burned only for Maraela.

On February 2, the monastery celebrated Candlemas Day, the

Purification of the Virgin, and then it was spring again and the little dog rose of Andalusia came to bloom and birds nested in the reeds along the river.

It was raining when I took the Wafer that Friday morning, and was storming tumultuously when Fray Juan came to my stall that afternoon, only a few minutes before my weekly respite, before my hour of Paradise with Maraela. He had a copy of *Historia Rerum Ubique Gestarum* under his arm and was eating dried beans again.

I feared a visit that might impose upon my leave and eyed the book suspiciously. Fray Juan laid it upon the bench and sat himself beside it with the resignation of a visitor who has no conception of time or his fellow man's intent.

My breeding, nevertheless, compelled me to ask his health and other matters of polite trivia, including his opinion of the weather, which was discouraging. He answered in monosyllables, as though his mind and tongue were asunder, and there were long, infuriating pauses between his words as his jaw revolved malevolently and his teeth crunched the beans. I was fidgety because the minute for my freedom was nigh and I could not depart Juan Ruiz de Medina without his sanction. In nervous anxiety I snatched for a subject to interest him and asked the latest news of Christopher Columbus, not that I cared a copper blanca about Christopher Columbus.

"With Cerda," Fray Juan said. "Still with Cerda."

"And how is Benjamin Marino progressing with his map?" I reached for another subject.

"Slowly." He clasped his hands around his knee and looked at the window and at the rain gushing against the stones, hiding the river while the sky lacerated the earth with lightning whips and the earth bellowed her protests in rolling thunder. For a long time he sat thus, and me straining, and then he said, "*Ruat caelum!* It is droll that Marino himself may be wrong. The earth is larger even than he thinks."

"Aye?" It was amusing that my fray should challenge the great map-maker. "That is droll." I assumed he would not fathom the subtlety of my pun.

His eyes left the window and fastened on my face and he smiled. "Benjamin Marino is not the only learned cosmographer in the world." I detected a yearning, a longing that I should know that he, too, was a man of letters, that this ugly specter and twisted Fury was one of God's creatures and blessed in mind if denied in body. It was piteously

72

sad and I was closer to him than ever before and could not leave him, even for Maraela, because he was so lonely.

"I was sent to the College of Seville——" The lie came easily. "I was sent to the Dominicans to profit by the knowledge of Fray Juan Ruiz de Medina."

His fleeting pride, yea, sinful pride, was reward for my perjury and he smiled again. "Absolution for that lie is given of God and, therefore, I am spared the truth. And thou, little brother, will forgive my vanity."

He was encroaching upon my time, stealing minutes from my hour of Paradise, but there was naught I could do and he betrayed no intention of going away. Another long pause and he said, "Aye. The earth is larger than Marino believes. Studious men have known since the days of Eratosthenes that the girth of our sphere is 26,000 miles. And Eratosthenes lived three hundred years before Christ."

"A Greek?" My interest flared immediately.

"A Greek." He nodded methodically. "A Western man, Rodrigo, and hence scorned by Semites. But all knowledge does not come from the East." He stroked his chin and scratched his bare toe along the stones of my floor. "Eratosthenes measured the earth with a rod, a well, a pole, and a shadow."

I leaned forward to catch every word and, seeing my heed, he spat out the bean hulls and wiped a trickle of saliva from the corners of his mouth. "This Greek was a librarian at Alexandria." He arrayed his facts and recited them. "At Syene, 520 miles from Alexandria, was a well that was lighted to its bottom on the day of the summer solstice. So the sun was directly overhead."

He peered at me, then continued. "Eratosthenes erected a pole at Alexandria and on the day of the solstice he measured the angle of the pole's shadow. It was 7⅕ degrees. Know you that significance?"

"No," I said truthfully.

"Then we will spend more time on mathematics and less on geography," he mumbled, grating the words in obvious displeasure. "Aroint! Even a dullard should know that if Eratosthenes' pole and Syene's well were extended to the center of the earth they would meet at the same angle, or 7⅕ degrees. Now, how many degrees in a circle?"

"Three hundred and sixty."

"Then the 7⅕-degree angle was ¹⁄₅₀th of a circle." He bore in like a starving rat that has smelled food. "Hence, the distance between the

73

pole and the well was ⅟₅₀th of the earth's girth. Multiply the distance, 520 miles, by 50."

"It comes to 26,000," I said.

"Exactly." He held out his left hand and it trembled as he extended his fingers rigidly for emphasis. "The Greek unit of measure was the stadium and we may have erred a trifle in changing the distance into miles. But let Christopher Columbus prattle of the Indies. Let Benjamin Marino scourge his brain for the secrets of the Ocean Sea. I tell you the earth's circumference is 26,000 miles." He clinched his fingers into a gnarled fist and struck his knee. "East by land, Cathay itself is less than one third that distance, even this far north of the Equator, and I am assuming a stingy figure. Hence, west by water, Cathay is at least 18,000 miles from Spain."

The fires that Teacher Marino had kindled blazed again in me and time was without meaning. "Then Cathay is beyond our reach," I said. "Westward by water."

"Not at all, Rodrigo. Not at all." He crossed over to the window and watched the rain, and the wind rustled his mantle and misted rain against his cheeks. "God commanded us to carry the sweet message of His Son to all men. Therefore, nothing is inaccessible, nothing impossible. There is land between here and Cathay and where you find land you will find men. And every man is your brother and his soul is your concern——"

This talk I did not relish. Geography, yes. Theology, no. And again I was vexed that he was poaching minutes from my hour of Paradise.

"The lands of the Unknown are a bridge to the Known." He was mumbling again and his face was graven against the window and etched sharp by the lightning. "Marino speaks of islands to the west. And 700 leagues. Beshrew! There are masses of land out there or else God gave man merely a speck for his habitation. And that land is nearer than we dare believe. Ptolemy knew it and I shall teach it."

His fervor was thoroughly Dominican, the zeal of Savonarola of the same order, who even then was shaking Italy into an ague of reformation.

"Eratosthenes," I repeated the Greek's name to remember it. "And 26,000 miles. Why has such knowledge been hidden from us, Fray Juan?"

"Nothing is hidden from those who seek." It was spoken as though the opening of a parable and I resigned myself for a metaphorical

74

harangue, and then he turned his back to the window and his face was in shadows while his head was lighted by the sky flames of the storm. "The tragedy of this age is man's assumption of superiority and his scorn of Antiquity's knowledge; our devastating conviction that we share the eldern earth and not its infancy. The Greeks, in many ways, were wiser."

"And how?" I asked. "We have the blessings of Him dead and risen. They had only the promise."

He left the window and stood by me and his artful eyes mapped my face in the manner of Inquisitors searching the conscience of man for one blemish of heresy. Was Fray Juan testing me? Were the fingers of the Inquisition feeling for a broken link in my Christian armor? The ears of the Inquisition against my breast to count the heartbeats of my conformity? I was bewildered, but I spoke out as an Andalusian and the son of the son of a Goth. "What is this meaning, elder brother? Why were the Greeks wiser? Is heathen ignorance the master of Christian wisdom?"

"What a Dominican you would make." He muttered the dictum, but I heard it, and I heard clearly what followed and measured the dogmatism for its meaning; for he said, "The Greeks bound their gods to events and discoveries. We bind events to our God and suffer the stupefaction of the Philistines."

These words from the Queen's Inquisitor! This could be a mesh to ensnare me and immediately, aye, instinctively, I recited my remonstrance. "That is Dissension, Fray Juan. And I call upon you to witness that, at sound of the words, I invoked my protest."

His answer was as calm as a summer dawn in the Sierra de los Santos. "Dissension?" He tasted the accusation and it obviously was insipid. "You retreat into mild expression, Rodrigo, for my words were heresy."

I stared at him, my mouth gaping and my tongue cloven. This was no artifice of the Inquisition's cunning. This man was speaking Truth as he knew Truth and was chancing his life to teach me that Truth, for in those days the voice of any accuser could indict at Quemadero's tribunal; the voice of the turtle-dove had loosed the lions in the street.

It came to me then why Juan Ruiz de Medina was ever a friar and never a prior, why Torquemada was Inquisitor-General and my tutor was only a lance bearer in the Army of Purification. This man was a Dissenter, one of those Dominicans who, like Savonarola, dared cry

75

repentance and reformation above the ashes of Quemadero's wrath.

He had handed me a quill for his Doomsday Book and I pretended naïvete and wanted only to be away from that place of gloom and wormwood and into the sweet presence of Maraela. "My fray," I said with measured dignity, "is a man of exquisite discretion whose prudence I pray to reflect. He also is a man of consummate justice and so, therefore, I presume to remind him that this is Friday afternoon and already much of my respite has passed."

"On a day such as this?" He flung his arm toward the window and the storm outside. "Would you brave such weather for a brief recess?"

"It is my right," I said.

"You may see your father tomorrow. I grant it. But not today——"

"It is my right," I repeated firmly.

He drew closer to me as though there was something he would say and then, after cogitation, he drew away again and was stern and aloof. "Aye, Rodrigo of Triana. It is your right."

One glance he gave to the *Historia Rerum* on the bench and another glance he gave to me, and was gone, leaving open the door between my stall and the grilled exit of the monastery. Quickly I pulled my jacket tight around my neck and dashed to the street, and raced to my father's shop, hugging the walls along the way to shield myself from heaven's anger of torrent and thunder.

My father was not there and the ledger was not on his desk.

And the gloom of evening was fast upon the land, and the sun going down into the riddle of the Unknown.

I hurried to the back room and old Mudarra was on his knees and scrubbing the floor and this, indeed, a mockery of his pride. He was startled by my sudden attendance, and to conceal his surprise he blurted his acrimony. "What here, Dominican scamp? Only fools and fish breast this weather."

"Where is my father?" I was in no mood for his disdain and my voice bespoke my temper.

He straightened and hurled the scrub rag into a corner and under the cask. "He went out with Amerigo Vespucci and it is obvious that the storm caught him."

"The ledger is not on the desk——"

"Then he does not want you to take it to Harana. That, too, is obvious, or should be." He growled the judgment and sat his bench, pumping his wheel furiously and glancing about the floor and then at me.

I returned to the salesroom and sprawled in my father's chair and was taken with a seizure of disgust and anger. The day was away and my liberty was up and, even if I chose to violate my monasterial duties, I had no acceptable excuse to disturb Harana in his own home and thereby see Maraela.

But urgencies always sharpened my wits and I opened the desk and there was the ledger and it was posted to that day. I assumed an oversight on my father's part, that he simply had forgot to leave the book on the desk, yet knowing the assumption was only a balm for my conscience. A fie on conscience! Bell and book for the monastery and a candle for Fray Juan Ruiz de Medina! I shoved the ledger under my jacket and walked boldly out of the shop and was aware that Mudarra could not hear my departure above the gush and clatter of the storm and the whirl of his potter's wheel.

The rain beat upon my hunched shoulders and I darted down the narrow alleys and along the riverway to the Street of Felicity. The cymbal shone yellow in the Furies' celestial lanterns and I swung the clapper, but the clapper of heaven's thunder drowned all earthly noises. Again I swung the clapper and again its echo melted into the thunder.

Instinctively, and without second thought, I felt for the latch and it loosened, and I stepped into the hallway to call Harana and announce my presence.

Mother of Mercy! My very guts quivered into a nauseous jelly of dismay and I was seized in a spasm of horror.

The dining table was adorned by a spotless white cloth and there sat Harana, the prayer shawl of Israel over his head, and Maraela with a taper, lighting the candles and shielding each with her hand in the tradition of Jewish women since the Babylonian exile.

*Judaizing!*

A gust through the open door flickered the candles and she looked up the hallway and saw me, and dropped the taper in paralytic terror. Then Harana saw me and shrieked his lament and snatched her hand. "The door! You did not bolt the door! We are lost!"

In his piteous bewilderment he bowed his neck and began chanting the Kol Nidre, the Atonement prayer, the plea for release from his vows; part wail, part psalm, and all sorrow.

Maraela yanked tight the drapes to the dining room and ran up the

77

hall and flung herself on me, scratching and screaming. "Beast of cloven hooves! Vile seed of Haman!"

Her nails raked my face like the claws of Triana's prowling cats and I threw up my arms to protect myself and all the while calling her to her senses. "Maraela! Maraela!"

"Swine and sperm of swine! Conception of iniquity! Filth of the Inquisition! Dominican spy!" She spewed the words at me and beat my chest with her sweet hands until I seized her wrists and made myself heard.

"Silence, Maraela! Silence this madness!" I shook her to free her from the devils that had possessed her. "Your secret is safe."

She stared at me and her eyes were wide in the imploration of her hope and then her eyes were closed and she sobbed her rending anguish. "Rodrigo. Rodrigo mine."

I held her head to my breast and stroked her hair. "Could I betray my love?" I asked in staunch resolution. "Could I behead my dreams with treachery's foul sword and scatter them on the barren ground of my own perfidy?" My assurance comforted her and I felt the waning convulsions of her terror. "Better that I tear out my own heart and hurl it to the passion of Quemadero than that I should pain the heart of my beloved."

She looked up at me, searching my face, and the panic was gone from her eyes and they were pleading. "Say you this?" she implored.

"This I say."

"Then swear."

"I swear."

Like a frightened bird with a broken wing she darted into the big room and snatched the poniard and sheath from the wall and raised the hilt to my lips. "By this you swear. This, the Cross."

"By this I swear," I said and kissed the Cross and the words of its admonition: "Trust God and hammer on!"

She thrust it into my hand and rested her head on my shoulder and close to my ear, and whispered, "Then wear it, Rodrigo of Triana, that the Cross of your faith and the steel of your honor may remind you forever of your vow."

And now I was as guilty as she and must share her guilt, for the secret of heresy was as heinous as its practice and the Inquisition tolerated no distinction between information concealed and apostasy done.

Her lips touched my ear in a caress of dew and she abandoned herself to my arms, suddenly whimpering and crushing my mouth and biting my cheeks and neck in frenzied bliss. The manliness of my breed scorned place and time and I imprisoned her in my embrace and looked from her to the couch, and she felt my resolve and slipped from the bonds of my rapture.

"You must depart." She opened the door and the rain misted her hair in glorious adornment and the wind sealed her raiment to her thighs and belly. "I must attend my father, Rodrigo. Farewell."

She encouraged me through the doorway, gently pushing, and closed the portal and I stumbled down the passageway to the Street of Felicity and the rain smarted my cheeks where her frantic nails had ripped my flesh before she kissed away the pain.

My first thought was of my father, to protect him from any knowledge that his associate was a Judaizing converso, and I concocted a story that Harana had not answered my knock and that I had taken refuge from the storm and had fallen on the cobblestones in my haste to return.

Woe the lies of youth. How foolish the conspiracies of heart and tongue.

My father was waiting for me at his desk and one glance dissipated my intent for deception; the haggard lines of his face and the indictment of his eyes. Besides, the poniard was at my hip and how could I pretend I had not entered the Harana home.

He motioned me to the bench and glanced quickly toward the back room to be sure the drapes were drawn between us and Mudarra. Some of the dread that I had first noticed on my father's countenance began to disappear and he said impassively, "Now you know."

I did not reply. I could not.

"This I would have spared you, my son. And the sin is mine."

"Yours?" The poignancy of my question touched him and his visage changed to infinite tenderness.

"Aye, mine." He nodded the verdict. "I have known all along that the Haranas are Christians by day and Jews by night. But I needed Luis and Luis needed me and it might have worked had not the heart of my son and the heart of his daughter become entwined in the mystery of youth's first love."

"I should not have gone there tonight." I sought solace for him in my own condemnation. "The ledger was not here. I opened your desk."

He got up and stood tall before me, he an Andalusian and the son of a Goth. "Never look back, Rodrigo, at the bridgeless chasm you have crossed. I should have been here to forbid your impetuosity. This day is the Feast of Purim, when Jews commemorate their deliverance from Haman, and the fealty of Esther, and the guile of their vengeance on their enemies."

I stood, too, and my head was as high as his and my shoulders as broad. "I have sealed my lips." The poniard was in my hand and I held it before him. "By this Cross I have sworn."

"Reckless warrant of love's duress." He flung up his arms in a gesture of exasperation. "Now you have the stain of their guilt. Even as I." He took the poniard and its sheath and put them in his desk and looked hard at me again and there was a glint of pride in his eyes. "But by the sky gods of your Gothic forebears, a man is born a man." He clasped his hand on my shoulder. "Alert, my son! The eyes of your tutor, of your own confessor, are mirrors for the Inquisition."

I nodded toward the back room and asked, "And what of Mudarra?"

"Mudarra has no tongue for Quemadero's ears. Now to your monastery and we will choose our course on the morrow. Begone in haste, rash youth! before the tempest of my apprehension rises to the tempest of this night that bedevils us."

I ran all the way to the monastery, panting and stumbling when I reached the door, and it was closed. Vespers had passed and the cloisters were still and I pounded on the door and Juan Ruiz de Medina clattered free the bolt and let me in.

Straightway I went to my quarters, pretending petulance and disgust, and straightway he came to me and put his candle on my bench and studied me in the yellow light of the revealing flame. Then he spake: "You were delayed by the storm, perhaps. It was most violent."

"Yes." I rubbed my hand across my face and the scratches were tender. "And very dark. The streets are slippery and the rose thorns sharp along the way." Let him think what he would, that I had been brawling or whoring.

He reached for the candle and the yellow light was in his yellow eyes. "You will fast tomorrow and remain in your quarters all of next week. Even Friday."

"Yes, my fray."

He stepped into the corridor and there he paused and looked back at me. "Shall I confess thee tonight, little brother?"

80

"If you choose." My eyes did not waver.

"It is for you to say, Rodrigo of Triana."

"There is no sin on my soul, Fray Juan." It was a lie to him and not to the Holy Ghost.

"Then good night, and peace attend you."

His shuffling footfalls sounded down the corridor and I crept to my straw. The storm was rumbling its death and I lay wild-eyed and watched the lightning exhaust itself from fiery tongue into meek aurora; and then to sleep.

# CHAPTER 7

*A*LL THE NEXT MORNING, IN SOLITARY CONFINEMENT FOR MY dereliction, I saw no face, I heard no voice, and soon after the meridian, this being the hour the sun crossed the river, my father came to my stall in attendance with Fray Juan.

The Inquisitor's bearing was obdurate and this troubled me muchly; my father's deportment was grim and this troubled me more.

After a perfunctory explanation that my durance was punishment for malfeasance Fray Juan left us, and my father's first admonition was: "Fear not, my son. Fear nothing except thyself."

"Is she all right?" I implored and kicked straw around the bottom of the door to muffle all sound. "And Harana, also. Are they safe?"

"The Haranas departed Seville this midmorning." He spoke the verdict without embellishment.

"Where?" My instinctive concern was that precipitative flight might attract suspicion.

My father shoved the bench near the window and sat down and rubbed the fatigue from his brow. "I know not. I did not see Maraela, only Luis, and unselfishly he spared us further knowledge of his plight and plans."

So she was gone, and my only prayer was for her safety. Some day I would find her, and soon, for at the blessed hour of my freedom from this doleful place I would call her name from every mountaintop in Andalusia and whisper my troth through every vale of Spain. "Their departure is evidence of Harana's discretion." My lips said it, but my heart said more. Oh, Maraela, flower of my youth. I will find you, and this you know.

"Luis is a man of unfaltering wariness," my father said with the prideful candor of his business training. "He closed his affairs with me in the presence of witnesses most reputable and he and his daughter went forth leisurely. On two fine mules——"

"Mules!" The word aroused my apprehension. "Did they have permits?"

My father's scowl was arraignment of my slothful speculation. "Naturally, Rodrigo. Think you that my friend is a fool? Edge your wits, boy. Luis Harana, a converso, did business on this day, the Jewish Sabbath. He applied for a mule license on this day and departed hastelessly as becomes a gentleman of exemplary repute and unblemished conscience."

The sagacity of the maneuver was apparent to me then and I bowed submission to my father's rebuke. "Aye, sir. Harana is a man of unfaltering wariness."

He directed that I sit on the bench by him and put his hand on my knee in the warmth of sodality. "And now for yourself, my son. I am sending you to Lepe."

"To Aunt Ronda?" My freedom was promised sooner than I had dared hope, and my search could begin while her kisses were still sweet on my lips.

"Aye. To my sister. And she will send you to the Franciscans, to the monastery of Santa Maria de los Remedios."

Even this edict disturbed me not at all. I was to be away from the indefatigable scrutiny of Juan Ruiz de Medina. There would be no opportunity for him to cull my thoughts and thus endanger Maraela, and I could begin my quest in Lepe, for Harana, being a merchant, perchance would travel toward the sea. I strove to conceal my delight and said, "Your wishes are my pleasure. Have you spoken to Fray Juan?"

"I have. He knows of my disassociation with Luis Harana and understands my sorrow that my business, henceforth, will not justify your continuance in this college." He smiled tactfully. "He knows you go to your Aunt Ronda, but I chose not to trouble him with our Franciscan plans in Lepe."

How the stones for the temple of my life fitted one to the other: Christopher Columbus was under the protection of the gray mantles of the Franciscans, Benjamin Marino was in their service, and now Lachesis was casting my lot into the net that was to bind the three of us in common cause and set our roles in the Odyssean drama that

84

changed the world. Had I been older, or wiser, this hint of coincidence might have impressed itself upon me, but I had no heed for this collusion of circumstances, cultivating my interest wholly upon Maraela, whom I must find, and upon Lepe, which sired the greatest sailors in the world; Lepe, neighbor of Palos and cousin to Huelva, Lepe of the Ocean Sea.

"When do I leave?" I asked my father, striving manfully to conceal any childish impetuosity.

"Monday. This day you will observe your fast. Tomorrow afternoon you will come to my shop for final instructions. And Monday you will take leave."

"By ship or barge?"

"Neither. A company of drovers are taking mules to Lepe. You will accompany them in the employ of one Pedro de Arcos."

(Arcos, my comrade! That you were alive to read this. You, the staunch arm of Palos, you whose hand held the tiller that miraculous dawn at San Salvador, you who steered our ship into the embrace of the New World and who quailed not at the mystery of the floating meadow. You a mule drover. By the Thirty Pieces, Pedro de Arcos! You a nursemaid for seedless asses!)

The name meant nothing to me, but the journey promised adventure as I knew, from hearsay, the overland route to Lepe, the highroad from Seville to La Palma, the gypsies along the way, the night campfires and the river Odiel; and this venture to be the opening of my quest for Maraela.

"Your pay will be a pittance." My father used his foot to rake the straw from around the door and made ready to take his leave. "Only 200 maravedis and food for the journey. This, however, is of no consequence. The sooner you are beyond the myriad eyes of Juan Ruiz de Medina, the smoother my humors will flow."

His farewell was a handclasp on my shoulder and then he went away, and all that afternoon I kept the fast and supposedly was alone, but I was not alone, for always the image of Maraela was with me and now the contemplation of my journey.

Fray Juan brought me a large wooden bowl of soup at twilight and had a small one for himself and sat with me and we supped together, and he ate most ravenously, gurgling his porridge, and it came to me that he, too, had fasted that day and had shared my chastening. Again I felt close to him, and in the shadows of night borning I could not see

85

his repulsive face, but only feel his presence, the strength of him near. And then he spake and his words were as gentle as the fringes of twilight, of dayspring to come.

"There is more soup, little brother." So sweet, so compassionate, and the miracle of such tenderness from the cavernous jaws of the Queen's Inquisitor.

The latent nobility of my own spirit, the benediction of my own saint, touched my tongue with a wand of charity and I spake goodly in this manner, and bless the moment: "I will have more only if my brother shares my plenty."

Juan Ruiz de Medina wept and his eyes glistened tears in the last light of day, and then instantly he was himself again and walked out and soon I heard his bare feet shuffling back up the corridor, and his steps were lighter than ever before.

He had two large bowls of soup in his hands and these he put on the bench and fumbled in his habit and drew therefrom a new candle, two oranges, two onions, a handful of dates and, praise all saints, two pieces of bread soaked in honey. This contraband, these prizes, he arrayed before me and his eyes danced the mischief of a culprit in empyrean.

"And now, Rodrigo of Triana, lay to." His handclasp on my shoulder was as warm, as strong, as my father's had been. "And remember always that the hospitality of the Dominicans is not stinted."

He blessed the food, and we feasted.

Then he lit the candle and the cell was cheerful, and us with full bellies and the light bright and warm. It was I, in the camaraderie of the spell, who first mentioned my departure from the college and for a painful instant I thought Fray Juan was going to offer me the facilities of the school without tuition or cost and thus create further complications. I should have known better. I should have known that he was too wise and too sensitive to offend the pride of an Andalusian by a tender of charity. His only comment was: "Your father confided in me."

"I have never been to Lepe," I said, a sop of the bread in my mouth and the honey oozing sweet in my throat.

Fray Juan licked the honey from his fingers and stared at the candle-light as though his lips hungered to say things that his vows forbade. "It is only a few miles from the Portuguese border," he said. "The influence of Lusitania is strong in Lepe and there will be many temptations, even before you go to sea."

86

"To sea?" I, too, stared at the candle and then up at him. "I am not going to sea."

"If you go to Lepe, you go to sea. It is always thus."

"But not I, Fray Juan," I protested. "I am going to my Aunt Ronda and when things are better I will return to Seville and enter my father's business."

Slowly he shook his head. "If you go to Lepe, you go to sea. It is as natural as breathing, as inevitable as death." He watched the wax spill down the length of the candle and reached for a daub of the stuff and rubbed it between his fingers. "I regret I will not be here on the morrow to bid you God's blessings."

Now this was an invitation for inquiry, a notice that he had something to say that he would not volunteer. I must not pry and, yet, good breeding dictated that I must expose interest. Such is the subtlety of manners in Andalusia. "You will not be here tomorrow?" It was a conflict of statement and query. "And it the holy Sabbath."

"I go to Cordova," he said. "To the court of the Queen." And then as an afterthought, he affixed these words: "And, thereby, to the court of the King also." It was a sly aspersion, not in the expression at all, but only in the tone.

The court of Ferdinand and Isabel had been in Cordova for several weeks, he to lead the campaign against Granada and she to gather into her saintly hands all the reins of the Inquisition.

There was more to the trend of his conversation than appeared on the surface and I probed a bit, skillfully, to be sure, and without any evidence of curiosity. "To Cordova and the court? Are the duties of the Inquisition so stringent that a Dominican must travel on the Holy Day?"

He looked at me in fastidious approval. "It is not the Inquisition, Rodrigo. It is a matter most pertinent." The wax between his fingers was shaped into a ball and this he put into his mouth and chewed thoughtfully. "Christopher Columbus of our earlier lectures arrived in Seville this morning, and departed this afternoon for Cordova."

This was news most savory; intelligence I should pass to my father if he knew it not. "To audience with the Queen?" I asked. "Has this Columbus the ear of our blessed Majesty?"

"No." He touched his hand to the candle and the flame seemed not to pain him. "But he has letters from Cerda and from Franciscans to several persons of most singular repute, and these include Alonso de Quintanilla and Luis de Santangel."

My ears tingled my excitement and, still, there was a foreboding in my preserving caution. Why should I, a youth, have the confidence of an Inquisitor? Here was obvious privity of state, and what was this to me? Alonso de Quintanilla was *Contador Mayor,* which is to say Treasurer of the Realm, and Luis de Santangel—woe the name—Luis de Santangel was the King's Minister of Finance and the most powerful converso in Spain. One of his kinsmen had gone to the stake for conspiring against the Inquisition and for the murder of an Inquisitor, but Luis de Santangel was the King's trusted confidant. He was a converso trusted and Luis Harana was a converso suspected, and this was ground I did not care to trod.

"Does one skilled in the ways of intrigue trust these matters to the ears of youth?" I asked boldly.

"I do," he replied without quibble.

"Does Juan Ruiz de Medina use his brother as bait for Quemadero's passion?" I demanded in temper.

"I do," he replied forthrightly.

"Then speak, Juan Ruiz de Medina, and the conscience of Rodrigo of Triana will adjudge thy command and weigh it with his loyalty to Crown and Cross."

"Bravely spoken!" His face lighted his pleasure. "Now hear me. At Lepe is the Franciscan monastery of Santa Maria de los Remedios. I am no dolt. Your father has dreams for you and hopes that your education is furthered. So where except at Santa Maria de los Remedios?"

I was pinned to the mast and, yet—witness all—I did not squirm, neither blink an eye, but answered in utmost prudence, "My fray has knowledge that is denied me."

He was all friar again, all master, and the camaraderie was dissipated. "What a Dominican you would make." He almost whispered it and then spoke out. "Students have keys that teachers cannot hold. I remind you that the path of Christopher Columbus leads always from Franciscans to conversos. If you attend the monastery, and you will, I ask you to sleep not——"

"And report to you an explanation for this affinity between Christopher Columbus, the Franciscans, and conversos?" I shook free the harness from my tongue and accosted him most valiantly. "I request, sir, the honor of unfettered perspicuity between you and me."

"I only ask that you sleep not," he repeated.

"You ask that I observe the intent and practices of the Franciscans and inform you of my findings. I say to you, sir, that coverture is repugnant to my healthy nostrils. Do you dare challenge the probity of the Friars Minor?"

He threw back his head and laughed in a manner most hilarious, a really unseeming merriment for a *caelebs* in Holy Orders. "Aroint! And crow fiercely my Andalusian cockerel. Have we, the Dominicans, suckled our student on verbosity?" He wiped his eyes on his mantle and fixed his penetrating gaze upon me. "One minute you speak as a man, the next as a child." He hitched himself closer to me and tapped my knee with his bony finger. "It is never the probity of the Minorites that harasses me, but their prosperity."

This, to be sure, was cake of a different flavor and I smiled at recollection of my own bravado.

Fray Juan obviously perceived my thoughts and his eyes sparkled merriment again. "The conversos, Rodrigo, are the richest group in Spain and the Franciscans have a key to their purse. I am weary of this Dominican college struggling on a pittance while the Franciscans have plenty. I want a chair of map making for this school. A chair of Arabic. I want the secret of Franciscan tenure on the moneybags of conversos so I may emulate them."

"That, sir," I said in undisguised relief, "is a wine of another vintage, and none of the bitter dregs of loathsome duplicity. My service is at your command." I was desirous suddenly of ending this talk of conversos for fear his inquisitive genius might lead to the Haranas.

"I ask only that you remain aware." He stretched his hands in exasperation that I should misconstrue his motive. "I know that students gossip and that young ears are keener than old ears. If you can learn, with honor, why converso sesame is so ready for Franciscan touch, then I ask you to share this knowledge with me, and thusly your Dominicans can swarm around the converso comb and perhaps find some honey for our cause." He doubled his fist and pounded the bench so hard that the candle shook and spluttered. "I will do any honorable service to build this college into a university."

I, too, struck the bench to emphasize my enthusiasm, a feigned assurance that I did well. "It will be a privilege to serve Seville," I said, and this a promise that I had no intention whatsoever of keeping.

Fray Juan gave every indication of contentment and, upon my soul, began querying me on the wisdom of Isidore, the theorems of Eratosthenes, and divers and sundry matters that he had taught me. He burrowed into my mind like a mole and wheedled and needled until my senses reeled under the constancy of his intellectual aggression. Then he relented, and growled, "You have learned a few things. The Franciscans and the world will not find you a vacuous idiot. What——" he jabbed his long finger into my chest and barked. "What is the most important thing I have taught you?"

Without hesitation I spake up: "*Vincit qui se vincit.*"

"Bravo!" He exclaimed his approval. "He conquers who conquers himself. And next?"

"That the world is larger than we think."

"Good, Rodrigo. It is spoken in the scholarship of thy brothers and the grace of thy God." He pushed the candle to the far end of the bench and touched the tips of all of his fingers together and chewed his lower lip in contemplation. "The urn is turned, little brother. The bowl is thrown. Search the stars of thy immortality and weep never for the clay at thy feet. Prattle not the beauty of truth with thy tongue if there be a lie in thy heart."

He put his arm around my shoulders and his counsel came in forceful exhortation: "Borrow naught from thy friends except friendship and this to be paid with interest. Count never your purse among your jewels. Your mercy for all men. Touch not a maiden without troth and cherish thy begats as vessels shaped by thy own hands. That is all." He stood and I, too, arose, and he lifted the candle and stepped to the door and there he turned and smiled his farewell. "And now, Rodrigo of Triana, trust God and hammer on!"

My fray was gone before I could shape a reply to my tongue and this discomforted me as there were things I needed to speak, my esteem and laudation, my gratitude to Juan Ruiz de Medina—Dominican, Inquisitor, teacher; lonely man of the midnight office, lance bearer in the army of his Lord.

My eyes were heavy but I could not sleep. My straw was clean but I could not rest. The night whispered in my window and her name was on every zephyr, Maraela of golden hair, Maraela of sky-blue eyes. They were changing the watches along the river, turning the glasses, and the lookouts called the ridings of the peaceful hour. My city, my Seville, slept the serenity of her venerable years and never again was I to see her in this mood, the tranquility of Sabbath borning, the awakening of the bells, the spring swelling her breasts in motherly abundance, and I, her son, filled with love for my fellow man and the sweet hopes of youth.

(Seville—my Andalusia. Tread of the Phoenicians, trod of the Goths. Do the stars still cradle in the spire of San Marcos? Is the blue haze over thy river yet? Does the sun still rise from thy meadow and shadow behind the Castle of Triana? The wine of my years is bitter on my tongue and, though my storehouse spills its plenty, I am impoverished, for my spirit is wrinkled and my hopes are mockery. Oh, Mita—my faith in Paradise for one hour in thy embrace. Ah, Andalusia—my honor, my turban, my soul! All these for one spring night on the motherly breast of my homeland. But, go plague! Vanish these fires of memory and leave me with the ashes of my desolation.)

# CHAPTER 8

*T*HE HOLY SABBATH WAS TURNING ITS OWN GLASS INTO THE long afternoon when I stepped from the portal of the monastery and blinked in the radiant light of my emancipation, then wended down the quiet streets to my father's shop.

Old Mudarra was on the corner of the alley and purloining glances at the women passing, and making ribald gestures and jests to those who raised their eyes to his licentious appraisement. I saw him before he saw me and he spoke to me while his gaze followed a slut down the way, her bracelets jangling the tocsin of her trade and her buttocks weaving an invitation to her couch.

"Ho! Young goat that seeks fresh pastures." The puta had vanished around the corner and reluctantly he gave me his attention. "So the Dominican shackles are smitten from your brain, and from your loins, I praise Allah."

"I am in no mood for buffoonery, Mudarra. Is my father in his shop?"

"In no mood for buffoonery, he says." The irascible Morisco cackled his disdain and bowed low to me in mockery. "And this the feast day of his benighted convictions——"

"Swallow your blasphemy, seedless ram," I said in tempestuous harshness. "At times your toothless gums and wrinkled brow are the only armor that protects you from my ire."

Old Mudarra jumped up and down in frenzied agitation. "Seedless ram, he says. Hear him, Messenger of Allah. Hear the yelp of this pup fresh from the den of Dominican eunuchs. Christian vanity! Andalusian arrogance! May his feeble saints wean him from the pap of Aquinas and the heresy of his barbarian forebears."

"Enough! By the withered cods of your lecherous prophet, enough!" I seized his shoulder in a grip that was firm but by no means rough. "I have long wearied of your sneers for my race and my faith. A Moor praises the howling simoom of his native desert and that is patriotism most valiant. A Jew chants the glory of his ancient Zion and that is tradition most blessed. But if an Andalusian raises his voice to the glory of his Cross and the sanctity of his hearth, then that is the hollow whine of a native fool. Away with such Semitic inanity. Now, where is my father?"

I released his shoulder and his sunken old eyes blazed his judgment of me and he reached out and grabbed my arm and felt its strength and looked me over from my heavy leather shoes to the wool stocking-cap slanted on my head. "You are ready," he muttered. "By the flourishing fields of The Messenger, you are ready. *Amir el bahr.* Your father awaits your presence." He turned from me and slouched up the alley.

"Mudarra!"

"Aye?" His face came around to me.

"Do you know whither she has gone?" All the anger was out of my voice.

He pulled his burnoose tight around his person and laid his hand on the crest of his turban. "I am the blood of Abraham, young Spaniard. The breed of Ishmael. Know you the story of the water glass and the drop of oil?"

"I know it——"

"Then remember it forever, Rodrigo. And forget Maraela Harana." He swung his back to me and trudged down the alley where the brothels stretched to the river and the putas lolled in the sun, while their enterprising sisters, the rameras, hawked in the street and, for two maravedis, sold themselves under the wharves. If the buyer had no money, a crust of bread would seal the bargain, and a loaf would buy a virgin, if one could be found in the squalor of Seville.

The door to my father's shop was closed and the shutters drawn, this day being the Lord's, but he answered my knock and admitted me into the stale gloom of his mart and, as my eyes accustomed themselves to the shadows, I saw the stranger. He was sitting at the desk and a flagon of wine and a tankard were within easy reach, and then I was presented to Pedro de Arcos.

As sturdy as a mountain jack was Arcos, his sandy eyebrows shaggy like the bristles of an angry boar and his black eyes squinting and darting and never still. He weighed me like a trader in the mule market and spake clearly his approval. "So this is the Bermejo colt I take to Lepe. Well, Vicente——" He lifted his tankard and drank his endorsement. "He has got salt in his guts and good bile for his humors. A stalwart son is a father's sweetest blessing."

"I thank you, Arcos." My father beamed his pride and clapped his hand on my shoulder in a gesture most manly and hearty.

Then he poured a tankard for himself and one for me and I joined that company of men and although the monastery was only minutes away it already seemed hours, and I was drawn to Pedro de Arcos as the needle is drawn to the Pole Star.

"My curiosity, sir, is a fault acquired and not inherited." I touched my tankard to his. "But you are not a stranger in Seville. I have seen you before——"

"Rodrigo!" My father snapped my name. "In these days no man has ever seen another man before."

My cheeks tingled my embarrassment and Arcos laughed. "Clear the scuppers, Vicente. The boy speaks forthrightly." His eyes darted from my father to me. "You have seen me before?"

"If you say I have, sir, I have." My instinctive caution had possessed my faculties again.

"How close have you been to hell?"

"Close enough," I answered immediately and thus proving that my wits and levity were as sharp as his.

My father chuckled his accord and Pedro de Arcos drew his brows together in a scowl most fierce and poked my chest with his stubby forefinger, and I saw the calluses thereon and the tar under his nail. "Or Galway? Or the Misty Isles? Even Thule. Mayhaps you have seen me there." He was a bit drunk and his words gurgled in his throat.

"A sailor," I said in obvious envy. "Now I know. I have seen you on the ships."

"Incredible wisdom." He laughed uproariously.

As I have told you before, and it bears repeating, I was never one to scorn jeers or accept ridicule. My father was watching me and I spoke clearly, albeit with no umbrage but firmly nevertheless. "This raucous mirth opens the door to friendship, or folly. Do Andalusian sailors drive mules?"

He cocked his right eye at me like one of the parakeets the seafarers

95

sometimes fetched from Guinea. "In these days, spurless cockerel, Andalusia's sailors do anything they can to take the slack out of their bellies. The seas belong to Portugal while our Ferdinand spends his realm's strength against the Moors and his own sperm into the cold belly of Isabel."

"Sir, she is our Queen," I protested indignantly.

"Sir, she is a fool." He pounded his tankard on the desk. "Not as insane as that witless Joanna she has breached, but a witling in her own right. She converts with conversos and consorts with saints while Spain's caravels rot at their moorings."

I might have replied, but my father shook his head at me and we let Arcos have his say. "I herded horses from Palos to Seville and now I drive mules back to Lepe. I, Pedro de Arcos, the best helmsman of Rio Saltes." He pushed the flagon aside and got up. "I will see you to Lepe and safe in the arms of your estimable aunt, whose betrothed was my comrade. We leave at dawn." He drained his tankard and nudged his elbow into my father's ribs. "And as for you, Vicente, I will be on the lookout for aloes if ever I get my hand on a tiller again."

He flung open the door and weaved into the alley, bellowing the chant of his calling:

> *"One glass is gone and another flows;*
> *It all shall run down if God so wills."*

We heard him to the street and toward the river and there was a silence between us and I spake first, "Then he knows my Aunt Ronda?"

"Aye. Since childhood." My father picked up the tankards and took them back to the water cask in Mudarra's workshop and washed them. "Never argue with a man after the third cup, Rodrigo," he counseled me. "Fight him if you must. Ignore him if you can. But never argue." He put the tankards on a shelf and dried his hands under the armpits of his doublet. "All is ready. You will spend this night at your home in Triana and at dayspring you leave the nest."

"Have you not forgotten something, sire?"

"I have not forgotten." He opened his desk and took out the poniard and himself buckled it around my waist. "Can you use this thing?"

"It was not one of my studies at the College of Seville," I said.

"You will learn. But until you do, mind your tongue lest you lose

96

it, and your temper lest you are brought bloodless back to me. Now we go."

I hooked my thumb under the belt of my poniard in a manner most proud and dashing. "But Mudarra," I reminded him. "I must tell Mudarra farewell."

"He has asked the privilege of accompanying you to the corral tomorrow where you will join Arcos. I granted his wish as I am not one for lingering farewells."

One quick survey he made of the shop, sniffing the air and peering into the corners, and then he opened the door and we went out in the sunshine; and me most puffed up to be at his side, her Toledo poniard on my hip and the promise of adventure that I was sure would lead me to her.

The strollers were out, and the carriages, and often my father swept his hat and hand into a graceful greeting to some worthy personage, and I, too, bowing even more elaborately than he, my left arm wide from my body lest it conceal the blade.

We crossed the bridge to Triana and to our home and my heart pulled the melancholy humors into my fancy when I saw the things endeared to my childhood and reminisced that on the morrow I would put these scenes behind me. My father, sensing my sadness and striving to hide his, set out a repast of wine and honey and cakes, and a jar of that devilish brew called coffee, the smuggled *qahwah* of Arabia and prohibited in Christian countries because its intoxicating mystery came not from grapes.

At sundown some of our neighbors came avisiting and enlivened the occasion with song and story. They remained to sup and together we sang the Salve Regina and together we repeated our prayers and then my father and I were alone once more, and the night come, and I to my pallet.

I was not asleep when my father tiptoed to my side and stood looking down at me, and knelt and stroked my hair and gently kissed my forehead. I lay still, pretending sleep, and when he was gone my tears cleansed my eyes and my resolve cleansed my conscience and enflamed my ambition to noble endeavor that the name of Bermejo would be honored forever. This was the only tribute I could pay my father for the gift of manhood, the only ransom for my freedom.

Again the ancient calls from the river, the all's well of the night watch and I lapsed into sound slumber.

My father's touch awakened me and I scarcely could believe that it was dawn, but the east was graying and the river was stretching into life. We broke our fast by candlelight, and each of us quiet in the sorrow of my going forth, and then Mudarra came with a long staff in his hand and a most doleful expression on his wizened countenance. My father embraced me, and Mudarra turned away, and my father kissed me. "Farewell, my son," he said. "The blessings of thy sainted mother attend thee, and the good wishes and love of thy neglectful father."

I followed old Mudarra down the steps and up the street and his staff tapped the cobblestones as we walked, and him in the reverie of the hour and me sadly contemplative and no longer exuberant at the promise of the journey.

We reached the outskirts of Triana and I was not aware that Mudarra had extracted my poniard from its sheath and then I saw it in his hand as he balanced it delicately, examining its beauty and appraising its temper. "A weapon for women," he growled. "But it will serve the hand of a master. Your father asked that I explain the poniard."

"It is a beautiful weapon," I said heatedly.

"A stone is better." He tested the point against his thumb. "Now, hear you and no argument, for the first time you hurl this blade I will not be there to guide your arm." He gripped the hilt and I watched. "To thrust, hold the wrist firm and strike below the chest bone and down to the heart. Or to the belly and up, but always the wrist firm and the shoulder will perform the chore."

In a twinkle, he had flipped the blade and the point was between his thumb and forefinger. "To hurl, loosen the wrist. This you will practice. Now vow."

"I will practice," I said. "Firm wrist for thrust, loose wrist for throw."

He returned the knife to me and grumbled again. "Would that you had the brave scimitar of Islam at your side instead of that trinket."

We reached the corrals of Seville, the stinking slaughterhouses at the edge of the meadow and along the river, and the place a confusion of animals and the cries of drovers. Mudarra led the way, scattering sheep with his staff and avoiding swine as though they were devils, which he believed they were.

98

Our company was at the far side of the yard, eating breakfast under a cork oak, and Pedro de Arcos shouted the morning's greetings and presented me to my fellows. I will not detain you, indulgent reader, with the names and descriptions of these ruffians, as they take no part in my narration; only one, and this one Gomez Rascon, called The Rabbit.

I was fascinated immediately by Rascon, for he was about my age although not nearly my height and his structure was somewhat like that of Mudarra's water cask, a barrel body on short, spindly shanks. His left arm was withered and his right arm was bent and there was a loathsome lump on his shoulder where broken bones had knotted into misshapen ugliness. His mouth came to a pucker when he breathed and his face resembled that of a rabbit, elongated from his enormous ears to his tiny nose that clung like a withered button to the contour of his visage. Yet, it was the most wistful face I had ever seen.

(Ah, Rascon, my comrade, my right arm. A ducat, aye, ten thousand ducats, little rabbit, to hear you call the hour again, and the Unknown Sea swishing under Arcos' tiller and the floating meadow lapping our brave *Pinta*. Unbend the mizzen! Put your back into it! Lace on the bonnet! Call it out, forgotten jester in the drama of time! We are almost there. *Adelante! Adelante!*)

I beseech you, kind reader, to forgive an old man his digressions, the moments I steal from you to pamper my memory of things that mean so much to me, if nothing to you; the wheedling voice of Christopher Columbus until his anger surged, the bright, bold eyes of Alonso Pinzon, and Arcos' muscles straining at the tiller as we parted the Ocean Sea into the wake that the lesser breeds followed. So forgive me, and we return to Gomez Rascon, called The Rabbit.

His knife was in a sheath of untanned leather, which was held high on his waist by a rawhide thong so his bent arm could reach it easily. Even at casual glance I saw that it was not fine Toledo like mine, but inferior Damascus made by twisting strips of steel together and welding them into a blade.

He was staring at my poniard, either in envy or admiration, when Mudarra bade me farewell and put his hands on my shoulders and said:

"*Assalamu alaik.*"

Rascon's face underwent a hideous convulsion at sound of the

Arabic and he spat his contempt. "Moslem filth. Is Quemadero a stranger in Seville——",

"Hold, you gnome!" I spun and faced him and clenched my fists and gave no thought at all to my knife. "One more insult of your betters and I will bury you in a swine wallow where you were born."

His mouth gaped his incredulity and he stared at me in amazement, and over at Arcos, and Arcos held up his hand for silence, and spake his command: "Clear the scuppers, Rabbit."

Rascon's knife flashed by my face and into the cork oak, and the hilt vibrated the force of the throw and then slowly was still; and my heart contracted into a hard knot, for I knew this was his warning, his pennant flying before battle. I breathed deeply to master my awe into composure and felt the eyes of them all and cringed inwardly in my dilemma.

Then Mudarra swung his staff and it swished under the noses of Arcos and The Rabbit and, disdainfully, he turned his back to them and stepped to the tree, and there he flipped the knife free with his stick and tossed it to the feet of Gomez Rascon.

"Your blade, young master." He was calling me master, an indication to all that I was superior to him in every way, in every thing, and I lifted out my poniard and tossed it to him. He whirled and threw and the dagger pierced the cork bark within an inch of where The Rabbit's had been, and the hilt hummed the vibration of the jaculation.

Arcos' eyebrows came together in amazement and The Rabbit actually beamed his commendation, his lips puckering rapidly like a fish nibbling bait. Mudarra ignored them and resumed his leave-taking.

"*Assalamu alaik.*" He said it loud for them all to hear, for the battle pennant of Mudarra was flying, too. "Do not begin your journey, young master, with the blood of your comrades on your hands." He pushed his staff into the crook of my arm. "This is the tool and weapon of drovers. And now, farewell."

He spat at The Rabbit's feet and cleared his throat and spat at the feet of Arcos, then walked away and the majesty of his going left the company speechless; a silence that Rascon broke by a childish giggle of pleasure at the skill and daring he had witnessed.

It was he who extracted my weapon from the tree and presented it to me. "This rightfully is the best poniard in our midst." His voice was thin and reedy, like a child's. "Perhaps the best in all Andalusia."

"Your excellent judgment belies your station," I said in prayerful relief of the events, but knowing I must speak boldly as these reckless coves would translate Christian forgiveness and gentlemanly behavior into personal weakness.

"And this staff——" He reached for it and balanced it and returned it to me. "It is the best in Andalusia?"

"It will serve me," I said.

"And you are the best mule drover in Andalusia?"

"I am no drover at all. That art I will learn from you."

All the company laughed and Arcos the loudest of all, and The Rabbit giggled again and addressed his petition to our leader. "If it pleases you, Pedro de Arcos, I will fare with this man."

"That you will," agreed Arcos, "and I, too. And, now, to the journey."

There were nine men in our company and we were divided into groups of three and each group to tend fifteen mules, to water them twice daily and at night feed them the fodder they carried on their backs and hobble them. And so, after many ribald farewells to the other drovers, we set forth on the road from Triana to Lepe, The Rabbit and I together and me nudging the mules with my staff to keep them stepping spritely and in line. The dust caked my face and cracked my lips.

Rascon allowed me to work myself into a froth and then grinned his good-natured disapproval of my energetic attention to the brutes. "Do not nudge them." He gestured lassitude with his bent right arm. "If they walk fast, we walk fast. They will follow the bell." He motioned toward the lead mule of our fifteen, around whose neck a bronze bell tingled. "The lovely buttocks of rich maidens will some day warm the backs of these beasts. Would that we were mules, eh, Lepe?"

It was The Rabbit who first called me Lepe because that was the town to which I journeyed, and because it was a simple name and one which a comrade is apt to bestow affectionately. And this, sirs, if you are vigilant readers, explains the infuriating discrepancies that attend my role in the various journals of The Discovery; the accounts of which, incidentally and only thirty-seven years after the fact, already are confusing scholars and courts, who, in reconstructing the miracle, insist upon associating known results with imagined causes, a common failing of literary and legal minds, and who seem determined to forget that Christopher Columbus digested his food like any other man.

Hence, the sundry records, authentic or forged, list me under three names while the perusers exhaust their wits to confound a matter that really is quite simple. The Juan Rodrigo Bermejo, the Rodrigo of Triana, and the Lepe of varying documents are the same man, and he is I; the Christian name of Bermejo, the birthplace being Triana, and the nickname of Lepe, given to me by Gomez Rascon, who was at my side that glorious morn when I saw it and screamed the tidings to him.

We had traveled only a few miles before I knew enough about The Rabbit to envy his experiences, for he was, by trade, a gromet, which is to say a ship's boy, who was tending mules to keep belly and backbone together because the ways at Palos and Cadiz were swarming with idle shipbuilders and sailors.

Like Arcos, he was a native of Palos and his withered arm had been his Cross since birth, but the shoulder lump came from bones broken in a shipwreck off Cabo Villano, and this he accepted with a mariner's Stoicism as he had been going to sea since he was nine. He had never heard of Christopher Columbus or Benjamin Marino and thought all Jews should be fed to Quemadero or exiled from Spain.

My own knowledge was a wellspring of delight to him and he questioned me slyly about many things: the Pole Star, the circumference of the earth, and the proper way to request the transitory favors of well-bred maids. This I did not know, and that he did not believe.

We paused at high noon long enough to rest the mules and ourselves and the dearth of journeyers on the road surprised me until Arcos explained that under the realm's stringent regulations travel was restricted on land as well as on sea.

There were no gypsy wayfarers to amuse me, and The Rabbit, leering and wholly misconstruing my interest in the Romanys, pointed out that gypsy women fled the empty purses and bestial lusts of drovers while their menfolk hid in the woods to escape impressment into Ferdinand's army.

The Merchants' Post passed us in midafternoon, the rider on an Arabian horse and so exalted in his own pomposity that he deliberately rode among us and scattered our mules and then was off in a cloud of dust while Rascon hurled rocks at him and cursed his forebears as far back as the brood sow that dropped his grandmother on a dung heap; and such grandiose fulminations I had never heard before.

We reached the corrals of La Palma, a healthy league from the town, at twilight, and the place teeming with cattle and drovers bound north to Badajoz, and we made camp by a stream and tended our animals and then supped on cold mutton and onions.

The campfires were burning and the beasts lowing and braying their discomfort when I, attended by The Rabbit, went among the camps and asked discreetly if any man had heard the whereabouts of one Luis Harana, merchant. Perhaps he had come this way, journeying to the sea, and he had promised me employment.

The drovers answered me in surly maledictions and all in the negative, and one tried to steal my poniard and The Rabbit kicked him in the groin and I laid open his scalp with my staff, and this in a manner most neat and deserving, and we ran back to our own camp. Rascon, seeing me discouraged and dejected, did not ask the cause, neither did he pry concerning Luis Harana, but disappeared for an hour and returned with two females, both exceedingly plump and exceedingly malodorous. He offered me my choice and was puzzled by my refusal, for to The Rabbit a woman was a woman, a doctrine I envied but could not practice; never with Maraela's kisses a remembrance upon my lips.

I saw her that night in the moon's castings, in the shadows of the campfire and, upon rising, I saw her in the dawn and then my imagery faded into the dust of the road, the grime, the heat, and the monotony of mule rumps.

In La Palma and in San Juan del Puerto, I asked of Luis Harana and vacant stares and shaking heads were my only rewards, and by the time we reached Cartaya I was convinced that they had not come this way but probably had gone east toward Cordova or northeast toward Madrid.

My discouragement was heavy upon me and even the antics of The Rabbit did not cheer me. "I will get you a gypsy," he said, assuming the cause of my gloom and promising a remedy that was hard to find. "But women are women, Lepe. All except Turks." He touched his grimy hand to his puckish lips and blew a kiss into the air. "Moslem women dignify love into the art that it is. And Jewish women, also."

I resented his words, and yet they entranced me, remembering that Maraela was a converso and a Judaizer.

On the fourth day from Triana, we hove into the corrals of Lepe and turned our mules over to the trader, who paid our wages and grumbled direly that men should expect 200 maravedis merely for driving animals eighty miles. He tried to deduct for our keep and Arcos' eyebrows bristled together and he scowled in the dealer's face, and we were paid in full.

Our company was disbanded and Arcos, Rascon, and I walked toward town and came to a bluff that overlooked the Valley of the Odiel and the Bay of Lepe. The river veered southeast to Huelva and the bay was fed only by the sea; the Ocean Sea that elbowed into the Gulf of Cadiz and the water arm of Lepe. The sea was beyond my vision, but the bay glistened and the gulls called, and there was a strange tug at my heart. I know now that the sea bewitched me the moment I first saw the Bay of Lepe, that it lured me into its fickle embrace as the Sirens lured Odysseus.

We sat under a tree, Arcos, Rascon, and I, and were silent and knowing our journey had ended. Arcos, picking his teeth with a straw, broke the spell, saying: "I go home to Palos. I have heard you talk, Lepe" (for now he called me Lepe, too) "and know that you are a hidalgo and a student of books. I have a fat wife in Palos and a foal of my own, a son of eight years."

"A son?" I asked. One always is envious of a man with a son.

"Three daughters and one son." He nodded his head slowly. "This son I cannot send to the friars, as I have no money. But if you are ever in Palos, I will steal a few blancas, if necessary, to pay you to tutor my son."

"Thank you, Arcos," I said, and his offer stored itself in my memory although I gave it no heed at that minute, for my eyes were on the bay and my mind was calling up the words of Juan Ruiz de Medina— "If you go to Lepe, you go to sea."

The Rabbit used his poniard to scrape mud from his sandals. "I, too, go to Palos. I have neither wife nor foals, that I account. If the ships are idle and there are no beasts to drive, you can find me at the wineshop of Francisco Gallego, whose daughter shares my pallet because her father beats her." He glanced up quickly as a thought awakened a memory. "For that matter, so do I. But that is different, eh, Lepe?"

I thanked him, too, and gave him my staff and we walked down from the bluff and into the town and passed the statue to Our Beautiful Virgin and to the home of my Aunt Ronda Bermejo.

She welcomed me with fuss and coos and allowed Arcos to kiss her blushing cheek, but eyed The Rabbit with obvious distaste. She gave us wine and cakes and we talked for an hour or so and then my comrades left us and went out the road to Palos, Arcos anxious to be home and The Rabbit ogling every woman he passed.

They scarcely were beyond sight ere Aunt Ronda was plying me with questions about my father. "I received a letter from him by Merchants' Post," she said. "It is a relief to me that Harana is no longer associated with your father. Good riddance, I say. Holy Water and the blessed Eucharist will never make Christians of Jews."

"I thought perhaps——" I was feeling my way. "I thought perhaps Harana came this way."

"Why do you concern yourself?" she demanded.

"Aloes, Aunt Ronda. Harana has a source for aloes, even the Medusa of Mauretania, which is the most valuable of all."

She lifted her bulk from her chair and glowered down at me. "A converso to Lepe? Never, Rodrigo. The Franciscans are here and keep the air purified of Jewish pollution." She patted my cheek and the scowl left her face. "We will eat chicken this night. And bread by my own hands."

"You honor me beyond my desert."

"You are my only brother's only son, and now a man. I have been baking for two days, since your father's letter that you were coming." She stepped back and looked at me, her head cocking from side to side. "The last time I saw you there was a velvet doublet."

The words probed a memory that was painful.

"Did I not tell you——" She was not sensitive enough to feel my misery and loneliness. "Did I not say that you would outgrow it within the year? Why, now, it would not meet around your waist where you wear that poniard with such elegance. Whence came that?"

"It is a Harana gift," I said in a tone that indicated the subject was closed.

She stared at me for a second and then shifted her gaze and said no more about it.

The chicken was fat and tender and I had two glasses of wine, the biting, bitter wine of the sea country and we sat at table and I answered questions until my lids drooped and the candle itself spluttered wearily as it burned itself away.

She showed me to a back room and my pallet and the straw was fresh and a flaxen cover was handy for my use. She felt the straw and fluffed it as is the wont of women and then fetched a jar of water and a bowl and waited without while I cleansed myself and crawled onto the pallet and pulled the cover to my chest, and sighed the luxury of the minute.

Aunt Ronda came in and kissed me good night and said, "Tomorrow you will go to the monastery. It is only a mile from here and near the bay. The blessed Franciscans will sweeten your humors and rid your heart of that Dominican gloom, and set your feet to the path they should trod."

Then she was gone and I heard her bustling about her room and then the house was still and I heard the night sounds of Lepe; the calls of fishermen hauling in, the calls of lookouts on the caravels, and they were deeper calls, freer calls than those of Seville.

The stars were so bright seaward that they shared my room, the wind steady from the bay and the gulf and the mystery beyond. I called her name and the stars mocked me and then I lulled myself to sleep with the beauty she loved so much, the sad lines of Alhakem:

> *I know not how it chanced that the fierce flame*
> *Of that atrocious grief consumed me not.*
> *Maddening I asked, "Where is my light of Love?*
> *My heart's sole treasure, where?" Yet there in truth,*
> *There didst thou lurk. Aye, in my heart of hearts,*
> *Where thou art ever; Pole Star of my life,*
> *Soul of my soul. Mine own! Mine own Maraela!*

# CHAPTER 9

*I* WAS AT NO TIME A STUDENT OF THE FRANCISCANS IN THE acceptable essence of scholarship and did not even visit the monastery on my first morning in Lepe, but, forsooth, pursued comportment most desultory and this being witness of two faults that have harassed me all of my years; respectively, procrastination and daydreaming.

At dawn's coming, I set forth from my aunt's abode in honest resolution to go directly to the friars and then the lodestone of my destiny seduced my intent and set my course toward the water front, an understandable delinquency inasmuch as I never before had seen a water front of the Ocean Sea.

The harbor itself was serene, the water lapping a grayish foam onto the beach and into the docks, and fishing craft rode the swells in rhythmical beauty. There was a score or more of these vessels, all at furl and riding the tide, for Lepe, as you know, is a port of excellent activity in the tuna and sardine trade and a gateway from Portugal both by land and by sea.

A caravel was crawling up the bay and, naturally, I was fascinated by her behavior, and time took no toll of my memory and gave no warning of its own deplorable inconsistency, its flight through minutes pleasurable and its lag through hours monotonous. The ship was lateen rigged and, as I watched, a capricious wind sprang up from the gulf and the caravel scudded before it and was brought about gallantly into a port tack with the wind abeam and lay to in a procedure most seamanly, and the watch doubled that she could claw off if the variable winds shifted leeward; and this execution running at least six sandglasses, or three hours, and me in a childish captivation like any dry-foot who had never dogged a watch.

The master and two seamen came ashore as soon as feasible, the master to report his manifest to his agent and the sailors to chart the vicinity for the recreation that men usually seek after a few days at sea.

No sooner was the master beyond hearing than one of the sailors asked me directions to the nearest wineshop and my reply that I, too, was a stranger in Lepe gave me a reason to engage them in conversation about their ship without revealing my insularism which, I am sure, was not apparent.

They were from Palos as was their caravel; and her name was *Nina*.

(Perhaps I should not put that so bluntly and here, in deference to your sensibilities, should attempt literary finesse, for I am quite aware that introduction of the noble *Nina* at this junction is, surely, something of a nonexpectation. But I must beseech your indulgence again inasmuch as I am a man for the point and, incapable of belletristic niceties, must, therefore, record this as it occurred even at the sufferance of ungracious obtundity. Also, I am quite aware that the *Nina* was, excepting the Ark of Noah, the most important vessel ever floated and this assertion you may challenge with mention of the craft that brought St. Paul to Rome, although no man knows her name, but I will not be moved. Perchance this seemingly is bias out of my own experience and if this be your assumption I will dispel it immediately by informing you that the *Pinta* was my ship on the Great Voyage, but the *Nina* made three voyages to the New World and sailed more than 25,000 miles under command of Christopher Columbus; so match that, if you can, and a blast to the wind for your challenge.)

And now because the *Nina* was the princess of The Discovery—the floundering *Santa Maria* was the queen and our *Pinta* was the courier —and now because of this I will tarry long enough to describe her, my recital being voice to my own observations as well as details furnished by the two sailors who are on history's roster as Gutierre Perez and Juan Ortiz.

The name *Nina* has been translated recklessly into "The Little Girl" and this is acceptable inasmuch as her sailors, in the sentimental fashion of our breed, did call her The Little Girl or The Little One. Actually, however, she was named for her owner, Juan Nino of Moguer, this Moguer, as you know, being a small river port a few miles upstream from Palos. But Nino is masculine and ship is feminine.

Hence, in the way of Spaniards, it was necessary to feminize Nino into Nina. Her patron was Santa Clara and thus to be consistent, and Heaven forbid such prosaic procedure, she should be called Santa Clara if the Galician is to be called Santa Maria.

She was of 57 tons, and that is to say her capacity was 57 toneladas, or tuns, of wine, and wine being a common cargo and always the best ballast. Her keel was 50 feet and her over-all length was 70, which, comparatively, was muchly smaller than St. Paul's missionary ship of at least fifteen hundred years ago. And whereas this report may startle you, I suggest that you be troubled not one scintilla, for we have learned in this age of advancement that a ship's worth is not in her size, but rather in her construction and in the salt of the men who sail her.

The Nina was a typical Andalusian caravel in all ways save one: her soul was greater even than my Pinta's and her heart as strong, although she was not as fleet.

I remained in conversation with the two sailors until the day was waning and then dreading the interrogation to which my Aunt Ronda was certain to expose me, I hastened to the monastery of Santa Maria de los Remedios and there to audience with a Franciscan, with whom I arranged to begin my lectures the next day, but only in map making.

And, of course, my aunt began her examination of my day's activities even before I had digested my sup and I told her I had enrolled for several courses, notably Latin, and this prevarication I confessed covertly and renounced most readily in my prayers.

My tenure with the Franciscans was an experience virtually of no profit and this diminution must be imputed to my own indolence and, in turn, my sloth directly was traceable to the perturbation that the sea's propinquity engendered in my humors and the melancholy persuasion that Maraela had disappeared into the labyrinth of Spain's derangement. My father wrote that he knew nothing whatsoever of the Haranas' whereabouts and suspected that they had gone to Cordova or Barcelona, and then came his message that he was convinced they had fled to Italy for reasons most expedient, and this his way of informing me that they had exiled themselves to escape the Inquisition.

And thus my beauteous Maraela moved from substance into fancy, from image into shadow, while I dawdled at the monastery in Lepe and there learned only two things that have any remote consanguinity with this narration.

Firstly, it soon was apparent to me why conversos favored Franciscans over Dominicans in matters of gratuity and this simply because the Gray Friars of the sea country were not as zealous in the Inquisition as the Black Friars of the inland cities and, in fact, I quickly learned that maritime folk generally are more tolerant of human frailties than their landlocked kinsmen and accept strangers more readily; that they are more lenient concerning differences of race and nationality, and even religion.

My Aunt Ronda was one of the exceptions.

Secondly, I came in contact, obliquely to be sure, with Bartholomew Columbus, the second brother of The Discoverer and himself a thread that Christopher Columbus stitched so carefully into the pattern that has mystified the world; and this pattern a part of the riddle perpetuated by himself, his heirs, and deifiers for purposes of vanity, glory, and avarice.

Bartholomew Columbus rode a mule into Lepe from across the adjacent Portuguese border but could not procede farther into Spain in the same manner without an official permit and, like his brother, this adventurer turned first to the Franciscans for aid.

It was the late summer of 1485 when he, dusty and irritable, appeared in the yard of the monastery, leading his mule and denouncing the asininity of the frontier guards who had warned him that, Portuguese visitor or not, he was forbidden to stride his beast until he had received proper authorization.

Upon learning his identity, the friars welcomed him and immediately set in motion his plea for permission to ride his mule to Cordova, where his brother was waiting for audience with the Crowns, either Isabel or Ferdinand or both; and they too occupied with affairs of state to hear the plans of Christopher Columbus for a costly venture of exploration.

The arrival of Bartholomew Columbus excited the monastery into a frenzy of speculation and I shared this ferment and on the second day of his visit I saw a member of the Columbus ménage for the first time. He was sunning himself in the yard and I presumed the prerogative of bidding him good morning and he answered most affably and in the best of breeding. He was a man of about twenty-three and perhaps an inch taller than I, and I was a youth of exactly five feet and six inches in those days.

He was of good countenance and every word he spake he weighed most carefully, thus giving an indication of caution and wariness. And yet he was voluble, almost glib, a thorough master of positive colloquy without really ever saying anything. Extraordinarily fluent he was and extraordinarily nimble, quite like the hawkers who paraded in front of my father's shop and called their wares in boastful assonance which, if clefted, had utterly no substance.

Now this Bartholomew Columbus was ignorant of Spanish geography in that he wasn't sure of the route to Cordova or even Seville and was a complete stranger to our customs, the delicate nuances of our ways. However, he spake our tongue in casual assurance, although frequently he called upon phrases of my grandmother's generation, a Spain I was too young to remember and so was he. I noticed particularly how asturely he heeded my modern expressions and how adroitly he imitated them.

I was taken most favorably with Bartholomew Columbus and, therefore, you can appreciate my delight when the friars announced that he would lecture our school and stated his qualifications: that he and his brother had participated in a map-making enterprise in Lisbon, that Christopher Columbus, muchly traveled, had contributed the data and Bartholomew Columbus the draftsmanship, and together they had sold charts, maps, and other notabilia of use to mariners.

This I believed and this I still believe because Bartholomew was a master at drafting, an art he demonstrated to exquisite perfection in his lecture to us, and spicing his discourse with anecdotes about the lands whose coastlines he sketched, and these lands Portugal, Spain, the Canary Isles, and the Azores. Now mark you this: he did not sketch, neither did he mention, the coast of Liguria, particularly of Genoa or any of Italy, and this a most singular omission inasmuch as Genoa reputedly was the native city of the Columbus household. Would not a man demonstrating map sketching almost instinctively use his native land as a model?

But, as God is my witness, he did not and at the time it seemed peculiar to me and then, in the doldrums of youth, I forgot about it. However, I did not forget the admonition with which he ended his lecture, for its presumptive impudence rankled my Andalusian pride.

"I am in an enviable position," he said, "to bring to you and to your countrymen intelligence most pertinent to Spanish requirements. Even now a valiant Portuguese mariner, by name Bartholomew Diaz, is readying an expedition to seek the Indies by sailing south around

111

Africa. He has requested, and surely will receive, 6000 reis from the Portuguese Crown for this worthy undertaking. Portugal, as you know, is most generous to her pilots who will dare unknown waters for the glory of her sovereign. She is concerned more with advancement of the Faith, of science, and of frontiers than with wars and Inquisition."

He let the taunt rest upon our cognition and then said: "I count myself among those who believe the shortest route to India is westward. Portugal has rejected a westward expedition to accept Diaz' southward venture. This is Spain's opportunity. The negligence will be shameful and costly if this, the most enlightened state of all Europe, fails to explore westward to challenge Portugal's southward expansion."

It was more than an inculpation. It was a threat, and yet how cunningly framed and hung for all of us to see and talk about later and pass along to our families and friends. For, mind you, the only westward expedition even in the egg was the unhatched scheme of Christopher Columbus to reach the Indies by crossing the Ocean Sea, and thereby make him and his family the richest and most honored household in the world.

The mule permit for Bartholomew Columbus to continue to Cordova was approved a few days later and he departed Lepe, the monastery receded into the humdrums, and I into the phlegmatism of my indolence. Aunt Ronda scolded me often for my sloth and threatened to write my father and this stirred the pith of my resentment.

I was weary of Lepe, was weary of everything, and only my filial loyalty shackled me to that place and held me from the sea, from a course between the Pillars of Hercules and into the Mediterranean, and to Italy where I might find Maraela.

I spent more hours on the water front than ever, just watching the ships and allowing my fancy the nebulous flights that are the heritage of youth; the clouds into castles, the bay into the Ocean Sea, and I into Don Rodrigo of Triana, my feet firm on my quarter-deck and my eyes on the horizon, and Maraela on her couch, awaiting the return of her Jason.

I was ripe for debauchery and I plucked easily.

It began in the wineshops and I so proud that the sailors sought my company and laughed at my wit and boasted to their women that I was their comrade and a gentleman of scholarship and purse—the few jingling maravedi that my father sent me each month.

A cup of bitter wine was cheap, but the dregs were costly, and the first one called herself Maria. The wine and the woman convulsed me into frenzied lunacy and in my loathsome appetency I pretended her into Maraela; a moment of bliss and then the consuming remorse.

I slank like a panting dog back to Aunt Ronda's house and quickly to bed before she saw me, my soul pleading God for succor and my heart pleading Maraela for forgiveness. The moon was full and I remember the superstition that the man in the moon was the sinner who had gathered sticks on the Sabbath to warm the harlot of his initiation. I shuddered my desolation and prayed myself to sleep.

The next night she was at the same place, and I, too.

The sequence was inevitable. Aunt Ronda learned from the Franciscans that I was attending lectures at widening intervals and, womanlike, she spliced effect to cause and then unraveled the rope and moaned her lamentations over each strand until she realized that commiseration is a worthless catharsis against the fever of Aspasia.

So she swelled into righteous anger and I often have wondered since if her wrath sprang from saintly indignation or virginal curiosity.

"Ungrateful libertine!" she railed at me. "Your indulgent father distraught in genteel poverty and you wasting his money in riotous profligacy——"

My startled reaction checked her arraignment and I immediately was aware that she had revealed a confidence between her and my father: that I was in Lepe at financial privation to him, and this, I vow, was my first inkling of my father's penury.

It came as a bitter torment that I had wasted his substance and was unworthy of his trust and forthwith, despite Aunt Ronda's profuse tears and copious wails, I wrote him that I no longer could accept his benevolence, that I was going to Palos to seek my fortune and justify his faith in me, that I had been offered a tutorship in the home of Pedro de Arcos and could be reached at the wineshop of Francisco Gallego, where lived my friend, Gomez Rascon, the one called The Rabbit.

My aunt took to her bed in feigned illness to deter me and I kissed her cheek and left her there and, buckling on my poniard, walked resolutely out of her house, and glanced back only once to see her at her window, watching me and wiping her eyes on her sleeve. There was no ship to Palos that day and, besides, I had no money and so I assigned myself to a pottery hawker who was journeying to Huelva and had need of my strong back to help with his wares.

We set forth from Lepe about midday and took the sandy road to the Odiel, the monger leading one laden mule and I the second. We reached Huelva the next afternoon and he gave me a few blancas for my hire and fed me in a public house, where sailors and merchants sat at a long table and vied each with the other in boasts and gossip.

Here I heard that Bartholomew Columbus had arrived in Cordova and that Christopher Columbus had not seen Isabel or Ferdinand because the court had moved to Madrid for the winter; and this opportunity I take to explain that the Spanish court was transilient, moving often from one noble's estates to another and remaining with each host only long enough to exhaust his larder and hospitality.

I asked the forum if any of the gentlemen present knew the whereabouts of one Luis Harana, merchant, and they all shook their heads and assured me that if he were on the coast between Portugal and Gibraltar they would know it, and that none had ever heard his name.

I arranged with the proprietor for a bed in exchange for services in the kitchen and then struck a bargain with a boatsman, my few blancas if he would row me down the lagoon that tied Rio Odiel to Rio Tinto, then across the Tinto to Palos de la Frontera.

We set out soon after dawn and the lagoon was high and swift with flood waters, but easily navigable until we came to the Tinto and there the harsh channel caught us and swept us below Palos, and I was put ashore directly across from Point del Sebo with instructions to walk the three miles to the city.

Hunger was my first concern as I trudged up from the riverbank to the road to Palos and there, lofty on a bluff, was a monastery and there, as a wayfarer in need, I pounded the gate and was admitted to the friary of La Rabida, where Christopher Columbus first had supped on Spanish hospitality and first had received Spanish encouragement for his venture.

This, however, was naught to me and I even forgot that his son, Diego, was in the friars' custody. I wanted only bread and directions and both were given gladly, the bread sopped in grease and a portion of cold mutton to stretch the skin of my belly into ample thews.

"The establishment of Francisco Gallego?" the friar looked closely at me. "Does one so young first seek a wineshop?"

"I have a friend there and one I need see." The wine he had given me was water-weakened and glowed my guts a bit, but had no sting.

"Then that is different, little brother, for a friend is a jewel in heaven's firmament or in a pigsty."

He walked with me to the gate and pointed up the road to Palos. "A mile, and no more, is the house of Martin Alonso Pinzon, mariner——"

Pinzon! The pilot on the barge at Seville and my father's friend—but, no, I must not lean on my father's name or impose on his friends. The world was mine to have with my own hands and my own worth.

"You veer from the road at Master Pinzon's residence"—the Franciscan shielded his eyes and swept his left arm outward—"and take a footpath riverward. It will lead you to the alley on which is located Gallego's shop. And, now, God attend thee, little brother."

The road wound to the crest of the bluff and I stood and surveyed the Niebla that had been the spine of Andalusia's African trade until our Crowns restricted commerce and left these ports to rot in their own stagnation; Palos, Huelva, Moguer. There below me, at Point del Sebo, the Odiel and the Tinto swept into confluence to form Rio Saltes and the roadstead of Palos, and there the Ocean Sea rolling grayish-green into timelessness.

The roadstead was empty and the Niebla was a sorry contrast to Lepe, which was near enough to Portugal to enjoy some of the bustle and expansion of that happy kingdom.

I hitched my belt an inch higher and raked my stocking-cap to the side of my head and trod up the road, and Alonso Pinzon's house evoked my envy as its dimensions and elegance testified to the master's affluence even in these trying times. Negro slaves were tending his personal vineyard and these blackbirds were among the few I had ever seen because the Guinea "mines" had been closed to Spain for almost five years in compliance with Isabel's injunction against the slave trade.

I veered riverward and there was Palos, cradled at the end of her harbor, and then I covered my eyes against the sun and peered at the only ship that gave any indication of activity.

*Santa Maria! Marigalante!* Old *Frivolous Mary*. There she was again, easy at anchor and sailors on her crossarms, and it was like unto seeing an old friend from a far place and she reflected my mind to Seville, to Fray Juan and Mudarra and my father. I must write him this night that I am well.

The path grew into a cobblestone alley and this I followed into Palos, and noticing the idle seamen in little groups on the corners and

Guinea barracoons built close to the harbor and stenching the air most foully.

It was my intent to inquire the exact location of Gallego's shop and I stopped at an apothecary's for this chore and my hand was on the door to enter when I saw the shelf of aloes in the window and in the center, like the queen she was, the hideous Medusa of Mauretania, her tentacles withered and dried like those of a dead octupus.

A passing sailor saw me transfixed and touched my arm and motioned his head toward the Medusa. "Worth more than a Guinea blackbird, that one is."

"Aye," I replied. "Whence came it?" Could it have come from Luis Harana? Was this horrible aloe to lead me to her?

"How should I know?" the sailor grimaced at me. "Am I one to break the Queen's law and trade with Africa?" Then he shrugged and smiled. "Perhaps it came from the Azores or the Canaries. They can be had, you know, if a man dares venture his neck into the Queen's wrath."

"I have a long neck." I met his stare and sought to read it.

"And an expensive poniard, I see."

"A sharp poniard. And the friendship of Pedro de Arcos and Gomez Rascon."

"Ah-h-h. But a stranger."

"An Andalusian is a stranger in no land, and a Sevillano is neither stranger in heaven, nor in hell. And now where is the establishment of Francisco Gallego?"

The wineshop was but a stone's throw down the alley and, reaching it, I opened the door to inquire of Rascon, and my heart leaped as his squeaky voice sounded from a rear table of the public house.

"A pox on you, Francisco Gallego, and a fie for your dreggy wine."

Then he saw me and sprang to his feet and spilled his wine in his haste to greet me. "Lepe! By the neglected cods of Paul and Silas. Lepe!"

# CHAPTER 10

*I* NEVER REACHED THE HOME OF PEDRO DE ARCOS; I WAS NEVER A tutor.

Alas! From this day until I was hounded into the role of Mudarra the bastard Moor, and that after The Discovery, I relegated all scholarship to the recess of my volition and rent the veil between me and the world of callous wit and sinewy hands, and this confession in the name of Heraclitus, the Weeping Philosopher.

The Rabbit demanded a jeroboam of publican Gallego's best wine and we drank first to our reunion and then to Arcos and to the Queen, to my father and old Mudarra and Fray Juan, to Maria back in Lepe and my aunt and a host of persons, only I did not mention Maraela, and I was soaked in loquacious bacchanalia when I remembered the Medusa of Mauretania and presumed to ask why such an exotic rarity was on display in this moribund port.

"If it crosses the sea, it will reach Palos." The Rabbit was eying me warily, his lips puckering rapidly like his cognominal mammal approaching a delectable morsel.

"By the Thirty Pieces, Rabbit!" I banged my tankard on the table in hardy enthusiasm. "I would give my left arm up to here for one of those aloes." I touched my elbow. "Aye, up to here." I touched my shoulder.

He shook his head to clear it and pushed his goblet away and his mouth ceased its puckering and began twitching. "Blackbirds are better articles of vendue, but if you have need for contraband aloes they can be had in the Guinea Isles, provided you are willing to risk a hundred lashes on your back and ten years in a dungeon."

Then he sought to shift the conversation and this I would not allow, but kept prying until, in exasperation, he glared at me as though I were a babe with a wet bottom. "B'rlady, Lepe! The sea is Palos' basket and the staunch paladins of the Niebla will never allow a dry-foot's law to starve us, even though the injunction be regal."

I weighed the import of his declaration and jibbed my course a bit. "Where sails the *Santa Maria*?"

"*Frivolous Mary*," he corrected me and reached across the table and shoved my tankard aside. "I am not the harbor master of Palos; only a gromet who can never be a mariner because of my affliction. To the point, Lepe!"

"Will you be here after the *Santa Maria* has sailed?" I stuck to the name because she was a friend from Seville and worthy of dignity.

"I will not." He glanced over his shoulder and waved Gallego back to the kitchen.

My resolution, spontaneous in its origin and obstinate in its purpose, borned the words that changed my life: "Is there a berth for another gromet on her?"

For almost a minute he did not speak, only looking at me. "You are a student, Lepe."

"I want aloes, Rabbit."

"The first lash draws blood, my friend. The last one you do not feel. You are unconscious."

"There are no welts on your back."

"You go mad the first year in the Queen's dungeon and after the fifth they forget you are there, forget even to bury you."

"When does she sail?" I demanded. "And will she berth me?"

"Iron in your craw, spurred cockerel!" He reached for the jeroboam and brimmed our tankards. "Salt in your guts, by Iscariot's issue! Gallego! Come in reverence, you puffed pinchfist."

The publican approached in unctuous servility and The Rabbit condescended to pour him a cup of our drink and then commanded: "Send to the residence of Pedro de Arcos and request him to attend me here. I have a happy lick for his humors."

Gallego bowed his exit and Rascon fixed his gaze on me. "On the morrow's tide the second ship of an unheralded expedition will arrive. The caravel *Pinta* from Cadiz. Home port is Palos. Her patron is Santa Catalina."

(Ah, valiant *Pinta*. Here I heard your name for the first time and from your servant, gnomed Gomez Rascon, who loved thee as much

118

as I. Had I but known the years, I would have lifted my tankard to every timber in thy keel, to every block and studding. Noble Mercury, my *Pinta!*)

"Then two ships for the voyage?" I asked, being convinced I could find a berth on one.

The Rabbit nodded. "You and I and Arcos for *Frivolous Mary*. We sail first for Coruna in Galicia, and take a legal cargo."

"Then where?"

"We will be at the tip of Spain and if the winds of the Ocean Sea are spiteful and we lose our course——" He shrugged his indifference. "Who is to judge where we anchor for food and water save God, and never the Queen. You have money?"

"Not a blanca."

"Confusion seize, pothunter!" His scowl testified that my poverty was most disconcerting. "You cannot buy aloes on your miserable pay. You will need money." He glanced at my poniard and his eyes lighted his mentation.

And this I read and so declared firmly, "No."

"You will not need it on the voyage. I have my blade and I will be at your side."

"No," I said, but less firmly.

"It will secure a loan from Gallego and if you return you can redeem it. If you do not return, you will not need it." He grinned the diabolic logic of his contention. "But, now, hear me. Your risk is your own."

I was most vexed that he should continue to treat me as a child and spake out in annoyance. "I am aware of the penalties for smuggling——"

"It is not smuggling!" The Rabbit slapped his hand on the table. "It is trafficking, and a useful enterprise although slightly illegal."

I smiled my amusement at his distinction between smuggling and trafficking, between black and gray, albeit there was a variance and upon this I will elucidate now in deference to your time and patience.

All intercourse between Spain and Africa being forbidden, there developed divers systems of profit taking and these included smuggling, which was an inefficient trade conducted by fishermen, gypsies, and other hazarders, and then the vast enterprise known as trafficking, and this an organized participation between shipowners, merchants, and public officials.

119

It worked thusly: a master leased a vessel by verbal agreement and often the owner then signed on as pilot or even as a seaman. A legal cargo was taken aboard and the ship lawfully cleared for an open port and, thence, by devious methods made for a second port and there traded in contraband. The goods were unloaded in Palos and picked up by merchants who pretended no knowledge of the voyage, for, mind you, the merchandise itself was not contraband. For example, slavery was not forbidden, it was only forbidden to import slaves. The merchants shared a pittance of their gain with various officials and the Niebla continued in trade.

From Cadiz to the Portuguese border, Andalusian seamen, masters, brokers, merchants, and functionaries were interlocked in trafficking, although the victims of the risks were the mariners who went after the cargoes and ran them up the Tinto, often under the blind eyes of thieving satraps.

Sometimes, to restrain or discourage investigations by the Crowns, the functionaries seized a ship, threw the master into a dungeon, branded and leathered the crew, and reported to the court that the Niebla was prosperous and submissive, and this by the grace of Queen Isabel and to the glory of King Ferdinand. Then the ship reverted to its owner who, nursing his welts, leased it to another master and the rigol of being prosperous and submissive whirled its merry course.

Rascon explained all this to me in drunken garrulity and brave gestures and was mimicking a lash-master when Arcos arrived and greeted me in a manner most fatherly and scowled at The Rabbit. "What now, imp? Has Gallego hobbled your roger as security for your debts?"

The little devil pushed the jeroboam and a mug before Arcos. "The cockerel goes crowing with us." His lips puckered rapidly and he wagged his head in glee. "We will berth him as a gromet on *Frivolous Mary*."

"What's this?" The ruddy stalwart shouted the inquiry and clamped his hand on The Rabbit's humped shoulder. "Lepe is a student and the son of Vicente Bermejo. Am I to see an innocent spread-eagled on the ladder of La Cosa's stinking jade?"

Rascon shrugged off the hand and nodded for me to defend his words and this I did. "I am no longer a student, Arcos. I am going trading."

"Trading, eh?" His blood reddened his countenance into flushed agitation. "Have you ever smelled bilge under your bed and picked lice from every hair on your body?"

"No, sir."

"Have you ever drunk slime in your water and eaten worms in your bread?"

"No, sir."

"And your bowels running blood while your guts choke your throat?"

"No, sir." I lifted my tankard to him and grinned. "But I am going to sea, Arcos. With you and The Rabbit, I hope, but if that is not your will then I seek a berth for myself. I ask only that you not dismay my father——"

"But you will write him?" demanded Arcos, a father himself.

"Tomorrow," I promised. "After I have taken the master's knife in bounded fealty to his command."

Rascon banged the table with his fist and laughed his delight in that effeminate tone of his, the grating contradiction of a squeaking voice from the callous throat of a cynical marplot. "Clear your scuppers, old one. We have a shipmate."

"Mother of men!" Arcos reached for his wine and quaffed its goodly mockery until a trickle ran from the corners of his lips. "Will glory of Andalusia ever die?" He filled his tankard again and lifted it to me. "If your father were here and younger, he would be with us. Now, to the voyage, Rodrigo of Triana, Lepe of our brotherhood. Your saint?"

"Christopher."

"Ah-h-h. The Christ-bearer. May he attend you."

We drank, and Gallego came and drank with us and it was Arcos who bought me my first sailor's smock, a garment that fitted well around my shoulders and with a hood to be pulled over my head in foul weather. The Rabbit gave me my first gorro, the red stocking-cap of his trade, and that was the garb of Andalusian sailors who opened the world to all men: a rough smock and a red cap. Feet bare, of course.

I kicked off my shoes and put the smock over my jacket and breeches, raked my gorro to the side of my head and raised high my tankard. "*Dum vivimus, vivamus.*" I toasted for all to hear and in my undutiful vainglory I wished most of all for Maraela to hear and admire my resolution, and chastise her own conduct for deserting such a worthy man.

Gallego fetched meat and bread and we reveled until Arcos' eyes reddened with his wine and his drooping lids and jowls sagged his face into a mummer's mask. He mumbled a parting and stumbled into the night and I, lively as a sprite and drunk as a Don, bargained with Gallego for my poniard. He offered 5000 maravedis and I cuffed his stingy cheeks and demanded 7000. We settled for 6500 minus my sup and drink; a small sum indeed for the memory of Maraela that I could feel at my side and touch with my fingers.

The Rabbit witnessed the transaction and tossed the empty jeroboam to the publican. "A jericho for your wife, foul usurer, if her aim is true. And now a couch for my brother."

Gallego led him to his bed and then showed me to a couch at the end of a dingy hall and I sprawled on the straw, knowing not the hour.

My mouth tasted of dregs and devils the next morning, but Rascon pulled me from my bearing and coaxed me to soup and a tumbler of watered wine, and then to the harbor where Arcos awaited us, and aboard the *Santa Maria* and to the presence of her master.

His name I will not disclose as his progeny now are gentlemen of eminent respectability, but this I will vow: he was not Martin Alonso Pinzon, whose wealth his enemies, the idolaters of Christopher Columbus, suggest was founded on trafficking. I know not and care not if Pinzon ever delivered contraband for vendue, but I swear to you by the five wounds of your sacred Lamb that I never saw him on the deck of a trafficker, and I sailed from the Niebla for almost seven years, from the winter of 1485 to the summer of 1492, the year of The Discovery.

The master, who also was captain on my first voyage, heeded the advocacy of Pedro de Arcos, the best helmsman in all Spain, and the impertinent demands of Gomez Rascon, the knave and jester, and signed me to his company as a gromet, a ship's boy to tend the forecastle, where much gear was stowed, and to make myself useful at commands of the master, the pilots, the boatswain, and the carpenter, who also served as surgeon.

I was to receive 3500 maravedis a month of twenty-two days, payable upon our return, and was allowed one seaman's chest of light wood, its size not to exceed five feet in length or three feet in width or depth. In lieu of this chest, I could have space in the hold for one blackbird, his keep to be deducted from my pay.

My own keep was furnished and, in fair weather, I could cook one warm meal a day on the firebox, just aft of the forecastle, and simply a tub of sand shielded against the wind and called "the pot."

I must lead my watch, if it be twilight, in the Salve Regina and turn the glasses on the half hours.

To all these I agreed and the master gave me my knife, a small Damascus blade with which I must cut my food and tend rope. It had a wooden hilt, but no bar to protect my hand and a slip meant bloody fingers or a bloody palm.

The deed was done and The Rabbit showed me about the *Santa Maria*, the 93 feet from her bow to stern, first the forecastle deck shadowed by the foremast, then down to the main deck, convexed to fit the arched beams, past the smoking pot and the forward windlasses to the great hatch into the hold, and this ballasted with rocks which served also as shots for the bombard, although there were leaden balls for the falconet, the only other piece aboard.

Then up to the half deck and the mainmast, and up still higher to the stern, and there the quarter-deck and the mizzen. Just under the quarter-deck was the captain's cabin, its door onto the half deck and windows in the stern and there a poop for the mighty.

Like all fitting craft of her day, the *Santa Maria* carried seven anchors, the sheet hook in the hold to be dragged out and dropped only in emergencies, and two always on the bows and two in reserve. Then there was a stern anchor to keep her nose in the swells and a kedge for forward headway in shoals.

Her yawl was lashed on the main deck in rough weather, but floated astern in easy seas.

Next Rascon and I, and me bubbling pride and curiosity, went from the quarter-deck to the tiller and this deep in the stern and just aft of the pilots' quarters, and there was Arcos at his compass and himself propped against the stout beam of his tiller, and this to the rudderpost and there a gaping port that could not be closed inasmuch as the tiller had need of ample play to control the rudder.

Arcos beamed the lordliness of his trade as he showed me the tiller and let me feel it and pointed up to a small opening in the quarter-deck and through this I saw a speck of sky and a bit of sail, and nothing more. And now in this way was the ship handled: the captain the lord of all and the master setting the course and the sails, and instructions to the pilot who kept his watch on the quarter-deck and close by his compass and calling the course down to the helmsman and he con-

123

stantly checking his own compass against the pilot's and then steering by the feel of the ship and the lodestone in his own spine.

We went back to the deck, and me dripping sweat even though it was winter, and The Rabbit tasted the breeze and pointed riverward to the caravel crawling into the harbor.

"The *Pinta*," he said as though it were nothing, and that is all it was to me that day; nothing.

She was small, much smaller than the *Santa Maria* and smaller even than the *Nina* I had seen in Lepe, but square-rigged and lively. She was called "The Painted One" in the fashion of amorous sailors, but her planking was mottled and sea-eaten. Actually her name came from her first owners, the Pinto family of Palos. Her present owner was Christopher Quintero, also of Palos, and her sobriquet of "The Painted One" merely was evidence of her sailors' longing for home and painted lips and tinted cheeks.

It was after noon, and the *Pinta* still inching in, when Rascon and I went ashore and there on a wharf and before a chandlery that bore his name was Martin Alonso Pinzon peering at me, and I alert to his attendance and with proper presentation of my identity, and this in utmost deference because my gorro was the signum of the cleft between Lepe the sailor and Pinzon the master.

"Rodrigo the son of Vicente Bermejo, eh?" His black, black hair was greasy in the December sun and his swarthy countenance bristled his morning's awn. "And I hear you are for the Galician with Arcos and that rogue at your side." He jerked his head toward The Rabbit.

My comrade twitched his face into an appearance most comical and bespoke Pinzon as though there was no station between Gomez Rascon and the richest man in Palos. "Belay the backstays, sire. Am I not the superior gromet of all Spain?"

"You are a superior imp from hell. Now, back to your whore bed, knave, while I talk to this man."

The Rabbit dangled his withered arm like a ratline in a breeze and budged not one foot and Pinzon laughed and then addressed me. "Your father knows of this venture?"

"He will, sire. I am writing him this day."

"Discretion is the handmaiden of valor, Rodrigo."

"That I realize, and caution is my watchword. And now, sire, when go you to Seville?"

"Within a few months. I sail this week for Rome. On a caravel I have leased. The *Nina* of this port."

"Perchance some day I can sail with you."

He tugged his hair that hung straight and short to his ears and straight across his forehead. "I do not ship men who are branded on their rumps. If I know it." He turned from me and into his shop, but mumbled loudly enough for me to hear, "But then I do not examine the sterns of my sailors."

Arcos joined The Rabbit and me for a meal of sardines and olives and then went to his home to bid his family farewell and Rascon went bargaining for a gorro with a tassel, and I wrote my father that I was going voyaging on the *Santa Maria* and for him to pray for me; and my esteem to old Mudarra.

We went aboard at dusk and The Rabbit showed me how to turn the glass and taught me the time song:

> *"Good is that which passeth,*
> *Better is that which cometh;*
> *An hour is past and another floweth,*
> *More shall flow if God willeth;*
> *Count and pass makes voyage fast."*

I sang it out and the seamen already on watch nodded their appreciation as my voice was hearty and resonant.

All time was measured by watches and glasses, and hours had no meaning, and this was the first evening watch, called the second dog-watch, and The Rabbit went to the quarter-deck, to the binnacle that housed the pilot's compass, and trimmed the lantern there, then held it aloft and chanted: "Amen and God give us a good night, sir captain and master and brotherly company."

His thin tone was praiseful, and this very meet and proper, and all the ship's company gathered and we sang our Salve Regina and the hymn floated across the harbor to Palos and beyond.

The *Pinta* was singing, also.

The officers had bunks in their quarters and seamen and gromets bedded down where we could, usually on deck, and Rascon quickly taught me the trick of bedding on the great hatch, which was level and in comfortable contrast to the arched deck.

He soon was breathing deeply the innocence of sleep, but I lay awake until the dogwatch gromet sang the time song, the glass turning and me watching the stars and wishing for straw for my back.

We were away on the flood tide, Palos still sleeping and the night growing old, and all hands aroused to haul in the anchor, and our *Santa Maria* creaked out of the harbor and into the Rio Tinto, then turned her bow toward the Gulf of Cadiz and the Ocean Sea. A lantern dangled on the bowsprit and the *Pinta* was in our wake, her running light dipping as she flexed her back and belly for the run through the gulf for Cape St. Vincent.

The Gulf of Cadiz is green and gray and the Ocean Sea is greener and grayer and nothing in all man's endeavor is more monotonous than a voyage in good weather, the tedium never varying under the stringent discipline of everything done the same time in the same manner by the same hands.

Even I, my feet scarcely damp, quickly was aware that the *Santa Maria* was a clumsy sailer (and remember she was a Galician and not an Andalusian) verily a flying pig, for the Niebla yet was off our starboard beam before the little *Pinta*, scudding without spritsail at her bow or bonnets on her main course, keeled by us and shook her stern in our noses and was gone.

And now, kind friends (and if you have come this far with me, I may call you friends) I will not here narrate the details of my first voyage or any subsequent voyages until The Discovery, and this in deference to your patience. One voyage is quite like another, all circumstances being similar, and I assume you are interested only in *the* voyage. Therefore, I will not serve tidbits here, but save them all for the feast and then tell you how we sailed across the Ocean Sea with Christopher Columbus, whose name means Christ-bearer Dove, to the New World that he believed was India.

It is sufficient that by the time we raised Cape Finisterre at the westernmost tip of Spain I had mastered all my duties as gromet and was with the ropes and sheets and in my apprentice as seaman. I learned readily, being an apt pupil and most strong for my years and of sharp faculties.

The *Pinta*, in ballast and rummaged, which is to say cleansed and sweetened after the voyage, was waiting for us at Coruna and we unloaded our cargo of wine tuns and a few dyed silks from Persia, smuggled in from Malta, and The Rabbit drew against his pay for an orgy in port and insisted that I accompany him.

126

This I refused to do, electing to remain on shipboard with Arcos and thus conserve my resources.

We remained in port a week before we were bound away and bow on into the Ocean Sea and hoping for weather that would give credence to the tales of storms we must report if questioned back in Palos. The winter gales, down from Flanders and England, struck us on the second day out and we close-hauled and ran with the wind, down into the Sea of the Mares, thusly called because so many horses died in shipment across those waters; hard down for the Canaries, and to anchor at Las Palmas.

The year had turned to '86 and the winter was breaking up and the Guinea Isles seethed with enterprises, mostly illegal; blackbirds and aloes from Africa, damask from Damascus, poplin from Avignon, gauze from Gaza, and iron from England, the home of those who put as much faith in metals as Spaniards did in honor.

Our master, with a purse of ducats at his belt, made arrangements with the proper authorities and then we were permitted ashore to trade and Arcos and The Rabbit bought two Negroes at auction while I went bargaining for aloes.

There were no Medusas in Las Palmas, a Portuguese bastard having traded for the last only a few days before, but I found some acceptable spider aloes and in these I invested all of my resources and put them in my sea chest and it filled with sand and soil.

The *Pinta* still was trading, and a few of our company also, when a Castillian sail was reported offshore, luffing against a wind that was leeward to us, and this good fortune we used to scud out of the harbor that night and, all lights doused and the pot covered, back to our course and the six hundred mile haul to Palos.

I could work any line, bow, bunt, or clew by the day we sighted the Point of Umbria in beautiful Andalusia, then across the bar and into Rio Saltes, to Rio Tinto and home.

I was a sailor.

My belly was hard and flat and the muscles knotted at my shoulders and flowed strong into my sinews. The calluses on my feet and hands were thick and rough and my hair crinkled and lay long to my neck. My eyes were blue clear and my beard was autumn brown, the growth of a long voyage.

I was a man.

So bold and greedy were the merchants of Palos that they did not wait for auction, but came aboard the *Santa Maria* and bargained openly for our contraband, and Arcos did well with his blackbird and The Rabbit even better by swearing that his man was an Ethiopian of the ancient land of Sheba's crown and a true descendant of Soloman's seed. He swore by the regeneration of Dismas.

I sold half of my aloes for a goodly profit and the remainder I kept to send to my father. Arcos helped me carry my sea chest to Gallego's place and there I redeemed my poniard and ordered wine for all present, then retired to a corner to read the letters my father had dispatched to this address.

I opened them in the sequence that Gallego had received them, the first written the preceding December. My father was well, and also old Mudarra and Fray Juan, and there was no censure that I had gone to sea, only hope and prayers for my safety and godliness.

Seville was overflowing with soldiers again, a new army to be fielded against Granada's Moors in a war that had become a ladder of sieges with King Boabdil falling back steadily but taking heinous toll while Ferdinand waded in the blood of his own warriors and strove mightily to conjure up the ardor of the old Crusades.

His shrewd spouse, the pious Isabel, was in camp with him and knotting the frayed strands of statecraft into the stout rope that was to bind all Spain into one kingdom, and she using her intuitive wits more profitably than he used his mailed fist. Already she was counting the princes of Europe to arrange a fertile marriage for her imbecile daughter, the piteous Joanna, who was a child of staring eyes and stagnant intellect.

Isabel's scheme was apparent even to the beggars of Europe: strengthen her own house and the Spanish arm of the Holy Church, maneuver the Moors out of the realm, unite the country, marry her issues into strong families, and then create an empire beyond the sea, and this meant Africa.

The fields were bare and the honey was exhausted, and the Spanish beehive was buzzing and soon the hungry bees must take flight or die, and the squirming gum needed only a queen, and this was Isabel, and the Queen needed only a captain.

She held all the reins of the Inquisition and skillfully manipulated them, checking the horses of the Apocalypse when her nobles frowned and lashing the beasts to a froth when her nobles turned their heads, and feeding converso heretics to old Quemadero that the smoke might blind the people and hide the barren fields, the withered vineyards, and the blood torrents in Granada.

The Queen needed time and a captain.

And the people, the bees swarming for flight, had ceased murmuring against conversos and now were crying out against the public Jews, who were not heretics in any manner, but stalwarts in their faith; the fathers snarling "Christ-killers" in the streets and the children shrieking, "Stone them out!" For fourteen hundred years, Christians and Jews had lived under the same starry canopy in Spain and for seven hundred years the Moors had breathed the sweet air of this land, but now the canopy was rent and the thunder was crashing through.

And Isabel was curling the whip over the backs of the frenzied horses of St. John's revelation, wheeling them into Granada's torment, lashing them through Quemadero's smoke, trotting them on parade for the nobles, jerking their heads into reverent bows for the priests.

All this my father wrote me, and sadly.

But hold! Benjamin Marino was back in Seville and with his family, his wife, a son, and a daughter, lecturing again at the college. His map was finished, and this instrument for the Franciscans, and this is all my father knew of the matter.

Yet hear! Christopher Columbus had seen the Queen and she most impressed, not by his knowledge but by his zeal, and now he was at the University of Salamanca to appear before a Commission of Learned Men and there espouse his cause under the aegis of Franciscan prestige and converso purse.

Of this circumstance, my father knew no more and I cared no more, for the same letter that gave mention to Christopher Columbus brought the news that Luis Harana was dead.

This unhappy intelligence, gleamed through the fingers of the Inquisition's long arm, was a token of bereavement from Fray Juan to my father that the house of Bermejo might know the woeful loss and mourn our friend.

Luis Harana, merchant, was dead of fever in the village of Porcuna near Cordova and there buried, and Maraela had gone to abide with kinsmen and of these neither my father nor Fray Juan had any knowledge; name or abode.

The letter lay loosely in my hand and the memories swirled through the pungent vapors of Gallego's wineshop, the high revelry of sailors home, the drunken boasts of The Rabbit, the cacophonous clamor and the oaths by bell, book, and candle.

I had not thought of Maraela in weeks.

A man forgets the taste of sweet wine if the vineyards are barren.

# CHAPTER 11

*I* DRANK THAT NIGHT TO THE DEMIGODS OF SPAIN, FROM HANNIBAL, who came this way, to The Cid, who sprang of this soil, and in my spirituous torpidity I wasted much of my substance from the voyage and insensibly pledged to help weigh the *Santa Maria*'s anchors within a week and hie for the Flemish ports on a licit expedition.

The Rabbit procured an array of women and Arcos sprawled at a table and bellowed, "Clear the scuppers, Lepe! Clear the scuppers, Rabbit!"

It was dawn-coming when Gallego and two seamen dragged me to the harbor and doused me into presentable sobriety and I shaved off my beard and slept until midmorning and then to the chandlery to see Martin Alonso Pinzon, himself recently returned from his voyage to Rome.

He was most censorious of my behavior the night before, having heard the harbor gossip, but agreed, nevertheless, to take my remaining aloes to my father on his next trip to Seville, and that before the new moon.

I sensed that he was anxious to talk to me on some matter of his concern, or of mine, and tarried until curiosity found tongue and he said, "You were a student at the College of Seville, uh, Rodrigo?"

"That is correct, sire," I said, volunteering nothing.

"Map making, perhaps?"

"Among other things."

Pinzon beckoned a servant, who set before us two goblets of excellent Roman wine, and I toasted the master's health, and this in utmost circumspection, for in the company of gentlemen I was their kind and at ease. He acknowledged my compliment, then looked at me searchingly and spake in a manner that suggested confidence without so saying: "The wisest geographer of the Niebla is Fray Antonio de Marchena of the monastery at La Rabida and he has gone inland to espouse the chimeric design of a certain Christopher Columbus to reach the Indies by sailing west."

"I have heard of Christopher Columbus, and muchly," I said and was somewhat vexed that he should think me ignorant of national affairs. "All Spain has."

"Spain will hear more," he said.

"This Columbus is a visionary." I spoke my judgment as though it were a learned pronunciamento. "He prattles like a mystic and wears the robes of prophecy."

Pinzon relaxed in his chair and folded his hands behind his head. "Visionary, uh? Christopher Columbus is a visionary, so they all say. And Alonso Pinzon is a realist, a practical mariner, master and merchant. Hear me, young worthy. The difference between a realist and a visionary is this: the realist will settle for half a cask of wine; the visionary demands all or nothing."

He turned and gazed toward the harbor, the *Santa Maria* and the *Pinta* at anchor and the *Nina* and other craft in dock. "I have a friend ———" He moved his gaze from the harbor and to me. "I have been to Rome."

"Yes, Captain Pinzon. All Palos knows you have been to Rome. Did you see the Holy Father?"

"I delayed you here for a purpose," he explained as though he had not heard my question. "All Rome is in a ferment of excitation and has fallen prey to Europe's latest plague—the fever of exploration. Even His Holiness himself has a rash of the epidemic." He peered into his wine goblet, then drained it. "Now, in the household of the Pope I have a friend who believes India is westward, for sure, but too far removed for a voyage in that direction."

All of this I had heard before from Fray Juan and from Benjamin Marino, and now the concept had seeped from the Holy House itself to Martin Alonso Pinzon, who was a sailor and not a geographer, a practical trader and not a dreamer. I smiled to myself, remembering the long hours in the College of Seville, the ardor of Marino, the zeal of Fray Juan, and the verbosity of the prior.

"The source of my agitation, this friend in Rome———" Pinzon clicked his fingernails and did not look up at me. "He is a steward who is close to the Holy Father and he believes there is land within 700 leagues of Spain and directly across the Ocean Sea, but unknown land and not India at all."

"The Marino theorem," I said casually.

His head came up with a jerk and his black eyes sparkled his sudden anticipation. "That is the name I wanted to hear. Benjamin Marino, the Jew. He lectured at your college?"

"Aye."

"Do you know him?"

Now it must be remembered that I was the son of a merchant and, extravagant as I was, I was ever one for a bargain. It was quite obvious that I possessed knowledge that Pinzon had need of, and, therefore, a barter was in order. I, too, peered into my goblet and was silent just long enough to indicate my willingness to trade, and then I said, "He was my teacher."

"Did he lecture on the unknown lands?" For a practical merchant, Pinzon was childishly eager. "Did he teach that land is only 700 leagues west? Did you see a map?"

I lifted my goblet again, turning it slowly in my hand, and quickly he motioned to his servant and the goblet was filled. "Benjamin Marino is the best map maker in Europe," I said, and, as you perceive, I really said nothing that all Spain did not know.

Nervously Pinzon nibbled at a bit of nail on his middle finger, and his eyes, sparkling the minute before, now were cloudy and cold. "Naturally," he said in aloof disdain, "there will be no fee for delivery of your aloes to your father."

"That is most kind," I replied.

"And that wine——" He nodded toward my goblet. "I brought two tuns from Rome and one of these for my good friend, Vicente Bermejo."

"The wine of our Pope's household, and this surely." I sniffed the bouquet, and my nose, trained to the bitter wines of water fronts, told me naught although my demeanor suggested a proficiency in such matters.

"Naturally," Pinzon said. "Red gold in Seville."

"You are most gracious, sire." I crossed my legs in the confidence of my status, and leaned back in my chair. "But you have digressed from our subject. We were discussing Benjamin Marino. He has prepared a map for the Franciscans, and naturally this you know."

"Naturally," he said in the mendacious assurance of a trader.

"The map possibly is in the possession of Christopher Columbus, whose cause the Franciscans espouse."

"Obviously," he said as though I were speaking trifles and yet I knew he was engraving every word on his memory. "Have you seen this map?"

I shrugged my shoulders and lifted my hands in a gesture of disvaluation. "No, Captain Pinzon. Do you need a map for your quarterdeck? I heard Benjamin Marino explain his theories. Therefore, I know his map." It would profit me naught to dangle the bait further, so I spoke out. "Teacher Marino's map, and of this I am positive, fixes the degree at 62½ miles and places *terra incognita* roughly 3000 miles west of Spain, and there legendary Antilia—the island opposite—and beyond Antilia a mass of unknown land." I relaxed and enjoyed the simplicity and accuracy of my declaration.

Alonso Pinzon glowered at me in search of a hint of trickery and, finding none, smiled his gratitude and struck his desk with his clinched fist. "It accords. By the portals of Purgatory, it fits! The Holy City agrees with Marino. The Church with a Jew."

And then his vanity came forth, as it must in all men, and he could not deny himself the aggrandizement of these words: "My friend, and surely on advice of the Holy Father himself, has suggested that I equip two caravels and go exploring westward."

"Why not?" I asked, instinctively calculating how I might profit from such a venture.

Martin Alonso Pinzon hesitated (ah, fateful pause in the lives of men) and then shook his head in rumination. "I have not the wealth to sponsor such an expedition."

"Our Lady's finger, sire! Is it remiss for a lowly gromet to remind the captain that the Niebla will be patron for such a voyage. One nod from you and the Niebla and all her ships and men are at your command."

The temptation was in his eyes, the warm glow of a great thing almost done, and he shook it off, and it passed. "I am unknown at court," he said. "I have not the sanction of the realm."

(Oh no, Martin Alonso Pinzon. No, no, my captain. Your name is on no speck of land in the new islands, on no spot of water, only because there was no imagination in your humors. The Fates knocked and you scorned them. One word from Rome would have opened every royal door in Europe.

(Never, my captain. It was not the realm's sanction, and this knowledge tormented you until your death. It was not courage, for you could sail a ship into the red jaws of hell and out again on Satan's saliva. No, Pinzon. You were first a trader—a blanca here to get two blancas there. The difference between you and Christopher Columbus was the difference between vision and substance, for he believed a dream and you dreamed a belief. The Fates caress those who cast their dice upon the waves and stake their lives that fortune's ivory will float, that the gods themselves will swirl the spots into the miraculous combination that ordains the wreath of immortality upon the brow of the one who dreams and dares. Aye, Pinzon, you were the realist of substance, the cautious disciple of the Philistines who will not believe ere they can see; you were the pragmatical stalwart—Christopher Columbus was the fool.)

I stared at Pinzon in the galled realization that he was a timid man, that he was a lance but never an arrow, that he was a captain but never a chieftain, a knight but never a king.

His eyes shifted to avoid my stare and he said, "I must think on these things."

(Did Jason ruminate in Iolcus with the Golden Fleece in Colchis? Did he reflect on the dragons' teeth sown?)

I departed that place and left the richest man in Palos to sip his sweet Roman wine and went straightwith to Gallego's lair and there ordered a jeroboam of the Niebla's strong, bitter vintage, which smelled of Spanish sun and tasted of Spanish earth; and The Rabbit joined me and asked whereof my melancholia and I told him not, but sipped the drink into eventual song and gaiety.

My funds were dissipated when we boarded the *Santa Maria* five days later and my sea whiskers were sprouting thick when we cleared the bar at the roadstead and our flying pig buried her nose in the gray waste, and we were away for the Flemish ports.

Our cargo was spun cotton and Andalusian pottery and, of course, wine for ballast, and the Flemish land was a sodden province of barbarians who never had heard of Salamanca or even The Cid; thence to Hull in England and that a region of perfidious tricksters and, by the bald head of Elijah and the hairy back of Esau, the most profane people in all the world. It was no wonder at all that The Maid of Arc had called them Goddammees and that in France an Englishman was Jean Goddamo.

We were out of Hull by late summer, a hold of English wool and salt for Lisbon, and off Cap de la Hague when misfortune's wile, shrouded by a Channel squall, brushed a sailor of the starboard watch and he fell from the crossarm of the main topsail and shattered his spine on the great hatch. Our surgeon lashed him to a plank and he departed us in blubbering agony and we committed him to the sea, a stone at his feet, and I was given his berth and became an able seaman, and this to the cheer of Arcos but to the stricture of The Rabbit, who balanced himself precariously on the falconet on the half deck and sang out: "I will nurse the embers of the pot and fetch drink to all gentlemen and mariners, yet no commands will I hear from Lepe the sailor."

I leaped to the falconet, balanced myself as agilely as he and seized him and heaved him into the arms of Arcos, and all the company laughed, and The Rabbit the loudest of all, for we were a merry crew and all Andalusians; beans in our bellies and warm bile for our humors and our *Santa Maria* grunting her way homeward.

Summer into autumn and we were off Lusitania, off Cabo Raso, and there a Portuguese galley of four bombards spake us and ordered us to proceed cautiously up the Tagus to Lisbon as the roadstead was swarming ships to witness the leave of Bartholomew Diaz. Our master acknowledged the order and The Rabbit gave the galley his stern and a blast and shouted that we were Andalusians from Palos and a fie for a Portuguese parvenu with four bombards.

The patrol did not hear him, God be praised, and our master cuffed his flippant mouth and we crept to the maw of the Tagus with fore-course and mizzen and then the breeze failed us and we went into Lisbon on an ash wind, working our long sweeps through the ports while The Rabbit squatted and taunted us, he being spared such labor, owing to his withered arm.

Even our haughty Andalusians were stilled into envious silence by the splendor of Portugal's capital, for here indeed was the most active port of all Europe because this realm looked to the sea and not to the ashes of old Quemadero. Never before had I seen so many ships or a people so happy in the blessed activity of accomplishments.

A harbor patrol, an innovation I had seen in no other port, boarded us and directed us to a slip and anchorage and sternly criticized the vermin and odors of our hold and ordered us to rummage ere we unloaded. Our master was indignant and the Portuguese shrugged their indifference to his spluttering wrath and there was no recourse save to do their bidding and cleanse ship.

We shifted our cargo and swabbed the hold with vinegar and water, and the rats scampered down the anchor ropes and swam ashore while the vermin curled and died and The Rabbit shrieked his bane on all things Portuguese and, in retaliation, foreswore the pleasures of Oporto wine and Lisbon women. "Let their loins wither for Andalusian solace." He spat in the Tagus toward the city. "Out upon! And the curse of the foam of Judas upon this realm."

The rummage delayed us for five days and for this I was grateful as we were still at anchor the morning Bartholomew Diaz' three caravels dropped down the Tagus for the voyage along the west coast of Africa, his search for a new route to India.

The water front was lively with buntings and ensigns and a multitude thronged to cheer them away. A bombard roared and the crowd danced its excitement.

(Aye, poor Palos and mean, this glory you should have witnessed, you who wept or gawked in silence when we departed you for The Discovery that frayed the lanyards of Portugal's proud standards and transformed our Niebla's drowsy lanes into a busy roadstead.)

The flagship of Diaz led the procession, her officers in splendiferous array on her quarter and the crew in boisterous babel on her main deck. The Rabbit sulked his envy that our *Santa Maria* was rocked by the wake of Portugal's adverturers and he, munching olives, spat the seed into their Tagus and mouthed his contempt. "They will drop off the end of the earth and good riddance and may their widows drop seven bastards each in commemoration of their extinction."

"There is no end of the earth." In the excitement of the spectacle I forgot myself and attempted remonstrance with the little imp, and took an olive from his hand and held it up. "Aroint, long ears! It is thus." I coursed the olive. "If you sail down this side and keep sailing, you will come up this side. There is no shelf on the earth. There is no end."

"Dominican proficiency." He snarled at me. "Hell's witchery." His face contorted into a grimace and he snatched the olive from my fingers and popped it into his mouth. "There is an end to everything."

Arcos' elbows were rested on the rail and his chin was on his hands, and he disdained our duologue but studied the Portuguese caravels, and his sharp eyes raked them from bow to stern and to topsail. "See you, Lepe." He nudged his elbow deep in my side and pointed to the quarter-deck of Diaz' ship. "That wheel. They steer with a wheel and their helmsman has sea and sun."

"More witchery," The Rabbit said. "It will not do. A helmsman must handle the tiller. It has been ever thus."

"But it does do," Arcos said. "These foreigners are clever, aye, Lepe?"

"At least they know the world is round." I gave my back to The Rabbit and shaded my eyes and conned the quarter and perceived at once how the wheel performed; the ropes to the wheel and through the deck to the tiller. Hence a turn of the wheel pulled the ropes, obviously through blocks, and maneuvered the tiller. It was as simple as that, merely blocks and stanchions to anchor them, and ropes and a wheel. Now this was a worthy discovery and a thing that well might bring profit and honor to me. And, of course, to Arcos who had noticed it first.

We remained on deck until Diaz' expedition was around a point and the multitude was thinning, and then we fell to and began unloading, and this enterprise with a will and a song as we were hungry for home. We took on a legal cargo of wine, cheaper and more plentiful here than in Andalusia, and ten blackbirds, and these contraband, and departed that orderly and thriving city on the flood, running with a flaming brazier at our bow as a signal that we were under way and must not be headed.

The Rabbit put powder and shot in our falconet and the master ordered the bombard stuffed just in case some Portuguese bastard, frisky in the triumph of Diaz' voyage, cut our bow to gloat and jeer the insularism of mighty Spain.

We were not spaken all the way to the sea, and for this a candle to our ship's saint, as The Rabbit had neglected to wad the falconet and a spark might have blown me into the arms of my Gothic forebears and all of us into the hateful embrace of the grisly Moerae.

The strong arms of Arcos, and his weight and skill at the tiller, held us true across the shank of the bar, and the tide ebbing, and then we were in the Saltes again and inbound for Palos; the *Santa Maria* creaking in every joint.

Our anchor ripples still were running when the merchant hagglers put out to board us and from them I heard my first news of Spain in several months, and this the fiasco of Christopher Columbus in his appearance before the Commission of Learned Men at Salamanca.

And now, just reader, let us tarry here and inventory our intellects if you wish sincerely to comprehend the triumph and tragedy of Christopher Columbus, an enlightenment possible only if you are capable of probity and can withstand the din of his deific advocates, many of whom have gilded the Columbus legend for personal gains, and the man's spirit scarcely risen.

Under the patronage of some of the most powerful forces in the kingdom, including the Franciscans, the adventurer had been presented to the Queen, and, glib as a street hawker, had made a likely impression upon Isabel because they had similar temperaments, a proclivity for enterprise and an abundance of Catholic missionary zeal, and both willing to hazard a flame at each end of the candle and themselves aglow with grandiose schemes.

The Queen entered his name on her royal accounts to the amount of approximately 63,000 maravedis a year and instructed that he be garbed appropriately, and then appointed the Commission to examine his plans and report to her; and this Commission under the direction of Fray Hernando de Talavera, the Queen's own confessor and a renowned Hieronymite, which is to say a hermit of St. Jerome's austerity.

Now, mind you, this Commission of Learned Men was not charged to approve or reject Columbus' plans, but only to hear them and counsel Isabel. This was done.

The petitioner was no friendless wayfarer pleading his dream to skeptical professors. He had influential partisans at his side and his premise to the Commission was that India was only a caravel's voyage west of Spain and that he could reach it.

This, naturally, the Commission could not accept because it was not true.

The earth is small, he argued, and India is beyond the horizon, perhaps only 700 leagues.

The earth is large, they replied, and India is half a world away.

He presented no maps, no charts, and this most singular, inasmuch as he had a copy of Toscanelli's map, purloined or not, and possibly the Marino map. Columbus offered no proof or argument whatsoever, only his adamant contention: "India is across the Ocean Sea and I can reach it."

Out of this council has sprung a most preposterous legend and nourished by The Discoverer's idolaters, who would make him a saint instead of a sailor: that the Commission disputed the shape of the world with Columbus. This, of course, is ludicrous nonsense.

The scholars did not dismiss the petitioner, but did as they were charged and heard his claim and advised the Queen that he was a mystic of magnetic personality and staunch in his dream that he could accomplish a miracle and find India where India could not possibly be. They advised her that zeal, courage, and hope were his attributes and that whereas his knowledge of geography was deficient he was a man of infinite conviction in his own destiny and that the gate should never be barred to a possible miracle.

So there it stood when I returned to Spain. The Queen had taken Columbus' cause under consideration and he was back in Cordova, her protégé and pensioner and augmenting this emolument by the sale of maps that he and his brother, Bartholomew, designed and executed. He could be found almost daily in the apothecary of Leonardo de Esbarraya, discussing exploration with the loiterers there and exhorting his bent to all who would heed, and these not many, for Cordova was a place of dreary insularism and her people of no mind for dreams of the Indies, but concerned only with matters at hand: the Moorish War, the Inquisition, and the clamor of the populace against all Jews, even those who strove to lull the heaving waves by opening their purses to good works and giving eloquence to pleas for mercy and justice.

I was paid 28,000 maravedis for the long voyage, the master rewarding me this stipend in gold excelentes, and I, joyfully affluent, was intent upon a return to Seville to see my father and old Mudarra, but first I must have good raiment that Seville might know I had done well. I priced a doublet and the seamer was most insistent that I buy, promising me the garment in a week, and there in his shop, fingering the velvets and silks, I remembered the admonition of Fray Juan that day he deprived me of my trophy: "Rodrigo of Triana, never again will you wear a velvet doublet until you have earned it."

Well, I had earned it.

Nevertheless, I did not settle the transaction, there being a troublesome tug at my conscience, and I departed the shop and my promise to return did not still the laments of the tailor.

I took myself therewith to Gallego's place, and this most fortunate as there were two letters from my father, the first that all was well and

the second that he was journeying into Granada to seek army contracts, particularly medicines and meat. The medicines I understood,
he being a dealer in aloes, but the meat surprised me, and this indicating either that he had come upon a supply of beef or must find
one, and this, in turn, being evidence that his pottery and aloes business
was not healthy.

Anyway, my father was in Granada and a visit to Seville would have
been useless, and so my gratitude to God that I had not wasted my
opulence on the doublet, such being a garment of no utility to a
sailor.

The Rabbit was at Gallego's, dissipating his weal on drink and, for
truth, he had purchased a gift for the ordinary's daughter, the dim-
witted bed warmer for my comrade, who customarily had naught for
her except kicks and curses and only such manliness that Palos' whores
did not consume. The token was a shawl of India cotton and she was
piteously proud and flaunted herself before the winebibbers, and The
Rabbit smirking his devilish perversity.

I declined his invitation to revelry and rid myself of the beard and
filth of the voyage and then straightway to Martin Pinzon's establishment. Yes, he had seen my father and had delivered the aloes and my
father most proud of his son's devotion. Aye, my father seemed in excellent health, albeit of gloomy humors because business was wretched.
The pottery market was glutted and aloes were scarce and, aye, he had
heard my father comment that he proposed to seek army contracts for
meat. No, he had no inkling of the supply, but then: "Your father is
an excellent trader, Rodrigo, and if beef is available he will find it."

Half of my excelentes I put on his desk and requested him to send
them to Mudarra by Merchants' Post with instructions that they be
held for my father and, aware that Pinzon was impressed by my
earnestness, I broached him the matter of the steering apparatus I had
seen on Diaz' ships.

"Now that is a Portuguese feat of much merit," I said, and reached
for quill and paper and demonstrated how I could equip the Niebla's
caravels with the innovation. I would secure two stanchions and to
these attach blocks, thence ropes to the tiller and through the blocks
and up to a wheel on the quarter.

Pinzon smiled at my enthusiasm and then shook his head. "I charter
the ships I sail," he explained. "All except one small craft that I own
and which I lease to the sardine fishermen of Lepe. Should I suggest

this novelty of your imagination to the owners from whom I lease they conceivably might commission you to install it, but surely they would increase the charter fees. It is not good business, Rodrigo." He picked up the quill and returned it to its well. "I can hire helmsmen for 7000 maravedis a month, and that is that."

My disappointment, I am sure, was obvious, as I had hoped to convert my design into ducats and thereby lessen my father's worries.

Alonso Pinzon perceived my disillusion and put his hand on my arm and spoke kindly, "There is nothing wrong with your father's business that aloes will not correct."

"Aye, sir," I replied and frowned my impatience at the platitude. "Aloes will cure anything. But where the aloes?"

"You fetched aloes on your first voyage."

"Captain Pinzon." I drew myself erect and was taller than he, and rested my hand on my poniard in a most seamanly manner. "Please do me the honor that my intelligence justifies. The aloes I fetched were inferior and meager. There is no profit in trafficking save for the owner, the master, and the merchant."

He studied me intently, his black eyes steady on my face. "Then come with me."

"Trafficking?" I demanded boldly.

"No. To the Mediterranean ports. I have chartered the *Nina.*" He picked up my gold excelentes and jingled them in his hand. "Leave these with me and I will buy for you. Also, I will hold back one half of your pay and invest it. But only in aloes, and in the licit markets of Italy."

"You are most kind, sire," I said and was deeply touched by his fatherly interest in me.

His smile was quick and warm. "Most sailors are wastrels, Rodrigo. Hence my presumption in this affair. I need your shoulders and capacity on my ships and for these I will exchange my acumen in the markets."

"I will not impose upon your friendship for my father." It was the polite remark to make and really of no meaning, as I was eager to sail with him.

"It is a matter of business," he assured me. "I have need of you and you have need of me. The *Nina* sails on the moon change. It will be a long voyage."

"Arcos?" I asked.

"Aye. Arcos."

"The Rabbit?"

He smiled again, then nodded. "The Rabbit."

In a buoyant ado, I pressed upon him all of my earnings, save keep money, and he insisted that I retain one excelente for the wine I might need.

I was in debt to Arcos when we boarded the *Nina* and I took the knife of Martin Alonso Pinzon, my vow to his service and my pledge to his discipline, and Arcos, Rascon, and I were given the port watch and then Arcos to his tiller, The Rabbit to the pot, and I to the rigging.

> *"Blessed be the light of day*
> *And the Holy Cross, we say.*
> *And the Lord of Veritie*
> *And the Holy Trinity."*

The dawn song and we sang it out, and Andalusia's east pinking and our anchors sucking mud. But up with them! And down the Tinto again, down the Saltes and across the bar, then an easy port rudder and *The Little Girl* scudded off Playa de Castilla, past the delta of the muddy Guadalquivir that winded inland to my Seville, past Cadiz and hard for Cabo Trafalgar, the Strait, and the Pillars of Hercules.

To our starboard was Africa, rugged and green and misty, and there Tangier of Portuguese pretension and Moorish domination, ancient when history was new, and named for Tinge, who wedded Neptune's son; and there the Gardens of the Hesperides, whence Hercules stole the golden fruit[1] and therewith gave oranges to Europa.

The Strait was shallow, the path of Hercules, who cleft the mountain that separated the Mediterranean from the Ocean Sea and builded the pillars that bear his name, and this watercourse the most important in all the world, for its shelf holds back the ocean and protects the Middle Sea, which, as all men know, is the cradle of mankind.

True into the Strait we sailed, our *Nina* pitching and squirming, and the mist shrouded Tangier and the African coast.

(*Magna civitas, magna solitudo.* Ah-h-h, Tangier, thou gem of antiquity and my prison of iniquity, for I sit today in Tangier, penning my story; I an exile, I an old man of many vineyards, but I find no pleasure in them; I an old man of many maidens and, woe to years, no

---

[1]Tangerines.

143

delight thereof, for I had Mita and God never has given man a taste for watered wine after a feast of plenty. My house is marble. My slaves are fat. But all this would I trade, and gladly, to cross yon finger of the sea and to my Andalusia once more. The water is gray on this morn and the clouds low, and yon—I point my finger to remember—and yon the Strait where our *Nina* sailed, and me young and almost ripe for the greatest adventure that ever befell mortal man: I saw it first.)

The lateen sails of our ship caused her to yaw most disgustingly in a steady wind aft and Arcos labored to exhaustion to hold her true. We were compelled to lower and hoist at the slightest shift and we roundly cursed her owner, who was too stingy to rig her squarely, but through the Strait we beat and into the Mediterranean, the Middle Sea—our sea.

An ebb, a flow, and each so gentle that it was days before we noticed it, being bred to tides, and this a lake, saltier than the sea, greenish at anchorage and heavenly blue at great depth, shadowing to purple in the first wind of storm.

We stood well off from the coast of Granada to avoid Moors, then around Cabo de Gata to Spanish water again and by Cabo de Palos, and this name a joy to us, and into Valencia, where our master began trading, this being a dry land of abundant wheat and esparto grass, of which sandals and rope are made.

The Rabbit made for the first wineshop he sighted and I, more in curiosity than in remembrance, inquired if the name of Harana were known thereabouts, and it was not.

Also, there were no aloes in Valencia and Pinzon traded in rope and we were away before The Rabbit had chance to teach his selected maidens the art of Andalusian lusting.

Around the coast to Barcelona, and then France, and Pinzon trading in every port and driving us as I had never been driven before; he in a frenzy, aye, a mania of profit taking: almonds and olives, wine and wheat, rope and leather, but no aloes to be had and me distraught in this knowledge, and the master driving on.

Aloes? Aloes? He asked in Marseille.

No aloes.

So we took horsehides instead.

Corsica and Sardinia and into the Tyrrhenian Sea, then up to Genoa and I forgot that hence came Christopher Columbus, or so they say. His name never crossed my memory and, besides, I sopped wine my first night in Genoa, and my humors melancholy in the conviction that aloes were not obtainable, that I was in for a long, long voyage under a hard master.

My determination for enterprise and decorum melted in the tedium and even the stalwart Arcos gave way to man's bestial bent and we sowed our seed and wined our thirst at every call.

"Clear the scuppers, Lepe!"

It sounded in Florence.

"Clear the scuppers, Rabbit!"

That was in Pisa.

(The scar on my shoulder is a memento from an unreasonable husband in Livorno, the one whose ribs I parted with a single thrust. This scar high on my forehead is a souvenir of Piombino, where The Rabbit left his poniard in a Tuscan's back, then stole a better knife in Syracuse.)

Rome was bloated decay and there The Rabbit bought a bundle of sticks to be sold in Spain as splinters from the True Cross and Arcos and I visited the ruins and wearied of them. Women were cheaper in Naples than in Palos.

Rome, Naples, Syracuse—the cities flowed past in musty senescence, and the months flowed into seasons and the seasons into a year, and Pinzon was a master possessed of profit fever and his crew lean and gaunt and threatening desertion ere he spake us from his quarter: "We are for home, my hearties. We stand for Palos."

Most of the men were too sullen to cheer, but The Rabbit leaped to the half deck and jigged. "By the boils on Job! You have decided well, Captain Pinzon, else the pining misery of Andalusia's maids be on your conscience."

Alonso Pinzon shouted down to Arcos to bring her about and the great tiller creaked and the rudder also, and *The Little Girl* bowed her nose for home and there was a song in the rigging and a chant from the deck.

I was summonsed to the quarter and the captain returned my investment, together with my accumulated pay, and was most regretful that he had been unable to obtain aloes for me. This whim of fortune I shrugged off as a cast of the dice and, to allay his dejection, I spake cheerfully. "It has been a profitable voyage for you, aye, sire? We have traded hard and now go home with a hold of good Italian wheat."

He conned the binnacle and, serving as pilot, called the course

145

down to Arcos, then looked up at me. "I drove all of you too hard. The voyage was too long. Nineteen months from home. Too long." He stared across the starboard bow at the coast line of Italy and chewed his lower lip. "Profit? Aye. But not enough. It will cost 4,200,000 maravedis to charter and equip two caravels for an expedition across the Ocean Sea. Neither I nor my family has that sum. This voyage was not enough."

Mother of Mary and Mary the mother! So that explained the back-and-forth trading in Italian cities, the *Nina* beaten and the men beaten. Alonso Pinzon needed money to go exploring. He had maps from the Pope's library and he had men and still he hesitated, and I know now that it was not gold that held my captain from the Unknown Sea. It was a fault of imagination, a demerit of vision, a want of conviction of his own destiny.

He was the greatest sailor I ever knew, and this truth into the teeth of the toadies of Christopher Columbus; but he would not challenge the Fates although Christopher Columbus, the Christ-bearer Dove, spat his dare into the hideous faces of Hell's Three Sisters.

I could not deny the words on my tongue and let them fall. "Captain Pinzon, the Niebla will furnish ships for you, and this you know. And rest this crew for a month and we will sail you to Polaris if you chart the course."

Instead of dismissing me as an impudent sailor, he argued with me. "My maps are not sufficient."

"There is always Benjamin Marino," I said. "He can be commissioned to draw maps."

"Marino is a Jew and all Jews in Spain are in scalding water. I heard in Rome that our Queen may order a new exodus."

The import of this did not penetrate immediately as my mind was on maps. "Bartholomew Columbus is a good map maker. I have seen his work——"

"Bartholomew Columbus is not in Spain. This, too, I learned in Rome." Pinzon glanced at his compass and shouted the course down to Arcos. "Bartholomew Columbus is back in Portugal. He has been to France and England to peddle his brother's scheme to those kingdoms."

"And Christopher Columbus?" I immediately was interested.

"Still in Cordova, the last I heard. And growing moss on his backside while the Queen mulls his case and Ferdinand smites the Moors."

"She has been mulling a long time." The *Nina* was yawing again and I felt Arcos steady her.

"Too long I fear."

"Then Bartholomew has interested France? Or England?" I was vexed by the thought that either of those backward realms might act while Spain faltered.

Pinzon laughed but without mirth. "They jeered him. But he is in Portugal now and that kingdom has ears for any reasonable plan of exploration. If Christopher Columbus will lower his price, Portugal will sponsor him tomorrow."

"Will he lower it?"

Now there was mirth in my captain's laugh. "By the five wounds! No! His garments are threadbare. He grows gaunt and wrinkled. But he will not compromise one mote. Instead of bargaining, the man raises his price every time he is questioned. A simpleton or a sage, this Christopher Columbus." He glanced quickly at the sky, then at his compass. "The wind shifts. To your watch, Rodrigo."

The voyage home was accursed and ere we raised Gibralter the rats were as thick as weevils in our hold and the vermin so thick in our beards that our faces seemed to crawl. Arcos took us across the bar into the roadstead of our Niebla and we crept up the Saltes to the Tinto and there fortune nailed us down with a strong wind on our bow and the channel too swift for our sweeps.

We anchored off La Rabida for the wind to change and Palos heard of our return and many friends came down and lined the river-bank and waved at us. Our captain's two brothers, Francisco and Vicente Pinzon, rowed out to the *Nina* and greeted us with praises of "bravo," then to seclusion and talk with the master. We lolled on the main deck, impatient at our luck, and soon the Pinzons joined us and gave us news of home, and their faces troubled by events of which we knew naught.

The Moorish stronghold of Malaga had fallen to Ferdinand's armies and Spain slowly was strangling Granada into submission, and all the country in a turmoil against aliens, and an alien was any person who was not a Christian.

"Praise God and the Queen," The Rabbit shouted. "She will cleanse our homeland of circumcision and chicanery."

"She will rob Spain of brains and purse," growled the helmsman of our starboard watch and himself a converso.

147

Old Quemadero was flaming brighter than ever and every city was celebrating Faggot Day and jeering heretics into the fire's embrace. No man cheered this report. We were sailors and we hated fire. If death must settle for heresy, let it be a good rope from a crossarm and God's breeze to cool the spirit before its eternal torment.

A cry was sounding throughout the realm to exile all professed Jews from Spain and already many had departed Andalusia, being torn from their homes and shipped to Africa and their property confiscated.

"Good riddance," The Rabbit gibed. "Their depravity is a pestilence."

"Close your hatch," Arcos snarled. "It is sinful to deprive any man of his home, and the Jews have been with us forever."

"And that is too long," The Rabbit taunted. "By the Christian blood they drink, that is too long."

"Silence." The order came from our captain and then he addressed his brothers. "Tell the men of Diaz. As you told me——"

"Diaz?" Several asked it. "That Portuguese bastard. Did his ships fall off the rim of the earth?"

The three Pinzons exchanged glances and Francisco, the youngest of the family, spake out: "Bartholomew Diaz has sailed to the southernmost cape of Africa and back. A route is open to India."

Arcos whistled his amazement, sucking wind fast between his lips, and we all were stunned, and I by the real significance of the news.

"Diaz reached the tip of Africa and named it Good Hope." Our captain now was speaking. "The way to India is open to Christian trade, and Portugal succeeded while Spain talked."

My mind went out to Fray Juan Ruiz de Medina and to Benjamin Marino, who had looked west instead of south, and then, for truth, my sympathy went out to Christopher Columbus, who had waited too long, and my disgust to our Crowns, who had pinned him down.

I was leaning against the port anchor winch and I called out: "The fortunes of the cast, aye, masters? And this clips the feather from the cap of Christopher Columbus."

"Aye, Lepe." Vicente Pinzon nodded agreement and waved his hand toward the shore and La Rabida on the hill. "He is there, the nobody. Visiting his son, Diego."

Arcos spake and shrugged his broad shoulders in unconcern of fortune's rebuke to Christopher Columbus. "He should have remained in Portugal. Spain has dallied his cause——"

148

"While he diddled in Cordova." Francisco Pinzon could not deny the witticism. "Spain has given him solace if not support, for he found a mistress in Cordova; a converso maiden who has borne him a bastard son."

"Named for a Franciscan, I will wager," The Rabbit jeered. "Or for the King."

"A mark!" Vicente Pinzon laughed. "He has named his colt Ferdinand in honor of the saint, albeit the name of our sovereign, who has the seed of San Fernando but none of his saintliness."

I, too, smiled and joined the levity. "By the navel of Adam. Our homeless Dove came to Spain to find the Indies and found an indention. I will wager he needed no map for that enterprise."

My fellows roared at my wit and Francisco Pinzon chuckled deep in his belly. "His bed help is most comely and meet, I hear. The name of Harana."

The gasp rasped my throat and my tongue clove to the roof of my mouth and I sucked it free and shouted the name. "*Harana!*"

All the ship's company stared at me and Francisco Pinzon was startled by my vehement agitation. "Aye, Lepe. Harana. The woman is Beatriz Enriquez Harana. A respectable family in Cordova."

The seizure departed my heart. Then it was not Maraela. A kinswoman, perhaps. She had gone to live with kin. My gaze moved from Francisco Pinzon to La Rabida there on the hill, to the monastery that sheltered Christopher Columbus.

He might know her. He might; if the Fates be kind.

# CHAPTER 12

*A*LONSO PINZON GRANTED ME PERMISSION TO GO ASHORE AFTER I explained that, for personal reasons, I had urgent need of communication with Christopher Columbus, and I rowed alone to the foot of La Rabida's hill and then walked up the slope to the Franciscan friary.

The bell clapper had rusted and broken and I rapped on the door and it was opened by Fray Juan Perez himself and he scrutinized my bearded face and calloused feet and bade me enter, and this I did; my gorro in my hand and my sailor's smock tattered from the arduous voyage.

I bowed gallantly to establish that my breeding was more than that of a common seaman and asked his leave for audience with the renowned Christopher Columbus, and for an instant the Franciscan hesitated and I said, "I am this day returned from Rome."

"Ah-h. With Captain Pinzon." He entwined his fingers and revolved his thumbs. "It is a joy to hear one so young speak so respectfully of Christopher Columbus, for, indeed, he is a man of renown, and a shame on Spain that our blessed realm dawdles his enterprise." Fray Perez motioned me to a bench. "And, now, may I ask the name of the mariner who hastens directly from Pinzon's caravel to seek audience with this monastery's guest?"

"You may," I said with a delicate inflection of hauteur. "I am Lepe, a sailor, and my business with the thwarted Christopher Columbus is of a personal nature."

Again he studied me closely and I sensed that his curiosity was whetted and that his bent was for converse with me. "Our guest is at matin," he said. "He is a man most pious. We will wait here, you and I."

The wile was artless and wholly unworthy of a man so nimble in artifice. I was vexed by his nosy deportment and elected to best him and perhaps teach him a lesson in Dominican stratagem. I spread my legs wide in a most jaunty manner and rested my hand on my poniard. "A man cannot long remain in this blessed spot and in this worthy presence without feeling the need of piety's virtue. Therefore, brother, I request the sanctity of your chapel for my Contrition."

He looked at me in unfeigned admiration and smiled. "Follow me." There was naught else he could say and yet he added, "An Act of Contrition is a fitting end to a long voyage."

Fray Juan Perez (and he an iron link in the chain that Columbus swung from Spain to the New World) led me down a corridor, thence along a cloister and to the chapel, and that holy place in calm shadows. My vision, accustomed to bright sun, was impaired by the gloom and I felt my way to a prayer stool and there knelt and was conscious of men all around me, some telling their beads and others mumbling penances.

I made my Contrition and then five Our Fathers and ten Hail Marys, and these to my father and my Aunt Ronda and my comrades, and I raised my head slightly and glanced around; and there he was, his head bowed to a statue of the Virgin and his broad shoulders garbed in the gray of Franciscans.

The first time I saw Christopher Columbus he was praying.

My eyes adjusted to the shadows and I audited the contour of his face, first the bold, hawked nose and then the high cheekbones and the stern mouth and thin lips. His hair was as white as clean sea foam, and fleecy, like a summer cloud over Andalusia's hills. He was but thirty-seven the first time I saw him; the frost-hair of an old man and the restless eyes blue as the steel of my Toledo poniard.

He was taller than his brother, as tall as I, and I am quite tall for a Spaniard, we being a breed that measures our strength in enterprise rather than in inches.

I watched him beat his breast thrice and then he arose and stepped by me and to the door of the chapel. There Fray Juan Perez laid his hand on Columbus' arm to detain him and nodded toward me, and I joined them in the cool recess of the cloister.

"This is Lepe, a sailor." The friar presented me to him and that was proper inasmuch as I was the younger, albeit of equal station.

The acute blue eyes, sheltered by long lashes and bristling brows, darted from my face to my feet. "By San Fernando!" he growled peevishly. "Does he need a compass for a nose to identify his trade? It is obvious that he is a sailor."

Forsooth. The first words I heard from the cunning lips of Christopher Columbus were an oath.

There were spaces between his upper teeth and a gap at the left corner of his mouth, where two lower teeth were missing, and this affected his speech a minim, and he hissed certain consonant syllables.

Immediately I discerned him as a dogmatist to be accosted forthrightly, that if given an upper hand he would press instinctively, that he was not one for the niceties or subtleties of Spanish palaver. Therefore, in order that he be enlightened that my gorro was not an emblem of servility, it behooved me to flick my tongue, and this sharply. "Your observation, sire, is more pertinent than your irreverence."

His ruddy face twitched his surprise and his demeanor changed spontaneously, and this an indication that he was not sure of himself or of my station. I might be a personage and in the early days The Discoverer was a veritable chameleon, never trodding toes of any man who might farther his ambition. His bow was polite, almost Spanish, and he directed it to the friar. "Your forgiveness, my brother. I am distraught, as you know." Then he addressed me. "Your pleasure, young man."

I vacillated not, but went straight to the point. "You have been in Cordova?"

An expression of bland imperturbation came to his face and he replied warily, "And if I have?"

Now you will heed that he did not answer me directly and this was a pronounced trait of the man: he rarely ever answered a question straightforwardly, but, as a rule, asked one.

My mission was honorable and there was no need for guile. Hence, I hued to the line and spake frankly. "My father is a merchant in Seville and, for family and business reasons, I seek an old friend. The name is Harana."

Fray Juan Perez glared at me and Columbus' eyes narrowed perceptibly. "Harana?"

153

I was annoyed by the repetition as I had spoken plainly, and this I did again. "That is correct, sire. Harana."

"Aye," he nodded and revealed no emotion whatsoever. "I have the privilege of friendship with a Harana family in Cordova."

"The one I seek is Luis Harana, merchant."

"Luis Harana? Merchant?" He frowned as he searched his memory and then shook his head. "I do not know Luis Harana."

"He has a daughter. Maraela."

"I do not know this family," he said.

It was a truth and I weened it as a truth and yet I persisted in the hope of refreshing his memory. "They are conversos, sire."

A flush surged to his face and he was seized of reckless anger. "Hold! The Haranas of Cordova are not conversos. This is slander and the tongue of slander is more evil than the assassin's dagger——"

"Hold, yourself!" I planted my feet firmly and rested my fists on my hips. "The Haranas I seek are conversos and a family of most envious repute."

The friar raised his hands for silence and addressed his guest. "Patience, Christopher. The young man uttered no slander. It is obvious that he seeks a different family." Then he put his hand on my arm. "I know the Haranas of Cordova. There is Pedro de Harana and his sister, Beatriz Enriquez Harana, who are orphans and live with a kinsman, Rodrigo Enriquez de Harana."

Beatriz; she was Columbus' mistress and mother of his son, but these names had no meaning to me.

"And they are not conversos," Columbus said and still in spirited agitation.

"Oh, come now, Christopher," Fray Juan Perez said soothingly. "You are making a mountain out of an ant heap. All Cordova knows that Pedro and Beatriz are the children of Pedro Torquemada and that when their parents died they took the name of their mother, who was a Harana."

"Torquemada?" I asked politely. "Did I hear aright? It is a powerful name in Spain."

"You heard aright," the Franciscan nodded. "Pedro Torquemada was a kinsman of our Inquisitor-General."

Now here was a fillip, a choice morsel indeed. The mistress of Christopher Columbus was a kinswoman of the Inquisitor-General and, by the Thirty Pieces, Torquemada himself was a descendant of a famous converso family, one of these being the Cardinal of St. Sixt.

The friar apparently kenned the implication of my smile, for he spake the words that were in my mind. "Torquemada is of converso strain. Aye. But several generations removed."

"It is meaningless," Columbus said and the flush remained on his countenance. "By such reasoning the Virgin Herself was a converso. Even our Savior, and the Apostles. They all were born Jews." He threw up his hands in a gesture of exasperation and stalked away.

I watched him walk down the cloister and he had none of the swinging gait of a sailor and then I shrugged my indifference. "He is sensitive. Perhaps more sensitive than sensible."

"He is sorely pressed, young man." Fray Juan Perez took my arm and walked with me toward the door. "Our Crowns have dallied his cause and he has appealed once more to Portugal, but Diaz' discovery will void that petition."

(It was years before I learned the sequence of events that the brothers Columbus set in motion when they first wearied of Spain's procrastinations: Bartholomew returned to Portugal and advocated his brother's purpose and then Christopher wrote to the King of Portugal for aid, and that monarch invited him to return to Lusitania and forgave him an unstated offense, and this possibly debt or illegal appropriation of details of the Toscanelli map. He departed Cordova and Isabel discontinued his retainer and ere he reached La Rabida there came news that Diaz had found the Cape of Good Hope and a route to India, and the King of Portugal had no need of Christopher Columbus.)

I thanked the friar for his hospitality and walked down the slope. The *Nina* was under way and I rowed my small boat up the Tinto to Palos, and this a strenuous chore that brought aches to my shoulders and petulance to my humors.

It was dark when I arrived and I hurried to Gallego's, and there my comrades already reveling, and the ordinary gave me my post that had accumulated for more than a year. There was no letter from Maraela and, verily, I had expected none. There was one from my aunt and three from my father and two of these I read hurriedly and was thankful that he and Mudarra were well. The third one, however, filled my heart with dejection and loneliness.

My father had married again, and his wife a converso nearer my years than his; and his business was flourishing as never before.

He used five pages to explain this to me. He was growing old and I was gone and he was lonely, so he had taken a wife unto himself. He had been awarded contracts to furnish meat for the army and had money for me if I needed it, particularly if I cared to continue my studies.

Another woman on my mother's couch, and this knowledge stirred my resentment and then my better judgment prevailed and I was happy that my father had found a measure of contentment in his late years. But I knew I would not return to Seville. I did not choose to face a stepmother of my own age in the house of my mother, and thereby embarrass my father's wife and perhaps my father, and surely myself.

*Ruat caelum!* And so be it. My father had no need of benefaction from me, and me with a heavy purse. I shouted a jest to The Rabbit and demanded the best wine of the house, and my lust was full upon me, but not my luck, as I lost three months' pay at dice.

And, now, forbearing readers, we reach that junction of my narration, that interregnum before The Discovery, when each word is a flight of time. I sense your impatience and sympathize therewith for I am as anxious as you to be away from these particulars and to the Ocean Sea and the Unknown beyond, but if you are to view my tapestry you must ken certain colors and shades of colors.

The limp hand of restricted trade was on Palos and even trafficking was meager and soon my resources were squandered and I borrowed from The Rabbit, who did well with his splinters from Rome. Alonso Pinzon gave me employment at intervals, dripping candles in his shop, mending sails, and posting his books. I made several short voyages, once to Cadiz, twice to Lepe (and my Aunt Ronda was well) and once to Vigo. But on almost any day in this weary interlude I could be seen at Gallego's. My jacket was ragged and my sandals worn and I was the malefactor of my own dissolution, caring not what the next sun brought as long as there was a little wine for my gullet and a slut for my straw.

Christopher Columbus returned to Cordova because his mistress was there and the court accessible at Baza, whence Ferdinand was commanding his last siege of the Moors, and there was ever the hope that the Queen might relent and send for him, although the Commission of Learned Men had reported formally that his offers were vain inasmuch as he could not reach India by sailing west.

But he needed to be nigh if Isabel beckoned and so he returned to Cordova, and riding a mule.

The dispensation of this boon was made by the dilatory alcalde of Palos, at behest of the Franciscans, and would have gone unnoticed but for two trivial events that swerved the course of Spain's history and turned the world inside out.

Christopher Columbus was a vain, sensitive man and was harassed constantly by a gnawing striction of insecurity and this he hid under a cloak of arrogance and aloofness. He was as unpopular in Palos as a visitation of the flux because he was an alien who boasted of his seamanship and yet scorned the camaraderie of his trade.

Ergo, his mule permit brought grumblings from divers nabobs whose applications for favors were gathering dust on the mayor's desk, and eventually these faultfinders wrote the Crowns' provincial magistrates at Seville that Palos' alcalde was slighting loyal Spanish subjects, and taxpayers, in partiality to an alien nobody.

This of itself might have aroused the magistrates, who, being public lords in the guise of servants, ever were alert to opportunities to further themselves by probing and pinching and pretending diligence for the state's weal. But to crown the circumstance, the mayor's clerk was a sloven cove, who, instead of forwarding documents to the magistrates as they were issued, allowed them to accumulate and sent them to Seville in lots of ten and twelve.

The officials, in the ineptitude of their ilk, assumed the permits were granted in recurring abundance and this, with the complaints from the dissenters, induced a veritable tizzy among the magistrates and they dispatched three lawyers to Palos to peep into our closets.

They came to investigate mules and remained to uncover trafficking.

And, now, inasmuch as this offense was a community enterprise, the penalty was assessed against Palos rather than individuals; and Palos was directed to charter and maintain two caravels for the Crowns' convenience, and this retribution to be in force for a twelvemonth, beginning in January of 1492.

The thrifty citizens of our town leased the two cheapest caravels available and these were the *Nina* and the *Pinta*, and their owners were instructed to anchor them in Palos' harbor in event some royal functionary had need of them.

Meanwhile Bartholomew Columbus, his star eclipsed completely by Diaz' exploit, took ship from Lisbon to London to present his brother's case to King Henry VII and of this voyage reported a most singular occurrence; that he was delayed by sea thieves identified, by him, as Sterlings or Esterlines, and these a people of whom no Spanish geographer had knowledge. Bartholomew insisted that the pirates reduced him to poverty, and this a cause of illness, and that he was destitute when he eventually was presented to King Henry as Bartholomeus Colombus de Terra Rubra, Genoese, an impressive appellation indeed although it did not charm the penurious English.

King Henry mocked his pretensions and dismissed him, for Albion, through her merchants at Bristol, already was involved in futile explorations and had employed one John Cabot of Genoese birth, christened Giovanni Caboto, to seek the legendary Islands of Brazil and the Seven Cities; and Cabot had essayed cautiously the seas to the west of Ireland and had encountered violent storms and variables.

Like a peddler rebuffed at the merchant's door, Bartholomew departed England and went to France in an attempt to interest King Charles VIII in his brother's schemes and adroitly pointed out that Portugal was casting south, that England was casting west, that Spain was watching both and that France's ships might rot at their moorings while her enemies seized the prizes. King Charles pondered.

Then out of the East, out of Jerusalem herself, came two Franciscans via Rome with a warning to Ferdinand and Isabel that the Moors of the Holy Land, the neutral ground, were threatening retaliation against Christians there unless our Crowns ended the war against Spanish Moors. Our King and Queen, glory to their valor, scorned the ultimatum of Islam and the pressure of Rome and sent their chivalry, the foremost knights of Christendom, against the City of Granada itself and this the last Moorish citadel in western Europe.

All Spain was aroused by Islam's threat of reprisals in holy Jerusalem and throughout the countryside swelled cries for death, damnation, or exile for all religious aliens, and the aliens were the Moors and the Jews.

Through this storm a light glimmered for Christopher Columbus, beckoning him to court once more, and he journeyed into Granada and, through intercession of partisans, gained audience with Isabel and encouraged her that his explorations would bring to her coffers enough gold to launch a crusade for Jerusalem, that Spain could smite Islam's chains from the Holy Sepulchre itself.

It was a tempting lure for the pious Isabel, but she was as wary in politics as she was staunch in the Faith. She did not discuss the geographic aspects of his proposal, for our Sovereign was not informed in this useful science, but with her realm in a frenzy against all things alien she hesitated to grant Christopher Columbus, himself a foreigner, the honors and titles he demanded. And the wily Ferdinand lowered his sword arm long enough to swear his impatience. "Aroint! And away with this dreamer. He prattles nonsense. I need swords, not sages."

Thus again Columbus was rebuffed. Isabel was too cautious to bolt the door against him and suggested that he return when the times were more propitious, that he reopen his case when the Moors were dispersed and the problem of aliens was settled.

Man's pride will suffer fortune's boycott in spiritual resignation for months and years, but not forever, and now it was that Christopher Columbus, in rightful disgust, turned his back to the court of Spain and took his leave in haughty disdain. Cerda had forsaken him at last and all of his powerful advocates, save the Franciscans and a few conversos, and these troubled more by the Inquisition than the plight of an adventurer.

Wherefor could he turn? Portugal had Diaz. England had Cabot. Italy had the Mediterranean. Only France remained. Bartholomew was in that kingdom, sounding the Columbus trumpets for all to hear and whispering rich promises into the thick ears of Charles VIII. The Unwanted, the Nobody, would join his brother in Paris and together they would launch a French expedition across the sea that Spain scorned.

But first he must rest and think and then lay his plans. Beatriz Harana was waiting in Cordova and their son, Ferdinand, but Christopher Columbus sought not the solace of his mistress. Nay, and by the Brother Sun and the Sister Moon of Assisi's beatification, he came to La Rabida, to the Franciscans, to Fray Juan Perez, who loved him, to Fray Antonio de Marchena, who believed in him and who knew good maps when he saw them.

I was in Palos, dripping candles for Alonso Pinzon for a monthly stipend of 3500 maravedis, when the wanderer came back to the place where he first had set foot on Spanish soil. I was in the chandlery the day Fray Juan Perez came in person and requested Pinzon to visit the monastery of La Rabida for the honor of the acquaintance of Christopher Columbus, mariner.

My friends: the Rosary of Triumph is the telling of each bead and none must be neglected, for if one is slighted wherefore is the chain not complete. It was Fray Juan Perez, a lowly Minor in the Order of Humility, who brought Christopher Columbus and Alonso Pinzon together. Perhaps it seems singular indeed that they had not crossed courses ere this day, but they had not, and this a truth to which I swear.

They met. They talked. And this no council of wizards splitting hairs, but this a junction of two sailors willing to stand their quarters over the rim of the world if land were not a caravel's sail west of Spain.

Pinzon vowed it was new land and produced charts he had kept for years. "The wind blows west from the Canaries. This I have observed, Captain Columbus. Cannot wind flow like rivers? Ever steady?"

"Aye, Captain Pinzon." And he rubbed his hands in the glee of the hour, for here was a man of his kind and without the shifty eyes of the court or the furrowed brows of Salamanca.

Fray Juan Perez fetched wine and Fray Antonio de Marchena watched the two mariners, and Pinzon drank with relish and Columbus with caution, and Pinzon pounded the desk in the exuberence of his conviction. "West of here it blows east, then veers southwest. But from the Canaries it is steady west. By the blood and bones of the saints, Captain Columbus. Are the winds of the Ocean Sea a vast circle? And if this is true, what forms the circle?"

"Land," spoke Christopher Columbus. "By San Fernando! Land, I say!" He rested his hands on the desk and stood tall above them. "It is India. This I know."

Pinzon shrugged. "*Fata obstant*, sire. But a taper for the candle. I have men and I can get ships, and I will sail for you. The court's consent is the mischief that plagues us. *Hoc opus hic labor est.*"

The wanderer closed his eyes and pressed his long fingers against his lids and relaxed in deep meditation and then he snapped open his eyes and stared at his companions, judging their probity and discretion, and forthwith revealed all of his contrivances: first the charts he had prepared and maps that he and Bartholomew had drawn.

Then the Marino map that placed Antilia 700 leagues west of the Canaries.

And then his prize; a copy of the Toscanelli map that he had arrogated from Portugal's royal archives.

Only Fray Antonio de Marchena recognized the significance of what he saw and he gasped his astonishment. "*Dei gratia!* Did you dare show this at Salamanca?"

"Never," Columbus said in petulance. "The Commission was against me from the start."

"The Queen?" demanded Fray Antonio. "Did you show it to the Queen?"

Columbus' gaze wandered from the friar to Pinzon, who, being a man without guile, did not comprehend at once the import of this talk, thence to Fray Juan Perez, and then Columbus, aware of his role in this drama, retreated into the ambiguity that was ever his fortress. "The Crowns of Spain and the Crown of Portugal are on excellent terms, the saints be thankful." His gaze continued to the window and he looked out on the Rio Tinto.

"Most excellent," said Fray Antonio, and addressed Fray Juan Perez and Pinzon. "That map——" He pointed to the document. "That is a copy of Toscanelli's map, which was prepared under patronage of the King of Portugal and solely for that kingdom's service."

(Those were his words, the words my captain repeated to me that night in the *Pinta's* cabin when we were homeward bound and the storm upon us, and the *Santa Maria* was no more and the *Nina* floundering.)

Even Pinzon, a novice in the rudiments of statecraft, grasped the full meaning and his eyes sparkled his appreciation of a seaman's ingenuity, but the face of Fray Juan Perez suddenly was pallid and his lips twitched his agitation. "Christopher." His voice was stern. "You have not answered Fray Antonio's question. Does the Queen share this secret?"

The Unwanted, the Nobody, kept his gaze on the window and the river beyond. "Has not Spain's Infanta recently wed the heir to Portugal's throne? Are not the kingdoms wedded by blood and Christian faith?"

"For truth," Fray Juan said. "Now, speak out, Christopher. And no parables."

"What if she knew this document was in her realm and in the hands of a foreigner she had received?"

"It might be most embarrassing. She would be compelled to denounce you."

"Would I embarrass my Queen?" Columbus looked at each of them and the bland expression of rectitude was on his countenance.

"Out upon, wayfarer!" Fray Antonio was a blunt man. "You would embarrass any mortal to serve your cause. And trifle not with my wits. The Queen knows naught of this map——"

"Why say you this?" Fray Juan interrupted.

"Because she has not denounced him."

"Perhaps she shares his secret and keeps it safe in her heart."

Fray Antonio laughed his derision. "Come, come, my brother. You know the Queen. You have confessed her. She is a Spaniard."

Juan Perez of Holy Orders and La Rabida opened wide his eyes in the light of the comprehension that awakened his wisdom. "*Aut Caesar aut nullus*. Of course she knows not. If Isabel of Castile had instrumentality to dim Portugal's maritime glory she would launch an expedition westward under God's grace and fortune's risk."

Christopher Columbus smiled for the first time in months.

Pinzon never knew, and, therefore, neither do I, the contents of Fray Juan's letter to Isabel. He retired to his quarters and wrote the message in his own hand and for no eyes but her's, and this wholly proper inasmuch as he had been her confessor and had access to her heart and mind. Pinzon was instructed to commission a trustworthy courier and he chose Sebastian Rodriquez, a pilot of Lepe, and himself paid for the horse that took the messenger to the Queen.

Now Ferdinand was poised for his final thrust against the Moors and had built a camp near the City of Granada and had named it Santa Fe, honoring the Holy Faith that was strangling the last breath from Islam in Spain.

So to Santa Fe rode Rodriquez and the letter to the Queen, and she dallied no more but directed Fray Juan to attend her as quickly as possible and counseled Columbus to remain in La Rabida and to be of good cheer.

Pinzon rented a mule for Fray Juan and arranged the permit and the Franciscan began the first span of the journey that led to the New World.

Mortal does not know, mortal will never know, what the friar of La Rabida told his Queen. The secret died with them. *Te judice*. As for myself, however, I have long been convinced that he told her that

162

Christopher Columbus had a Portuguese map that, God willing, could lead him to new islands across the Ocean Sea and thereby bring her realm manifold honors and great wealth. He was a man of God, her confessor. Should he not know more than the wise men of Salamanca? He had faith and faith could will lands where no lands had been before.

"Send Christopher Columbus to me," she said.

Fray Juan brought the tidings back to La Rabida and also 20,000 maravedis from the royal purse with which the Nobody was to purchase raiment suitable for his presentation to the most brilliant court in all of Europe. However, and ever the dramatist, he did not garb himself in splendor, but chose the simple attire of an honest mariner, the humble garments of a poor dreamer, perhaps a poet.

And then he rode for Santa Fe, surely watching the lazy ears of the mule Alonso Pinzon had purchased for him and envisioning the golden trappings that someday might bedeck his shoulders if the gods be kind; the titles, the heraldry, a Nobody into a Somebody.

The Fates began smiling. They have always loved poets. They have always seduced dreamers.

Isabel received him in privy council and again no mortal knows their words. The smirking hints that he charmed her are calumnious, and this from me who came to hate Columbus and the Crowns of Spain. Let the dead bury the dead. Isabel of Castile was more queen than woman.

She summoned another Commission and in this one were several grandees who knew that Spain must expand or wither. Ferdinand was in the field, but his household was represented by Luis de Santangel, converso and Minister of Finance, and Juan Cabrero, converso and the King's own chamberlain. The Church was represented by Fray Diego de Deza, converso and teacher of theology at the University of Salamanca. The Queen represented herself.

Columbus did not reveal his hand to this Commission, only enough of it to show its strength. Isabel approved his plans in principle and asked his terms. He spake them:

Knighthood and golden spurs, and heraldry and titles perpetually and these to include Admiral of the Ocean Sea.

—The grandees blinked. An alien knight in Spain torn by racial and religious dissension? An alien admiral for Spanish ships? And this title to his son, and the son of his son, and on forever? Only Luis de Santangel was calm.

One tenth of all income accruing to Spain within limits of the Admiralty, and this reward to be free of taxes.

—The grandees scowled. Santangel smiled.

The right to invest in any or every expedition and to take profit thereof.

—Even the Queen turned her head.

The title of Viceroy and Governor General over all lands he discovered and this right also in perpetuity.

—"*Satis superque!*" Isabel was vexed by his presumptuous demands. "Have you increased your terms?"

"Has Your Majesty increased her interest?" the Nobody asked.

The Queen dismissed the Commission and directed that Columbus remain in Santa Fe while she pondered the issue. After all, the kingdom was at war and she could not be expected to launch his risky venture until the Moors were conquered.

Laughter from the Fates, for their favorite scarcely had settled himself in the camp ere Spain's chivalry hurled itself against Boabdil's battlements before the City of Granada, and the walls fell and thus fell the Moorish banner, the Crescent of Islam, the Star of the East. Christian victors gazed up the hill to the Alhambra and shouted for their saints to bear witness as their swords carved the epitaph to seven hundred years of Moorish tenure. Spain was united at last.

Boabdil wept and his mother said, "Thou dost well to weep like a woman for that which thou hast not defended as a man." Then he banished himself and, in departure, paused on a bridge near Granada and looked back and forever more the bridge has been called "The Last Sigh of the Moor."

His followers were commanded to accept Christianity, death, or exile, and many of them trailed their king to Africa and this encouraged the people to cry louder for the exile of all religious aliens, especially the Jews. The Inquisition could not molest public Jews but had found heresy rampant among conversos and the Crowns were caught between the rock of duty and the winds of expediency, for many of their counselors and financiers were New Christians whose kinsmen stood convicted of Judaizing.

Thus it was on the day when the Queen sent for Christopher Columbus and rejected his proposals *in toto*. His price was too high.

Pedro Gonzalez de Mendoza, Cardinal of Spain, pleaded Columbus' cause, but she was adamant; she dared not taunt the people's wrath by honoring a foreigner with the highest titles at her command.

Strong minds entreated the Nobody to soften his ultimatum, and he scorned them and would not alter his demands one single mote, not one paltry scintilla. He had cast his dice. *Unguibus et rostro!* Claws and beak! Tooth and nail! It was all or nothing.

So Isabel bade him bye and Columbus did not bend his stiff neck in her presence, but only his waist.

"Whither now?" she asked, and surely sadly.

"To France," he said.

He saddled his own mule, for his purse was light and there was no gratuity for a groomsman. He mounted and rode away and the red dust of the camp settled on the ears of his beast and on his own white hair.

Six years he had worked and waited and now he must begin all over again.

Can you not hear the raucous cackle of the Fates? Do you not see the dice spinning from his hands and onto the gaming board that man calls life?

The dust settled behind his mule and Luis de Santangel was announced into the presence of Isabel of Castile. The dice swerved and stopped, and the Fates ceased their cackling, and wove and snipped, holding their laughter for the final act.

There is no living memory, no written word, to tell the counsel given by Ferdinand's Minister of Finance to Ferdinand's wife, but conjecture is the pith of any stimulating compendium and my assumption is as meritorious as any man's and superior to most, for, whereas I never saw the Queen or Santangel, I was with Christopher Columbus at his hour of triumph and then in the year of his tragedy, which was my revenge.

Luis de Santangel was the most powerful converso at court and was not one to wheedle or banter. Therefore, straight to the point.

—The loyal conversos, many of excellent purse and faithful purpose, are deeply concerned over the excesses of the Inquisition and mortified that other nations are mouthing indictments of bigotry against the saintly Isabel of Spain. A most unhappy circumstance. But, now——

Yes, Luis de Santangel.

—A liberal gesture would do much to alleviate the strain under which the faithful conversos writhe, those whose kinsmen breathe daily the smoke of Quemadero. And what could be more liberal than to grant favors to an alien, an exemplary Christian, provided he can fill a contract that, if successful, will be most advantageous to the realm. Such is sound statecraft, and sound business.

His price is too high, Luis de Santangel.

—Is it? If he fails, there is only the trifling cost of the expedition. If he succeeds, this realm will resound of glory into eternity.

I believe in this venture, Luis de Santangel. Gladly would I surrender my jewels into usurious hands to finance this voyage.

—A trifle, Your Majesty. The Crowns have two idle caravels at Palos. He will need a third. I estimate that 4,000,000 maravedis, perhaps 5,000,000, will launch this enterprise. A pittance. I will raise this sum or furnish it myself.

Bring back Christopher Columbus, mariner. Bring back Don Christopher Columbus, grandee!

An Andalusian stallion raced by the barracks of Santa Fe, through the gate and to the plains, and the red dust settled on the purple trappings of the House of Castile. The courier found the Nobody on the Bridge of Pines, where he had paused to rest himself and his mule.

Come back, wanderer. Come back, Somebody.

The Capitulations of Santa Fe were drafted by Fray Juan Perez and Juan de Coloma, another of Ferdinand's men, and his mother a Jew. That was in February of 1492 and the document was presented to the Crowns and again action was postponed, this time while the State prepared the edict that exiled all Jews from the land that had succored them since destruction of Jerusalem, and many even longer than that.

This decree also was drawn by Juan de Coloma for Ferdinand and Isabel and on March 30 was proclaimed the law of the realm. After July 30, no Jew could remain in Spain or in any of Spain's possessions, including Sicily and Sardinia. The alternatives were baptism or death. They could take with them no gold or silver or coins.

A few hurried to the priests for conversion and safety, but mostly they began moving out, the rich and the favored into Portugal and some into ships for the Levant. The multitude, however, began wandering with no place to go and no money to take them anywhere, trickling toward the seaports and chanting prayers that God would deliver them into a new land.

166

It was done and the Crowns turned their attention once more to Columbus and on April 30, 1492, signed and executed the Capitulations of Sante Fe and thus unshackled the dreamer at last.

The Lord Don Christopher weighed each word of his contract, and weighed it again. The Indies were not mentioned. Perhaps he himself was no longer sure what lay beyond and a faulty word might blemish the agreement. Also, India might suggest Toscanelli's map and King John of Portugal was a vengeful monarch.

The Lord Don Christopher purchased his first velvet doublet and chose a white mule for himself and set out for Cordova to see Beatriz Harana before journeying to Palos. The roads were choked with wandering Jews, but Columbus rode on. Every demand had been met. He had reached for the stars and the firmament had fallen.

Now only one more miracle remained in the womb of his true mistress, the Fate he had wooed, the Fate he had ravished—only a voyage across the Unknown Sea and a voyage back home again.

Trust God and hammer on!

# CHAPTER 13

*C*HRISTOPHER COLUMBUS CAME BACK TO PALOS IN MAY AND straightway essayed to circumvent Alonso Pinzon, for, now that he was a Don and the Queen's chosen instrument, he assumed he need trouble himself no further with counsel or support from the hostile provincials of our Niebla who looked upon him as an imperious interloper.

The Rabbit and I, reduced to menials, were drudging at a rope walk and cording Spanish grass when the bell of the Church of St. George summonsed the populace to the plaza and there the notary, one Francisco Fernandez, read the Crowns' order to Palos. Don Christopher himself was not in attendance, never deigning to mingle with the multitude, and there was a tinge of drollery in the voice of our notary as he recited the lines that Columbus supposed would send Andalusian sailors scampering aboard his ships and singing his praises as we pledged our lives to his mastery.

"Ferdinand and Isabel, by the Grace of God King and Queen of Castile, Leon, Aragon, Sicily, et cetera, to all the inhabitants of the Town of Palos, greeting and grace."

The notary's intonation sounded to the far end of the plaza and the people gaped or smiled or scowled. The Rabbit grinned.

"Know ye that whereas for certain things done and committed by you to our disservice you were condemned and obliged by our Council to provide us for a twelvemonth with two equipped caravels at your own proper charge and expense.

"And whereas we have now commanded Christopher Columbus to

go with three caravels as our Captain of the same, toward certain regions of the Ocean Sea, to perform certain things in our service, and we desire that he take with him the said two caravels with which you are thus required to serve us.

"Therefore we command that within ten days of receiving this our letter you have all ready and prepared two equipped caravels, as you are required by virtue of the said sentence, to depart with the said Christopher Columbus whither we have commanded him to go; and we have commanded him to give you advance pay for four months for the people who are to sail aboard the said caravels at the rate to be paid to the other people who are to be in the said three caravels, and in the other caravel that we have commanded him to take, whatever is commonly and customarily paid on this coast to the people who go to sea in a fleet; and we forbid the said Christopher Columbus or any others who sail in the said caravels to go to the Mine or engage in the trade thereof that the King of Portugal our brother holds.

"Given in our City of Granada on the 30th day of April, year of our Lord Jesus Christ 1492.

"I The King.          I The Queen."

The functionary squinted at his neighbors when he finished reading, and the Palenos looked at one another, first in rapt amazement and then in devilish amusement. Obviously Don Christopher had approved this document, his nature being such that he must review every word that concerned him, and this document established that the said servant of the said queen was a said fool.

Examine the command, kind reader. First it was flagrantly ambiguous as to the number of caravels to be taken. The *Nina* and the *Pinta* were in harbor as Palos' penalty for trafficking, but the monarchs, now including Columbus, were seemingly confused as to how many ships we must forfeit to service of the Crowns.

And whence the crew? Palos was given no authority to impress seamen. Who was to sail the undetermined number of ships into the Unknown, and why? There were no offers of reward; either money or titles. Had Christopher Columbus convinced Isabel that her Andalusian subjects were idiots?

Equip an expedition in ten days! Was any man so ignorant of ships and provisions?

All of this entertained my reflection, and more, for, note carefully, the document commanded for Palos' ears did not grace the Columbus name with a title. He was Christopher Columbus in the public instrument, only Don Christopher in private instruments. And obviously he had persuaded the Queen that the Niebla would support him. He had used Pinzon's reputation at court and now was ignoring Pinzon at home. The whole scheme reeked of odors most foul, of duplicity most hateful.

Palos, and praise her valiant name, turned her lean backside to Christopher Columbus. He fumed in impotent fury and then, disregarding the admonitions of the Franciscans at La Rabida, even dared order Arcos aboard the *Nina* in the Queen's name. The helmsman shrugged his shoulders, recited his fealty to Isabel, and went his way. Don Christopher for the first time encountered, and never understood, the nature of us Andalusians, who since the days of Rome had evaded unpopular decrees by the simple maxim of: "This law is to be obeyed but not carried out."

We were most respectful to the royal order and to the Queen's explorer, and tended our own nets and nothing more. Columbus was a suspected stranger among us and we bowed low to his face and smiled behind his back.

Albeit, we had other problems to concern us withal his nefarious project to exploit the Niebla for his own aggrandizement. The exodus of the Jews was a boon to all seaports and many of us turned an excellent profit in service to those haunted and wailing exiles by escorting them to the border of Portugal, a haven they might enter if they had purse or prestige, or by ferrying them down to Cadiz, where waited ships to haul them, swinelike, to Africa or the Levant, and this for a price, of course.

Many of these ships were intercepted by pirates, who leveled ransom on the passengers, and these, being Jews and without a country, could appeal to no sovereign for protection, neither to any church, but only to their God. Numerous were the homeless who were lost at sea that the captains might make faster voyages and accrue better profits.

Some Palenos, those with sufficient resources for substantial enterprise, shrewdly augmented their fortunes by conniving with Jews to pay them gold for their properties, at fantastic discounts, and then reporting the Jews for attempting to smuggle gold out of Spain, thereby earning an informer's commission, usually ten per centum of all gold recovered from the miscreants. The Jews, quite naturally, could not seek redress inasmuch as they had conspired to circumvent the royal edict against removal of gold from our enlightened and blessed realm.

All that summer the Jews wandered to the coast from the interior of Spain, wailing their laments and tearing their hair and beating their breasts. A most noisome people.

Jewish women could be had in Palos for a loaf of bread. A virgin for a piece of cheese large enough for the family.

They came in droves down the dusty roads and the poor had their goods and their babies on their backs, and their rabbis paced the processions and their eyes burned a fervor that disquieted me; this their Dispersal.

The rich rode horses and lifted the hems of their garments as they passed the straggling rabble and the multitude shook their fists at the more fortunate and cursed them as usurers and filth.

They camped on the outskirts of Palos, waiting for ships, and every day officials went among them and searched them for gold and often the Jews, particularly the women, swallowed their coins and jewelry and subsequently searched their own filth for their treasures and swallowed them again.

It became the custom of certain scavengers, both Christians and Jews, to spy upon the women in their privacy and then rush upon them and drive them away and scramble for the gold, the Jews to swallow it themselves and the Christians to spend or hoard. And this depravity returned my memory to Benjamin Marino and I was saddened and wondered his fate.

Wave after wave came the homeless and at irregular intervals, and never once did I see Christopher Columbus on the days when Palos swarmed with exiles. He remained in the sanctuary of La Rabida, but after each wave moved on he showed himself and strove to organize his expedition.

It was he who chartered the *Santa Maria*. You will remember that this ship was owned by Juan de la Cosa of Santona, and he brought her to Palos possibly for a cargo of Jews, although of this I am not positive, and Columbus immediately entered into negotiations with him.

Santangel had sent several million maravedis to his protégé and Columbus was able not only to charter the *Santa Maria*, known hereabouts as the *Frivolous Mary*, but also to hire Juan de la Cosa as her master, and Cosa was charged with the task of recruiting a crew. The

Andalusian sailors gave him no heed whatsoever as we had no intention of trusting our lives to a Galician.

Thus Columbus was baffled again. He had his three ships and a master for one of them and naught else save his maravedis. It was then that he proclaimed, with fanfare, that he had chosen a marshal for his fleet and this worthy was Diego Harana of Cordova, a cousin of Don Christopher's mistress and a dry-foot whose nostrils had never inhaled salt air.

Maraela had become only a dim shadow in my memory and, therefore, the arrival of Diego Harana brought only cursory interest to me and, yet, I must ask about her to appease a longing that never had vanished entirely. It was his wont to join Juan de la Cosa at the plaza each day and together they harangued sailors to take the knife of Christopher Columbus and sail for riches and fame, and, incidentally, to obey the Queen's directive, and could not fathom the undisciplined evasion of Andalusians of a law we did not approve.

I walked from Gallego's to the plaza and there joined a group of sailors lolling in the shade while Harana and Cosa extolled the seamanship of Christopher Columbus and exorted us to come with them. I studied Harana closely and there was no resemblance to Maraela as I remembered her.

The marshal of a fleet that did not exist and the master of a ship that had no crew talked themselves into a dripping sweat and no man moved, and Juan de la Cosa stalked away in disgust. Diego Harana visibly was puzzled and he was staring vacantly toward the harbor, where the *Santa Maria*, the *Nina*, and the *Pinta* rode their anchors, when I approached him in proper deference and accosted him in utmost civility.

"Who are you?" he asked and his voice was pleasant.

"Lepe, a sailor," I replied and only then did I remove my gorro and this gesture solely because he had greeted me most affably.

"My admiral——" he was the first I ever heard who called Columbus an admiral. "My admiral needs sailors. Why not come with us?"

I noticed then that he was staring at my poniard and from the beautiful Toledo steel to my ragged jacket and bare feet.

"I am a poor sailor and not worthy of participation in such a glorious enterprise." I bowed gracefully in expressing my regrets. "Withal I have an injury. My back, sire. A most devilish affliction." I put my hand to the small of my back and groaned my misery.

173

Harana scowled his disapproval of my deception inasmuch as my broad shoulders and healthy countenance belied my words. "Then why do you detain me?" he demanded.

"Your name, sire." I placed my hand over the hilt of my poniard and covered it. "I once had a friend, or, rather, my father had a friend, who was named Harana. A most excellent compatriot and a pious Christian."

"It is a large family. Do you recall his full name?"

"Luis Harana," I replied. "A merchant."

"In Seville?"

"Aye. Years ago." He knew him. I sensed that he knew him.

"A cousin," he said, and wholly without guile or hesitation and this being evidence that he did not suspect Luis Harana of Judaizing, as no man willingly would admit kinship to a Judaizer. "Luis Harana is dead."

"My father will be sorely grieved," I said and bowed again, this time in reverence to the dead. "And there was a daughter——" I strove for indifference and cursed myself that my cheeks should flush suddenly in the agitation of my hope.

He obviously did not discern my fervency as he answered most readily. "A daughter? Yes. Her name was Maraela."

"Is she well?" My composure now was affirmation of my will.

"I know not," he said. "She is a distant cousin and we have not heard from her in years. And may I ask your interest?" He was looking closely at me again.

"We were children together. That is all."

He tugged at the collar of his doublet to loosen it and cool his skin, and ran his fingers around his neck and flipped the sweat away. "I am sorry I can be of no service and it is shameful that families should be separated. But times are trying. I had not thought of Maraela in years until this minute. After her father died I know not whither she went. It is my shame."

"The times——" I shrugged and quickly took my leave as I read the suspicion in his eyes that I was not a sailor born and cared not for questions from him.

I strolled back to the harbor and eventually to Gallego's and there drank with The Rabbit and Arcos, and Maraela was returned to her niche in my memory, a hollowed place to be sure, but one I seldom disturbed. More than six years had passed since that terrifying evening when she shielded the candle in the way of a Judaizer, and then tormented my lips in the way of a woman.

It was late June of 1492 and Christopher Columbus was wasting his days and patience in a futile struggle against Palos' contempt for his power and the complaisant evasion of his orders. The decree was to be obeyed but not carried out, and he was learning far more about Andalusian obstinacy than he had learned about the Ocean Sea. It was then, goaded to folly, that he ventured an imbecile manipulation: he obtained from the Queen the prerogative of amnesty for any criminal in all the Niebla who volunteered for service in the caravels. This proclamation was made public at Moguer, a few miles up the Tinto from Palos, and this was a precaution most wise as Palos surely would have demonstrated against Columbus had he dared read the fatuous document at the plaza.

Four prisoners, under a sentence of death, took his knife with the plea that service under a fool was preferable to the gallows. One of these men was a murderer and his comrades had been convicted of liberating him from a dungeon, and Don Christopher traded them berths for their necks. The Niebla's other prisoners, none facing death, announced scornfully that they preferred bars to service under a lunatic who was mad enough to sail the Ocean Sea with a crew of criminals and dry-feet.

And now we pause and tot the account. Summer was half away and Columbus had three ships, four criminal seamen who had never pulled an oar, a master, a marshal, sufficient money, a royal commission, and a purloined map.

Only the saints can conjecture the consequences had not the Franciscans at La Rabida taken upon themselves to extricate their lay brother from the dilemma in which he had ensnared himself by his insatiable lust for power, his ignorance, and his deceit.

Fray Juan Perez and Fray Antonio de Marchena wearied of his errors and eventually admonished sternly that the Queen soon would become fretful at his delay and send magistrates to inquire into the cause, and this a thing that Don Christopher did not want above all things.

He humbled himself a little and deigned ask their counsel and they advised: "Send for Pinzon."

"I have no need of Pinzon," he argued.

"Accept Pinzon or expect the Queen's prying emissaries."

Reluctantly he acquiesced, for, although he was jealous of Pinzon's skill and suspicious of his intent, he nevertheless was aware that he alone could never launch the expedition regardless of his resources and commissions. And thus it came to be that, at behest of Fray Juan Perez, Captain Martin Alonso Pinzon presented himself at La Rabida and then into privy conference with Don Christopher.

Death has long since hushed the words they passed and any written agreement between them has vanished in the chicanery that attended Columbus even in his hour of triumph. Years and years of litigation have failed to establish the promises that the Queen's captain made to my captain. I can contribute naught to this sordid controversy in the way of legal evidence, but I, who knew them both, am convinced that Christopher Columbus pledged a share of his rewards to Alonso Pinzon. Otherwise, why should my captain have sailed? For the paltry pay of a six months' voyage?

Nay, loyal readers. Never. Never. There was a promise. The proof? The contract? My captain would not have haggled over a contract. He was a sailor and his handclasp was his vow and his oath was his bond.

Captain Pinzon not only agreed to raise the crews and ready the ships, but he advanced 500,000 maravedis to Admiral Columbus and this sum was invested in the expedition in the admiral's name, and this obviously because only Columbus had the Queen's permission to invest in the enterprise.

Let the magistrates wrangle themselves to distraction. Let them labor to separate the soup from the cup, and the beans and the strength and the stock from the broth, but this I know: Martin Alonso Pinzon walked out of the conference with Christopher Columbus and mounted his horse at the gate of La Rabida and rode for Palos, and this was a late afternoon in late June.

I was at Gallego's and drinking with The Rabbit and Arcos and several other sailors, including Juan de Jerez, Juan Sevilla, and Garcia Alonso, who was father of six sons and fourteen times a grandfather.

We were discussing the exodus of the Jews and two converso Judaizers who that day had been sentenced to the stake when Pinzon appeared at the door of the wineshop and waved his hand before his face to dissipate the fumes of wine and sweat. The Rabbit saw him first and called out, "Avast there, Captain! The shank of the day to you and your saint's blessing."

176

"Avast yourselves, you merry wastrels, while I sweeten my guts with bitter drink. No wine like a sailor's wine, aye, Arcos?"

"Aye, Captain."

"Aye, Lepe?"

"Aye." I saw his poniard at his right hip and the Demascus blade at his left.

The Rabbit passed him a tankard and he held it high and drank to the Queen and wiped his mouth on his sleeve and pounded the back of old Garcia Alonso. "The clemency of God upon you, old man. And how with the sons, my comrade?"

"The brood is well," said Garcia Alonso and he, too, noticed the Damascus blade and stared at it.

We all quickly were silent, watching Pinzon, and he spread wide his feet, rested his hands on his knives, and burned his bright, black eyes into ours. It was The Rabbit who spake, always The Rabbit whose impudence scorned propriety. "Does a Pinzon grease his rich belly with the cheap wines of Gallego?"

"A Pinzon greases his belly with the wine of his comrades."

The Rabbit tilted his head and laughed his effrontery and then slapped his hand on the table and arose. "By the ceaseless flow of Mother Eve's breasts, sire, count us not as fools. You are puffed and pregnant with your secret. Speak it, Captain Pinzon. Whither away?"

"*Adelante!*" He hurled the challenge. "Westward, you rogues. I am for the Ocean Sea!"

I sprang to my feet and scattered the tankards and bearded him. "With the Dove? To the Unknown with Don Christopher?"

"With God and Andalusians." He stepped close to us and snatched a cup from Arcos' hand and drained it. "The wine we share! The glory we seek! The death we jeer!" Then he fingered the Damascus knife and drew it free.

"Terms!" It came from Arcos.

"Five thousand maravedis a month for able seamen."

"Food!" It came from Juan de Jerez.

"Biscuits, one pound daily. Wine, two liters daily. Meat, two-thirds pound, daily."

"Shrouds!" This from Juan Sevilla.

"Clean sails, old woman. The cool sea for your bones and a breaker for your monument. The west wind for your requiem and the tears of your comrades for holy water. Who will follow Pinzon to the Unknown?" He flung the knife to the table and its point was buried in the wood and its hilt vibrated. "Gold for all. Roofs of gold in cities of Paradise——"

"Our bones in a shark's belly," spoke The Rabbit.

"Aloes and pearls," shouted Pinzon and we watched the blade until it was still, and no man reached for it.

"Our guts strung on the floating meadow and our eyeballs in a gull's beak." Again spake The Rabbit.

"Aye, knave." Pinzon cuffed The Rabbit's cheek and cursed his ancestry back to the goats and swine of Phoenicia. "But they will be the guts of men who died nobly in God's sweet air and not at the sot table of a stinking wineshop." He leaned forward and seized my tankard and dashed the wine on the blade. "Blood red it is, but heed! It drips clean from the good metal. None clings to hard steel. Now hear this! *Adelante!* Glory or death. Who will take the knife of Pinzon?"

The old one reached first, old Garcia Alonso. Six sons had he and fourteen grandchildren. He grasped tight the hilt and his eyes blazed the fire of another world. "I take the knife of Pinzon. By my mother's saint and my father's seed. *Adelante!*"

He turned his face from the captain to Arcos and spake thus: "The hilt is cold to my touch. Steady my hand, my friend, lest it falter."

And Arcos placed his strong hand over the old hand and vowed: "By the loins whence I sprang, I, Pedro de Arcos steady the hand of my comrade and take the knife of Pinzon."

The Rabbit hawked clear his throat and spat at my feet and reached forth and pressed his dirty fingers against the Damascus steel and then dashed wine upon it, and the wine clung where his flesh had touched. He jerked free the knife and held it before Pinzon. "Blood red is the wine, sire, and it clings where mortal hand has warmed its temper. But by the increase of Sheba's womb I will tend your glass and chant your watch else your luck forsake you at the shelf of the world."

He licked the wine from the blade and stepped beyond Pinzon and grimaced at me. "Shall I steady your hand, Lepe, as Arcos has steadied the old one's?"

"My hand is steady," I said.

"Then move your hand, Savillano, else I pierce your tankard."

"My hand remains."

The Rabbit's diabolic grin spread into a smile and he flicked the knife, and the blade passed between my forefinger and my middle finger and into the leather cup. The group was hushed and watching me, and slowly I pulled free the steel and balanced it on my palm. "Now hear this! I, Rodrigo of Triana, of Lepe, take the knife of Pinzon and this by——" I felt for an oath, and found it. "And this by the wisdom of Benjamin Marino and the Faith of Juan Ruiz de Medina."

(Aye, Mita. I swore by his name and remember you this in Paradise and forgive me, and plead God's forgiveness of my transgressions. Yes, beloved, it is true and may a measure of joy attend you in this truth: the name of Marino pledged me to the service I performed, I who saw it first.)

Jerez was the next to take the knife and then Juan Sevilla and all the Andalusians in Gallego's who were not signed to other masters, and Pinzon advanced us money against our pay and filled our tankards. We drank to him and to the Queen and one to the other, but no one to Christopher Columbus.

Pinzon departed us and we shook the wineshop with our songs and boiled into the street and to the plaza, jostling the Jews who milled there in lonely resignation, and down to the harbor where our three caravels were shadows on the Tinto. All that night we wined and all the next day, and then slowly we sobered and cursed our intemperance and empty purses.

Pilots and mariners were flocking to the beckon of Alonso Pinzon and the lists were filling fast. First there was his own family. He himself chose the *Pinta* as his command and selected his youngest brother, Francisco, as her master.

The *Nina* was given unto the second brother, Vicente Pinzon, who took a cousin, Diego Pinzon, a mariner, and this sailor was called *el viejo*, meaning "the old boy."

Second in prominence was the Nino family of Moguer, who owned the *Nina*. Juan Nino was master of his ship, but under Captain Vicente Pinzon. Peralanso Nino was assigned to the *Nina* as pilot and Francisco Nino as gromet.

Then came the Quintero brothers of Palos, Christopher and Juan, who owned the *Pinta* and were signed on as seamen.

These appointments were made by Captain Pinzon and approved by Admiral Columbus, but he himself chose the men for the *Santa Maria*, which was to be his flagship because it was the largest of the three. Jaun de la Cosa he picked as the master, Diego Harana as marshal, Rodrigo de Escobedo as secretary, Rodrigo Sanchez de

Segovia as comptroller, and Luis de Torres as interpreter, and this hapless man a converso who spoke Hebrew and Arabic.

I was sure that Pinzon wanted Arcos for his helmsman and me for his deck and that he would not separate The Rabbit from us, and in this I was not disappointed, for when the lists were drawn and posted on the door of the Church of St. George we were together, and on the *Pinta*.

The *Santa Maria* headed the pronouncement and her complement was forty men. Then the *Nina* and thirty men. And then:

*Con le carabela* Pinta

*Martin Alonso Pinzon, capitan, de Palos*
*Francisco Martin Pinzon, maestre, de Palos*
*Cristobal Garcia Xalmiento, piloto, de Lepe*
*Juan de Umbria, piloto, de Huelva*
*Bartholomew Garcia, contramaestre, de Palos*
*Juan Perez Vizcaino, calafate, de Palos*
*Garcia Hernandez, despensero, de Palos*
*Juan Bermudez, marino, de Palos*
*Cristobal Quintero, marino, de Palos*
*Juan Quintero, marino, de Palos*
*Pedro de Arcos, marino, de Palos*
*Rodrigo de Triana, marino, de Lepe*
*Garcia Alonso, marino, de Palos*
*Juan de Jerez, grumete, de Palos*
*Juan de Sevilla, grumete, de Moguer*
*Juan Rodriguez, grumete, de Molinos*
*Diego Bermudez, grumete, de Palos*
*Francisco Garcia, grumete, de Moguer*
*Francisco Gallego, grumete, de Moguer*
*Gomez Rascon, grumete, de Palos*

A company of twenty, with six able seamen, and five ordinary seamen who had the same rating as ship's boys and all were gromets.

And two scamps—The Rabbit, whose name trailed all the rest, and Francisco Gallego, who was called Chico and who sang the Salve Regina even more sweetly than my impish comrade.

All told, we were ninety for three ships and only five aliens among us and these on the *Santa Maria*: Christopher Columbus himself, then

Anton Calabres, Calabrian; Juan Arias, Portuguese, Jacome el Rico, Genoese; and Juan Vecano, Venetian.

There was one Spaniard from Murcia and ten from Galicia, and these followers of La Cosa, but all the others were Andalusians and for this all Christendom should be grateful, for it assured success if success were possible.

The monthly pay was posted as follows:

| | |
|---|---|
| Masters and pilots | 10,000 maravedis |
| Able seamen | 5000 maravedis |
| Ordinary seamen and ship's boys | 3000 maravedis |

No soldiers were signed on, not even a crossbowman, for we were commissioned only to explore and never to raid. Each ship carried one bombard and one falconet to be used only for signals until we could outsail or outmaneuver any adversary. There were four fire-pieces aboard our *Pinta* and more aboard the other ships and these were the matchlocks called harquebuses by the French and hook guns by the English.

Every officer and sailor had knives and there were swords for all, but these were stored in the captain's cabin and to be broken out only at his orders.

Christopher Columbus deposited 5,000,000 maravedis, the sum advanced by Santangel in the Queen's name, and invested the 500,000 maravedis he had borrowed from Pinzon. Ergo, a total of 5,500,000 maravedis was available, but the venture needed only 5,040,000 maravedis.[1]

Every seaman was sworn to loyalty; first to the flagship and her standards and then to his own ship, and this by the Blessed Cross and at the admiral's command, and this was done by placing the right thumb across the right forefinger and thus forming the Cross, and this we kissed.

The wrath of Andalusia's fiery summer curled the grass and curled our skin and, under Pinzon's vigilant eyes and the marshal's stern rod, we beached the ships and scraped them and treated the hulls with tallow and oil and helped the caulkers; and these were arduous tasks that strained our patience and our tempers.

Captain Pinzon was with us every day and the admiral came among

[1]About $7200.

us at those times when the Tinto was free of Jewish migrants and he was most cordial to all of us, pausing often to exchange pleasantries and these usually about the fiendish weather. Yet, never did he bend, and always he wore a long doublet and walked with measured stride, his white hair crinkling in the sun and his skin red and peeling.

We saw him not on the days when the Jews passed through and at these piteous times he remained at La Rabida and studied his maps and worked on his heraldry and his arms to be a field of gold with a band azure on a chief gules, the third quarter a few islands and sea waves.

There also came among us, to talk and counsel in the manner of old men, one Pedro Vasquez, who was a water-front vagrant, a nimble-witted old codger who badgered us for drinks and told us tales of the exploits of his youth. I had heard his story a dozen times and each time it was different. He had sailed westward forty years before, aye, with Portugal's Diego de Tieve and they had reached the floating meadow and then, fearing the Beyond, had turned northeast.

We welcomed his visits to the ships because his tales broke the monotony of our labors. He came one day, and this early in July, and borrowed two blancas from Arcos and stretched on the ground and watched us scrape the *Pinta's* bottom.

"You do not clean ships as well now as when I was a boy," he said. "I sailed with Diego de Tieve——"

"Go buy your drink, old goat," The Rabbit jeered him.

Pedro Vasquez ignored the taunt and slowly shook his head in remembrance of his youth. "We missed the prize, for we turned back. But I saw the floating meadow."

"Did the sea grass hold you?" The Rabbit snickered. "Did serpents board you? Did you occupy a mermaid?"

"Insolent pimp," the old man sneered. "Now hear this! All of you, and damn your eyes. Fear not the floating meadow. Leagues and leagues of grass, but sail on. Land is beyond——"

"Why say you this?" I asked.

"You can feel it. You can taste it. You can smell it. Land is beyond, but we turned back."

We noticed not the admiral, standing near, until he addressed old Pedro, and most kindly, and gave him several blancas and invited him to La Rabida. The grizzled mariner doffed his gorro and bowed and followed Columbus, shuffling after him and beseeching his blessing and a few more blancas.

"The old goat will be drunk by night," The Rabbit said and splashed tallow and oil on the planking.

"Don Christopher heeds even fools," Arcos said. "The truth is not in old Pedro."

We saw the shiftless mariner at Gallego's that night and he had a gold ducat and treated us to wine and drank the health of Christopher Columbus, and then got sot drunk and mumbled over and over, "Leagues of grass. And it parted so easy. The wind was steady. But we turned back."

It was July 12 when the ships were floated again and we rummaged our *Pinta* and sweetened her hold with water and vinegar and ballasted her snug with stones, and began provisioning.

Wine and biscuits and salted flour—sufficient for a year's voyage, and this caused many eyebrows to lift and many men to wonder. Then wood for the pot, and candles and oil and purging aloes. Sails and blocks and rope, and these stowed in the forecastle. Then salted meat and chick-peas and onions, and the admiral boarded us and was alert to every duty and checked the gear most critically and the provisions.

"Watch closely the merchants, Captain Pinzon," he ordered. "By San Fernando, they are swindlers."

"Aye, sire. I have chosen the best."

"Small onions, Captain Pinzon. Only the small, hard ones. The large, juicy onions rot too quickly. A ship sails on the bellies of her crew. Wine and onions, Captain, and a warm pot."

This encouraged all of us and The Rabbit watched him and Pinzon go aft and then spake our thoughts, "Wine and onions. By the Womb, mayhaps he is a sailor."

"He swears only by San Fernando," I said. "A foreigner, but he swears by a Spanish saint."

"There is none better," said Arcos. "I hold with The Rabbit. Mayhaps he is a sailor."

The standard of Isabel, the Castle and Lion of Castile and Leon, was hoisted on the mainmast of the *Santa Maria* and Columbus directed that the Cross be painted on the main and fore courses of all the ships, and that each command take gross and sleight wares, to wit: pins and needles and charms, and colored bonnets and mirrors and beads and other trinkets to be traded with barbarous heathens.

Savages? In the Indies? Marco Polo had found no savages.

This did not trouble most of the sailors, for they had traded in Africa and particularly at the Mine for blackbirds and thought that all races, save Europeans, were savages. However, I was concerned and I puzzled this mystery. Was he really to seek the Indies? Or unknown land? Or was he merely being cautious and prudent, and taking trinkets in event the Indies were not there at all, but strange land and savage people? This I accepted: Columbus was preparing for an exigency, for any riddle he found beyond the Beyond.

July passed and the ships were ready, and he had posted on the door of the Church of St. George the pronouncement that any claims against the enterprise, or the men thereof, must be filed immediately; that the expedition would weigh anchor at dawn on August 3.

Now this date was an omen that boded evil and this sufferance plagued us, for August 3 was Friday and we wondered, and were troubled, that such a pious Christian as Christopher Columbus would fix upon the Sad Day to go forth. Sunday, the Day of Resurrection, the first day of week, was the day of good omen.

There was much talk among us on this matter and many of us longed to be away from Palos and therewith spared the misery of the morrow, which was August 2 and the day on which the last of the Jews must be out of Spain. Two caravels were waiting in the harbor to haul the remnants off, the stragglers, the infirm, and the dying.

These, the last of the rabble, were encamped on a meadow near La Rabida, the same spot where the stake was erected on Faggot Day, and they must be away by sundown of August 2 or die on the public gallows or the chopping block. This, the last going, I yearned to be spared, but, nay, we would be here. They must depart at sundown and we the next dawn.

It was the afternoon of August 1, and I took my gear aboard our *Pinta* and then went to Gallego's and wrote letters, the first to my father and one to Aunt Ronda, and a long message to Fray Juan Ruiz de Medina. I pleaded that he pray for my soul. I also wrote to old Mudarra and thanked him for all the things he had done for me, and beseeched that he attend my father most faithfully and that he pray for me.

I spent the night at Gallego's. The Rabbit took wench and, seeing that I was alone, he offered to share her with me, and this hospitality I declined for there was no lust within me, only an empty loneliness.

My slumber was disturbed by awesome dreams and long ere dawn I heard the Jews tramping into Palos and down to the harbor, and they wailed most piteously and chanted their psalms in the weird mien of the East.

It came to me then that this was their season of Ab, verily, this the ninth of Ab, the day of their black fast, the horror day on which Babylonia razed their First Temple and drove them into exile, and the very day on which Rome razed their Second Temple and drove them forth to wander. Again it was the ninth of Ab, and again the Dispersal.

I went to Gallego's doorway and watched the soldiers herd them aboard the caravels and search them for gold, and some of the Jews cried out for mercy and some of the soldiers gave them bread.

"By their lost foreskins, they did less for the Savior." The Rabbit was at my elbow and his grinning whore was at his side and he kicked her into the street and we stood there watching the Jews until our marshal's pipe commanded us to the plaza and to the fountain where flowed sweet water from the ancient Roman aqueduct.

All morning we filled casks and hauled them aboard, and the Jews swarmed the decks of their ships and many called to us for mercy, but some cursed us for Christian dogs and filth.

"No heed!" Captain Pinzon ordered. "No heed to them!"

We were piped again to the plaza and Don Christopher led us into the Church of St. George and we were confessed and all took the very holy sacrament of the Eucharist, and then we were assembled before the church and Marshal Harana announced, in the name of the admiral, that we would board our ships at sundown.

A wave of protests swept the men and The Rabbit's was the loudest of all. "Seize upon, Marshal! We have the right of the last night ashore——"

Diego Harana brought his rod down hard on The Rabbit's back and Arcos and I moved at the same instant, but Captain Pinzon pushed us aside and braced himself before the marshal, and his eyes were blazing anger. "Marshal Harana, now hear this! You will not strike my men. I alone will judge and I alone will mete. Your authority is confined to the decks of the flagship. See to it."

The marshal retired in embarrassment and Pinzon addressed us: "I know you have the right of the last night ashore, but that right is abridged and by the admiral's orders."

185

"But, Captain——" It came from a dozen throats.

"And in this I concur. I will not have your strength wasted this night on women and wine. We will need clear heads and strong backs for the dawn. Now, follow me."

He led us to the harbor and we boarded our ships and soon the word spread that we would not be ashore again and some of the Jews leaned over the sides of their ships and jeered us, but others prayed that they and we have safe voyages, they to the East, we to the West.

The Palenos began lining the river, the wives and children to weep and the men to call farewell.

Fray Juan Perez boarded the *Santa Maria* with Don Christopher and blessed the fleet and then the admiral vanished into his cabin and the friar was rowed ashore and walked through the crowd and to the road to La Rabida.

The bells of St. George tolled the hour and it was sundown and the two caravels bearing Jews weighed their anchors and dropped down the Tinto and the wails of the exiles rent the sky and the women of Palos waved to the wanderers and then waved to their loved ones on our ships, and sobbed their misery and fears. The last Jews were gone. Dawn was the hour for us.

Chico and The Rabbit cast dice for the honor of leading the Salve Regina and Chico won, and The Rabbit cried trickery. Nevertheless, it was Chico who led our sundown song and then the watch was posted and I stretched on the great hatch to sleep.

But there was no sound slumber, only fitful naps. All night the women kept their vigil, calling to their men and to our God. The lights of Palos went out and the town was still, and the women huddled in groups and munched food and called all night:

"A thousand Hail Marys for you, Arcos. Aye, ten thousand."

"God attend you, Juan Umbria."

"Six masses I will have said, Juan Quintero. And candles for Her until you return."

Pedro. Diego. Francisco. *Quede usted con Dios.*

Gallego's daughter came down and waved to The Rabbit and wailed her lament as though she were a respectable wife instead of a wineshop slut, and he shouted ribald jests at her until she dried her tears and began laughing. I stood on the great hatch and she saw me and cupped her hands and called:

"*Quede usted con Dios, Lepe.*"

186

It was my only farewell.

Chico turned the glass at 4 A.M. of Friday, August 3, and I heard the boat alongside the *Santa Maria* and then the splash of oars and Captain Pinzon said, "Our admiral goes to pray for us."

The crowd mumbled when his boat was docked and he passed among them and up to the plaza and to the Church of St. George, and there he took the Wafer again and returned to the *Santa Maria*.

It was almost five o'clock, the glass almost run, and a light blinked thrice on the quarter-deck of the *Santa Maria*, but the command sounded first on the *Nina*. "All hands!"

Then from the *Santa Maria*, from Don Christopher himself: "All hands!"

Arcos was at our tiller and my watch was on the main deck and waiting, and Captain Pinzon rested both fists on the binnacle and shouted: "All hands——"

"*Ole!*" The Rabbit took it up. "Bend your backs, you merry bastards. *Ole!*"

My starboard watch sprang to the windlasses and broke the anchors free while the port watch sucked the pumps until they flowed easy, and then to the sweeps and our brave little *Pinta* brought her nose around and toward the channel of the Tinto.

The *Santa Maria* was in the river and standing downstream and the sun came up red and touched her Crosses, and her pennant on the mizzen and the ensign of Ferdinand and Isabel on her foremast and the Royal Standard on her mainmast.

The *Nina* was in her wake, still under sweeps, and we felt the channel take us and then Pinzon sent the port watch to the forecourse and the dawn breeze of Andalusia billowed our sail and rippled our standard.

The heat smote us ere we raised Point Sebo to starboard, and I looked back toward Palos and there was La Rabida on the hill, and beyond, on the meadow where the Jews had camped, the Queen's men were raising old Quemadero again, for this was Faggot Day and two Judaizers must die.

We were in the Saltes and across the bar and my watch was on the main course, and we trimmed it sharp and laced on a bonnet, and were away for the Ocean Sea; we the first of the bees to fly west from the swarming hive.

# CHAPTER 14

*A* SEA BREEZE CAUGHT US WHILE THE SALTES STILL WAS VISIBLE to starboard and Arcos steered south, which was as near the wind as he could bring our spritely little *Pinta*. Our headway was a deplorable two knots and this a sluggish commencement for the most auspicious voyage in all of man's endeavor.

All that day land was in sight and the clouds massed over the sea line and all who were not on watch gathered at the rail and stared toward Spain and home, and no man spoke frivolity. Captain Pinzon was at the binnacle and his black, burning eyes were steady on the needle and the needle was steady, hard north, which, as you know, is the source of the mystery that holds the needle. He called down the course to Arcos, chanting it down, and Arcos checked his own compass and sang back the course and we moved on, bound for Lanzarote and her sister Canary Islands that sprinkle the sea just off Africa and northwest therefrom.

This rendezvous, the easternmost of the Canaries, was 700 miles and eight days from Palos and Pinzon knew the course as he knew the passageway to his wife's soft couch. He was as fractious, as alert, as a merchant at vendue, for a voyage to the Canaries ever was parlous. These islands are reef-bound and whereas Spain enforced sovereignty over five of them, the remaining two were unconquered and at the mercy of the ferocious natives, the heathen Guanches.

I sensed a trepidation among the men and to alleviate this malady I broke into song and the men joined me, all singing:

> "From the far regions of Calcutta
> With toil and strict attention to business
> We have brought here many sorts of spices."

Pinzon nodded approval of my finesse, but The Rabbit scorned my enterprise and snarled at me, "Have off, Lepe. Do you expect a berth on this wooden jade by licking the backside of your officers?"

The *Santa Maria* was to our port, lumbering and so close I could see Juan de la Cosa conning his helmsman through the hatch that was a step or so forward of the binnacle. Alonso Roldan, the pilot, was at the binnacle and the admiral[1] himself was on his poop, the breeze in his hair and his face resolutely south and by west, the route to the Canaries.

The *Nina* was beyond the flagship, her lateens gasping for breath, for the breeze had exhausted itself and was as weak and as tepid as a spent mistress at dawn.

We changed watches at vespers, which were the third hour after the full sun, and that being high noon. Now, watches were set in this manner: at 3 and 7 and 11, although in those days we did not measure time by hours but by glasses, prayers, and watches, there being eight glasses to the watch and three canonical hours a day—tierce, vespers, and compline.

The morning watch began at tierce, the seventh hour after midnight. The mid-day watch was set at 11 A.M. and was on until vespers, at which time the late day or dog watch came on and worked until compline. By common consent, we divided the vesper watch that the men might change their night watches and thus get more sleep.

The helmsman worked two glasses on, then rested two and we had done our vespers when Arcos joined us in the shadow of the foredeck, where my watch was lolling. He had a cup of watered wine in his left hand and was nibbling a biscuit and an onion.

Francisco Gallego, the one called Chico, spake him cheerily and The Rabbit cuffed the boy and silenced him with an oath that, as a gromet, he had not earned the privilege of fraternization with a helmsman. Then The Rabbit addressed Arcos, smirking his vantage over Chico. "Aye, my stalwart. Suck up a wind! We creep and nothing more. How goes it below?"

Old Arcos grunted and rinsed his mouth and swallowed. "The tiller

[1]This is an error of habit. On the outward voyage, Columbus was captain-general and was not admiral until The Discovery. The narrator, or the translation from Arabic, errs also in speaking of "knots" in measuring nautical speed and time. Knots did not come into use until the sixteenth century, when the narrator was an old man. On The Voyage, distance and speed were measured by Roman miles although the league also was used to measure distance.

is jumping like a jack at his first spring stand. This flying pig will never cross the Sea of the Mares and may the Mother forbid her the Ocean Sea."

Pinzon shouted all hands to the courses and we trimmed her tight and he called "Well the halyard, belay!"

We slacked off and went back to the shadow of the foredeck and The Rabbit broke out his dice, but there was no man to game with him for we all were watching the *Santa Maria* steer closer, her rudder hard over. A seaman dropped charcoal into the brazier which hung over the stern of the flagship and then one of the ratings doused it with a wet canvas and a ball of smoke spread into the still air and this a signal that the *Sant Maria* would speak us.

Pinzon stepped to the quarter's rail and cupped his ear and Diego Harana, assuming a prerogative that was not the marshal's, spake for Columbus, saying: "My master is of good cheer. A man of faith and the blessings of St. Francis."

Faith, indeed! By the torch of St. Elmo! We all were men of faith and the dirty skin of Chico was as precious to him and to God as the anointed temples and brow of Christopher Columbus.

The flagship veered away, yawing badly like a pup-full bitch trying to gnaw her own tail, and the sun headed down red and the land misted and was blurred, and then was gone. The compline watch was set and The Rabbit turned the glass and chanted:

"*Good is that which passeth,*
*Better is that which cometh.*
*The eighth is past and the first floweth again.*"

Chico led the Salve Regina and Juan Quintero was chosen by the quarter-deck to lead our prayers and this most fitting inasmuch as the Quintero brothers, Juan and Christopher, owned the *Pinta* and had shipped as seamen to be with their ship, which had been commandeered without their permission and to their bitter resentment.

" 'Whoso dwelleth under the defense of the Most High, shall abide under the shadow of the Almighty.' "

We said it together, The Rabbit the loudest of all, and then darkness was upon us and the coals of our brazier glowed red and the little oil lamp by the binnacle glowed yellow and the candle in the captain's quarters glowed yellow, too, and the *Pinta* creaked her timbers.

Diego Bermudez, the quarter-deck gromet, was ordered by the

master, young Francisco Pinzon, to fetch charcoal from the forecastle and this he did and put it on the pot and we warmed our food into a broth of bread and meat and onions.

The mizzen filled and then a goodly wind was upon us and it backed strong to the north and all the courses bellied tight and the bonnets were full. Our *Pinta* shivered her delight and bit into the sea and was a wooden jade no longer, nay, neither a wallowing pig, but a bird that had found her wings.

Captain Alonso Pinzon, naked for the night's repose, came to his quarter and smelled the wind and studied all courses, the big sails singing and the *Pinta* plunging, and then he conned the helmsman and shouted down for him to feel for the best offing, and that south and by the west. "The south wind and one half of the west wind." Our captain sang it out.

"—And one half of the west wind," the helmsman sang back.

The needle was fast on Polaris and that star bright in the north, and Spain was down beyond the horizon and beyond our eyes. The brazier on the *Santa Maria* flamed and then a pitch torch showed once, and twice, and thrice. Columbus was setting the course and calling our *Pinta* and the *Nina* to follow him.

*Sur cuarta del sudoeste.*

For the Islands! Ho! for the Canaries.

The south wind we knew well. But the west wind we knew not at all.

Captain Pinzon retired to his quarters and Master Francisco Pinzon took the quarter and Pilot Garcia Xalmiento was at the binnacle. Juan de Jerez, a gromet of Palos, went to the forecastle and cut rope, severing the rough Spanish twist into handy lengths. He fetched these to the main deck, to the lee of the forecastle deck, and there, by the light of the pot, he trimmed them and nipped the harsh ends of the hemp. I joined him and trimmed rope even closer than he.

We whispered as we worked and little Juan de Jerez told me of his home, his father a worker in mortar and his mother a cheerful woman, and of sisters four and brothers two. He was fearful of the voyage, for were there not huge beasts at sea and a shelf at the end of the world? He had taken Pinzon's knife to earn the pay and someday he hoped to be a mariner and then a master and own his ship and fish for sardines off Lepe. "If we return," he said and smiled at me.

"See to your rope, boy. A chain of onions and this rope are more important to a good voyage than a kind master. As primary as the wind rose."

In those days we called the compass the wind rose because it resembled a rosette, or rather a roundel, and we steered by the winds and the halves and quarters thereof.[2]

The gromet and I took the rope spans to the rail and secured them. Then back to the pot and Juan de Jerez doused the fire and bade me good night and went to the quarter to attend the needs of the master and the pilot. I felt for a soft plank on the great hatch and stretched my ease and courted sleep until the consummation came with dreams of misty seas, and Maraela there and laughing and then vanishing as a swirling wraith and then my father there, and he pale as a corpse.

I awoke in affright and Arcos was snoring like a bear in a cave, and, for a minute or more, I refreshed the dream in my memory and pondered why I should dream of Maraela after all these years, and, then being a man of no superstitions, I put it away. The pilot was bent low over the binnacle and our *Pinta* was heeling slightly and curling the sea; and thus ended the first day of that momentous venture that remolded the world in my lifetime, and changed me even more.

Juan de Jerez roused me for my night watch at the twenty-third hour, two hours before the first, and I went to the lee and relieved my bladder and then sweetened my stomach with a shallow of wine and hurried to the bow, to my lookout.

The *Nina* was off our port stern and the *Santa Maria* was abaft her wake and thus, at the beginning, the flagship led us not at all, but followed. We had furled our mizzen and had blanketed our forecourse to keep the others in sight, had hobbled our *Pinta* else we sail away from the clumsy *Santa Maria* and the awkward *Nina*.

Arcos, taking the air on his hour off from his tiller, joined me and grumbled his anxiety for the helm. "The fin is lurching," he said, "and this ship handles like a sluggish jade. The rudder slues its gudgeons."

"Aye?" I said it of habit and no heed gave I really to his grouse, for

[2]There were no useless letters on the compass, as most sailors of this age were illiterate. The eight prime winds were pointed prominently on the wind rose: N (marked by a fleur-de-lis) and NE, E, SE, S, SW, W, NW. The between winds, 24 of them, were half winds and quarter winds and were designated by diamond figures of various sizes and colors. The wind rose had 32 points, but "points" and "degrees" were unheard of.

Arcos at sea ever was one for pessimism and verily a Job's comforter.

"She handled easily in the Tinto, but the tiller has been lurching since we made the bar and out-bounded into the sea. I smell mischance, aye, mayhaps adversity."

Now, mind you, there was no hint in his words of culpability, no indictment of the brothers Quintero who owned the *Pinta*, the two who had shipped as seamen to be with their ship, the two who nourished acrimony that their *Pinta* had been seized for use by that unwived alien, Christopher Columbus.

The words of Arcos gave phrase to his honest trepidation that mischievous hap was brooding, forasmuch, as a sailor, he knew that the winds of chance are fickle winds. He accused no man of intrigue nor of meddlesome deed at the tiller, but charged only the deviltry of the Fates, and they are women, and his dictum was the unsuspecting locution of a fretful sailor, and on this you may wager.

All was well that watch on the deck which was my tour, the bow lookout, the forecastle, and the pot. The pumps were sucking steadily, although the bilge already was stinking the slops of our waste and the slime of the sea. The pot fire was harmless coals. The gear in the forecastle was trim, the ropes coiled and the tools secured. My relief, and he was Garcia Alonso of Palos, an estimable seaman of no teeth and a spittle trickle at the corners of his mouth, laid his hand on my shoulder at the third hour and I told him that all was well, and he blessed me in his saint's name, and this St. Joseph; and I turned in and quickly to sleep in the exhaustion of our first day out.

The bustling of the dawn watch stirred me to half-sleep as the gromet saluted daybreak in his chant from the quarter:

> "Blessed be the immortal soul
> And the Lord who keeps it whole.
> Blessed be the light of day
> And He who sends the night away."

Then came a Pater Noster and an Ave Maria, and old Arcos, weary but beyond sleep, stirred at my side and mumbled his prayers—"pray for us sinners, now and at the hour of our death"—and I deduced his mood and weighed it into the substance of apprehension and this surely over the performance of the tiller.

That watch, always the noisiest and most irksome aboard, began the last duties of their tour, lowering buckets into the sea and hoisting

194

water to the deck and spilling it and then scrubbing the deck down with brooms of stiff Spanish grass.

The Rabbit, his voice rasping like sand on glass, broke out my watch at the seventh hour, when he scampered to the quarter and chanted his summons: "On deck, and off your hinds, gentlemen mariners of the starboard, you of the gentleman pilot's watch. On deck! Time moves and so need we."

He turned the ampolleta, as we called the glass, and smirked his demoniac grin as we scampered for onions and biscuits to appease our hunger. Then we lowered the jardines forward and aft and, seamanly, to the lee, and these jardines simply planks rubbed smooth to prevent splinters in our backsides, and each man chose his length of tarred rope and I certes to title of the particular swatch I had prepared for my own comfort.

Many were the carlish and vulgar obscenities as we balanced ourselves in obeisance to Ajax, and The Rabbit, damn his eyes, led a chantey of ridicule to our ungentlemanly postures.

Master Francisco Pinzon, his watch completed, lifted the slate by the binnacle and studied the reckonings he had posted during his vigil and entered them in the log and The Rabbit wiped clean the slate.

Captain Alonso Pinzon came to his quarter-deck and The Rabbit fetched him a cup of watered wine and two biscuits and then hurried below to tidy the captain's cabin and empty the buckets and these, the little bastard, he flung wide and some of the contents sprayed the men who were lingering on the jardines and they cursed his sire's ancestry to the serpent of Eden and his dam's line to the scabby whores of Babylon.

The off-watch helmsman reported the course to Master Francisco Pinzon and the master repeated it to Pilot Juan de Umbria. The pilot repeated it and passed it to Arcos, the on-duty helmsman, and Arcos repeated it.

"The south wind and one half of the west wind."

As lookout, I went forward and scanned the sea and cupped my hands and sang to the quarter-deck that the yawing *Nina* was about three glasses off our stern and the clumsy *Santa Maria* about five glasses, maychance two miles. Captain Pinzon cocked his ear to take my report and then looked aft at the other ships and returned his attention to the binnacle and to talk with the pilot.

Juan Perez Vizcaino, our carpenter, primed the pumps and, inasmuch as we had taken water during the night, he set a detail to two hand pumps and sucked her dry.

The deck hands swayed up the rigging and tightened the lanyards and our *Pinta* curtsied her gratitude and was away, dancing the waves. Master Francisco Pinzon retired to his quarters and Captain Alonso Pinzon called out a cheery *gracias à Dios* for fair weather and wind. The sun was at the yardarm and our day was begun, and this Saturday, August 4, 1492, our first full day at sea and the pattern for the many to come.

We had chick-peas that day, boiled with slabs of dried meat and seasoned goodly with garlic and onions. The next day was the Sabbath and many prayers were said and supplications made and our captain issued a liberal portion of wine and ordered every man to eat dried fruit to sweeten his humors and lax his bowels. The Rabbit broke out his dice again that afternoon and Juan de Sevilla was foolish enough to game with him and lost 100 maravedis and reported this loss to Captain Pinzon, and our captain entered in his accounts that Juan de Sevilla was owing to Gomez Rascon the sum of 100 maravedis, to be deducted from wages and paid to the winner.

The *Nina* and the *Santa Maria* were yet to our stern and under full sail to keep us in sight and our *Pinta* only half dressed, else we run away from them. We lolled the deck that Sabbath afternoon, and even after the twilight Salve Regina, and talked of the things that sailors ever talk about at the beginning of a voyage; of women—The Rabbit rending us to laughter and jeers with his tales of virgins won and abandoned and his rodomontade that no man aboard dared measure staffs with him on wager of a month's pay. *Ay Dios mío!* That Rabbit.

And then it was Monday, the sea choppy, and my watch was stirred out at the seventh hour and we had run up the jardines and cleansed our ropes and were ready for compline when the *Pinta* jibbed wildly to port and Arcos bawled to the quarter-deck for furtherance. Captain Pinzon shouted for the Quintero brothers and they dashed below. The pilot steadied us and we all knew what had come to pass, that our rudder had jumped its gudgeon, and this the socket attached to the sternpost to hold the rudder pintle.

Calm were we, as behooved Andalusians, and seamanly, as befitted the brave crew of earth's foremost sailor, our own indomitable Alonso

Pinzon. Master Francisco Pinzon swung to the quarter-deck and was naked, he being quickly from his couch and of no moment to garb himself. Our *Pinta* lurched her helplessness and shivered the mortification of her predicament. Her fin was awry and her nose swung to port and the waves slapped her in contemptuous abandon.

The master sent all hands to stations in a ringing order and we broke out the sweeps to keep her out of the trough. Then we showed distress signals, and these braziers at bow and stern. The Rabbit, his prying eyes missing naught, scampered below and brought back the bruit.

"*Ave María Purísima!*" He delayed his report to enrich the heroics of his disgusting histrionics. "It is as I thought. The rudder has snapped from its socket. Bend your backs to those sweeps, you merry cockerels, or else you have bunged your last barrel."

"Drown him," shouted Juan Bermudez. "Drown him in the captain's bucket. The little cyst of filth——"

The master silenced the raillery. "Bend to those sweeps, Andalusians! Keep her bow ahead. Your captain, who is my own brother, is at the tiller. And the good Arcos. And so, too, the stalwart brothers Quintero."

"*Toma!*" We answered him in one voice.

He flung back his head and spake his pride in us. "Now hear this, you brave ones: She strains a gut in her labor and snaps a tendon. If you quail before mishap in the Sea of the Mares, then how stand you for the Ocean Sea? *Andar!*"

We undressed her save for the forecourse to keep her steady and the *Nina* came alongside and we waved her away, and she stood off and then the *Santa Maria* lumbered up and Christopher Columbus himself was on the quarter, the wind in his hair and his zealous countenance contorted in anxiety.

"What ho, there?" He called it himself. "What deviltry?"

"Our rudder is fouled, sire," replied Francisco Pinzon. "*Mira!* It is a mischief."

"Where is your captain?"

"Below, sire. At the cradle of our misfortune."

Columbus vented his impatience that he, the favored of the Queen and of God, should be compelled to discourse with our master instead of our captain, but Francisco Pinzon, and quite properly, neither bespake nor hinted any intent to summons his brother from his duty without a command from the admiral, and this command Columbus deemed wise not to speak.

The admiral conferred with Juan de la Cosa, the master and owner of the *Santa Maria*, and then shouted his decision. "Captain Pinzon is a gentleman of energy and ingenuity. He will not need my aid. We will draw off and stand by."

Chico himself, the fledgling of our company, stared at the great man and gulped his amazement at the sophistry of the pronouncement. The admiral's aid? Mother of God! What service could he perform? Launch his boat and board us? That would cost hours. And then what? Christopher Columbus knew less about shipwrightry than did I of the *Malleus Maleficarum*[3] and I vouchsafe to you that that was naught, at that time.

The sea was running too high for the *Santa Maria* to tie to us and work her tackle to ship our rudder, so, as any witling could perceive, his only intelligent behavior was to trust our captain's judgment and himself pull away and heave to.

This he did and our gentlemen bent to the task and all that day and all that night we kept our *Pinta* head-on while our captain and Arcos and the brothers Quintero labored at the rudder; and before tierce the next morning, and that on August 7, Captain Pinzon came to his quarter-deck and, dripping exhaustion but exuding triumph, signaled the flag that we were shipshape again and then ordered us under way.

Now hear this: in the drifting, the expedition had lost the course and there was much signaling and shouting as we sought our way. The admiral (is error ever possible with an admiral?) in the events that followed, usurped even the detail of this matter and, in his covetousness and urbanity, pretended the course was revealed through his godly wisdom and by assistance of the saints who tended his wants like lackeys at court. Punish that hateful face! Curse the body of that head and belly! It was Captain Vicente Pinzon of the *Nina* who deduced the true course and it was he who spake it, and the admiral concurred and all the ships were under sail again by vespers, still the south wind and one half of the west wind.

But, as all Andalusians know, the whims of the sea are jealous whims and cavort in pairs and on August 8, six days out of Palos, and that a

[3]*Malleus Maleficarum* was the handbook of the Inquisition and defined the five categories of heretics upon whom sentence should be passed.

Wednesday, our *Pinta's* rudder fouled again and we began to take water, and this only a few hours after we had found the true course, the course of Vicente Pinzon.

Columbus spake us ere twilight and Captain Alonso Pinzon took the summons and the admiral informed him that the plan was changed: we were to rendezvous at Las Palmas on the Grand Canary and avoid Lanzarote, the first port of call.

His plan was sound, and does not this admission establish that I am capable of commendation where commendation is earned?

There were forges and other facilities at Las Palmas, for it is a larger port than Lanzarote. There we could repair our *Pinta*, or, failing that, the admiral might charter another ship to take the stead of our crippled *Pinta*.

Thus, having spake his command, Columbus ordered us to mend our ship and follow his *Santa Maria* and the *Nina* and this we did, limping in their wakes.

We raised the Grand Canary at dawn of the next day, and that August 9, and then a dead calm was upon us and for three dreadful days the expedition lay off the island while Christopher Columbus implored his saints for succor.

A fresh breeze came to us on the third night (surely the saints) and again Columbus changed his mind. We were commanded to take our *Pinta* into Las Palmas and repair her if we could, while the *Santa Maria* and the *Nina* proceeded to the port of San Sebastian on island Gomera, which, as you know, is one of the westernmost of the Canaries.

Now here, with our *Pinta* struggling for the roadstead of Las Palmas and the *Nina* and the *Santa Maria* under way for San Sebastian, I arrogate a minute to elucidate on the whyfor did the admiral divide his fleet ere our blessed voyage scarcely was begun. His was a decision most exemplary and bestirring no whit of deceit.

Neither the *Santa Maria* nor the *Nina* could serve the *Pinta* and therefore it was wise seamanship for them to seek a harbor and send us into the nearest port for repairs.

But, now, cogitate you this: the island of Gomera was a possession of Castile and under the hereditary rule of the Herrera y Peraza family. The mistress of this family was that ambitious and beauteous widow, the youthful Dona Beatriz de Peraza y Bobadilla. She administered the affairs of Gomera as guardian for her son, for he was immature in body and intellect.

This noble lady, whose first name was the same as that of the mistress of Columbus, the forlorn Beatriz Harana, had enjoyed an amorous adventure back in Spain. Isabel herself had named the comely maid to her court, only to suffer the flagrant humiliation of a passion between her attendant and her own stud, the vigorous Ferdinand.

To the court (mayhaps the whims of the saints again?) came Hernan Peraza of Gomera to answer for the murder of a rival plunderer in the Canaries. The wise Isabel forgave his crime in return for his promise to marry the maid and remove her from the beckon of Ferdinand. This came to pass and thus the young bed warmer of the king became Dona Beatriz de Peraza y Bobadilla and, most fortunately for all, her husband was assassinated after seducing a native girl and Dona Beatriz was left to govern Gomera in the name of her pup.

To my knowledge, Columbus had no acquaintance with Beatriz Peraza, but he had a way with women, a careful eye, and manly equipment. Perhaps Beatriz Peraza might be persuaded to charter him a ship to sail in *Pinta's* stead, provided, naturally, our ship was beyond repair.

So to San Sebastian he sailed and then only to find that Dona Beatriz was at Las Palmas, the very port that we of the *Pinta* were trying to make.

Confusion seize! And by the foal of Hagar, and he being Ishmael himself.

To worsen this intricacy into chaos, our rudder was beyond restoration and for two weeks, aye, two Stygian weeks, we drifted off the Grand Canary and were at the mercy of offshore winds and on-shore tides until, by the very dint of desperation, we warped the *Pinta* in, using sweeps to handle her and our dinghy to tow her.

Now that was August 24, we being twenty-two days from home, and scarcely had we tied up at Las Palmas ere we learned that Dona Beatriz had sailed four days earlier for San Sebastian.

There was no news in Las Palmas of the *Nina* or the *Santa Maria* and, spurred by the affright that our *Pinta* might be left behind and we compelled to sail another ship, we fell to willingly to mend our pet.

Captain Pinzon made contract with Las Palmas' smiths to furnish tools and forges and straightway, despite our exhaustion, we began forging new pintles and gudgeons for our ship.

And, now, hear this and despair not: the next day, on August 25, the *Santa Maria* and the *Nina* joined us. Columbus had passed Dona Beatriz in the night and he was forlorn at this whim of chance and from his crew we learned all that had passed.

In San Sebastian, awaiting the lady and the 40-ton craft of her ensign, Columbus set the men to gathering provender and wood and water. And yet no Dona Beatriz to warm his heart with her beauty and, forsooth, her boat. So therewith Columbus dispatched one of his men to Las Palmas to acquaint us with his adversity and we, at that time, drifting off the Grand Canary. The messenger began his journey on a coastwise craft.

For nine days, the Admiral of the Ocean Sea cooled his heels in San Sebastian and then, in a veritable froth, ordered the *Nina* and the *Santa Maria* to raise canvas for Las Palmas.

He passed Dona Beatriz' ship the first night out and on the second day he overtook the coaster on which his messenger had sailed. Mother of man! What a propitious augury for the most noble venture in all the span of tide and climate.

And other truths learned I from the Andalusians of his company, who muttered vows to forsake his command and jump his *Santa Maria* and return to Spain. "He is no sailor," they mouthed. "His eyes are on the stars and never his deck. He whispers to his saints while his marshal curses us. *Al asesino!* To the hell with him."

"And no tar for our ropes," wailed an able man of Huelva. "My backside bleeds and rasps like a hung sheep. His marshal, that Harana filth, that converso pig, will give our gromets no hour to tar rope, but uses them for his own service and for the admiral's beckon."

"We are treated as Portuguese——"

"As Genoese and Venetians——"

Thus ominously did they vent their grumbles, these free Andalusians who had neither fealty nor respect for their alien master.

And from them did I learn that the ratings of the *Santa Maria* had fanned a rumor that the Quintero brothers had fouled our tiller in protest against the seizure of their *Pinta* by the Crowns. That Pinzon himself, meaning Alonso and not Francisco, had reported mischief aboard our caravel and this mischief surely man-work and impossibly the chance of the dice, the fortune of the game.

God's mercy! You readers whose wisdom has passed your suckling mew. Had Alonso Pinzon suspected the Quintero brothers, he would have accused them on his quarter and in the presence of his company and, if guilt be their lot, he would have hanged them as high as Mordecai hanged Haman.

And had he not, then we ourselves would have flung the culprits into the sea.

Flummery and nonsense. The lives of the Quintero brothers had been in the same balance as our lives. Would they suicide? They loved their *Pinta*. It was their livelihood. Do sane men destroy their bread and roof?

Nay, I say to you who weigh these words—nay.

This report, now fast in chronicle, was the guile of Christopher Columbus. He was the favored of God, the anointed, and, therefore, in the magisterial conceit of his ilk, in the mystic convictions of his dreams, he could never admit even to himself that any hap to his ambitions was the chance of the hunt. He was God's chosen instrument, beloved of the Host and persecuted by men. Hence any mischance to his deification, his dream-stuff apotheosis, was the mischief of jealous men, for God could not be against him.

*Vox et praeterea nihil.*

For seven days we labored in Las Palmas to forge the fin for our *Pinta* and so ceaselessly did we toil that at night we flung ourselves down to sleep and were too weary for merrymaking in the port.

Our repairs on the *Pinta* were equaled by work on the *Nina*, for, at suggestion of Vicente Pinzon, the sails on his command were changed from lateen to square, the better for her to hold the westerly winds, which, at this season, blew steadily from the Canaries and into the vastness of the Ocean Sea.

We were trim again, all ships and men, on September 1, and that Friday, and after vespers our brave fleet sailed from Las Palmas for San Sebastian to pick up the provisions Columbus had caused to be stored there.

And to visit Dona Beatriz? Who was to deny our saintly admiral a breath of sweet life before the ordeal of possible death.

That night we sailed close to the southern shore of the island of Teneriffe, one of the largest of the Canaries and unconquered, and her volcano was belching red and we stood to starboard and watched it, and were awed; aye, and prayerful in the presence of such mysteries.

Bravely and surely we sailed into San Sebastian the next day, the westerlies on our sterns, and anchored in the roadstead, and then to shore in our dinghies, or tenders if you prefer.

The governor's castle of stone faced the harbor and hard by, on the brink of a barranca, was the Church of the Assumption and there waited Dona Beatriz and her retinue, and she as enchanting as a garland, as ripe as a springtime cherry.

Your propriety and delicacy shall be spared the obscene interjections of The Rabbit, but *Mira!* even stalwart old Arcos and gentle Chico were aroused to lustful approbation. She was as beautiful as I had remembered Maraela to be, a pomegranate bursting its seeds and limp-hanging for the subduction.

Don Christopher tugged tight his doublet and, sweeping his plume, gave her a leg, the gust and grace of which I thought he was scant capable. Aroint! A gallant! And I deign confess my envy, and I an Andalusian.

He and his captains went first with her into the church for prayers and thence to the castle and so high his spirits that he instructed his marshal to give us leave that we might take our pleasure in the town.

This we did the night of September 1.

The next day we began loading our fleet with the provisions he had stored on his previous call and again, in justice to truth, I must report that he had purchased well of wine and meat and some prize cheeses. The natives helped us at our tasks and many were their stories of land to the west, of islands they had seen in the Ocean Sea.

We loaded for four days and the moon was swelling full for her autumnal tryst with winds and tides and in the starry hours of September 6 Columbus assembled us at the Church of the Assumption and proclaimed that we would sail on the flood.

"I have received bruit——" He spake it himself in that sharp voice of his that reeked of modern Portuguese and old Spanish. "I have bruit that Portuguese men-of-war have come to defeat my expedition, which, under God and our Queen, shall not fail."

The men stared at him and then at one another, I staring at Arcos in the mellow light of the African moon. Portugal? Men-of-war? Balderdash! What manner of flummery was this? Was the admiral conjuring a vindication for himself should his labors fault?

We were not dolts. We were Andalusian sailors and every man jack among us knew that the King of Portugal dared not lift a lance against Spain.

Duplicity again, and evil sham. The stealthy machination of a legist and not the steady resolve of an admiral, fitting unto his emblems.

Dona Beatriz walked from out the shadows of the church and joined him and stood at his side and her rapture and satiety were apparent to all, and he spake us further:

"Westward on the flood."

"Seven hundred leagues westward and there we will not navigate between midnight and dawn."

He smiled at us, and this we took as his unspoken assurance that we would find land at 700 leagues and therefore should fret not at decisions in those parts.

Then he held high his right hand to command our ears and eyes and thus he spake: "Our gracious Queen has instructed me, her instrument, that the first man to sight land shall receive her pension of 25,000 maravedis per annum, and this gratuity for life."

"*Ole!*" We cheered this promise.

"And I, Don Christopher Columbus, will bestow upon the man who first sights land my own reward—a velvet doublet."

Again we cheered, for here indeed were prizes to quicken us: a velvet doublet of a gentleman and the Queen's pension to honor it.

He and Dona Beatriz turned into the church and his captains after him and then the ratings and then us, the men who must do it.

We took the Wafer, and Chico weeping and The Rabbit smirking, and old Arcos solemn and me filled with longing and loneliness.

At the door of the church, Don Christopher embraced Dona Beatriz and this sweet farewell we did not cheer, only smiling our benediction, and grateful that our admiral was a man for beauty. And might his fortune continue.

Down to the ships and aboard and the moon waning, and up anchors and up sails and we moved out, our *Pinta* obeying her fin with alacrity and Arcos bellowing a happy chantey as he manned his tiller. A bombard sounded from the castle and we fired our falconet, as did the other ships, and creaked out of the roadstead and squeezed for the south wind to drop down to the westerlies, the good south wind, whence came the parrots and the blacks, and then the unknown west wind.

But the south wind was frail and all that day and all the next we dawdled between island Teneriffe and island Gomera, and the *Santa Maria* down to one knot and heavy at her bow until her storage was shifted, and then her nose lifted and she showed spirit. The *Nina* was most spritely under her new rigging and our *Pinta*, quite naturally, even more spritely.

It was the eighth glass of my watch and this the third hour of September 8, and I at the lookout and I felt the north wind rising and this tiding I called to the quarter-deck. Master Pinzon sent The Rabbit scurrying for Captain Pinzon as our sails bellied taut and the fleet plunged southward and to the west.

The moon was full and the master held the oil lamp close to the binnacle and Captain Pinzon squatted and squinted his compass and then computed our speed, bearing on the juts of Gomera and Teneriffe. Next he judged the wind and the easterly compass variation and, computing these factors, he deduced his reckoning. Then he pricked his chart, laying the line, and when the glass was turned on the half hour he stroked a mark on the slate to record time on course; and thus we began.

Our three, the *Santa Maria*, the *Nina*, and our *Pinta*, were abeam and almost huddling, as though each sought comfort in the other, and then the signal flared from the flagship, the bold command of Christopher Columbus, who at last stood on his world, his own quarter-deck, and prayed mastery of his destiny and mastery of the Unknown sea.

*Oeste!*

The west wind and only one quarter of the southwest wind.

Not yet due west, but down fast to the steady winds from Africa, westerly into the horizon, into the mist.

At vespers of Sunday, September 9, the volcano of Teneriffe was visible astern and at compline only a hazy trace was wavering to the east. Chico led the Salve Regina at twilight and we lifted our faces to heaven and then we looked back once more; and there was no land.

*Oeste!*

The West!

Now trust God and hammer on.

CHAPTER 15

*T*HE WIND CAME FAIR AND NEVER WAS A SEA SO CALM; NEVER
God's grace so bountiful.

We scudded. Mother of Suffering and Our Lady of Seven Sorrows
—how majestically we scudded, as though God pillowed His head on
those clouds of silver fleece and gently wafted His sweet breath into
our sails.

Like a bird our *Pinta* skimmed, aye, like a boatswain bird, and the
cheer in our hearts was a thanksgiving and the lilt in our voices was a
laughter.

Even The Rabbit was gay as he called the watch to our first full
dinner at sea, singing out the call: "Table for sir captain and the
master and good company. The meat, the water. God bless the Queen
of Castile; and who will say not amen gets nothing to drink. Table,
table."

There was meat and cheese, and Arcos belched his gratification and
then made a wind so sturdy that it was heard on the quarter-deck and
Captain Pinzon laughed and called "Ah! *de popa!*" and The Rabbit
beat his own thigh and shouted, "Ah, Arcos! Bend your backside
westward and you will blow us to the Indies."

We were half a league before the *Nina*, and she under all bonnets
and sailing gallantly, and a full league before the *Santa Maria*, and
even that old jade scudding merrily in a prance.

Our tender was a good rope astern and was swishing in our wake,
the hawser taut and her bow full lifted.

We fixed on the bubbles that boiled from our *Pinta's* nose and,
checking the glass, we adjudged our speed and I could not believe my
own reckoning, for it computed at five knots. And this I would not

accept until Captain Pinzon took count and bellowed to us that we were making better than five knots.

*Hola!*

Pinzon sent The Rabbit for his sheepskin charts and made points from the dead reckoning he had fixed off Gomera. By deducing time and speed, he estimated the distance come, then laid his stick parallel to this course and nearest the west rhumb line on his chart and pricked a new point west.

And that our course. Hold to the line, and that due west.

The winds came fat and breathed in puffy gusts and were constant on our stern, and our *Pinta* lifted and rolled in a rhythmic cadence.

We made 118 miles that first day in which we were full in the Ocean Sea, that first day wholly beyond land. And hear this: on the third day we made 175 miles.

By the submission of Mohammed! We were birds.

Columbus journalized (as I later learned) that the weather was like spring in Andalusia and the only thing wanting was to hear nightingales. The sunrises were roses and the dews were heavy on our decks and on the ropes and sparkled on the sails. This then the Ocean Sea? This placid cup the Terror? Gray deep it was and as serene as a mother nursing her first-born.

A squally rain bathed us from low clouds above and our tender caught water and Juan de Sevilla dived into the sea and swam to the tender to bail it dry, and so buoyant and warm the sea that he called to us to join him and we, too, dived in and the captain himself shucked his garments and jumped in and washed himself.

The dread came on September 13, and not in sea or wind, but in the illimitable mystery of God's firmament. Our compass faltered. The true needle deceived us.

It was night and the stars blinked close and the ships had come abeam to share the sunless hours in comforting reunion. There came a cry from the helmsman and then sudden agitation on our quarterdeck and the master and pilot studied the compass and, in the yellow light of the binnacle lamp, I saw that Francisco Pinzon's face was contorted in dismay.

He sent for his brother and our captain stared at the compass and then north on Polaris. The deck sensed distress and yet the sea was calm and the wind gentle. A light flamed on the *Nina* and quickly on the *Santa Maria* and there was much perturbation on both ships and a hushed stillness on our ship.

The *Santa Maria* came close and the admiral himself hailed us, and to his glory let it be recorded that his demeanor was calm. "*Hola!* Captain Pinzon!" He cupped his hands and called. "Ahoy! And what of your compass?"

Our captain looked down at us, at the deck wide-awake and the faces staring up at him and my own heart pounding my ribs. "The needle, sire——"

"What of the needle?"

"It bears west of north, sire."

A gasp came from old Arcos and a moan from Juan Quintero. The needle had played us false. It should be a tittle east of Polaris, but it was west.

The Rabbit cackled his disdain of our affliction. "Pray, you bastards," he taunted us. "Never again will you taste Guadalajara's grapes or mount the thigh of an Andalusian maid."

Arcos slapped him into silence and Chico began the prayers—"Our Father who art in heaven"—and we all joined in, reciting it rapidly to have it done and perhaps an indulgence at the Throne.

"Board me!" The command came from Columbus and Captain Pinzon gathered his charts and we hauled the tender alongside, and I to the tiller, and we rowed the span to the flagship, then aboard.

I followed my captain to the quarter-deck, as was proper, and then he quickly to the admiral's poop and Vicente Pinzon already there in consultation with Columbus. I was near the *Santa Maria's* binnacle and I looked at the compass and the needle was west of the North Star.

Now you may scoff our fears for now man knows, because of our endeavor, that there is a westerly variation, but we knew it not and the needle was our life, our only hope, besides God, and it had faulted.[1]

I had seen the needle vary to the east of Polaris and this a wonder we accepted, yet on this night and in this climate it was west, and the West was the Unknown.

[1]This was the magnetic variation, a truth these times did not understand because even the most learned were not sure of magnetic north. Mariners used Polaris as due north. Some authorities say that Columbus "discovered" the earth's magnetic variation and the diurnal rotation of Polaris. Others insist his pronouncement that Polaris rotates was a lucky hypothesis. Anyway, he was right.

The brothers Pinzon were in fervid debate and Columbus was impassive and scanning the charts and then he silenced the brothers Pinzon and I heard him speak: "But Benjamin Marino says——"

He reached for a map and unfolded it.

(Aye, Mita. That I heard and that I saw.)

We remained on the flagship all night, the captains in deliberation and the men quieting as the hours turned and no evil befell us. And on the morn when the sun was up and the dew was gone, lo! the needle varied to the east of north, and this a comfort to us all.

Captain Pinzon left his charts with the admiral and we returned to our *Pinta* and there was much rejoicing and our spirits rose again and that day we made more than 100 miles.

On the next sun, however, the needle again was unsteady and in this suspense and quandary we lived and sailed until dusk of September 17, when Columbus instructed all pilots and masters to take the north, to palm the pilot's blessing. Captain Pinzon pressed his palm between his eyes and fixed on the North Star, then lowered his hand until his center finger was on the star, then his hand straight down and true on the star.

The needle was deviating west of north and almost a quarter of the wind, and this, indeed, caused us a melancholia in our humors and a dread in our being. There was no panic, and our officers were steady and most of the men also. Chico wept and The Rabbit, God bless him, comforted Chico and used those dreadful hours to teach him to throw the blade and made lend of my poniard for the lessons.

No man slept that night and at dawn the north was marked again and the needle was true. These deviations of our wind rose, these fickle mysteries of our Fates, did rasp the quick of the men and confound us all into misery. Another conference was held aboard the *Santa Maria* and this one in the admiral's quarters and it was following this council that Columbus announced: "The needles always require truth. Therefore, the star moves."

Polaris without anchor? The true star not fixed, but a wanderer? Then our needle had been true and had swung with the star and north was still north.

We were comforted by his assurance and I say to you that I know not if the Pinzons and the pilots believed him, or if the judgment was agreed upon in the council in order that we be quieted and confident once more.

At that time, and here I digress perforce and report information of after years, I knew not that Columbus was keeping two journals and these he called his "true" journal and the "false" journal. As admiral, only he had the prerogative of an official report to the Crowns and, even in this, he deceived us—we who sailed him into immortality.

His "true" and secret journal recorded data, as accurate as he could determine, on the expedition's speed and distance. His "false" journal cunningly minimized both speed and distance. In later years his explanation for this deception was that he feared for his ignorant seamen to know accurately how far they had come from home, that he kept his "false" journal to prevent dismay among the men if the voyage proved long.

That will not do. Sailors never have access to the admiral's journal. It mattered not the data he posted as we saw not his papers. Mary, Joseph, and Child! Do admirals share their journals with seamen? Then why a double log? To deceive his captains? That he could not do, for the Pinzons were better mariners than he.

Now hear this: I put forth that Christopher Columbus was prepared to deceive the Queen if that be to his advantage. In confusing all data, only he would have the key to discovery. But his saints were honorable, if he were not, and it came to pass that his "false" journal was more accurate than his "true" journal, for he himself erred shamefully in his computations and gave himself the profit of more miles than we truly had sailed.

So be the lie, and let him live it.

We began to see birds, and September half away, and some of the men believed these augured land, but Captain Pinzon, never a man for trickery or disillusionment, spake frankly his knowledge to us: that they were boatswain birds and frequently flew far to sea, and proved naught.

The weed soon was forming at our bow and swept free and floated by us and some of this weed we scooped aboard and found it green as though only lately had it torn free from some land. It could not be the mainland, Columbus told us, as he judged the mainland farther on. Surely, then, the weed was from an island near by, and on the next day when we found a live crab in the weed he told us that such crabs never were found more than 80 leagues from land; and this intelligence lightened our spirits muchly and we all sharpened our eyes and each was determined to see land first and thereby win acclaim and the Queen's pension and the admiral's velvet doublet.

On September 18, we ran 159 miles, and the next day it fell calm and the wind was sown to a whisper and we made only 72 miles and this our poorest day since Gomera. The pilots totted our position and our Christopher Xalmiento reckoned it as 420 leagues west of the Canaries. The *Nina's* pilot set it as 440 leagues and the *Santa Maria's* pilot adjudged it 400 leagues. Now we know that the *Santa Maria* was nearest correct, that in ten good sailing days from the Canaries we had sailed about 1300 miles.

Match that, any mariner. Stuff that in your craw.

Columbus, and, aye, our captain, also, were confident that we were sailing between islands, but why the admiral did not beat to windward and discover these islands I know not, save that he told us that his desire was to follow right along to the Indies, but on the return voyage, please God, all would be seen if the weather be favorable.

We all saw and the admiral recorded a "marvelous nosegay of fire fall from the sky and the air most balmy, and it a great pleasure to taste the mornings."

The old moon passed on September 20 and we ran away from the goodly winds and into variables and, to stay under way, we altered course slightly and bore west one quarter of the northwest wind. More birds winged by and some sat our yardarms and Chico did knock down one of these birds with a stone, the same he sneaked from ballast while the ratings' backs were turned.

Our moods and humors were most lively, for we believed that land was nigh. Then came a light calm and Columbus ordered soundings and each ship hove its line and there was no bottom at 200 fathoms.

Like innocents we slept that night and on the morn the sea was a meadow of grass, and this then the floating meadow of which we had heard, and into it we crept, although some of the men feared it would seize us and hold us fast, or that sea beasts would rise from it and devour us.

The *Santa Maria* went first and it was one of the few times that ship led the way and Columbus was on his poop and beckoned us to follow him, and he betrayed no affright and his valor was like unto a sign to all of us; and this a sight for his saints—the sea a wilderness of grass and the ships nosing through. A new moon came that night and the meadow was dark green and the flying fish leaped and, aye, a veritable host of finny creatures in the verdure. Dolphin we saw and bonito and larger fish, but none ferocious, and, indeed, myriads cavorting and squirming in the meadow.

The wind forsook us, and for awesome hours we lay in the meadow and some of the men spake fears that there would be no winds to take us back and then as the grumblings took fever, and many of the words against Columbus himself, the sea did rise and without wind, and this an astonishment to us. And the admiral, knowing the tempers of his men, did tell us that such a high sea without wind had not happened except at the time of the Jews when they went out of Egypt with Moses who was leading them out of captivity.

The sea without wind rolled us to a break in the meadow and there we saw a whale, and this a sign of land, and we were wetted by rains with no wind, and this, too, a sign of land.

The *Santa Maria* came close by our *Pinta* and Captain Pinzon and Columbus exchanged charts, hauling the sheepskins on lines, and did shout back and forth about islands in those climates, but we saw no islands and oozed out of the meadow and into free sea and the breeze down to a whiffet, but the sea running high.

Columbus called it a miracle, but Pinzon surmised that a line squall was on the northwest wind and beyond the squall a frightful storm[2] and that we were fortune's babes to be out of its path.

In five days we made only 200 miles and doubts came to us and a creeping fear that we had passed the wind shelf of the world and that there would be no wind to take us home. Yet the sea was as placid as a lake, and warm, and we swam every day, diving from our tenders, for the three ships were huddled for safety and the masters talked our plight.

At these times we of the *Pinta* commingled daily with the crew of the *Santa Maria* and most morose were those men and resentful of Columbus.

"He knows not where he is or where he goes," they said.

"He is no sailor, only a dreamer."

"There still is no tar for our ropes. We are treated as dogs and not Andalusians."

"We should bury that alien godkin in the meadow else the Furies bury us."

[2]Probably a hurricane as the expedition was nearing the incubator of these storms and in the hurricane season.

Now there was no such talk among the men of the *Pinta*, or even the *Nina*, for our captains had shared our woes and we knew them to be sailors. And on the *Pinta* and *Nina* we all were Andalusians, while the *Santa Maria* had a mongrel assortment.

By September 25 the suspirations had reached the quarter-decks, and the Pinzons and the admiral in frequent conference and it was twilight of that day, and I off watch, when Captain Pinzon rushed to his poop and pointed southwest and shouted: "Land! Land, sire. I claim the reward!"

Some of us scampered to the rigging and others fired the bombard and others lifted their faces and thanked God. Columbus dropped to his knees and led us in *Gloria in excelsis Deo* and ordered us to the southwest wind, and I scanned the seas, and was that land or sky, there where the sky touched the sea?

In my elation, I, too, mused it land, for fancy is the father of hope, and, if any officer were to win the prize, I was happy that it was our Pinzon.

But suffer you not in anticipation: it was not land.

All that night we sailed the southwest wind and on the morn we knew it was a false landfall and were sorely depressed and Columbus announced that what we had thought to be land was sky, and he was not as sad as we, but commented blithely on the soft, sweet air and the placid sea.

"Did I not tell you we must sail 700 leagues?" he said to us all. "We have come only 500. Whimper not. I have come for the Indies and I shall sail on till I find them with the help of the Lord. *Oeste!*"

West. Empty to the northward. Empty to the southward.

The doldrums set upon us and our humors biled and even we of the *Pinta* were in gloom and of sharp tempers. The talk long since had passed from women to food to home and now was to the hard, primitive things of life: the bowels that cramped us, the crepitations that eased us, the lice that crawled us, and the reeking stench of the bilge.

West. Nothing northward. Nothing southward.

The Rabbit, pretending cheer now that we were sullen, tried to lift us with a Salve Regina and some of the men cursed him and growled that Chico sang it better and to give them Chico. The Rabbit spat at them and one of them slapped him. I freed my poniard and Arcos reached for a marlinspike and we advanced upon them and Captain Pinzon leaped among us and scattered us, and reviled us. He sent us back to our chores, and these meager inasmuch as there was no wind, and time was a burden.

We made a scant 350 miles in six days, crawling on the glassy water. The wind was on our stern, but only timid capfuls and the tedium gnawed us and gave us leisure, a deadly thing at sea, and we were fretful and melancholy, and then the Terror was upon us.

But Captain Pinzon held us steady.

The flagship, though, was seething and the grumblings against Columbus rose to outbursts of anger and there were open cries of imposter and charlatan. The Pinzons, both of the *Nina* and our *Pinta*, looked to the admiral for decision and discipline, but he did naught and was aloof to the danger and spake frequently of the gentle weather, and meditated with his saints.

He used soft words instead of his marshal's lash. Saint or fool—let the years judge him.

On October 1 the variables began breaking and again the pilots totted the distance and Columbus announced that we had come 584 leagues. But now hear this: his secret journal, his "true" account, showed his reckoning at 707 leagues. Therefore, by his own deductions and his spoken vows, we should be near the Indies, aye, in the very shadow of the East.

Little wonder then that his own brow furrowed and his eyes clouded and he paced his deck in nervous agitation. He had deceived us, his people, but he could not deceive himself, and his record showed 700 leagues.

That he was wrong is of no import here. He thought he was right, that he had come the distance and yet the West was empty, and nothing northward and nothing southward.

The moon was coming full and there came a wind that lifted the ships to life, but not the men, for now stern-wind meant only increase of the world from home. The ships deserved more confidence and our little *Pinta* the most of all because she danced her delight in heaven's good offering and bent to her destiny like the birds passing overhead. Seven knots she gave us. She was leaping the sea and so far ahead of her sisters that we had to undress her to hold her down, else she run away from the *Santa Maria*, under bonnets, and the *Nina*, under main and fore courses.

But by the grace that gave her soul, even seven knots did not appease our *Pinta* and on October 3 she was at eight knots and straining for more, and on that day the expedition made 182 miles, and this the best day's run of the outward voyage.

And now at night, between the last glass and the dawn, we navigated no more, albeit the ships came to covey and waited out the darkness and we all remembered Columbus' pledge that at 700 leagues we would not navigate at night. This then was 700 leagues?

Yet no land, and the crew of the *Santa Maria* was in such discontent that Marshal Harana addressed them and praised them and gave them of wine and cheese from the admiral's stores, and we sailed on speedily until the sixth of October, when the wind dropped and we limped into variables again.

It was that night, and the moon high, that Pinzon sailed our *Pinta* under the stern of the *Santa Maria* and shouted to the admiral that we should change our course to the southwest wind.

"Cipango!" he shouted and pointed southwest, for he seemed convinced that island lay that way and that we were sailing it by, hull down.

Columbus held to the west wind.

The next day was Sunday and the *Nina* showed a flag and fired her bombard and this the signal for land. But there was no land, and the admiral was vexed and caused orders to be given that the next man who made a false landfall would disqualify himself for the reward: the pension and the doublet.

Mark that well. The next man who erred was disqualified for the prizes.

Came vespers of that Sunday and we all to prayers and Columbus leading his men and Pinzon leading us, and as we prayed there came flocks of birds winging low and these steady for the southwest. We all saw and marveled, for they were countless and on a bead, fast for the southwest.

The sun down and then twilight and then the moon fulling and soaring high, and Columbus came to his quarter-deck and paced it and prayed, and, aye, I saw him on his knees and in supplication, and the birds winging between us and the moon; and calling.

Columbus arose and himself gave voice to the command and his words rang across to us and on to the *Nina*: "The west wind and one half of the southwest wind!"

So be it. We broke our long course, the weeks due west, and veered to port and into the southwest, and this almost, but not full, the identical course that Alonso Pinzon had urged the night before.

Then Columbus was following Pinzon? The admiral was heeding the captain? Now, this you know and so with all men: I, Rodrigo of Triana, I, Lepe the sailor, I, Mudarra the bastard Moor—I loved Pinzon well, and better than most, but Columbus did not follow Pinzon, and this conviction I swear: that Christopher Columbus followed the birds, and they winging free and calling us.

*In rerum natura.*

If there be a dove for ancient Ararat, could there not be birds for a new world?

The glass was turned, spilling its sand, and the gromets chanted their tidings and Monday was born and died. The men long since had lost faith in Columbus' prayers and now even in the birds, still winging us southwest, and when the wind ran away—this being Tuesday, October 9—there was a tumult aboard the *Santa Maria*. Angry shouts echoed in our ears and mutinous threats, and Captain Pinzon stared toward the flagship, whence came this clamor, and then loosed his sword and fixed his eyes upon us, and no man moved.

The *Santa Maria* signaled us and we went alongside and Columbus spake our captain: "Martin Alonzo Pinzon, the people of this ship are grumbling and are desirous of turning back since we have been sailing for so much time and have found no land."

I and even Arcos and all of our company were eager to cheer, but the jubilation was stillborn, for Martin Alonso Pinzon spake thusly to Christopher Columbus: "Sire, let Your Worship hang half a dozen of them or throw them into the sea; and if this is not dared then I and my brothers will close upon them and do it, for a fleet which sailed mandated by high princes is not to turn back without good news. Forward!"

These brave words brought a din of recantation from the Galicians of the *Santa Maria*, and we of the *Pinta* crowded our rail and fingered weapons, for, as Andalusians, we would stand fast with our captain, albeit our fears were tremulous and the Terror was nigh.

Columbus extended his hand toward us as though to quiet Pinzon and then spake his submission: "Let us keep the peace with these gentlemen and sail on for three days, and if by then we have not found land we will consider what we are to do."

Flattery and unctuous obeisance. But his "gentlemen" were not pacified and increased their clamor and it came to me that Pinzon was debating with himself whether to take the command and save the expedition, and then the sea rose quickly and all hands scurried to the courses to trim for a wind, and this event did disperse the mutineers of the *Santa Maria* and set their hands to labor.

The sea ran heavy all that night and the sky was overcast on the morn—and that Wednesday, October 10—and again the rebellious clique on the *Santa Maria* howled for open mutiny. The sea was too turbulent for us to board the flagship and enforce discipline, but the admiral cajoled his men into restless acquiescence by promising they would turn back within two days unless land were found.

This was the day Pinzon told us: "If the admiral wishes, let him turn back, but I am determined to go on until land is found or return never to Spain. *Adelante!*"

Now, mind you, we were as fearful as they, but so bravely spake our Pinzon that we cheered him. "*Adelante! Adelante!*"

The salute rang across to the *Santa Maria* and the malcontents heard it and many of them came to their rail and shook their fists at us, and did revile us with obscene gestures, and, Mother of God! as they stood there one of the mutineers did swing a hook into the sea and lift out a green branch that resembled the dog rose of Andalusia.

This he held high and they took it for a sign of land, and they ran to the quarter-deck and waved it before the admiral's face and again I saw Columbus bend to his knees and thank his saints and bless that day.

The olive twig for old Ararat? Then the rose branch for the New World.

Next the *Nina* recovered a bough, and the greenery was all around our *Pinta* and we fished out many branches and The Rabbit hung one around his neck as a garland and jigged his elation, but Arcos kissed the signs and Chico fashioned one into a Cross.

We also fished a board and a span of cane from the sea, and these bodements of land did still all doubts and all of us on all three ships were of much joy and peered the horizon, every man tense and hopeful of being the first to see land.

But immortality passed that day by and the sun went down clean on the fifth glass of the vesper watch, and we to our evening worship, and then a signal from the flagship that we would navigate that night, for the morrow was the third day since the admiral's plight to turn back if no land be found in that time.

The ships were at six knots under a whistling wind and the course had been changed to due west again, and why I know not, save to take all the wind and make as much distance as possible before the third day.

At full dark the sea roughed up in a stiff wind and we were at seven knots and the braziers glowing on all ships that we might each sail within sight of the others. The vespers watch was relieved and the compline watch stood to, but no man slept and Arcos and The Rabbit and I were on the forecastle deck and scanning the night. The moon soon must up and the sea was foaming from the bow as our *Pinta* pranced her joy of good sails and good men, of good wood and good wind.

The sixth glass of the compline watch was turned and the Salve Regina was sung and in this hour of truth and at this place did Christopher Columbus fulfill his most hateful deceit—the lie of the Light of San Salvador.

Now, hear me and judge you the truth: I know not when he falsified his journal, be it before or after The Discovery, but I do know, as do you, that he recorded the light that no man saw save he and his henchman, and that being Pedro Gutierrez.

A gale was making and the bottom was beyond our fathoming, and yet The Anointed would dare beguile mankind that he saw a light— like a taper of wax that rose and fell.

He summonsed Pedro Gutierrez (or so he recorded) and that toady vouched the light and then the admiral sought confirmation from Rodrigo Sanchez of Segovia, bookkeeper for the expedition and a crony of Gutierrez.

Rodrigo Sanchez denied the light, and every man of the expedition was watching for signs and yet only the admiral saw the light and it rising and falling like a candle.

A candle in a gale? *Non sequitur. Non nobis Domine.*

Then fishermen, perhaps, and they with a torch. Or so Columbus hinted when all wise men scoffed his perfidy.

Men do not fish in a gale on fathomless seas.

Then a fire on land?

By the torch of St. Elmo! If his ship were near enough to land to see a fire, why did he not show his signal? Nay, I say, and this to you and to all men, it will not carry, it will not hold. He dared not signal, for it was a false landfall, and by his own law a false landfall would have denied him the reward.

And now hear this: why did he not come about if he saw a light? A gale and his ship to the lee of strange lands and mayhaps reefs? Even the weanlings of sailorfolk know that a ship must be brought about in the lee of unmarked shores. But he plunged on.

There was no Light of San Salvador, neither an illusion, but only an evil lie.

Of these events we of the *Pinta* knew naught at that time; we were in the rigging and at every vantage point and scanning the sea. The moon came up bright and our *Pinta* was leading the others and the *Nina* was to port and close upon us and the *Santa Maria* was to starboard and half a league aft.

My watch was called on the twenty-third hour, and this two glasses before midnight, and I went straightway to my lookout at the bow and there, his duties slack, The Rabbit did join me and we made converse, the nature of which I do not recall.

The sand flowed into the first hour of the new day—the Friday of October 12 and the third and last day since the promise—and all men exceedingly watchful and some in the rigging and others on the forecastle and the ratings on the quarter-deck.

Long the minutes and wild the sea, and wide, and The Rabbit did leave me then and went to the glass and turned it and chanted:

> *"Good is that which passeth,*
> *Better is that which cometh."*

I was alone and the moon was wasting to the port quarter and then, blessed be the grace of the Almighty, the faint glimmer dead ahead.

My eyes froze to the spot and an ague was upon me and I trembled to give tongue and, yet, I doubled my senses.

Then a smear gleaming in the moonlight and that surely sand and the waves pounding high; and God gave me voice and I turned to the quarter-deck and shouted: *"Tierra! Tierra!"*

The Rabbit bounded to my side and I was shivering my agitation and he saw also, and he called: "Land! By the blood of God. It is land!"

He ran below to break the tidings to Arcos and then the Pinzons were at my side and many of my shipmates and they all were screaming, and Captain Pinzon did command the pilot to bring her about, and did command his brother Francisco to break out the signals and Juan Quintero to fire the bombard.

The echo boomed into the night and then did the *Nina* discharge her bombard as testimony that she, too, had seen, and the *Santa Maria* came up fast, and hard about, and Christopher Columbus greeted my captain:

"Aye, Martin Alonso Pinzon, you have found land!"

My captain answered, "Sire, my reward is not lost."

And Columbus replied, "I give you 10,000 maravedis as a present."

Then did my captain embrace me and say for all to hear: "Rodrigo of Triana, I and all this company do bear witness to your triumph. Andalusia is your servant and your father will bless his seed."

The velvet doublet was mine and the Queen's pension to honor it, and on this fortune I thought and mayhaps with unseeming pride, but, before God, on another thing thought I more: I had seen it first—the new hive for the swarming bees.

# CHAPTER 16

E JUDGED WE WERE FIVE MILES OFFSHORE AND THERE WAS no leisure for gala, for the ships must be served else they, being in the lee, blow onto shoals. Therefore, we furled all sails except the main-course and braced its yard and did jog on-and-off in strait tacks and with the wind abeam.

A south drift caught us, and this not worrisome, and at dawn we were off a southeast jut of rocks and reefs and the land either an island or a peninsula. This brought spirited speculation that we had arrived at Cipango or the mainland of Cathay and we expected soon to be greeted by a Khan and to be borne to his palace in litters of gold and ivory, and there to disport ourselves.

No craft met us and we were near unto the land and no cities in view, so we made sail and did move west and then north around the shore, and the land surely a small island, and we did come windward and into a cove and there dropped anchors in five fathoms.

It was done. *Gloria Tibi, Domine.*

We were thirty-three days out of the Canaries and seventy days out of Palos, and Captain Pinzon did order a brimming cup of wine for each man and we toasted our health, for the expedition had crossed the Ocean Sea without ailment or accident to any man.

And then we raised our cups to the land and saluted it, and this with strange forebodings as no living signs bestirred, neither smoke, nor man or beast. This then the Indies, this sandy waste in a sapphire sea?

It came to me, in the desolation of my doubts and bewilderment, the wisdom of Benjamin Marino (Aye, Mita, it is true) that not the

Indies lay 700 leagues from Spain, but *terra incognita*, an unknown land—a new world.

On these things I was cogitating and then people, or creatures, did creep timorously to the beach and did peer at us across the narrow water, and they were unlike any people I had ever seen.

Small were they and armed with pointed sticks, almost spear length, and a few with blowguns, and of color they were light brown and more like the Guanches of the Canary Islands than the Eastern folk of Marco Polo's accounts. The women were wholly naked and most comely (we had been at sea a long time) and the men wore cod bags to protect their genitals, and these cloths were their only raiment.

They made no warlike gestures, only staring at us, and Columbus ordered the bombards manned and then three parties to shore in the tenders. Arcos was chosen, and I, and The Rabbit did leap into our tender and grin at Pinzon, and the captain let him be and we pulled for shore.

We all were sworded and the admiral in his most edifying apparel and holding firm the Royal Banner. Our Pinzon also did carry a standard, the Green Cross, which bore the initials of Ferdinand and Isabel.

Our boats scraped the beach and we leapt out and the strange creatures did flee and then peered at us from the brush, and Columbus raised high his hand, and we to our knees, and he did pray:

"O Lord, eternal and almighty God, by Thy sacred word Thou hast created the heavens, the earth, and the sea; blessed and glorified be Thy name and praised be Thy majesty, who hath designed to use Thy humble servant to make Thy sacred name known and proclaimed in this other part of the world."

The natives, witnessing our peaceful intent, did venture closer to us and we saw that their heads were pressed flat and to a bulge at their foreheads and The Rabbit did ogle the women, and they to giggling, and Pinzon did scowl the little scamp into behavior meet for the circumstances.

In ceremony most fitting, and raising his sword as the Cross and kissing it, the Admiral of the Ocean Sea and Viceroy of all lands discovered did christen this island San Salvador, and summonsed he Rodrigo de Escobedo, the secretary of the expedition, and Rodrigo Sanchez, the comptroller, and they, with quills and inkhorn, did write down his words; and therewith and under our witness he claimed possession of this land for our Sovereigns and these people for their subjects.

Now, even the dullards of our company were confused by this perpetration, for if this land be the Indies then it belonged to the Grand Khan and these people were his subjects, and we were not armed sufficiently to tilt with Cathay's navy or to enforce our will in any manner whatsoever against a prince of any power.

We had come as friends to barter and to make treaties, and yet we had seized.

In this conundrum, many of us assumed a secret agreement between the admiral and our Sovereigns and if Spain was to be served and her glory furthered, then our duty was to obey and riddle ourselves not in the machinations of diplomacy.

The natives, proclaimed Indians by Columbus, were most curious of our behavior during our prayers and ceremonies and crept quite close to us and I smelled them, and their odor neither offensive nor enticing, and then several of them did jabble at us and made gestures toward the heavens.

Columbus ordered his interpreter, the converso Luis de Torres, to make converse with them and he spoke all of his tongues, even Arabic, and they understood him not. And some of them did disappear and returned shortly with more of their kind and some of them had painted faces and streaks of black and yellow and red across their cheeks.

So docile were they, so childlike, that the admiral gave them little red caps and glass beads and they grunted their delight and fetched us viands, and these being fish and a succulent lizard which they called iguana and a most tasty meat which we learned later was dog.

Again Columbus sought to make discourse with them and asked of their king and of gold and they did stare at him and feel his raiment, and one of them came close to me and fingered my gorro and touched my poniard and I smiled at him and he did smile at me, and I knew there was no malice in them, only simplicity.

The day was waning and it was too late for exploration and the admiral rested on the beach and talked to the Pinzons concerning the natives, saying they would make good servants in Spain and that he would arrest some of them, both men and women, and return them to Spain that they might learn our language and then be fetched back to spread the True Faith and to serve our Sovereigns.

"They are simple people," he said, "and our Highnesses may wish to have all of them borne to Castile or keep them all captives on the island. Fifty armed men can keep them under our sway and make them do all our blessed Sovereigns may desire."

No man raised issue with the admiral, and quite naturally, and yet there were many doubts. If these Indians be subjects of the Grand Khan, then whyfor seize them and bear them away? Slavery be slavery under any appellation. Therefore, if they be subjects of the Grand Khan and this be the Indies, then the admiral was advocating a belligerent foray against the Khan whom he was seeking for trade and treaties.

And now wherefore he had claimed this island for Spain, these people were subjects of our Sovereigns and themselves Spaniards; and Spaniards are not slaves. Was he suggesting slavery upon subjects of our Crowns? Do you wonder then that doubts burdened us, and confusion? But, aroint, Christopher Columbus was a master of confusion and this a deliberate tack that he personally, and his brother, Bartholomew, and his chosen coterie, might profit from intricacies of his own making.

During this interval I was nigh unto the admiral and did hope that he would greet me and, in the presence of those assembled, honor me for my triumph and vouchsafe the pension and the doublet upon our return to Spain. Yet he heeded me not and this, for truth, of no concern to me as I knew him to be troubled by problems of more consequence to him than my reward.

The twilight was upon us, the pink of evening, and we returned to our ships and the Indians kindled fires on the beach and many of them stayed the night by their fires and watched our ships, and these people truly guileless Arcadians and befitting of Christian fellowship and never of Christian bondage.

At dawn the he folk swarmed into the cove and to our ships, many swimming and others in dugouts fashioned from boles of trees, and they climbed aboard and cavorted most joyously and did beg trinkets of us.

The admiral, in the *Santa Maria*'s tender, set forth to explore the coast line and, ever suspicious, forbade us the land in his absence, but soon he was returned, as the island was very small, and then our parties to shore again and to exploration of the island.

We found a lake of considerable dimension and an elevation, and from its top we could see all the island and it only about ten miles long and five miles wide. Our men were divided into small parties, and mine under Juan de Umbria, and we explored southward and came upon a village, and maidens here gave themselves to us in wanton abandon.

We rendezvoused at the cove and the admiral in a froth as he strove to make talk with the Indians and eventually, through arduous endeavor and by signs, we gained knowledge that the island was one of many thereabouts and that the enemies of these people lived to the south and were called Caribes; and that these Caribes did eat human flesh.

It was at this time that one of the Indians approached Diego Harana and, in buffoonery, wiggled the marshal's sword, and the other Indians had childish glee at their comrade's antics, as though they thought the sword a tail and their countryman a jester indeed and, also, a bold fellow.

Diego Harana, the insufferable dolt, then did unsheathe his sword and, in jest, did point it at the simple fellow and even suffered him to grasp the naked blade; and then did the Indian shriek his surprise and pain, and stare at the blood from his fingers.

May it be recorded that Columbus, to his merit, rebuked his marshal scathingly and sought to alleviate the Indian's hurt, but the sufferer withdrew from us and his people gathered around him and were frightened as they looked at his wound and then at us.

And thus it was that the trust was broken, that the unspoken covenant was sundered. If we be deities, we were gods of trickery and pain, and their idolatry became doubts and their faith became fears.

Thereafter they shunned us and, to our questions, always waved their arms to the south and west and this to have us begone forever. Gold? To the south and west. The Grand Khan to the south and west. Only flee us, they seemed to say. Begone and away.

Then Columbus had six of them seized and detained aboard the flagship as guides and we did depart that island, named for the gentle Savior, on the Sabbath afternoon of October 14, and sailed southwest for Cipango or Cathay.

That same afternoon, and quite late, we sighted another small island and we lay to that night and one of the captives from San Salvador leapt overboard and escaped. The next day we explored the shore line and the admiral named the island Santa Maria de la Concepcion[1] and this for the disputed doctrine of the immaculate conception of the Virgin in her mother's womb, a tenet that Columbus accepted and hoped some day would be dogma.

We went ashore the next day, and another of our captives did escape, and we found that island to be like San Salvador, and the natives, warned by those who had escaped us, waved to the south and west when we asked of gold and Cipango and Cathay. We tarried there only a day and straightway sailed to a larger island, and this close by, and Columbus did name it Fernandina,[2] and the Indians thereof paddled out to meet us and we gave them trinkets and molasses, and this muchly prized as their only sweetening was wild honey.

The people of Fernandina were more numerous and more sedentary than those of San Salvador and their thatched huts were quite snug, and this a blessing inasmuch as rain wetted us every day and this wet season a blight of these climates.

On this island we saw no animals except dogs, but many strange things we did see and among these was cotton ripe in the boll and a tall grass that fruited to an ear, and this a grain of some kind that was esteemed by the Indians as a nutriment.

Now, none of these marvels did Columbus take aboard, for on Fernandina did we see the first trinket of gold and this a nose ornament in possession of a native. All else was forgotten as this fellow was questioned and our excitement surely frightened the people as they, too, waved us to the south and west and babbled of the lands of Colba[3] and Bohio.[4]

Was Colba Cipango? And mayhaps Bohio was the fabled Quinsay[5] and then surely Cathay was nigh.

We were eager to be away, but tarried on Fernandina long enough to impress guides into our service and to explore a village, and in this village we saw our first hammock.

Now, this utility was a sling and loosely woven and suspended between posts and some of them large enough to sleep two or three persons. Cool and strong they were and most restful, and it was Gomez

[1]Now the island of Rum Cay.
[2]Long Island in the Bahamas.
[3]Cuba.
[4]Haiti.
[5]Hongkong.

228

Rascon, our droll little Rabbit, who fetched the hammock to the *Pinta* and slung it on deck and rested therein like a potentate, and took it down and stowed it when the deck was busy.

We weighed anchors from Fernandina on October 17 and went seeking Colba and Bohio and that night I did approach Captain Pinzon and did converse with him concerning my promised rewards of the Queen's pension and the velvet doublet, and expounded to him that the admiral had not mentioned these things to me and that almost a week had passed since my triumph. My captain lulled my impatience and pacified my apprehensions by explanation that Columbus could not bestow the rewards until we returned to Spain and that his mind now was troubled with matters of more import.

I should fret not, the captain said and in utmost sincerity, for every man of the expedition knew that I had sighted land first and that my prizes would be forthcoming at the proper time and place.

This reassured me and willingly did I put my back to my shipboard tasks and kept an astute lookout on my night watch as we sailed from Fernandina. The Rabbit slung his hammock on the forecastle and slept therein and, my watch done, I pledged him a blanca for its use for a week and rested myself in its comforts.

Your patience, my readers, shall be spared details of the next ten days, when we did sail by and to numerous little islands, and one liken unto the next and none with gold or jewels, and on October 27 we made landfall and the Indian guides did assure us that is was Colba, which land I hereafter will call Cuba, inasmuch as that is more nearly the pronunciation the Indians gave it, than Colba with its Spanish resonance.

Spirited were we in anticipation of the morrow when we would land, for the admiral was convinced that at last we were at Cipango and that we would be welcomed by potentates and honored in cities of gold and glitter, and that we would burden our ships with jewels and spices and aloes.

We anchored in a river soon after sunrise of Sunday, October 28. There were birds to greet us, and nothing else.

A brooding verdancy had this Cuba, and flowers and fruits along the river, but no potentates to welcome us, no cities to shelter us. No alabaster; only mud. Marco Polo had written of trumpets and temples, but we heard only the sweet calls of birds and saw only the forest before us and a mountain in the distance.

The humors of the men and of the captains were seized of melancholia and doubts, but the admiral himself was not depressed, which is to say visibly, and ordered a landing party to the tenders, and this done and we did row up the river and there found a village of thatched huts, and no inhabitants thereof.

In the huts were primitive fishhooks of bone and, roaming the village, were sulky yellow dogs that barked not, only emitting a strange grunt and this most unnatural.

No sheep. No goats. Nay, naught except the thatched huts and the dogs, and the birds calling from lofty trees, and a soft rich earth under our tread. Then did I refresh my memory of all that Marco Polo had written of Cathay and of all that Benjamin Marino had said of a new world, and I knew not what to believe, but one thing I knew in that hour and at that place: Cuba was not Cipango, neither Cathay.

The men were most forlorn and dispirited. The vastness and the silence awed us and Columbus himself was downcast, yet this he strove to conceal from us and ordered us back to the ships and there announced that Quinsay was to the west.

"By the wrinkled pickle of St. James the Lesser——" The Rabbit shrilled his oath. "That madman knows not where he is."

Arcos cuffed his cheeks and reviled him. "Give your words to prayers, you loathsome wart, and not to blasphemy."

And, a light wind having sprung up, the admiral set us to sail and we crawled west and at vespers of that same day, and it Monday, October 29, we came to a large river and a bay thereto and here we found an Indian village and the people as simple as guileless as those on San Salvador, and their language and customs the same. We took food and women for our pleasures and searched thereabouts for gold, and there was no gold.

Now one of these Indians was more alert than the others and we showed him pieces of gold and, by signs and gestures, he indicated that his Khan and gold were to the west. Therewith the fellow was taken as interpreter, and know you that this is the Indian who returned willingly to Spain with the admiral to be christened Diego Columbus (James Dove) in honor of the admiral's legitimate son.

We weighed and windwarded west along the coast of Cuba until a north wind came upon us and, it being dangerous to skirt land to our port with the wind northward, Columbus properly did command us about and we scudded back to the river and arrived there on November 1.

The moon was coming full and the admiral took position by fixing on the North Star, or what he thought was the North Star, and, judging its altitude with his quadrant, determined our position to be in lattitude 42 degrees north[6]; and this estimate, naturally, in the manner of Ptolemy's ancient reckoning by climates and winds. And now hear this: he also determined that we had wested 3600 miles from the Canaries.

Even the gromets of our company were aware that something was wrong. We had not sailed 3600 miles. And we could not be as far north as the admiral adjudged, for we had sailed due west from the Canaries and those islands are south and west of Spain.

By the holy mantle of the Chosen! The world was upside down.

The Pinzons did plead with Columbus that his quadrant was faulty and this he resented and particularly any suggestion from Alonso Pinzon.

Juan de la Cosa, the master and owner of the *Santa Maria*, did submit that what seemed to be the North Star was not the North Star at all, but one of the guards.

The admiral scorned all counsel and majestically did proclaim that we were not on Cipango at all, but on the mainland and in Cathay. Therefore, the Grand Khan must be nigh, and his cities of gold and alabaster. In the name of the seven devils cast out, how mad is madness!

Sharply did he interrogate the natives and they gestured what he wanted to hear: that the golden capital of Cathay was only a short march away and that there the Grand Khan awaited the pleasure of Spain's noble viceroy. Columbus asked of *El Gran Can*, the great king, and the Indians replied "*Cuba nacan*," which we know now to mean the center of that section of Cuba.

So an expedition was arranged to march to the golden city and inform the great king that Spain's envoy awaited a visit of state, for Christian viceroy must not go to heathen king; the king must come to him.

Luis de Torres, the converso, was chosen to lead this expedition because he understood and spoke Hebrew, Aramaic, and some Arabic and it was he who chose me because I, too, knew Arabic as well as

[6]This position would have placed the expedition off Boston.

Latin. Then he chose Rodrigo de Jerez, who had visited in Guinea. Our Indian interpreter, later to be named Diego Columbus, also was selected, as was one of the Indian captives from San Salvador.

The admiral did ready us with all manner of diplomatic means, and these including a letter from Ferdinand and Isabel, a passport, an image of the Virgin as a gift to the king, and beads to trade for food and maybe gold. We departed our comrades the morning of November 2 and with instructions to return within six days.

By the breasts of Khadija, who comforted the Messenger and tested the Angel! We were going to see the king.

All that day we walked through a valley of loveliness and by fields cultivated to cotton and to the tall grass of the yellow fruit.[7] I sought aloes and found an abundance of prickly plants that resembled common aloes, albeit not the Medusa, and tasted them and determined them useless.[8] Also did I find a viney plant which roots tasted of cinnamon and chestnuts.[9]

And a measure of all these marvels I gathered for myself to take to my father. There were Indians in the fields and they did gather around us and impede our progress, and they bowed down to us.

But hold! And hear this, and this I swear: these farmers did dry a weed and roll its leaves into a little faggot which they called tabacos, and one end of the faggot the user inserted into his nose and lighted the thing and did breathe the smoke thereof.

They pressed lighted tabacos upon us and Luis de Torres and I, being Andalusians and nothing daunted, inhaled the smoke and straightway were seized into a spasm of coughing and then into a dizziness that lightened our heads and mellowed our humors, and then to vomiting. Surely this weed was a drug and all the natives used it and perchance that accounted for their debility, for, indeed, they were a fragile people; seemingly not ill and yet never robust.

I chose one of the most stalwart as my carrier and intrusted to him the marvels I gathered, and these being three hammocks and many tabacos in addition to other things.

We slept the night in a farmer's hut and insects swarmed upon us and bit us, and willingly came maidens to us and I occupied one and

[7]Corn.

[8]Agave, the common century plant.

[9]Yams.

232

then she did remain awake all night and fan the insects from my flesh.

The birds called at dawn and the maids fetched food to us and lighted tabacos and I did shun the firebrands and brushed the lice from my garments and made myself ready for the journey. Runners preceded us and gallantly we marched into the golden city of Cathay.

It was a village of thatched huts and insects and stench and the king awaited us in the largest hut. His crown was a feather and his raiment was a cod bag of crude cotton and he smiled at us and we gave him the image of the Virgin and asked of gold, and he stared at the image and put it aside and held out his hands for beads.

Gold? He repeated the word after us and his people did laugh. He knew not its meaning and neither they.

Luis de Torres wept and I, too, was most downcast and, being a man of compassionate bent, my commiseration went out to Christopher Columbus, for never had man come so far to find so little, never had man been so wrong.

We did not present our passport to the Indian potentate, neither our letter from Ferdinand and Isabel. But Torres addressed him in many tongues and the prince and his people beamed upon us and begged beads. Then our interpreter spoke and through infinite patience, an art that Columbus never practiced, we learned that the prince was the chieftain of all people thereabouts and we showed him a bit of gold and, upon seeing it, he and many of his people set up a clamor and were sorely afraid and waved wildly toward the east and jabbered of Caribes and Canibales and Bohio. Also they did speak of Babeque and we took their signs to mean that on Babeque the Indians gathered gold on the beach and hammered it into bars.

The chieftain ordered a feast for us, and the food was beans and roasted dog, and did tell us his wish to return to the river with us and himself see our winged ships and our viceroy, and mayhaps beg more beads.

We consented and he bowed to us and did grant his people the boon of kissing our feet and ordered a hut for each of us, and I to the largest for he took me to be our leader, and this natural inasmuch as my bearing was more impressive than the others'.

And that night the chieftain himself did give me my choice of his village's jewels—the maids who tended the needs of the unwed men.

No gold in Cuba, but many jewels. *Ilias malorum.*

233

*M*Y LORD, DON CHRISTOPHER COLUMBUS, ADMIRAL OF THE Ocean Sea and Viceroy of the Indies, could not bring himself to accept our report of failure until we presented the chieftain to him and then he sunk into a despondency and into the misanthropism that, forsooth, was a part of his nature.

The ships had been careened for cleaning and he fêted the chieftain aboard the *Santa Maria* and interrogated him most tenaciously and the simple Indian, in bewilderment, offered Columbus tabacos in lieu of gold, and these the admiral scorned.

Furthermore, he instructed all of us to shun the tabacos and pronounced the herb a parlous drug and ordered that none be returned to Spain. He knew not of my tabacos, now safely in my sea chest, nor of my other marvels, nor of several hammocks I had concealed in the *Pinta's* forecastle.

His humors, steeped in the brew of his failures, were most vile and then he ascended into the isolation of his mysticism and communed with his saints and gave himself to long vigils at prayer and meditation. The men chafed and the captains were harassed.

They, too, believed in prayer and they, too, loved the saints, but the hour of decision was nigh. The expedition had failed, for, despite our courage and forbearance, we had found nought except silvan isles and heathen Arcadians. Our Sovereigns, both addicts to parsimony, surely would credit the expedition to folly and chance and tie their purses against any further exploration in these parts.

Therefore, the captains talked among themselves and Columbus did sense the winds and he came from out his reverie and assembled the company and faced us all. His long white hair had grown to his shoulders and his blue eyes were serene although wrinkles had gathered at their corners.

"Know you this," he spake to us. "These lands are peopled by creatures who know not the True Faith and it behooves us here, and our Sovereigns in Spain, to disseminate the Word of God to all these islands."

He was shaping a plea to justify his failure, a case to lay before the Crowns. No gold, nay, but always the Gospel.

"Now, you, all of you, bear witness to the submissiveness of these people and know you that these lands can furnish servants to Spain. I will arrest some of these people and take them to Spain as evidence of their servility and, to keep them content, we will seize several heads of women, as we have learned in our experience with blacks from Guinea that men servants are more tractable if their womenkind are with them."

Slavery. By any other word, it still was slavery. First the Cross and then the Crown of Thorns, for if the True Message would not impress the Crowns then slavery might. The riches of our Indies was bondage. No spices, but sweat. No gold, but chains. And all in the name of God.

And then in the fervor of his zeal Christopher Columbus did pledge all of us to a vow that Cuba was a part of a mainland, and if this be a mainland then Cipango was eastward, and surely Bohio if not Babeque,[1] where natives picked gold from the beach and rolled it into bars.

The captains, led by Alonso Pinzon, demanded a conference with the admiral and straightway they went to his quarters on the *Santa Maria* and I know not what transpired at the meeting although I heard angry shouts, and our Pinzon's the loudest of all. He was exasperated and this we all knew, and this we of the *Pinta* understood, for Pinzon was an Andalusian and given never to indecision as was that Genoese charlatan.

Columbus fattened on confusion, but it sickened Pinzon and, therefore, our captain did beard the admiral. I know not what was said, what threats were spaken or promises made, but I do know that after the conference Columbus masqueraded a martyrdom and unctuously pro-

[1]Great Inagua Island.

claimed in wheedling self-pity that the expedition would sail for Babeque and thence to Bohio.

A council of Indians boarded the *Santa Maria* to bid him farewell and he did kidnap five of them and sent a raiding party ashore to seize several heads of women, and the band taken numbered seven heads of women and three heads of children; and we departed that place on Monday, November 12.

For many days, eight as I recall, we sailed along the east coast of Cuba and into coves and rivers, seeking gold and finding none, and all the time feeling for a wind to take us to Babeque, and we were full at sea and bearing for that place when a dangerous sea made up to the east and Columbus signaled us to turn back for Cuba, and this we did and then the wind shifted and blew northeast and Pinzon swung our *Pinta* until she caught the wind, and we were away for Babeque.

That, I remember well, was the dawn watch of November 22. The moon was wasting and clouds were low and all lookouts were alerted as the wind was brisk and the sea running. The *Santa Maria* was perhaps a mile away when we came about and the *Nina* even nearer, and I saw no signals.

Now this is the hour in which Columbus pleads that Alonso Pinzon deserted him, that our captain broke away and dashed for Babeque to snatch the gold and then to sail for Spain and usurp the triumph.

Inane flummery! Think you that Pinzon would desert his own blood, they of the *Nina*? His own brother, Vicente Pinzon? Then you know not Andalusians.

The wind was right and we thought the *Santa Maria* and the *Nina* would follow us as Babeque was the announced destination of the expedition. All that morning and far into the afternoon the *Santa Maria* and the *Nina* were in sight and we saw no signal nor heard one, neither smoke nor bombard.

So let Columbus whine his calumny. We made Babeque because our captain was a better sailor and took the wind while the *Santa Maria* luffed and dared not the sea, and Columbus kept the brave little *Nina* at his side.

And now we did make Babeque in two days' sailing and there found the natives as primitive as those of Cuba and straightway Pinzon gave them beads and bells and dispatched them over the island with letters to be given to Columbus if he came that way en route to Bohio. Then we sought gold and, again, there was no gold.

But this we did see: the Indians bearing torches at night and walking the edge of the sea and catching fish, and these fish they threw on the beach and other Indians rolled them into a substance and this they roasted over an open fire. The gold on the beach was the food of the sea and thereafter we roasted fish and called this method of cooking after the isle of Babeque.

And we did depart that place on November 30 and did sail southeast and in two days were skirting the coast of Bohio, seeking anchorage and hopefully sight of the *Santa Maria* and the *Nina*.

We came safely offshore from a lofty prominence which, from the sea, resembled a tent, and east therefrom we found a river and there did anchor and our captain named the discovery Rio de Martin Alonso in his own honor.

Indians swarmed to the roadstead to watch us and ere we landed we knew they were different from all others we had seen, for the natives of Bohio had bows and arrows and their bearing bespake dignity.

And many of them wore trinkets of gold.

Our prayers of gratitude ascended to heaven at sight of this gold and hurriedly we made a camp and then to intercourse with the natives. We gave them beads and asked of the gold and they were most cautious, albeit friendly, and spake no directions until their prince arrived, and he was called the cacique and was as naked as they.

A trader of more finesse than the Genoese, our captain did not press the cacique concerning gold, but first fêted him aboard the *Pinta* and sought intelligence of Columbus and the other ships, and then he wrote letters and the cacique dispatched them to all the villages of his domain with instructions that the messages be given to the white gods should they appear.

Pinzon gave wine to his guest and the cacique smelled it and tasted it and spat it out, and then he invited our whole company to a gala in his village up-river and we drew lots to determine who would remain aboard and guard the ship. Arcos was among those who lost.

The Indians scorned our tender and fetched long canoes of the finest wood[2] I ever had seen and these we boarded in ceremony and soon we were skimming upstream like waterfowl. A league or so and the sea was behind us and we fast in the most lovely land of all the world. Tall were the mountains and wooded, and sweet the breezes,

[2]Mahogany.

and soon we were arrived at the village, and it a collection of thatched huts along the river. The feast was spread under the trees and I asked not what manner of meat we ate, assuming it was dog. Later I learned it was a large rodent.

We ate our fill and belched our appreciation and the Indians did likewise, and only then did Pinzon get to the matter at hand. He fingered a gold trinket in the cacique's nose and bespake more curiosity than desire and the cacique solemnly walked into his hut and returned with a handful of golden ornaments and I heard The Rabbit suck in his breath and saw his greedy little eyes bulge.

Pinzon scowled us to silence, and to open the trading he gave the cacique two tiny bells and to his amazement the cacique did give him two golden trinkets. Upon seeing the transaction, the other Indians pressed their gold upon us and demanded bells, and we fell briskly to trade: bells and beads for gold.

We asked the source of the gold, and politely of course, and they waved toward the mountains and said, "Cibao."

Each of us looked at the other. Cibao? Cipango? But if this be Cipango, then Columbus was right, and Cuba, to the west, was the mainland of Cathay. But if this be Cipango, we had discovered it and not he.

Pinzon requested the cacique to lead us to the mines of Cibao and he shook his head and explained that the mines were deep in the mountains and that the wet season had flooded the rivers and the way would not be open again until dry weather.

And many other things he made known to us: that this, too, was an island called both Cibao, meaning middle ground, and Bohio, meaning hut. There were more islands to the east and these the home of the awesome Canibales who devoured human flesh. I interpreted his gestures and grunts to mean that Cuba likewise was an island, but Pinzon took issue with me and accepted Columbus' dictum that Cuba was mainland.

We returned to the mouth of the river and made a camp and the Indians willingly erected thatched huts for us and were honored to serve us and we gave our days to the trading for their gold, and our nights to their maidens. Pinzon allowed each of us one half of the wealth we acquired and took one half for himself (or the Crowns) and this the way of all barter in new lands and acceptable to us.

December was running out and still no word of Columbus and we

239

fretted our fears that the others had returned to Spain, but Pinzon assured us that his brother Vicente never would sail the *Nina* homeward without first seeking us in every cove and inlet of this island. Fear not, he told us, and hold fast until we had word of the others and then we would find the mines of Cibao.

Christmas was a day of many devotions and much merriment and some of us were of minds to fête the Indians and give them beads, but Pinzon cautioned us against such extravagance inasmuch as our store of beads was running low, and our bells were almost gone.

And then the Feast of Epiphany graced us and that, quite naturally, was January 6 of 1493, and we were at tierce when the Indian runner brought news that a ship liken unto our *Pinta* had sunk on shoals to the west of us. We were away within an hour, but ere we departed, and this I journalize with heavy heart, Pinzon did emulate Columbus and kidnap six Indians. Outside the river we caught a fresh breeze and scudded west with every man at station and I on lookout at the forecastle bow.

The vesper watch was half away when we raised the *Nina* clawing to windward, and we scudding, and we gave vent to shouts. Gladsome were we at sight of that noble little Andalusian bird and, yet, a foreboding was upon us, for if a ship were down it must be the *Santa Maria*. Then what of the admiral and the others.

Gracefully we swept to starboard of the *Nina* and about, and there on her quarter was our lord Don Christopher, and Juan de la Cosa, and others of the flagship; and we did raise another shout and were exceedingly thankful that they had been spared.

We escorted the *Nina* to anchorage west of the prominence that resembled a tent and Columbus did greet us most affably, and there was no hint of virulence until he learned from us all that we had learned and only then did he call us traitors and lewd fellows, only then did he accuse us of deserting the expedition back off Cuba.

But what of his adventures? His triumphs and tragedies and the loss of the *Santa Maria*? I report these circumstances as they were reported to me by the Andalusians of the *Nina*:

After the ships were parted, and we for Babeque, the *Santa Maria* and the *Nina* explored the coast of Cuba and, finding nought of worth, sailed for Bohio, intending to try for Babeque from that quarter.

Eventually they touched at Bohio, after divers exploits and uneventful haps, at a point they named Puerto de San Nicolas and remained there only one night and thence to an anchorage that Columbus named Puerto de la Concepcion, but which the men called Mosquito Bay.

It was there, on December 12, that the admiral raised a Cross and assumed seizen of the island of Bohio and christened it La Isla Espanola[3] and this land properly called Hispaniola in Latin. They saw Indians there, but no gold for barter, and moved eastward along the coast, discovering bays and capes and valleys, and one they named Valle del Paraiso, the Valley of Paradise.

They did meet and fraternize with many Indians and came, on December 20, to a beautiful bay, which was named Santo Tomas, and there did encounter Indians with trinkets of gold, who joyously traded their wealth for bells and who burdened the white gods with gifts of food and cotton. And now it was from those Indians that they heard the story of the mines of Cibao and they, even as we, took Cibao to mean Cipango; and on December 24 they departed Santo Tomas and sailed east to spend Christmas Day with the Khan of Cipango.

That twilight of Christmas Eve they came to a rocky prominence that they named Punta Santa[4] and the wind died and the *Santa Maria* crept forward without soundings, off a strange shore and in the shadow of a headland.

The watch of the midnight hour was awakened and Don Christopher Columbus, Admiral of the Ocean Sea, betook himself to his couch, and to slumber. Master Juan de la Cosa also sought sleep and the flagship presumably was in the hands of a pilot.

The *Nina*, in the command of an Andalusian Pinzon, was sounding and all hands were on the alert, but the flagship drifted in and on the first hour of Christmas Day the *Santa Maria* ground onto a reef.

A gromet was the first to give tongue, screaming the alarm that brought the admiral and the master to the quarter. Columbus ordered the master and a crew to the tender that they might kedge her off. Juan de la Cosa had his own idea about that. The *Santa Maria* belonged to him and he had sailed her many years and understood her nature.

So he rowed to the *Nina* to determine if she could help—perhaps anchor fast and windlass the flagship free, but the *Nina* could not assist and launched her own tender. The reef quickly opened the

[3]Now the island of Haiti and Santo Domingo.
[4]Cape Haitien.

seams of the *Santa Maria* and it was too late to kedge her free, and Columbus and his men were rowed to the *Nina* and the flagship filled and settled in shallow water.

And, now, for this accident, the admiral did blame everyone save himself. He charged Juan de la Cosa with treason, yet dared not punish him. It was not treason; it was Genoese and Galician carelessness, and carelessness at sea is stupidity. Now hear this: the admiral even blamed the gromet who was on duty. Merciful Mother! Does an admiral blame a cabin boy, a king a page?

It was the Indians who served them best. They gathered on the beach and, at command of their cacique, paddled their long canoes to the *Santa Maria* and unloaded her and ferried the stores to the *Nina* and to shore and nothing was stolen, not even a needle.

Columbus wept and the cacique comforted him with promises of a feast, but most of all the Indian people comforted him by pressing gold upon him in exchange for bells.

Then Columbus went ashore and was fêted and traded for gold and was told that the mines of Cibao were in the mountains and could be reached when the rivers receded. It was then and there that he decided to establish a Spanish colony at that place and he proclaimed his plans and his men were dismayed.

The Admiral of the Ocean Sea had not been commissioned to colonize, but again the Fates had drawn him to their bosoms and nourished him. If Spaniards were left on Hispaniola then Spanish ships must return and since Columbus kept the journal and the charts only he knew the way. He was strengthening his case to come back to these lands even if the Queen was displeased with his discoveries. She could not abandon Spanish subjects on a far island.

And thus he spake to his men: "Our flagship was wrecked on the Holy Day of the Nativity. Was that not a sign from Heaven? Aye, it was the will of God that the *Santa Maria* be lost that we might here colonize and trade, and acquire gold and spices; and all the gain of this enterprise shall be spent for the conquest of Jerusalem and the recovery of the Holy Sepulchre."

Therewith he did order a fort built of timbers from the *Santa Maria* and a village thereabout and christened the place Puerto de la Navidad in honor of the Nativity.

He pleaded that the little *Nina* could not ship all the complement of the *Santa Maria* back to Spain and that those who remained on

Hispaniola would be richly rewarded. He could return Indian slaves to Spain, but there was no room for Spanish freemen.

By cajolery and promises, he secured a company to man the fort and this company numbered thirty-nine and included Diego Harana as commander, and Rodrigo de Escobedo, the secretary of the expedition and the one authority who might have had the ears of Our Highnesses, who might have revealed the perfidy of Christopher Columbus. The converso Luis de Torres also was to be left behind, as was Pedro Gutierrez, the man Columbus said also had seen the Light of San Salvador. Gutierrez was never to have opportunity to reveal his story in Spain, to speak for himself that he had seen the Light or to give the lie to his admiral.

Then on December 27 Indians brought word that our *Pinta* was anchored only two days to the east and Columbus did write a loving letter to our Pinzon and begged him to come to the fort that we all might be united again and enjoy the favors that Our Lord had shown us.

The messenger returned to the fort without delivering the letter. Then Columbus did strengthen the fort and equip it and took leave of his colonists and on Friday, January 4, the *Nina* weighed anchor and sailed east to find us.

We were reunited on January 6 as has been recounted heretofore.

The admiral was most benevolent to our captain until he gathered the reports of our exploits and fortunes and then did he turn vehemently on Alonso Pinzon and revile him and utter all manner of evil against him and against all of us of the *Pinta* and called us lewd fellows and mutineers.

Our Pinzon defended us and himself and tried to caution the admiral to reason and then warned him to discretion. "No Genoese adventurer calls an Andalusian a traitor to Spain!" I heard him say it.

Then all the Pinzon kinsmen spake confidence in their filiation and sided with our captain against the admiral and admonished Columbus to tend his tongue and temper, and take heed else the dissension wax into strife and the sailors relax all discipline.

Columbus sulked; and did seek sympathy from Bartholomew Roldan, a pilot of the *Nina*, and told him: "The Pinzons are a mutinous lot and an undisciplined people who will not obey my orders and who say many improper things against me. Therefore, we will make haste for home, for I will not suffer the deeds of lewd fellows devoid of virtue, who contrary to me who conferred honors upon them presume to do their own will."

Thereupon he demanded all the gold that we of the *Pinta* had traded for, and we surrendered only a part of it and Alonso Pinzon did not reveal our holdings. We turned eastward again on January 10 and anchored in Rio de Martin Alonso, which name Columbus spitefully changed to Rio de Gracia, and there he did order our captain to free our Indian captives and did send five of his Indians to the *Pinta*.

We moved eastward and Columbus trusted no man with his plans and we knew not that we were heading homeward. Both ships were leaking and Columbus blamed that on the workmen of Palos. We had been at sea more than five months, yet he blamed Palos for our leaking timbers.

The foremast of our *Pinta* was sprung and we needed a replacement, or surely time and place to repair it, and I assumed we soon would come to beach and caulk. But, nay, we sailed on and it was soon thereafter that we sighted the mermaids whose presence Columbus so gallantly proclaimed in fancy tales to our Queen. I saw the mermaids plainly. They were hideous and resembled sea beasts of some kind, and were grotesque and clumsy.[5]

On January 12 we anchored for a landing and a party was sent ashore for food and no sooner had they disbarked than a company of Indians ran out of the forest and discharged arrows at them.

A portent? Aye, an augury. This was the first time the natives had evidenced one scintilla of belligerence and it was obvious to all of us (save perhaps the admiral) that our ruthless behavior was bearing harvest, that word had spread to trust us never more. And we, true Spaniards, were leaving a company of compatriots on that land, with those people.

The arrows did no hurt and our party slashed a few backsides with their swords and the Indians howled and ran away, and all of us did sword ourselves and most of us joined our comrades on the beach, but the natives molested us no more and we named that bay the Place of the Arrows.

This was the spot to careen our ships and replace the *Pinta's* mast. Columbus gave no such order, however, and on the next day a cacique came bringing gifts of gold and cotton, and he told us the Isla de

[5]The mermaids were manatees, the seacows.

Caribe lay to the east, as did the island Matinino and it inhabited wholly by beautiful women, vertiable Amazons, who accepted visitations from men at one season each year, for the purpose of impregnation, and then drove the men away or killed them.

There was something sinister about this place and our men were uneasy and the admiral sensed the moods of the men and ordered us aboard our ships and we weighed anchors and were away, and the Place of the Arrows was the last land my feet trod in the New World.

We departed that place on January 16, 1493.

The admiral signaled the course as the northeast wind and one quarter of the east wind[6] and we all knew that we were homeward bound. *Ole!* And by the holy hump of the camel Al-Kaswa that bore The Messenger, if that Genoese sophist could sail a leaky *Nina* to Spain then we could sail a leaky *Pinta*, and the devil take the weakened mast.

We were northing steadily, long tacks to windward, and soon were in the floating meadow again and the moon new and our spirits high. We still were in the sea of grass when the moon came full on February 1 and the North Star was riding high. Then out of the meadow and the weather quite cool and there was much signaling between our *Pinta* and the *Nina*, and we set our course due east, and that on February 4.

And scarcely had Arcos settled her down before a northwest gale was upon us and our *Pinta* and the *Nina* verily seemed to rise in the sea and skim like birds.

From vespers of February 5 until vespers of February 6 we ran 198 miles and in four days did sail 600 miles, sometimes at eleven knots. The gale was light and we scudded fast and it was during this run that Captain Pinzon first mentioned his illness to us: that of nights he was seized of an ague and that of days his brow fevered.

His brother Francisco compelled him to his couch and soon thereafter the gale eased off and we fixed our position as east of Madeira, although now we know that we were east of the Azores and much farther north than we had reckoned.

A lazy weather was upon us and it was during this lull that Columbus contrived his letter to Luis de Santangel, the King's Minister of Finance, an affirmation designed for public consumption that the

[6]This course would have taken them to the Arctic Ocean.

245

people might encourage the Queen to continue exploration of the admiral's Indies.

This artifice was dated "Off the Canaries," although he was nowhere near the Canaries, and the letter did expound eloquently, albeit deceitfully, on the wealth of the discoveries and on marvels that no eyes had seen, nay, neither the dream-stuff eyes of that visionary Genoese.

Cautiously did he conceal all routes and distances lest some adventurer seek his prizes, and he assured Santangel, and, hence, the people, that the *Santa Maria* was left at Navidad for the colonists. This, some say, proved him a man of tact, a diplomat, but I say there were prayers on the lips of Christopher Columbus and a lie in his heart.

Our Pinzon, and may God rest his soul, took not quill in hand to exalt himself, but lay sick acouch and demanded frequent reports on the weather and the condition of his ship.

The weather began making up on February 12 and ere twilight the sea was to tempest and our foremast snapped like a twig. Pinzon, despite the protests of all, took command on the quarter and showed his distress signal and the *Nina* answered, although, of course, she could not serve us, for the sea was running wild and the wind was rising.

Pinzon ordered dry trees and we bared the main and mizzen masts and let her run before the wind and then he commanded us to clear the wreckage of the foremast, and it was done. All the night he stood his quarter and the wind like demons and, sensing our apprehension, he led us in prayers and held us steady, even though he was near to faint and could take no nourishment except watered wine and a few garlic cloves.

The storm mounted the next day and the waves broke over us and our *Pinta* took them bow on and shivered, and every pump sucking to keep her afloat. Pinzon ordered a small course slung low on the mainmast to lessen the strain on that pole and we scudded madly.

And then flares did show on the *Nina* and we answered in kind and the night was about us and the storm full upon us; and the *Nina* vanished into the abyss of darkness. Again Pinzon led us in prayer and this time for the *Nina*, for his blood kin were aboard her.

Throughout that night and all the next day we were in the palm of the Almighty and Pinzon had himself lashed to his quarter-deck and, by the grace of God, he did bring us through the storm and the wind moderated on the compline watch, even as Chico and The Rabbit were leading us into the Salve Regina.

We bore our captain to his cabin and he almost delirious and burning of fever, but he ordered the course pricked and commanded, "On the east wind. Due east for Spain."

I attended him often in the days that followed, and the weather mild, and he did encourage me to fret not that I might be denied the rewards I had won. For, he told me, if the *Nina* be lost, then he and all the others would bear witness that I had seen land first and had earned the Queen's pension, and that he, Alonso Pinzon, would see to it that the mayor of Palos or the mayor of Lepe awarded me a velvet doublet for the honor I had brought to the Niebla.

And many other things did he tell me: that he had underwritten a share of the voyage and would have his share of the honors; that if the admiral were lost, then he himself would present the facts at court; and that if the admiral were alive and attempted deceit in Spain, then he, a Pinzon and an Andalusian of merit and station, would press for an audience with the Crowns.

He said to me: "I have neither royal office nor appointment, but I need neither leave nor license to communicate with my Sovereigns. The truth shall be revealed and all proper honors and prizes shall be bestowed."

The winter sea began making up again and the winds to howl and we all knew that our *Pinta* could not weather another storm and so, with prudence to the devil, we gave her sail and dressed her full and scudded as no ship had scudded before, and dashed frantically for home.

It was February 26 and the sky low and a gale biting at our heels, and God did bless us through The Rabbit and give that hellborn imp good eyes and voice and caused him to see land and to give loud tongue. "Spain! Spain!" he shrieked. And there she lay, the rocky coast of Galicia, and all of us to our knees in thanksgiving for our deliverance, for hallowed Palos was south around Portugal and only 400 miles away.

A new age was on our sails, a new world in our knowledge and we headed hard in, and the foam was splashing our *Pinta's* bow; and we the first of the bees back home again.

We made the little port of Bayona, not far from Vigo, and the Galicians doubted our exploits until we showed them the Indians we had fetched and our other marvels, and then they set up a clamor of excitement and believed all of our tales and even The Rabbit's fable of women with nipples of pearls.

There was no news of the *Nina*.

Pinzon was taken ashore and he was wan and near unto collapse and yet he insisted on an audience with Bayona's mayor and did proclaim for all to hear that Don Christopher Columbus had discovered the Indies to the west and that we were his associates and maychance the only survivors of the expedition.

The court of Isabel and Ferdinand was at Barcelona, and that city more than 800 miles overland, and ere Pinzon surrendered himself to the ministration of physicians he requested quills and inkhorn and composed a letter to the Sovereigns and put forth all intelligence and informed them that, within a few days, he would proceed to Palos and there await their pleasure.

Then he put himself into the care of physicians and they announced his disease as of miasmal nature and bled him and treated him with herbs and frog entrails, and we were given the liberty of Bayona and were honored in all manners of drink and food and song.

Arcos sought a soft couch and The Rabbit a public house, but I to a public bath and there saw myself in a mirror. My hair was as thick as a ram's winter coat and long to my shoulders and was browned almost to black. My skin was bronze brown, as brown as the fine wood of the long canoes of Cibao, and my shoulders swelled my jacket.

I did have myself shaven clean and my hair trimmed to a straight line across my forehead and then full over my ears and sharp and straight around my neck, in the manner of Pinzon, and I purchased a leathern jacket and stout breeches, and shoes to cover my calloused feet.

From many towns thereabouts came multitudes to honor us and to see our marvels, and The Rabbit regaled them with fanciful tales, but I restrained myself within the dignity that behooves the one who first had seen land and I was pointed out as The One.

Our time in Bayona was two weeks, and yet no news of the *Nina*, and then Pinzon was strong enough to stand his quarter, albeit still wan and drawn, and we sailed from that place on March 12 and into contrary winds off Portugal.

But our *Pinta* was snug again and our foremast had been replaced, and we gave no concern to the running sea but curved the waters for home and then raised Cape St. Vincent and the Saltes bar, and across the bar and into the blessed Tinto and there La Rabida on the hill and the smoke of old Quemadero from the meadow, for this was Faggot Day—Friday, March 15.

And there Palos and there the miracle, for the *Nina* was creeping to berth, her sails furled and her anchors splashing.

Aye, it is so. There she lay; to Palos an hour before we and all hands safe.

All Palos was at the water front and cheering and all thought we had arrived together and none suspecting that we had been separated for a month. Columbus looked back at us, staring at us as though our *Pinta* were an apparition, and then gave himself into the care of the Franciscans and paraded in triumph to the monastery of La Rabida.

We rowed Pinzon ashore, and the crowd still cheering, and he was borne on a sick litter to his house near La Rabida and then to that house came Christopher Columbus and a group of Franciscans, and the doors to the house of Alonso Pinzon were closed.

To Gallego's wineshop we went, arm in arm with our fellows from the *Nina,* and there demanded jeroboams of Guadalajara's nectar and swapped accounts of all that had befallen us since the storm and the separation.

Columbus had prayed the *Nina* through the fury and assumed that we were lost and on February 15 sighted Portugal's Azores and there suffered difficulty with Portuguese authorities and imprisonment of many of his men. But, by San Fernando! the admiral threatened the Portuguese with Spanish wrath and did bluff them into releasing his men and, on February 24 and that two days before our *Pinta* made Bayona, the *Nina* made sail for the run to Palos.

But another storm lashed them, the one that scudded us, and they made anchorage in Portugal and thence to Lisbon.

Mind you that. Why did he go to Portugal? The storm? I know not and only the Doomsday Book will reveal the truth thereof, but I do know this: our *Pinta* touched not Portugal's Azores or Portugal's mainland. Only Spain for us. And Alonso Pinzon was on Spanish earth while Christopher Columbus dallied in Portugal.

There again he encountered complications and convinced the authorities that he had sailed not to Portuguese claims, but to the Indies. Then the King of Portugal did intercede and Columbus produced his warrants from Ferdinand and Isabel and the King of Portugal wisely did not dare an affront to our Sovereigns but honored the warrants and also Spain's Admiral of the Ocean Sea.

Furthermore, he furnished a royal messenger that Columbus' letters and documents might be speeded to the court at Barcelona and thus it was that those letters reached the court before Pinzon's letter.

The deed was done. The lie was fastened.

For Christopher Columbus castigated every man of the expedition except himself, and now who could approach him and bring him down because the Franciscans were his shield and the Queen believed him and entitled him The Very Magnificent Lord Don Christopher Columbus.

Alonso Martin Pinzon died on Sunday, his third day at home, and Columbus and the Franciscans were at his bedside and the bells of La Rabida did toll us the word.

He gave up the ghost at the vesper hour on that Holy Day and the doors of his house remained shut and the Bishop of Chiapa spoke kindly of him and said, "He died in a few days after the voyage and there occurred nothing more to me that I might say about him."

No papers found. Neither contracts nor agreements between Pinzon and Columbus, nothing; only death and silence.

His secrets were buried with him and his funeral a private one and we, who loved and followed him, were denied the rites, were denied a minute at his bier.

And then, ere the worms to the flesh of my captain, Don Christopher Columbus did proclaim that he was forming a processional for Barcelona, that he would walk a pilgrimage to his Queen and pray at every shrine between Palos and the court.

And that he had discovered the Indies, that he had seen land first—the Light of San Salvador.

Therefore and forever more he was taking the Queen's pension unto himself and bestowing it on Beatriz Harana, the mother of his bastard son.

There was no mention of the velvet doublet.

CHAPTER 18

*I*N PALOS, IN LEPE, IN ALL THE NIEBLA, THERE WAS NO PATRON FOR my advocacy, no personage of station to espouse my cause or remonstrate against The Very Magnificent Lord Don Christopher and his Franciscan paladins, because the Queen, the State, and the Inquisition were captives of the insatiable Friars Minor.

The Pinzon family, now that its leader was gone, was stricken of indecision and anguish and had neither minute nor mood for my sustainment. Even the sailors had scattered, many of them following Columbus in his processional across Spain and to the court, and others to sea and others to luxurious debaucheries.

Arcos was in the hinterland, seeking to purchase an olive grove or a vineyard to settle himself and his family far from the sea, and only The Rabbit was with me and he spent his nights in carousals and his days pounding Gallego's tables and shouting that his shipmate Lepe had seen it first and that truth had been seduced and justice outraged.

For weeks I drank and wenched my indignation into stagnant lethargy and then slowly my manly anger nourished itself into a determination for vengeful endeavor. I was twenty-four of years and strong and the son of a hidalgo, an Andalusian who had tasted the cup of triumph and drained it to bitterness, and I would suffer no more this heinous fortune.

I thought of my father and, forsooth, my neglect of him did trouble my conscience and I resolved to journey to Seville and renounce my prodigality and honor the wife he had taken, and prostrate myself that he might forgive my omissions and succor his only son to attainment of the renown that was rightfully mine. And failing this I would lay my plight before Juan Ruiz de Medina and petition patronage of the Dominicans.

Therefore, it came to be that my resolution sired execution and, with the mule law still in force although the Moorish War was concluded, I purchased a horse of long stride and steady gait and bade the bye to my comrades.

I set forth for my beloved Seville on April 16 and was of a mind to travel by Lepe and do homage to my Aunt Ronda, but the Odiel was at flood and so I took the post road, the one I had walked as a drover, and in three days did come to the Guadalquivir River and the dog roses were in bloom again and the birds nestled in the reeds.

The streets of Seville were crowded with soldiery, for Ferdinand, despite all treaties, was scheming to strive against France for domination of Italy. Already the ruthless House of Trade had been established in Seville to monopolize shipbuilding, and eventually the New World trade; and this house was hand in glove with the nobles, whose sheep, by royal decree, roamed the countryside and denuded the land and thus compelled the peasants into debt and bondage. Chains for debtors and the stake for Judaizers, and the public Jews banished forever and the Franciscans at the tiller.

Thus it was, but on these tragedies and portents my mind dwelt not, for I was filled with the joy, and the sweet sorrow, of homecoming.

I stabled my beast in the hostelry of Muntaner and there secured accommodation and cleansed myself and my garments and set forth afoot for my father's shop.

It was closed and spiders had webbed on the front door and dirt and filth were on the threshold.

Puzzled, but not alarmed, I sought old Mudarra and could not find him and I knew none of the shopkeepers thereabouts. Their faces were new and strange and when I asked of Vicente Bermejo and Mudarra, the Morisco and potter, they stared at me and turned their backs as though I were unclean.

Then, remembering old Mudarra's consuetude, I hurried up the alley to a public house and the putas there shook their heads to my queries and said, "We know not such a man. We have come here only lately from Cadiz."

At that time while I harangued them for news, a crone who tended their beds and basins hobbled into my presence and gaped at me. "You ask of Mudarra the potter?"

"Aye." I tossed a blanca to her. "I seek Mudarra."

"He is dead."

Now this report was most disheartening to me, albeit not startling, as old Mudarra was a wasted vessel and his days long had been numbered, and so I crossed myself and blessed his memory and spake further: "And what of Vicente Bermejo, the hidalgo?"

A grimace contorted her withered face and she snarled at me, "Why seek you Vicente Bermejo?"

"He is my father——"

Her shriek halted my words and she shooed her chicks to their quarters and slobbered vituperation upon me. "Begone, you seed of iniquity! Why molest this house with your hapless fortune? Away!"

She darted at me as though she would claw me and I backed out of the doorway and to the alley and for a minute was in puzzlement, and then I was seized of a premonition and ran to the street and was intent for my father's house in Triana; and then I remembered I must pass the College of Seville and, surely, Juan Ruiz de Medina could untangle this arcanum for me.

Rapidly I walked, sometimes running, and darted between strollers and jostled two drunken soldiers and they cursed me, and I spared no moment for umbrage, but hastened to the college and pounded for admittance.

A young friar, one I knew not, unbolted the latch and I pushed open the door and demanded that I be taken to Juan Ruiz de Medina.

"He is at prayer," the neophyte protested.

"Take me to him!" I shouted the command. "At once, you sapless nursling, else his prayers be for you to free your soul from purgatory."

The young monk fled the room and I strode the floor in petulant turmoil and then I heard the measured tread on the cloister and the vulturous frame of my boyhood mentor filled the doorway, and his jaw was revolving that incessant motion that I remembered so well.

"Fray Juan!" I greeted him fondly and he held out his arms and embraced me and I felt the tears on his cheek.

"Rodrigo, my brother." He gripped my shoulders and studied me. "You are home a man."

"What of my father?" I demanded. "His shop is closed and the

253

neighborhood is alien to me. I know that Mudarra is dead, but what of my father?"

The benevolence left his eyes and the inscrutable rigidity was there. "You do not know?"

"I know naught." I fastened my grip on his arm in troubled agitation. "I am only a few days from Palos and only some weeks from the Indies with Don Christopher Columbus. What of my father?"

He drew away from me and straightened his shoulders in the pride of his orders and the poverty of his black mantle, and his voice came in sepulchral strain like an echo from the Valley of Doom. "Vicente Bermejo is dead."

"Say not," I begged. "Spare a penitent son this accounting." My sins of neglect and dissipation did fill my soul with contrition, and I wept my misery and desolation. "That his only son was not beside him to comfort him. When did it happen, Fray Juan?"

"More than six months past, Rodrigo."

"And what of his wife, the one I never saw?"

"I do not know. She left Seville."

I sought the easement of a bench and buried my face in my hands to blot out the vision of my father dead and to collect my wits that were dulled by this torment. "Did God spare him pain?" I raised my face. "Or did he linger in agony?"

Juan Ruiz de Medina lifted his eyes from mine and toward heaven and spake the pronouncement: "Vicente Bermejo died at the stake."

Spin our threads, eternal Clotho! Dispose our lots, everlasting Lachesis! Hold fast, inflexible, Atropos! Cackle, old hags. You Moerae of hell, you Fates of the nethermost. My father in the embrace of Quemadero. The thorns for the brow. The sweat for the passion.

And I, in the fullness of my youth, suddenly was into an old man and my blood of no warmth and my spirit had fled. A moment passed, an eon, and I found expression on my tongue that had no liaison with my intellect, neither my heart. "Be this cruel jest of error? Or vile truth?"

"It is holy truth, Rodrigo."

"Then what crimination against my father?" Were those calm words mine? I, his son, and sitting there in craven dejection while the beads of his misery were told in judicial omnipotence.

"The crimination against Vicente Bermejo was that of selling sacrificial animals to the Jews. The Inquisition found him guilty and the State exacted punishment; as it is written."

The chicken feathers in Mudarra's shop, the lambs' wool and the odor and sight of fresh blood. It came back to me then and the apathy of helplessness and horror was fastened to my will. "What of Mudarra? What of his death?"

"Mudarra the Morisco was in the pay of the Moors. He had spied on Christendom for years and was beholden only to Mohammed. Mudarra died on the rack."

The images, long swirling in my mind, began to take shape and to stand out in their awful saliency. My father, and perhaps Luis Harana, in conspiracy to sell animals to the Jews, and the rabbis to the shop for the slaughter, and Mudarra sharing in this and himself in the pay of the Moors against the Crowns. The contours blended into the broad vista and, for an interval, I was ashamed of my birthright and contemptuous of Mudarra's perfidy. But the whole feast of humiliation I must digest, aye, to the last morsel. And so I persisted. "Did Mudarra accuse my father?"

The Dominican, having tightened the tapestry on the frame, now wove the pattern and spared me naught. "The eyes of Mudarra were blinded by searing rods. His nails were torn from his flesh. But he died defending Vicente Bermejo and praising Mohammed and cursing all Christians save Jesus, the One he called a prophet."

The finality of the recitation pricked my cowed spirit and aroused it and I pressed for the point that was concealed somewhere in this mire of delusion. "Then who accused my father? If not Mudarra, then who?" I brought my eyes into the focus of his and held his gaze. "Did you sit in judgment of my father?"

"Nay." He spake it quickly for the relief it promised. "Torquemada himself sat in judgment." He moved across the room and took bench there and it came to me that his misery was to the depth of mine, and his jaw slowly revolving and his cheeks as pallid as a corse only a few hours void of the soul. "I counseled with Vicente Bermejo," he said. "I pleaded that he accept the second category of the *Malleus Maleficarum* and confess to heresy that is relapsed, that he be penitent and thus save his life. Vicente Bermejo did jeer my counsel and did fling the challenge of the Goths at Torquemada, and he died singing the war chants of The Cid."

"Then who accused him?" I gripped the edge of the bench and felt

255

a warm quickening of my spirit. "Who did charge him and who bore witness against him?"

The jaw was stilled and a mask of impenetrable closure came to the Dominican face. "Vicente Bermejo and Mudarra the Morisco were accused by deposition executed in Cordova, and signed by Maraela Harana. She bore witness."

"Seize upon, Black Friar!" I sprang from the bench and stood trembling before him. "Is my sanity to suffer more stones from the sling of fortune most mad? My father and her father were associates and she has been unaccounted for years, for I have sought her. Weigh carefully your words, Dominican, lest they burden your soul to perdition and lighten my arm to vengeful speed."

The words flowed free and tumbled forth in brave defiance and yet I knew he spake true and that the last grim thread was woven into the tapestry, that the last knot was tied. Slowly he arose and stood taller than I and compassion was on his countenance. "Harass not my words, Rodrigo, and I will reveal a true account of this abomination."

"Speak forth, Fray Juan." I locked my arms over my chest and felt the beat of my heart.

He paced the floor in measured tread and in the silence of contemplation, and then he stopped and faced me. "No sooner had Christopher Columbus——"

"Again!" I cried out. "Must that name haunt me even in this hour——"

He held up his hand. "Harass not my words, but hear me out. No sooner had Christopher Columbus been favored of the Queen than Maraela Harana appeared in Cordova, and from whence I know not. And she established kinship to the Harana family of Cordova and ingratiated herself into the esteem of Beatriz Harana, the mistress of Don Christopher and the mother of his bastard."

My arms fell to my side and I bowed my head as his words chiseled the image of Maraela's betrayal, of the depravity of the one I had loved. And he spake further: "But she was suspect of Judaizing, and to erase this blot she did confess transgression and did plead that it was in the days of her innocence and at the behest and insistence of her father——"

I raised my face to challenge the lie and saw his eyes upon me and I lowered my face to avoid the temptation to speak and his avowal poured forth.

"Therefore, Luis Harana, long dead, was tried by the Inquisition and his guilt was set and his bones were dug up and burned. But she had cracked the door and could not stay the haps that flooded like a tide and threatened her inundation. It was then and to save herself that she accused Vicente Bermejo and Mudarra the Morisco, and bore witness against them; and they denied it not."

He paused and I spake: "In her innocence she Judaized? Was that her say——"

"Hold, Rodrigo!" It was the cold warning of death's wings before the flight. "You know the law. If Maraela Harana Judaized after the age of innocence, then she must die. But if any man knew that she sinned and did not accuse her, then he, too, is guilty. Let not your rashness destroy your reason. And one thing more——"

"Aye, Fray Juan." His warning was sufficient and I buried my knowledge deeper into my memory, for I could not speak against her else I, too, feel the wrath of the Inquisition.

"I know that you sailed with Christopher Columbus and I have hearsay that it was you who first saw land."

"It is true." I was returned from the Valley of Doom to the summit of my own triumph and my pride quickly had seize of my resolve. "I saw it first, but Columbus cheated me of the honor and of his avowed rewards. You, my teacher, denied me a velvet doublet I had not earned, but he has denied me a doublet I have earned. I, therefore, pray your patronage that I may present my case to the Queen and receive that which rightfully is mine——"

"And beard Don Christopher Columbus?"

"And beard the devil himself if need be." No longer was I in bondage to my mortification, a slave to the outrageous malevolence of schemers. My father and Mudarra were no more. Christopher Columbus had betrayed the knife of Pinzon and my covenant. Maraela Harana had betrayed my love. Now let them beware. Vengeance is a dish to be served cold.

Juan Ruiz de Medina stroked his forehead and then slowly shook his head. "You cannot accuse Don Christopher to the Queen. He is her favorite."

"With Dominican patronage I can face Don Christopher and, aye, even the Franciscans themselves——"

"This patronage we must not give." He spake it in contemplative finality. "We Dominicans must not raise cry against Franciscans, for schism is evil, far more evil than the wrong that has been done to you."

"Then I am alone?" I demanded.

"Impetuosity is never the lance of a wise man, Rodrigo. Let this dog sleep until time awakens it; until Christopher Columbus hoists himself upon the poniard of his own ambition. Patience is your watchword."

Patience is a virtue only for women and old men, and I, an Andalusian, was no more the hapless creature of fortune's whim. I felt my anger surging into fury and the steel in my heart was the coil for my decision. "But I am betrayed, Fray Juan! Must I drain this cup?"

"You must sip it, Rodrigo. But spare the dregs to be hurled into the evil faces of your tormentors——"

"Dominican conciliation!" I cried. "Peace where there can be no peace. Christendom condemned my father and my Sovereigns burned him. Now hear this, Black Friar: I will drain this cup unto the dregs and sicken thereon, and then spew my vomit on all that have passed this cup to me: my Faith, my state——"

"Hold! 'Tis blasphemy——"

"I hold not!" I raised my face to his and then to heaven. "By the Holy Cloth that sopped the Blood, I hold not. Christopher Columbus shall know my wrath and Maraela Harana my curse."

And so saying, I felt for the poniard she had given me and drove it into the wall of the College of Seville. "Leave it there, Fray Juan. For it is witness of the vow of Rodrigo of Triana. I shall be revenged on this earth, though I be condemned in heaven."

Then I looked at him scarcely a moment and saw the deep hurt in his eyes, and then I turned from him and walked into the light of Seville's spring and swung tight the door behind me, and heard the latch catch and knew that I was alone.

But I was free. I was without parents, and they the first responsibility of life. I was without church, and that the second responsibility. I was without country, that blinding responsibility of manhood. And I was without woman, the most tenacious let of all.

I squared my shoulders to the world and strode down the street and so resolute was my tread that even the soldiers stood aside and let me pass and stared after me. First I must wine and feed my humors and then chart my course, and so to the hostelry of Muntaner I directed my steps and to the common room, and there I ordered wine and spun a ducat on the table that the hosteler might know he was serving a personage of merit.

I appraised not the fire of the wine, neither did I assess the agitation of my humors, and soon my blood was coursing the heat of the grapes and my tongue was loosed and I surrendered myself into bacchic revel and foolish vaunt.

The publican joined me and poured my wine, and took my ducats, and honored me as a hidalgo and confided to me that he, too, was a man of consequence and a descendant of the great Ramon Muntaner whose narratives I had read and approved.

"*Ruat caelum*, host!" My tongue, indeed, was free from my reason. "I need not the name of any kinsman to vouch my merit. Know you who this is who honors your hovel?"

"A hidalgo, 'tis obvious," he whinnied.

"The son of a hidalgo," I corrected him and pounded the table with my cup. "But I am The One who first called land on the voyage of Christopher Columbus."

He smiled at me and poured more wine and I was angry that he believed me not, and this anger did spur me to reckless demeanor. I stood on my bench and shouted for all to hear that I had seen it first and that Christopher Columbus was alien filth and the spawn of gutters.

The host sought to quiet me and, failing that, he moved away from me and the other drinkers stared at me, and these numbered several soldiers, who watched me in benign amusement for awhile and then in hostile suspicion.

But nothing daunted me and I reviled Christopher Columbus and stood on my table as though it were the forecastle of the *Pinta* and called out, "Land. Land."

And at that time there came from the kitchen a maid who gazed at me and her eyes were wondrous bright and black as the rainy nights of Cibao. A mere kitten she was, scarcely to my shoulders, and her face pinched and piquant, and wise beyond the few years since her puberty. I returned her stare and she withdrew quickly to her pots and pans, and I continued my revel.

All afternoon I drank and longed for The Rabbit, and the night was upon Seville and the soldiers wearied of my babblings and warned me to silence. And now this did agitate me into a frenzy and I hurled my cup at them and cursed their ancestry in a manner that would have pleased The Rabbit, and, in the lunacy of my drunkenness, I did publicly revile the Sovereigns they served and the Cross they followed.

The soldiers counseled among themselves and then stomped out and the hosteler was in a fit of anxiety and came to me and pleaded thusly: "They will seek your arrest. So in the name of God have meat and begone, else you bring misfortune to this house." He removed the bottle from my table and called toward the kitchen, "Be alive, Mary, and to your chores. Fetch sup for this man and then he will be away."

The girl of wondrous eyes, the one he called Mary, hastened from the kitchen and was flustered to a predicament of visible confusion and in her bewilderment she paused at the linen corner and took forth a clean white cloth and spread it on my table, and this to my amusement.

'Twas only a Friday, yet she dressed the table as though for the Sabbath, and I said naught lest the host rebuke her for her disquietude and for her nervous forgetfulness. Truly, she thought me a personage.

But harken, patient reader. A humming cord to things long past awakened my memory and livened my brain, as besot as it was of wine. A white cloth on Friday? What, now? What meaning? This was no signal, but an instinctive gesture on her part, the compulsion of long training that revealed itself spontaneously in the agitation of her solicitude.

Then she fetched candle and taper and lighted the flame and instinctively did she shield it and, suddenly aware of the implication, she stared at me in frenzied helplessness and then around the room.

A white cloth on Friday. The candle shielded in remembrance of the exile to Babylon. Her inculcation and her excitement had betrayed her, for this girl was a Jew and no Jew could live in Spain.

I alone had seen it and I alone had read the meaning, and so I touched her fingers, and they were clammy cold, and I whispered, "Caution, maid, else the Inquisition return you to the bosom of Abraham whence you sprang."

A sudden terror blazed in her eyes, a dreadful horror, and she trembled as a wasted leaf and gripped my hand. "Mercy, sire. In God's name—mercy. And begone."

"Why? I welcome indictment before any magistrate that I might speak my arraignment of Christopher Columbus."

"Impetuous fool!" She hissed at me and clung to my hand like a derelict to a rock. "You cannot pull down idols as Samson did. Flee this snare——"

"I have no place to go. And no friends nearer than Palos."

"Then to my house. I need talk to you. Free yourself by some ruse and I will await you at the rear door of this place."

She returned to the cookery and I, after casual hesitation, made discreet inquiry of the host as to the proper place for my privacy and he nodded toward the back alley and there I went, staggering purposely although I no longer was drunk, only tipsy. The girl was at the rear door and she pulled me into the shadows and along the alley and we came to a street and soldiers were passing and we crouched in a doorway until the way was safe.

"The hosteler will be happy that I am gone," I whispered. "But he will follow you."

"He knows not where I live. I have served him only this day."

"Your name is Mary?"

"That is the name I gave him. Now, quiet, and follow me."

We hurried across the street and into another alley and it led us to the river and she took my hand, for it was very dark, and guided me among the hovels until we came to a refuge of stone and clay, and she opened the door, and this was her abode: a single room, a bed and a pitcher, and a peg on the wall where hung her threadbare garments.

She closed the shutters and bolted the door and then she lit a candle and in the light of the candle her face was bewitchingly wistful, the face of a girl and the black, darting eyes of a woman. She motioned that I should sit on her couch and she melted and stuck the candle on a bench and sat there, peering at me. "You were with Christopher Columbus?" It was her first question and she trembled the intensity of her words.

"Aye." The admiral and the Indies seemed far-away at that hour, for my blood still was warmed of the wine and never before had I seen a chick so ready for the serving. "I am Rodrigo of Triana and called Lepe the sailor. 'Twas I who first saw land."

I reached forth to take her and she drew away and studied me closely and said, "You remain heavy in wine. Your wits are dulled. I have need of you sober."

"Come to the couch," I directed. "I have gold and also desire for Jewish enchantment."

She fastened her eyes upon me and there was no fervor in them, but they reflected her deliberations and this fretted me as I had no intent to beg favors from a Jewish waif who surely was whoring for her bread while hiding her faith from the Inquisition. Why she still was in Spain I did not know and did not care. I had plans to make and work to do and if she must feign constraint and modesty then the tryst was not worth the toll.

So I arose from the bed to take my leave and she sprang before me and cried out, "No, no! You must stay here." Then she pushed me to the couch and held high her arms and swayed like a Sybarite and her eyes suddenly smoldered her fervor and the candle's flicker transformed her into the wand of Aphrodite and I called out, "Llamita—a little flame."

She smiled at me and again I called, "Llamita." And she smothered my words and my voice trailed into the name she will bear forever—Mita. Mita, my beloved.

The memory of that bliss is mine alone, but she kissed me into hush and held me as a nymph who has plucked a dragonfly from a reed and has shorn its wings and who holds it gently in her hands. The candle burned low and the flame within me was consumed and quenched, and on this day, when the Fates had smote me with their cudgels of fury, I had trod from Sheol and into a brief freedom, and now into joyous slavery, for I had found Mita.

## CHAPTER 19

THE RIVER AND THE SWEET CAURUS OF ANDALUSIA REFRESHED our bower and the Guadalquivir swayed her ships and the sailors on watch chanted their night calls—the Salve Regina and the songs of the East, and there was an empyrean peace within me and I knew that nothing, neither sails nor pride, could separate me from Mita.

She kissed my eyes and sealed them and slipped from the couch and into raiment and then into the night and soon she was returned with food, and she fed me and bathed my face with a cool cloth and nestled my head in her lap and stroked my brow.

"Rodrigo of Triana." She whispered my name in loving possession. "Out of the night you came to me and in the sun of day you shall remain with me, and the night and the day shall be one, and into the years of this covenant between you and me."

"Never shall I forsake you," I vowed. "My life had been an emptiness and now it is filled."

And we talked on, in whispers, of the things all lovers talk and she guided my converse to my adventures and to my triumph and I told her of the New Land, the isle I had sighted first and the people thereof and their customs, the tabacos and the hammocks.

Then I directed our familiarity to her and discreetly sifted for her story, for I knew not even her true name or her birthplace. But in this I did not persist, fearing I might nettle a secret and bring her to misery, and knowing that, in God's good time, all would be revealed to me.

But she was not secretive or furtive, only contemplative, and then did she ask me the course we had followed to The Discovery and many other things nautical, and I was pleased that she had knowledge of the elements I loved: the sea and the winds. And I was not surprised at her wisdom, for she was a Jew and the Jews have witnessed everything and have forgotten nothing.

"Did Don Christopher Columbus follow the charts and maps of Benjamin Marino?" The query came in casual objectivity and I was by no means astonished by her curiosity for, remember, Benjamin Marino was also a Jew and there is an affinity between Jews that is beyond the ken of Christians, albeit they trust not their own kith and, God knows, they disdain all people save their own.

"Marino?" I reached forth and felt the lobe of her ear and the hole there where a jewel had been. "He was my teacher at the College of Seville and the greatest man I have ever known."

The shudder almost was imperceptible, like the shadow of the raven's wing over the tombs of the past, but her fingers tightened on my arm and there was animation in her voice. "Did Columbus use the maps of Benjamin Marino?"

"I know not, Mita. He had Marino's maps. I saw them——"

"You saw them! Then think carefully, Rodrigo. Did Columbus use the maps? Did Marino's wisdom lead Christopher Columbus across the Ocean Sea?"

"I know not if he used them or followed them. But they were at his service as was Toscanelli's map." I was vexed by her sudden obstinacy and frowned my displeasure. "And of what concern?"

The shadow on her face, the gravity in her eyes, warned me of the truth before she spake it, yet even then the amazing utterance came as a wonderment:

"I am Leah, the daughter of Benjamin Marino."

I sat bolt upright and seized her shoulders and stared into her eyes and cried out, "By the burning bush and the rock that flowed water! Have miracles become pandemic? Is my life to take further thrusts from fortune's lance?"

She lowered her head against my chest and gave herself unto sobs and laments and I did comfort her and did hear from her own sweet lips of her flight through the Valley of Torment.

Benjamin Marino was dead, and his wife, and both at their own hands in alternative to exodus from their native Spain. They died ere I sailed Palos and the Queen's soldiery left their bones in a field for the dogs to gnaw.

"There was a son," I said. "I remember now that Benjamin Marino sired a daughter and a son. What of him?"

"He, too, is dead." The tears left her eyes and the flint of Edom was there, the wrath of Esther. "The edict of expulsion sickened my father into melancholia and he took my brother and me to the sanctuary of a converso's home in Burgos. Then he returned to Salamanca and he and my mother drained the cup of Socrates that their sacrifice might impel the Queen to spare the Jews who had served her so well. But fie!" Mita spat her contempt and her spleen. "That ambitious she-wolf was beyond mercy and suffered my people to be banished."

"Aye," I said. "Your tribulations are equal unto mine. So I harken. Bare all the truth, Mita, that I may share your distress."

Her voice came as the sound of a soft wind imprisoned in a chasm and seeking escape that it might summons its wind-kin and strengthen its vengeance into fury. "My brother sought to flee to France. The Queen's soldiers hunted him down with dogs and wounded him and sported with him and then gave him, still breathing, unto the beasts."

I shuddered the horror and she spake further: "And, now, Rodrigo, I tell you what you will always remember. I am a Jew. The recusancy of that converso's house tormented my soul as I could not live the Law only in darkness and worship Christian gods in the sunlight. Therefore, I ran away and I lived in caves and in the forests and with gypsies, and I fed my belly on the fruits of my wits and my spirit on my abhorrence of Spain and all things Spanish.

"I was in Jerez when news came that Christopher Columbus had returned to Palos from his voyage and I knew that my father had furnished maps for this enterprise. Forsooth, if Columbus, the Queen's favorite, would proclaim that a measure of the merit should go to Benjamin Marino, then, certes, the Queen would bless my father's memory to the honor of his people and vindicate his name, and I could live again in the sunlight with my God and the Law."

"Thought you that Columbus would share honors with any man?" I muttered.

"Hope, my love, is the raindrop that freshens springs that swell the rivers that move the mountains." She sighed her resignation to the will of God. "I planned first to go to Palos and then heard of his processional to Barcelona and that he would pass through Seville, and so I came here.

"He worshiped in the cathedral and rested in the Castle of Triana, and I waited upon him there and he scorned me and swore that he used not the Marino maps but followed his own guiding star."

I smiled at her indulgently and patted her hind in playful forbearance. "You, an outcast, waited upon The Very Magnificent Lord Don Christopher Columbus? What ruse, Mita?"

"No ruse. Merely a message marked by an obscure sign of David and stating that I was a maid of the Colom family, conversos of Catalonia. It is no labor for a Jew to arrest the ear of another Jew, only sometimes a task."

The significance of her avowal escaped me momentarily, for my wits were dozing, and then the dictum did prick my intellect and arouse it. "Colom? Conversos? Jews? What has Christopher Columbus to do with Jewry?"

She turned her eyes upon me and searched my face as though seeking betrayal of my banter and, seeing that I spake solemnly, she seemed amazed at my benightment and said, "Know you not that Christopher Columbus is a Jew?"

"Arrant nonsense!" I scoffed her words. "Columbus is pious in Christian rituals beyond all obligation. He walks with the saints. A Franciscan, Mita. Do not test my reason."

She pulled away from me and her ire sparked her mettle into Satanic temper. "Aroint, dullard!" Then she spewed forth the scurrilous invective of Spain's gutters. "I say that Christopher Columbus is a Jew. His soul is in bondage to Christian delusion, but he is the seed of Shem; he is a son of Abraham."

Mita was as earnest, as serious, as a Judahite canting the Law, and the direful implication of this revelation smote me as a tongue of lightning. Don Christopher a Semite? Incredible. I pressed her further and was most cautious not to fire her anger by my skepticism.

"Sevillian dolt!" She was vexed by my wheedling. "All Salamanca and most of the court know that the Explorer is a Judaist. He is a Spanish Jewish refugee come home to great honors——"

"Beshrew, girl! Is this fancy conceived in hate?"

"How thick is your skull, Rodrigo? Praise be that your other parts are not so insensitive as your head. The one you call Christopher Columbus was born Christoforo Colombo in Italy's Liguria. His father was Domenico Colombo, a worker with wool, and his mother was Susanna Fontanerossa. To this family were born four sons and one daughter; the sons named Christoforo, Bartolomeo, Giovanni, and Giacomo, and the daughter named Bianchinetta. Giovanni is dead. The others live."

266

Her factual recitation intrigued me to rapt attention and she put her hands on my shoulders and held my gaze and spake her declamation:

"Father Domenico Colombo was given stewardship of the landgate to the tower of Capo de Faro in Genoa, the cape lighthouse, and there Christoforo Colombo was born. Now, heed this: the Colombo family were refugees to Italy, either grandfather Giovanni Colombo or his father. The family's hearth, the one never forgotten, was in Spain's Catalonia and there the family's name was Colom, and the Coloms were conversos—Jews by blood and Christians by water."

She removed her hands from my shoulders and stretched on the couch and closed her eyes and I kissed her mouth and she pulled me to her. "Now do you believe me?"

"Is there more to the annals? I would know the last word in this narration."

She flung her arms above her head and relaxed her tension and squirmed the sensuous gratification of her couch. Like the serpent in Eden. Mita was the serpent at Creation and I the adorer; she the siren and I the idolist.

"More?" She pressed my hands hard to her breasts and then pushed me from her and sat erect. "Aye, there is more. The converso Coloms were persecuted in Catalonia and fled to Italy and the name became Colombo and thereafter the sons, even unto Christoforo, were instilled of Christian rituals and Jewish tradition. The family clung to the ways and the words of the fatherland and thus explains that Columbus' tongue twists to a Catalonian inflection and why his phrases are out of the century past."

"That for true," I said. "That I know. He speaks quaint phrases. And he writes in Spanish although he was born in Italy."

"Because his family kept the old ways," she explained. "And he set his course as a young man as truly as did Saul or David or any of the anointed. You know of his surreptitious arrival in Portugal, the mantle of mystery he put around himself and of his perfidy there. It is an ancient custom, Rodrigo, the sleight of the East to confuse that which you cannot conquer by effrontery. But he was suspect in Portugal and came to Spain, and the greatest of the converso Coloms came home when that man's feet touched the mud of the Niebla. So again his name was changed and this time to Christopher Columbus. And now the Queen's wreath is on his brow and the Cross is on his forehead, but the Ark of the Covenant remains in his heart."

I tasted all the words and digested them and many things I did recall of Columbus' bent—his traits that pointed to Semitic origin as surely as the needle to the Star: his mysticism and convictions in portents, his mobility and wiles. By the rod of Aaron! I remembered clearly the characteristics, the mannerisms. His pride in the history of the Jews and his acceptance of the prophet Esdras. The allurement of jewels rather than land, and the urge for barter. His morose silence on the expulsion of the Jews and his insistence to sail on Friday, a day of good omen for Jews albeit the black day for Christians. And, more than all, his affinity for conversos, for Luis de Santangel and others. Then, too, whom did he trust on the voyage? Diego Harana, the brother of his mistress, and Luis de Torres, both of Israel's seed.

"Can you prove this thing?" I demanded, for I was aware that this thunderbolt well might tremble the foundation of the realm itself. The Queen's favorite not only an alien, but of converso brood. She burns conversos on Friday, yet crowns Columbus' brow with laurel. She exiles all Jews by edict, but honors one of their sons with titles and trappings and her royal boon for his heraldry. The potentials were appalling with Spaniards in a frenzy of patriotic fervor and hating all things alien, particularly Jew things.

"Prove it?" In the way of her breed she answered my question by asking one. "Must you prove that the stars shine or that the Guadalquivir flows?"

"Hold, girl! I will have naught of travesty and Jewish hairsplitting. We have the weapon to fell Christopher Columbus, the chain to pull down the idol——"

"Is it so bad to be a Jew?" Her tone had the nettlesome superiority of her people, the one facet of her nature that always annoyed me most. Then she sensed my vexation and pressed her bare foot against the calf of my leg and pinched my flesh between her toes. "Who will hurl this weapon, Rodrigo? I, a Jewish waif who must crawl in the shadows? Or you, an orphan sailor who has blasphemed your church and reviled your state. Nourish your wits, sweet lover, and remember that vengeance is a fruit and not a soup, and it takes time for fruit to ripen."

Her wisdom, and this I willingly admit, was more devious than mine, albeit superior in some things, for her's was the patience of antiquity and I, the son of a Goth, was more direct and impetuous. Therefore, I heeded her and she said, "A tare planted in the wind will spread to the wheat and destroy it. But it takes time. Hence, our requirements are three. The first is safety. The second is power. And the third is patience. Now, what of these marvels you fetched from The Discovery?"

I was impatient of her seeming digression and yet I reined my antipathy and answered forthrightly. "They are in my sea chest at Palos. But what have these things to do with us? They are only tokens of my adventure."

"Ne'er the less, I am curious to see them. And if I am curious then others will be. For know this: that next to man's appetite and vanity, the best source of profit is his curiosity. We must first to Palos and into possession of your marvels."

"And then what?"

"We must flee Spain." Her prescription was as calculated as a conjurer's recipe. "We must find sanctuary and a way to power and then plant our tares."

"But where?" I was tolerant of her chimera and indulged her dream. "Every door in Christendom will be shut to me."

"Aye, but the shadow of the Cross has not blighted all lands. Islam is open to the submissive and Islam burns not the Jews."

"I am no Jew, Mita."

She looked at me in the forbearing taunt of the self-Chosen. "No, you are not a Jew. Are you a Christian?"

"Have I not renounced my Faith?" I, too, could avoid direct answers.

"Then you are naught," she said. "And Islam's tent will shelter us both. You can wind the turban, Rodrigo of Triana, for even a Spaniard knows that expediency is the shaft to the crossbow of revenge."

I was no longer superciliously indulgent of her reverie or afflicted with the indolence of my own caprice, for the boldness of her plan was a stimulant to my imagination and quickened it. I spoke Arabic. I knew, broadly, the message of Mohammed. A turban, a burnoose, and who was to reveal that my heart was not submissive to the five obligatory duties of the Moslem: the recital of the Creed, the five daily prayers, the fasting, the pilgrimage to Mecca, and the almsgiving.

I could assume the name of Mudarra, the sonship of that loyal guardian, and thereby honor his memory and assure his lineage. Upon the honor of the beard I must grow, what a plan! Verily, I would walk upright into a deceitful labyrinth that my vengeance might brew into poisonous vapors and then blow as the sirocco from Islam's wadies and sear all those who had wronged me.

And, now, this I say to you: that if man can focus his fate on any event or compress his life into any tide, then that was the hour when I became Mudarra the Moor, and the Moerae cackled their sanction of my audacity and turned from me and spat their spite at The Very Magnificent Lord Don Christopher Columbus, Admiral of the Ocean Sea and Viceroy of all Newly Discovered Lands.

I hugged Mita in the jubilation of our planned deliverance and we gave ourselves to more pleasure and then to strategy. She counted my gold and put half of it in a tiny sack and this sack she secured to her waist. We would leave my horse at the hostelry and walk to Palos, journeying by night. It was my suggestion.

She dissented immediately. We would leave naught. There is a time for stealth and a time for daring, and this was the time for assurance. The hosteler was asleep and the soldiers already had searched the place, and the stableboy was surely drunk, as was his wont. Therefore, I should enter the stable in a bold manner and lead forth my horse, and if the stableboy threatened an alarm I should tempt him with pay, but only a blanca. Failing that, I should clout him on the head and leave him at peace in his hay.

And, forsooth, she did dress herself in all of her garments and slipped one on top of the other until she bulged at her belly and was padded thick at her hind, and these garments piteous and threadbare and yet she would leave them naught. Then she lifted a jar and peered in it and spilled forth a few drops of oil and rubbed it in her hair in the way of brides of the East. For Mita was a bride.

No blessing of state. No cant of prelate. But Mita was a bride in the insoluble covenant of a man and a maid, and she oiled her hair with the few paltry drops and her hair smelled of musk and I kissed her hair and her lips, and we stepped bravely forth into Seville's night and neither was alone e'ermore, for we had each other.

Then we parted, me for the horse and she for the bridge to Triana where we would meet, and she instinctively slipped through the shadows while I walked erect up the street as becomes an Andalusian.

The stableboy was pleased to earn a blanca, for his wine was gone, and he even led my beast from the stall and bent his back for me to mount, and this I did and rode blithely away, emulating a sailor heavy in wine by singing a chant and sitting my horse in a fashion most awkward. The garrison soldiers, those on sentry and those whoring the night, laughed at me or cursed my vociferance, and molested me not.

Mita was at the bridge and she mounted behind me and we clomped across the Guadalquivir and through Triana's sleeping streets and ere the cocks crowed the morning's vigil we were on the road to Palos, and confident of our security because it would take days for the State to grind its indictment against me and proclaim its want of Rodrigo of Triana who had reviled Spain's blessed Queen and Christ's True Church.

So Mudarra rode forth, and Mita. *Magni nominis umbra.*

The sun came hot and my horse lathered, and Mita's bare legs were wrapped tight to his belly and her arms around my waist and she cradled her head in the dip of my back and slept, and the sweat of her breasts wet my back and the musk odor of her hair was heavy in my nostrils, and pleasing to me.

We rested and ate in the woods and took rapturously from each other that which each offered without stint and on the third day we sighted the harbor of Palos, and the *Nina* still at anchor, but the *Pinta* gone.

I first sought The Rabbit and learned from him that no alarm had been sounded for me in the Niebla and I confided in him and he thought me mad, and then he saw Mita and thought me the most fortunate man since Adam. He, the vile hellion, did dare suggest she share her favors and she cursed his paternity to the dungheaps of Sodom, and this delighted him and, mockingly, he knelt in obeisance and kissed the hem of her tattered raiment and swore fealty.

Then he led us to Gallego's and she examined the marvels in my sea chest and said naught, but therewith entered into barter with The Rabbit for a boat to take us to Tangier, across the Strait of Gibraltar and in Africa.

He went for Arcos and that stalwart left his vineyard and his grove and, in Moguer, they chartered a sardiner with main and mizzen and brought it down the Tinto to Palos and provisioned it, and I to a smuggler to dress my Mita in suitable raiment and myself as becomes a Moor.

Mita protested my extravagance and railed like a fishmonger at the merchant and called him a Syrian filcher and pretended a faint when I indulged two ducats of gold for my drawers that billowed to the ankles and a blue shirt with dainty buttons and coiling loops, and a blue coat with long wide sleeves. My burnoose was of camel's hair and yellow, and yellow were my slippers. The turban, of course, was white, and white I must wear on my head until I had seen Mecca.

For Mita I stacked four gold ducats before the smuggler's greedy eyes and chose her garments with the elegance of an Andalusian virtuoso. First, the fine gauze to cover her thighs and a cotton bodice for her breasts. Then the pantaloons and next the haik to cover her from neck to feet and this haik was fourteen feet long and five feet wide to drape in luxurious folds around her body. This cloak was of wool and was blue and yellow, and her slippers were of pale yellow. Mita being a Jew, the veil was not mandatory, but I bought for her a thin black kerchief to cover her hair and to be drawn tight across the forehead. And then, in the inspiration that comes to lovers, I bargained for a silver anklet with a tiny bell.

The parsimonious nature of my beloved melted before these gifts and she clapped her hands like a child and flung the haik around her shoulders and gathered it loosely at her waist and paraded before the merchant, and when that dupe expressed licentious approval, she tickled his ear and wangled a braided sash from him.

We stored our finery aboard our vessel and secured it against the weather and on the morning tide of May 2, 1493, Arcos, The Rabbit, and I stroked the craft into the Tinto and raised our maincourse and dropped down to the sea again.

Mita had never been to voyage and she sickened as we skirted the coast toward Cadiz and the Strait. The Rabbit jeered her misery and she cursed him. By the holy fleas of Mecca, how she cursed him while I cradled her head on my lap and doused her face, and she was embarrassed of her retching and, this I swear, it was the only time I ever saw Mita vexed into humiliation.

The wind came good and we raised Cabo Trafalgar and veered hard for the Strait and for Tangier, and the sea was choppy as it roughed toward the Pillars of Hercules and the Mediterranean. Arcos steered and The Rabbit and I tended sail and the moon drifted free and the low outline of Africa was off our bow. Arcos ran her into a cove, known to all freebooters, and if any Moors saw us they bothered us not, surely thinking we were smugglers from the Niebla and bringing good Christian gold for their aloes and spices.

I changed into my Moorish raiment and Arcos helped me wind my turban, and Mita, the vixen, stripped naked of her clothes and washed her body and Arcos was dismayed of her immodesty, but did stare at her, and The Rabbit beat his fist against his head and called out for the gods to witness the fortune of his comrade, Lepe the sailor. I fastened her bodice and old Arcos helped her drape the haik and The Rabbit was pleased only to fit the slippers to her feet and he kissed her feet, and she raised her haik and directed him to fasten the tiny bell to her ankle.

Then she kissed his wizened cheek and the cheek of old Arcos and I embraced my comrades and they swore that my summons would bring them to Africa, or to India, to any place under the sun.

Arcos lifted Mita into his arms and bore her to the shore and I lifted my sea chest and followed them, and Mita and I stood there and watched the vessel ease out and around, and raise sail for Spain.

The sea was dark and quickly swallowed them and there was no sound save the bark of a Moorish dog and the roar of the sea but the stars were gleaming bright; on us here in Islam and on Christians there in Europe. Mita snuggled close to me and we watched the stars and, hear me, one star flamed across the sky and was gone, as though a sign of the flames to come.

For, even at that hour, Christopher Columbus was planning another voyage across the Ocean Sea. His brothers, Bartholomew and Giacomo, were hurrying to the Spanish feast, Bartholomew from France and Giacomo from Italy.

Beatrize Harana was disporting the Queen's pension that belonged to me and, mayhaps, Maraela Harana was tending her wardrobe.

In Rome, Pope Alexander VI granted Spain title to the Indies discovered and then divided areas of discoveries between Portugal and Spain by drawing a line from Pole to Pole and one hundred leagues from the Azores and Cabo Verde, and thus established he knew more about God than about the geography of God's footstool.

In the far Germanic town of Mansfeld, the boy Martin Luther wrestled his Latin and chafed under the discipline of the monks while his pious father grumbled protests against the fees for indulgences and other ecclesiastical bargains.

In England, in the town of Bristol, John Cabot convinced the king who had hired him that, despite failures to find the Isles of Brazil, he still could find new lands to the west and asked a ship and royal commission.

In Portugal, Vasco da Gama looked south and petitioned his king for a grant to confirm what Diaz had shown: that the Orient could be reached south around Africa and east to India.

In Barcelona, where Columbus' processional received the plaudits of the multitude and the blessings of the Sovereigns, one Ruy Diaz de Isla, physician, noticed strange festers on some of his patients, and wondered the source.

While in Seville, Amerigo Vespucci, agent for the Medici, culled all bruits of The Discovery and wrote all merchants and bankers of the Medici that virgin land lay beyond the Ocean Sea and perhaps profit for traders of enterprise. He signed the reports: Amerigo.

Aye, the stars flamed over Europe and gleamed in placid luster over San Salvador and Cibao; and Europe, hungering unto death, raised her bony arms in supplication, holding them westward in prayer that the Ocean Sea might succor her and the misty isles save her—the land that I was the first to see.

I balanced my sea chest on my shoulder and Mita and I walked toward Tangier, and the dawn showing pink, and Mita close to me, she my star and my lodestone, and I an exile forever.

# CHAPTER 20

HE PEOPLE WE PASSED, ALL TURBANED AND SOME LEADING
burdened asses to market, gave us stares but no interruption and soon
the full sun was fervid upon us and compelled us to intermission at
the base of a slope, and this ascent the burial place of Antheus, the
founder of Tangier and the son of Neptune.

Once upon a time the Gardens of the Hesperides were nigh and
here, where we rested, Hercules slew the dragon of a hundred heads
and purloined oranges from the Gardens and took them to Greece.

The city was eastward and the mosque reflected the sun and the
minaret fingered the sky and, the day being pure, we could see the
jetty and sea tower of Tarifa across the Strait and in Spain. My native
land was only fifteen miles distant and the Spanish Pillar of Hercules
was but thirty miles distance and yet beyond our sight, for mist clung
to the gate where the Ocean Sea did tryst with the Mediterranean.

And now, patient readers, that you might understand all subsequent
events I must here record prosaic data concerning Tangier else you
fret for my safety in a strange land.

The seaport of Tangier, and never forget, is on the arm of the Ocean
Sea as it bends to Gibraltar and, hence, commercially looks to Europe,
for even England is nearer than Egypt and, geographically, Rome is
much closer than Mecca, although spiritually that Tiberine Babylon is
separated from Islam by the hell-deep chasm of Christian barbarism.

For years Tangier has been the weasand to freedom for Moors and
Jews fleeing Christendom's faggots and racks and the city's populace
is far more an amalgam than any city of blighted Europe.

Islam dominates Tangier, but not with branding irons, and the
people are a conglomeration of creeds, with the Moslems, naturally,

in superior numbers, wealth, intellect, and position. Next in prominence are the Jews, but also there are colonies of blacks, both free and slave, and Greek Christians, and Coptic Christians who trace their faith to ancient Egypt and scorn the Romans as usurpers in the Kingdom of Christ.

The seneschal of the Copts was one Hannas ibn Nomus, salt merchant and enterpriser whose name was known to all the Niebla, for his house was the clearing place for aloes and spices smuggled into Spain, and this Hannas was the princeling whose amity I eventually would need and yet I must be devious, for a stranger in a new turban did not artlessly present himself to that house and seek the patronage of Hannas.

And here I beseech your indulgence for one further verity that you might comprehend the circumstance in which Mita and I deliberately had placed ourselves, for I will inflict no heroics upon your credibility, but only scriven my journal to its conclusion and that, patient reader, not far removed.

Christian Portugal, in the customary manner of Europe's grandiose assumption, did claim suzerainty over Tangier, but this was a specious representation to the Pope to prevent a similar pretension by Spain. Actually, there was neither Portuguese power nor garrison in the city and all authority was vested in a caliph who licensed Portuguese traders (but no Spaniards) to buy in Tangier, albeit never to sell. And the regnant Enterprise of Trade was the Lisbon branch of Di Negro and Spinola, the Genoese house for which, remember, Christopher Columbus, in his early manhood, had traveled as a salesman of woolen goods.

And now, having pinched salt into the knead, let us on to the crust and the crumb of this narration, and so, if you be pleased, you will rejoin Mita and me as we rested at the base of the slope and nigh unto Tangier.

The dust and the clatter of hooves on the road we had trod sharpened our perspicacity and out of the dust rode a patrol of Moors and they numbered three and their scimitars dangled at their waists and their beards were stiff with sweat. They reined before us and looked down at us, at my new turban and at Mita's unveiled face and there was no enmity in their demeanor, only bemused curiosity. I spake the greeting of the land: "Peace be unto you."

They answered in kind although their eyes darted from me to Mita and it was apparent that my precise Arabic nettled their inquisitiveness, and the leader dismounted and addressed me: "Does Spain now send walking baggage to Islam rather than gold for our aloes?"

I stood before him and spake forth rightly: "We are from Spain and seek sanctuary of Islam, for it is written in the second sura of the Koran: 'Verily, they who believe, and the Jews and the Sabeans and the Christians—whoever of them believeth in God and the last day, and doth what is right, on them shall come no fear, neither shall they be put to grief.'"

"You are a Morisco?"

"I am the faithful."

"And she?" He nodded toward Mita and that adroit Thespis was standing with head bent and eyes lowered, the very image of modesty and humility.

"She is a Jew."

"Do the faithful in Spain take Jews to wife?"

"The faithful in Spain take what is offered, for the servants of The Servant are maltreated in that land."

"Your name?"

"My name is Mudarra."

"Mudarra!" He glanced quickly at his companions and they scowled at me.

I felt Mita's bare foot press mine and a premonition was upon me, for if I changed the story we had woven between us then surely I would ensnare us. Therefore my only course was to recite that which we had rehearsed so carefully, and trust to the mercy of God.

"My name is Mudarra," I repeated. "A name honored by the suffering faithful in Spain and hated by the Christians."

"Your father?" He spat the demand at me.

"He, too, was Mudarra, and dead on the rack in defense of the Faith."

The Moslem soldier studied every detail of my face, the fresh beard that was scraggly in its beginning and my bright blue eyes. "Where did your father die?"

"In Seville." I hewd to the line.

"Then he was Mudarra the potter and an amir of Islam."

I was trapped and dared not look at Mita, but heard her heavy breathing and then, because she was there, my courage flinched not and I spake boldly, albeit with proper humility: "My father told me naught of his stature in Islam, for he was a man of much modesty and consecration." I flung the fold of my burnoose over my shoulder and braced my feet wide apart. "But ere he was dragged to his torture he counseled me to flee Spain and return to the cradle of his people, and I am come and I demand the esteem that my father earned for his seed."

"And the opprobrium of bastardy?" The impeachment fell like a hammer blow and I steeled my sinews else I spring for him and die in the folly of my courage, for I was without weapon. A minglement of thoughts and furcations swirled in my brain and I lowered my head to assess my stratagem and this gesture he assumed to be evidence of my shame and the Moor spake further, and in a measure of compassion, "Rueful is the hour when a man is forced to flee his roof and into the odium of bastardy."

"Hold, craven libelant!" I opened my burnoose to show that I was unarmed. "Your advantage spurs you to calumny most cowardly. My mother was a gentlewoman of Lepe."

He took no umbrage whatsoever of my taunts, but shook his head sadly. "It is written that a man's lie for his lineage is not a lie at all. But, forsooth, seed of misfortune, it is known throughout Islam that Mudarra the amir never took wife and that in his youth he pilgrimaged thrice and each time did vow celibacy, and did exile himself to Spain that he might serve the harassed faithful in that benighted land."

The snare was about my shoulders and there it must remain, for I had springed myself through my ignorance of the true stature of old Mudarra. I cast down my eyes in dejection and Mita touched my arm and comforted me, and I ruminated my lot.                           •

Bastardy is more oppressive in Islam than in Christendom, albeit not so frequent, for if a maid or widow be bigg'd in this land of polygamy then the man takes her to wed, save she be of such low caste that she cannot honor his name. Therefore, if he wed her not, it is accepted that she is of mean station and, mayhaps, a whore or an adulteress. Anon, and the seed of this planting is inferior in the eyes of all men, and his riches or wisdom cannot hide the stigma or lessen inferiority.

I was not an outcast, neither a pariah, but a nonentity, and though I stack my gold as high as the Pillars of Hercules I could not be friend to men of worth and merit. I could not game with them and to table with them, but only to trade, and must always withdraw from their presence at any hour of sociability else I suffer their snub.

I, Rodrigo of Triana, I who had seen it first, now was nobody and this tether I must wear as penalty for my sworn vengeance.

On these things I was thinking, and in morose despair, and from the minaret came the echo of the call to prayer, faint and far-away, and I heeded it not until Mita kicked my shin and I glanced frantically about me and saw that the Moors were facing the East and humbling themselves.

And quickly, though clumsily, I made supplication, but instead of mumbling my worship I was in such a state of agitation that I cried out the message to public prayer and in a voice as clear and as strong as the immortal Bilal, the black slave who first called it:

> "Allah is most great.
> I bear witness that there is no God but Allah,
> I bear witness that Mohammed is The Messenger of Allah.
> Come to prayer,
> Come to progress.
> God is most great.
> There is no God but Allah."

The Moors gaped at me and in their superstition assumed that I had been a muezzin in Spain, else why could I cry the message so nobly and why did I cry it instinctively.

Mita was the first to sense the advantage and to press it and she stood rigid and her face was uplifted as she exulted in a voice as clear as mine and even more melodious, chanting Sura 100:

> "By the roaring panting steeds
> Striking fire flashes with the hoof
> That scour the land of Dawn
> Darken it with their dust
> Split apart the Enemy.
> Verily, Man is to his Lord ungrateful,
> Verily, he is keen after this world's goods."

The astonishment of the Moors was no whit more than mine (but Mita was an everlasting wellspring of surprises to me) and they muttered their amazement. "She is a Jew?"

"Aye," I said. "Of the seed of Abraham who was the father of Ishmael."

"But she chants a sura of the Koran. Is this the way of Jews in Spain?"

I was as hard put as they for an explanation and Mita still was exulting, and now in Sura 101, but my mind was agile again and I made discourse in the surety that my wits would seize upon a profitable exegesis. "Did not Abraham and Ishmael build the Kaaba at the well of Zemzem?" If I could not explain, I could confuse. "Is not Islam from the tents of the Ishmaelites, and the Ishmaelites from the tents of Israel through the seed of Esau who wed with Makalah, the daughter of Ishmael?"

" 'Tis written," they said in unison and were impressed.

I touched for the point and urged it into eloquence. "This woman, my spouse, is of such blessed consecration that she reveres the words of The Messenger as she reveres the words of her prophets."

The Moors withdrew to the shade of a eucalyptus tree and counseled among themselves and frequently cast puzzled glances toward us, and Mita leaned close to me and whispered, "You were slow to invest the opportunity I offered for their confusion."

"For only a minute was I remiss," I protested.

"And then you garnished the soup with a heavy hand——"

"Hush, Mita. They are watching us."

"My deportment was a ruse. Therefore, deceive not yourself that I revere the babblings of Mohammed as I do the Law and the Word of my people——"

"Silence, shrew!" I commanded. "The forked tongue of a woman is the weapon of a serpent."

Her face had not changed expression and it still was benign and angelic when the Moors rejoined us and they were most deferential to Mita, and this an unusual approbation inasmuch as women seldom are honored by Moslems. Naturally, they addressed me, although their words were for her. "A woman of such piety is pleasing to Allah and verily she can lessen her master's pain of bastardy. We are blessed that you have come to us and shall so report to the caliph."

Mita's obeisance was histrionics for Thalia and, without my permission, she opened my sea chest and displayed my marvels to those dolts and volunteered that I was the only Moslem who had accompanied

Christopher Columbus on his voyage across the Ocean Sea and that I first had seen land, and this to the glory of Allah and His Messenger.

The turbaned provincials had heard naught of Columbus or our expedition and were entranced when I deigned report some of the things I had seen and as I explained the use of a blowgun, of tabacos and the hammocks. Mita strung a hammock between a scrubby wild olive and an acacia and timidly they stretched in it and then giggled like girls at the bath and sought to purchase one for all the gold between them.

I was for sealing the bargain, but Mita pretended shock, as though they had asked to buy the heirlooms of her family, and spake craftily: "These possessions are not for barter, but send your women to me and I will teach them this art."

"But where?" they asked eagerly.

"We must have a shop, my master and I." She returned the marvels to my sea chest and closed it. "It should be nigh unto the Kasbah that the caliph and his household might visit our establishment without incommodation to themselves. And it should be in the bazaar and, therefore, accessible to all the people, for my master will have many trophies to show Tangier and much knowledge to impart."

The Moors knitted their brows in thought and then the face of one did wreathe into triumph. "I know such a place," he said. "The stall of Ambar where beggars were trained in contortions and ribaldry and fit-throwing, and other arts of their trade."

"The very place," they agreed. "And empty for more than a year."

"The rent must be within reason," Mita insisted. "It is a delicate subject that offends my master's pride, but I tell you that we once were rich but have been persecuted into poverty by the avaricious Christians."

They agreed that the rent was moderate (and if not they would see that it was) and were so engrossed of us, and my marvels, that one of them lifted my sea chest to his horse and secured it there, and another did mount with his comrade and thereby provided a beast for Mita and me.

She straddled the horse, a thing most brazen for one so pious, and wrapped her arms around my waist and tickled my belly and we set forth for the city, and the bell tinkled on her ankle and she nuzzled my neck and whispered:

281

> "By the roaring panting steeds
>   Striking fire flashes with the hoof——"

"You are a vixen," I said. "A djinni of a race that learned whoredom from their Babylonian masters."

"You are my master, Mudarra the son of Mudarra, the bastard issue of an amir. This night you shall pay for your insolence." She snuggled to me and caressed me and I was compelled to restrain her else I embarrass my dignity.

Thus we entered Tangier and first through the prosperous section of the Jewish quarter and the wives of the merchants resplendent in black velvet gowns and brocades with gold and silver designs, and each with a white veil under her chin and to a knot on the top of her head and each with a vivid kerchief, either blue or green, plastered across her forehead.

"Aren't they beautiful," Mita whispered and smiled at them.

"Gaudy," I replied. "And they stink of oils and grease."

" 'Tis better than the onions and sweat of Spaniards," she hissed.

And then into the poorer section and the women in shapeless India shawls and sprawling in their doorways and nursing their fouled young, and shrieking at passing peddlars and beggars and such a babel I had not heard since Cibao, where parrots screamed at daybreak. Dirt festooned the glazed tile walls of the houses and filth littered the floor.

"Aren't they beautiful?" I whispered to Mita.

Her temper flared into vile malison of me and my ancestry, for to her even Jewish filth was superior filth. "You ridicule the poor and the unfortunate," she railed and almost loud enough for our Moorish escort to hear. "You forget that Christians have persecuted them into this depravity."

"This is not Christian land," I persisted. "This is Semitic land and these Jews are blood-kin to the Moors——"

"Spanish jack!" She seized my flesh between two knuckled fingers and twisted it into hurt. "It is impossible to reason with arrogance, and all Andalusians are arrogant."

My laugh was a torment to her and she bore her fist into the small of my back and kept it there as we rode through the quarter, and she smiled at the Jewish mothers and the elders, but all the while her hard little fist was paining my back and I could do naught for fear I might reveal that my Mita was not a wistful seraph at all, but a she-devil with a forked tongue and loins of velvet.

We came to the bazaar, and the Kasbah on a hill near by, and the Moors halted their horses before the empty stall of Ambar, and Mita slid from our beast and examined the shop and proclaimed naught in its favor and pretended swoon at its dirt, although to me she confided, "It will serve."

The escort even fetched the landlord and, to prove my own acumen, I haggled with him and secured the shop for three gold ducats, one to be paid immediately and two at the end of the month. And there was no interest.

The Moors announced their intention of departure, to report our arrival to the caliph, and I was of mind to bestow a gratuity for their assistance, but Mita scowled me to inaction and gave them naught save a promise that they and their families, each family to the number of ten, might view our marvels on any single day of the next week by payment of only five copper coins, which, she assured them, was one half the toll to be charged all others.

Then we were alone, except for children and beggars and ribalds who gathered at the door and stared at us, and I sat on the sea chest to rest, but Mita did urge me into a frenzy of labor. She sent me to rent couch and brazier while she higgled cloths and pitcher from a neighbor and set to scouring our place.

We hung a curtain and behind this placed our couch and the brazier, and arranged my marvels in neat array near the door and then darkness was upon Tangier, and Mita blew charcoals into glowing heat and cooked our sup on the brazier.

And this food was a soup of fishheads and seasoned in the Jewish manner of oils and herbs, and she denied me garlic and even wine, for wine was costly, she explained, and, too, being a Moslem and the son of an amir, I should shun the grape.

My disposition was quite sour, and my belly gnawing, but I held my tongue until she lit an oil lamp and placed it by our couch and then did harangue me that I had overpaid the landlord.

"I perceive, my lord," she said in sarcasm, "that we shall survive on my wits."

"Harass me not, Mita." I was most gentle, albeit firm. "Our beginning has been auspicious and we should be thankful."

" 'Twas I who bested those Moors and fetched them groveling at our feet."

" 'Twas you."

"But my reward was your vilification of my people. Because they are poor and persecuted——"

"Silence, woman!" I seized her arm and shook her. "I have eaten your oil and fish and am a man of temperate humors. But my house shall not be a pigsty of Jewish grease or a tabernacle of Jewish babble."

She spat at me.

And I was goaded into unchivalrous demeanor and pinioned her arms and lowered her pantaloons and then did redden her hind with my palm. She clawed and scratched me and I lifted her to the couch and blew out the lamp and caressed her into purring tremor and the duteous submission that behooves all women.

"Tomorrow," she murmured, "there shall be garlic in the house of Mudarra."

Then she lay her head on the curl of my arm and to sleep, and her sweet hair tickled my nose.

The muezzin awaked us at daybreak, calling: "Prayer is better than sleep; come to prayer."

I faced east and recited a sura and Mita was pensive as she watched me, and after supplication, and this I swear, I felt cleansed and of airy spirit, and I rejoiced. Mita said, "My people know that Islam bestows more grace upon a submissive soul than does Christianity." It was she who suggested that this day I prepare a kibla, which is the niche in every Moslem home that indicates the direction of Mecca.

The mosque was open and I was of a mind to go there while Mita prepared breakfast but ere I had completed my morning ablutions, people began arriving at our shop and pleaded to see my marvels, for our escort of the day before had spread wide the news of our arrival, that I was the bastard of the amir Mudarra and bore his name, that my spouse was as pious as Reihana, the Jewess concubine who served Mohammed, and that we had trophies of a new land and tales more alluring than Arabia's tales of the Thousand Nights and a Night.

Mita collected a stipend from each and I showed them the marvels and they were intrigued mostly of the tabacos and raw cotton and, of course, the hammocks. We strung two of our three hammocks in the shop and for extra coins Mita allowed them to swing in the hammocks and to lie in them, and all the while I answered questions about The Voyage.

"Tell them, Mudarra," Mita said, "about the beautiful mermaids that wantoned about the bow of your ship, of the two-headed dogs that bark not, and of the isle that is ruled by maids with nipples of pearls."

I ignored her urging to fraudulence and honestly sought to inform them of the things I had seen, but, having heard Mita's bidding, they thought I was withholding the truth and pressed money upon me to loosen my tongue.

They wanted to believe in mermaids and two-headed dogs and in maids with pearly nipples. And so I accommodated them, for their money loosed not only my tongue but my imagination, and long before the muezzin called for the day's fifth prayer I had brewed a story so fantastic that it bore no resemblence whatsoever to truth; and my jaw was weary from wagging, but Mita's purse was stuffed with coins.

To glean a few more coppers, she took the women aside and, with downcast eyes and virtuous modesty, whispered to them the things I had told her of Indian maidens and their methods of love-making. The Moorish women bent their heads that their ears be closer to Mita's lips and several of them did hasten therefrom and to the houses and harems.

By nightfall the crowd was so thick before our shop that we were compelled to close the door else they press upon us and, perchance, pilfer some of our marvels. And then we closed the shutters and counted our toll and, upon my beard, our money was more than my pay had been for a month's service with Columbus or Pinzon.

Mita gave me good mutton for supper and offered me wine, and this I declined as a Moslem should, but she drank it and smacked her lips and kissed me that the breath of the grape might tease me and the tang of the wine pass from her lips to mine.

She took the remains of our feast to the Jewish poor and upon her return she unfolded to me more plans than I could harbor in my mind, and that very night we labored until we were jaded, arranging our prizes to better advantage, rehearsing my fables and preparing flour and water into tiny potions and a story that I had fetched them from the western isles and these sure to warm the ardor of any man and bring forth good djinns and to cure all manner of ailments save leprosy and lunacy, for it was contrary to law to sell fraudulent nostrums and elixirs for those maladies.

With curtains and rugs, Mita prepared a sanctum where the women could have privacy as she related the customs of Indian maids. (And God knows what Mita might tell her patrons as only a dryad would dare attempt to instruct Moslem women, particularly Turkish women, in any new form of the love art.)

We were so busy the next day that only the five prayer calls gave us surcease and, to my amusement, more Jewish women purchased the love and luck potions than did Moslem women, and this, and my smirks, perturbed Mita and she announced publicly that we had disposed of all charms and philters that I had fetched from the voyage, and thus did she seal that lucrative well forever. " 'Tis evil to deceive the ailing," she told me.

There are those who say even now that the fortune of Mudarra was built on tricky theatricals and deceitful dramaturgy, but I tell you that the foundation of my wealth was woven from the hammocks of Cuba. For of all the trophies we exhibited, the hammocks aroused the most interest, and the women came in goodly numbers and begged Mita to teach them the secret, although a hammock, as you surely know, is only a swinging couch made of rope, hemp, or even canvas, and of the simplest formation.

And thus it came to be that Mita entered into agreement with the women of Tangier that she would furnish hemp, but never canvas, and teach them the craft and for each hammock any woman made for herself or family she must make one for us; and this pact was made inviolate by the sacred oath of Moslems—a grass stalk in the fist and the vow: "By the life of this stem."

I urged that the Jewish women also take a sacred oath and Mita was piqued that I should think that her people needed binding, but I had my way.

Ramadan, the month of fasting, came with the summer that year, for Islam's calendar is lunar and not solar, and Ramadan varies in seasons, and as a gift for the holy month, Mita presented me a prayer rug from Medina and a vase of fine oil for my beard, which had flourished into elegant form, brown and wavy, and which I kept trimmed in meticulous refinement.

These expenditures chafed us not, for our leathern box was filled with coins of copper and silver and Mita's waist sack was heavy with gold. We had abode up the hill near the Kasbah and high above the stench and babble of the bazaar, and our Arcanum of Marvels, as we proclaimed our enterprise on gaudy signs and in the calls of professional shouters, enticed the curious from as far away as Algiers, and the caliph himself was a somewhat frequent visitor to our shop and I had presented him one of my rare tabacos.

I was steward of this business while Mita tended our hammock venture and directed the women who procured materials from her and wove and looped our merchandise under her rigid surveillance, and most of our hammocks were of cheap hemp that the poor could buy, although some of them were of good cloth with yellow silken tassels.

It was the hammocks and the trade therein that brought Hannas ibn Nomus to my board and cup, for being a Copt he was not rigorously fastidious concerning bastardy, especially if a profit might accrue through friendship to any man: Berber, barbarian, or bastard.

Mita and her black serving girl from the Mine (and this baggage is bondage to us through trade of a hammock to her master) prepared costly viands for the Copt, including a sheep's head, and after the repast Mita did not retire to seclusion, as a woman should, but remained at table and poured wine for Hannas and pampered him into loquacity.

He asked of our hammocks and she bargained with him in strident frugality and pledged to distribute hemp hammocks through his house and this, to me, only a bagatelle, for, being an Andalusian, I was a gamester at business as at life and the time had come to uncup the dice and cast them before the Moerae.

Therefore, and to Mita's consternation, I contracted with Hannas to furnish me aloes, particularly Medusas from the Atlas Mountains, and for these I would exchange fine hammocks of linen and cotton. But with this proviso: that he send to me agents of Di Negro and Spinola.

This was done and the salesmen of the great house (a garrulous and gluttonous lot) waited upon me and I instructed them as follows:

Their profit was to be twenty per centum and they were to deliver my aloes to Amerigo Vespucci in Seville and say to him that more were forthcoming, all that he could sell to the apothecaries of Spain; and that they came from Mudarra, a worthy native of Aleppo and now an enterpriser of Tangier. Under no circumstances, and upon my vow of reprisals, were they to reveal that I was a native of Andalusia or that I had voyaged with Christopher Columbus.

These salesmen were not witlings to betray a confidence if a profit were to be turned and they agreed with alacrity to all of my terms, and some of them remembered Columbus when he sold woolen goods for their house and they reviled him, possibly at the urge of envy, albeit probably to flatter me, whose hatred of the charlatan was known from Tangier to Tripoli.

Mita served rare *qahwah* and dried figs to the men and heeded all converse and held her tongue until it surely burned her mouth and then she spake out and harangued them to pry and spy and determine if Christopher Columbus had used the maps of Benjamin Marino for The Discovery.

"Marino?" one of the men said. "I have heard of him. A Jew."

"A Catalan," Mita replied promptly. "And an astronomer and scholar at Salamanca."

"He is dead," said another. "And all of his family. The Inquisition and the banishment." He shrugged his shoulders and sipped his costly brew.

Mita flushed her gratitude for the intelligence that Spain assumed her dead and darted her look at me as notice that again she had furnished an opening and that I should thrust in.

"Aye. Marino was a Jew," I said. "A public Jew and he and all of his family are dead by the malignity of Isabel, while her favorite, Don Christopher the converso, and his lewd mistress of the Harana family flaunt honors and pensions they have not earned."

"Columbus a converso!" The agent, an elder of the company, wagged his head in disagreement. "Nay, Mudarra. I knew the Genoese in his youth and he is born and suckled a Latin Christian and pious to tedium."

I gesticulated my apathy for such trivia, but carefully dropped another seed onto this fertile ground. "A Christian, mayhaps. But of converso breed. Through his grandsire, as all informed men know."

Aroint! It was a clever thrust inasmuch as meritorious salesmen are not afflicted of taciturnity unless it profit them, and the one thing that rankles them is ignorance of public facts or rumors because, as you know, they peddle bruit to all lands as well as merchandise.

One of the younger men, and surely to impress his comrades, volunteered that he had heard that the admiral's prestige would suffer upon close scrutiny of his annals, but knew not if the insinuation referred to his family or his amours.

288

"By the beds of Khadiji and Sawda and Aisha!" I feigned vexation. "I am astonished that you men are not better informed and riddle myself in fret that you are unworthy to tend my affairs. All wise men know that Columbus is of the Colom family of Catalonia, conversos who fled to Italy."

Several of the company sucked in their wind and exchanged glances and I read their thoughts: what a feast for their Spanish customers, what a morsel for France and Italy—Isabel's favorite himself was of the breed she had persecuted.

They took their leave and Mita and I sat at table and smiled proudly each at the other, for the seed of the tare was sown and time and tidings would spread it. We indulged ourselves on honey-water and almonds, but drank not the Arabian brew called coffee, Mita because it was so expensive and I because it now was forbidden good Moslems, who, in previous years, habitually had used it to keep awake during the long services in the mosques.

In one maneuver we had thrust for the Achilles' flaw in the mail of Christopher Columbus, the needle eye's vulnerable speckle between his pride and his secret, and had opened our trade routes to Spain, where aloes were more costly than jewels.

Our hammocks were delivered to Hannas in exchange for aloes, which we moved through Di Negro and Spinola, and their establishment, in turn, purchased our vendibles and distributed them first in Portugal and then throughout Europe, and especially to England,[1] whose admirals were the first to ken that a ship's complement could be enlarged through use of hammocks, and that each man-of-war should have a single command and the captain thereof proficient both in arms and navigation, and this learning eventually of much hurt to Spain.

The autumnal simoom blew hard from the East and bore sand even to Tangier, and Mita and I moved to a more sumptuous abode, with fountain and garden, and increased our slaves to three, and one of these to tend my personal needs, to trim my beard and freshen my garments and serve my bath, and this menial a toothless eunuch at my insistence after Mita forbade me a maid-slave for this function.

To this house Hannas came often, but never brought family or friends to share our viands, our garden, and our patio. He could not

[1]The narrator's bitterness leads him into error. Spanish ships apparently were the first to use hammocks, although England's navy did best Spain's through superior organization.

expose them to the stigma of the hospitality of Mudarra the bastard; and by this tide the women of Tangier whispered commiseration for Mita and not because she was mated to a bastard, but because I had a manly beard and virile bearing and she was without son, even daughter, and her belly flat as a child's, and her breasts dry.

Allah the Clement, Allah the Merciful. Mita and I were lonely and we did welcome visits from the salesmen who came from Portugal to roister at our table and guzzle our wine and coffee, and occupy the maids who worked at the Arcanum of Marvels and at the hammock establishment.

Always they came with news and gossip of Spain and it was from them we learned that Christopher Columbus had sailed again for the Indies, and this time from Cadiz with a grand fleet of seventeen vessels and more than twelve hundred men, including colonists, soldiers, ecclesiastics, and his younger brother, Giacomo, who had changed his name to the Spanish Diego and had been titled by the Queen.

The Sovereigns had counseled him to take Fray Antonio de Marchena, the Franciscan who had abetted him so successfully, but Don Christopher did not comply with this suggestion, for Fray Antonio was an astronomer and the admiral would share no secrets with any man, even one who had befriended him.

Aye, he took soldiers and cuirasses and crossbows and musketry, seeds and horses and servants, but he shipped no scholar who might penetrate his deceit or chart an open course across the Ocean Sea.

The armada was assembled and equipped under the skillful watch of Don Juan de Fonseca, Archdean of Seville, and the Crowns, perforce wisely, granted that worthy considerable authority for his task and this infuriated Don Christopher, who would tolerate no supplement of any kind, neither surveillance, even at the polite suggestion of his Sovereigns.

("Ah-h-h," one of the salesmen nodded knowingly. "The crafty viceroy fears his Jewry will be detected. 'Tis obvious.")

And while Columbus visited his mistress in Cordova and made a pious pilgrimage to the Hieronymite monastery of Guadalupe and there to pray at the feet of Our Lady of Guadalupe—the image carved by St. Luke himself—Don Juan de Fonseca struggled with the details of the fleet, and only to have the admiral carp and complain and to assert publicly that the court had been duped by evil men who had not the welfare of Church and Spain at heart.

Fonseca—aye, the same who later became bishop of Badajoz, of Palencia, of Burgos—smarted under such falsity and took a tuck in the viceroy's hem by informing the court that Don Christopher had taken unto himself a food taster, a mighty prerogative as only the very great could assume their lives in danger of deliberate poisoning, and that he had commandeered a personal bodyguard of men in continuous service and this, indeed, a royal prerogative.

Isabel was vexed and Ferdinand was angry.

And, further, he rechristened his flagship the *Santa Maria* in honor of the one he had wrecked. Our *Pinta* was not chartered as she was in trade to Italy, but brave *Nina* was in the line.

The armada departed Cadiz on September 25 with much pageantry and no Pinzon was aboard, not one of that deserving family, and but a few of the sailors who had made the first voyage and those through the dint of necessity because they were destitute.

(Arcos, The Rabbit, Chico, the brothers Quintero—what of them, I was wondering, and my hands aching for the feel of rope and my cheeks for the feel of wind.)

"A magnificent sailing," one of the salesmen said. "And only one trivial blemish to mar it. A hanging."

"Aye?" My mind was at the floating meadow, on the lookout of the *Pinta*, in the mountains of Cibao.

"Aye. And some say an augury, for the gallows bait was a sailor of Palos, a noisome cove named Gomez Rascon and called The Rabbit."

My pores spilled forth the juices of my agony and Mita's cark of anguish was piteous and she stared at me in horror. My glance warned her to silence and I steeled my tremors and spake without visible emotion: "Why should the death of a simple sailor be an augury?"

"Because this one exhorted publicly against Christopher Columbus and shouted that the admiral had defrauded one Rodrigo of Triana, called Lepe the sailor and the comrade of Rascon, and this Lepe sought by the King's soldiery for blasphemy against Church and State."

"A touching fraternity, but a foolish demonstration." I forced the words from my mouth and they seared my lips. "But do they hang Spaniards for exhorting against an admiral?"

" 'Twas more. This knave was convicted of aiding his comrade to escape. All Cadiz made a gala of the hanging, but Columbus was most distraught and took to his couch and was ill on his sailing day." The guest lifted one of our silver goblets and drained it and the wine drooled from the corners of his mouth. "And, an abortion of justice it was, because soon thereafter came one Pedro Arcos, a vinedresser of Moguer and once a helmsman, and this Arcos appeared before the magistrates and swore that Lepe the sailor had not escaped at all, but was dead of drunken debauchery, and this Arcos bore witness that he had helped bury the blasphemer in a pauper's hole near Palos."

The pit of my stomach quivered and I was nigh unto retch and wetted my lips with honey-water, and shifted the converse to lessen my misery, and Mita's. "Other news?" I asked. "Do you bring other news from the courts of Europe?"

"Courts? Nay, Mudarra, save the everlasting shams of monarchs. But Peter Martyr, that inveterate gossip-monger——"

"That Italian expounder? The one with ambassadorial letters from Ferdinand and Isabel?"

"The same. He has written that The Discovery is not the Indies at all, but a new world." The salesman laughed his ridicule and his fellows joined him in raucous mockery. "Are there no bounds to folly?"

A new world. The dictum came to my ears like the joyous prophecy of an oracle. A new world, and Benjamin Marino had taught that man would find a new world across the Ocean Sea; and I had seen it first. Surely his associates would recall his words and proclaim them, and his name would be remembered even if mine were forgot.

I glanced at Mita to reassure her and she had heard it not, for she was in a trance and staring toward the Strait, the mist rising and Spain beyond. Then she aroused herself from the torpor and lit a candle and put it on the table and this I knew to be her candle for Gomez Rascon.

*Memoria in aeterna.*

# CHAPTER 21

ND NOW, AND TO ALL WHO READ THIS CHRONOGRAPHY, I HAVE
set myself to the task of scrivening this journal, even at sufferance to
my privacy, that you may know the truth concerning The Discovery of
the New World and appraise the events that brought Christopher
Columbus naked and helpless into the talons of my vengeance.

Therefore, I deem my hymeneals with Leah Marino of no purpose
to this recital except as our unblessed spousal alloyed the fetters that
pulled down the charlatan from his throne of vanity and avarice.

Sufficient, accordingly, is my instruction that we flourished, that
our wealth accumulated as silt in a river bed, as sand in a wadi, until
the enterprise of Mudarra the bastard Moor was known throughout
Islam and in all the estimable marts and countinghouses of Europe.

Our palace we built on the Marshan plateau, which rises sheer from
the sea and constantly temperate in the wafts of the sweet breath of
Atlantis. White marble pillars, in number eighteen, surrounded our
patio, where a fountain to Hebe showered soft water into a pool of
tile that was glazed azure. From this sanctuary, save the sky be angry
or captive of night, we could see Spain where the horizon melted into
the rim of the world.

And here we sat each afternoon, Mita and I, and sipped honey-
water and nibbled spicy cakes; and everlastingly alone.

For Mita was barren, and thereby both of us were pitied in Islam,
albeit shunned, and even our slaves envied us not—because Mita's
womb never had throbbed the warmth of son-feel or her breasts the
miracle of sustenance for our image—and I forever in the shadow of
bastardy, the lie I lived in my bondage to vengeance.

Thus the lots were cast for us and wherefore, having writ, I command your attention away from Tangier and to the Ocean Sea and the Second Voyage of Christopher Columbus. The events thereon, and subsequently, I will only sketch that I might hasten this journal to its consummation, and this fulmination in his old age and in my middle years.

His armada sailed farther south than had we, and he did discover a necklace of islands, and one of these Guadeloupe, and these islands the home of the awesome Caniba, who castrated boys and ate them and even their own sons when born of women seized in forays against their enemies. And Columbus gave shirts to these Caniba that he might create a demand for cloth and thereby establish trade.

Thence to Hispaniola, and the colony of La Navidad was in desolation and the bodies of the Spaniards he had left marooned there were rotting in un-Christian exposure, for the Indians, goaded to savagery, had risen against them and slain them.

Now hear this: Instead of meting punishment to all who had spilled the blood of his countrymen, Don Christopher, with soldiery at his beck, marched not against the murderers but treated with them, and then, in degrading compromise, abandoned the site and moved up the coast to be nearer the gold mines of Cibao and there founded the colony of Isabella.

A company of hardies was sent inland to explore Cibao and they brought back rumors of El Dorado (but no gold) and reports that the natives were most docile. Thereupon Columbus dispatched a captain to Spain with letters to the Crowns, and these memoranda bewilderingly ambiguous save for a suggestion that a slave trade be established. This effrontery troubled Isabel, and irked Ferdinand, for Spanish vassals must not be slaves, even though they be naked heathens freshly claimed.

It was at this time, the spring of 1494, that the chief accountant of the expedition, himself explicable to Spain's Ministry of Affairs of the Indies, prepared a privy inquiry into the viceroy's conduct and this cabal was discovered, and Columbus suffered his judgment into an insane rage and imprisoned the accountant and hanged one of the conspirators. Aye, he treated with savages who butched Spaniards, but hanged Spaniards who pried into his affairs.

Next he went exploring into Cibao and left the colony in the control of a council, and the council was in the control of his brother Diego (Giacomo) Columbus, and this fellow a dolt.

There was no El Dorado in Cibao and only mountains and stones, for, of course, it was not Cipango, but "Stoneland" inasmuch as ciba was an Indian word for stone. However, he found some gold and left a garrison in Cibao and returned to Isabella and found the colony in deplorable circumstances.

Most of the food had rotted and the Spaniards were starving, yet would labor not for themselves with Indians at hand, and they beat the natives and tried to compel them to labor, but the Indians ran away. And now in this emergency Columbus was resolute and ordered all hands to work, even the gentlemen, and rebellion threatened and the viceroy, quite properly, hanged a few of the parasites and gave lash to others. This severity aroused Friar Bernardo Buil, the spiritual head of the expedition, to reprimand and he laid Columbus under an interdict and denied him the offices of the Church. The viceroy retaliated through a stoppage of the friar's rations, and soon Columbus was receiving spiritual aid again and Fray Buil was receiving food, but the damage was done. Fray Buil was the Queen's spiritual agent and the Pope's delegate and Columbus had blundered into a conflict between spiritual and temporal, between his own authority as viceroy and the Church's supremacy.

To worsen matters, Columbus had three Indians arrested for petty thefts and ordered the ears of one severed and the others to chains and when they protested he did hang all three of them.

This brutal impetuosity dismayed the natives into frantic bewilderment, for they knew not how to deal with a man who compromised with murder but hanged for pilferage, who pampered with one hand and cut off ears with his other hand.

And now I tell you this: the basal mischief in Hispaniola was labor, the service that Christians, as you know, hold to be the sacred and legal duty of menials. There were two trinities in the colony, the blessed Trinity of Father, Son and Holy Ghost and the trinity of work, thrift, and loyalty—for the lowly born.

The aborigines of the New Land had no conception whatsoever of the sanctity of property or the obligation to labor. Always they had tilled a few acres, speared a few fish, copulated, and died, and they comprehended not why they should toil unto exhaustion for strange masters who seized their baubles and occupied their women and gave them naught in exchange except alien rituals and a vague, mystic promise of reward in a second life.

Aye, Spain, wise behind her hoary walls but foolish beyond them, dared spill oil into a glass of water and then smashed the glass because the oil and the water would not mix.

And thereupon, having stirred the broth unto boiling, Columbus left his vacillatory brother Diego in charge of the colony and went exploring again, this time to the south coast of Cuba, then westward along that coast. A few more days and he would have learned that Cuba is an island and not the mainland, and still a few more days and he surely would have reached Yucatan and mayhaps the wealth of the Mayas.

But, nay. He now was robed viceroy and no longer reckless adventurer and the Fates jeered him and caused him to heed intelligence that an island to the south was overflowing with gold, and so he turned away from Cuba and the route that would have led him to truth and to the gold for which he hungered. And so he turned away and came upon the isle of Santiago.[1]

No gold. Nothing to grasp in his hands or send to the coffers of his Sovereigns. So westward he sailed along Santiago's fringe and again the winds of his fortune nudged him on, urging him toward Mexico and shrines of gold and silver and the sooth that my cry from the *Pinta* was the call to a virgin world, to a new hive for the swarming bees.

The west had failed him never, the west was his star and his destiny, but, alas! he denied his kismet, he refused the brimming cup and again he turned back. And why? Privations? By the glory of the Alhambra, brave Spanish hearts are not binded to gnawing bellies. Unworthy ships? He had the *Nina*.

Then why? Because he believed Cuba was the mainland, a finger to Cathay, that Santiago was an island near Cipango, and that the gateway lay south. The Indians told him Cuba is an island, but he would not believe. His calculations proved the Indies and no man could convince him to the contrary. He must be a learned cosmographer and not a sailor, a viceroy and not an adventurer, and the Fates would have it not.

Whereupon he persuaded his men to take vow that Cuba was the mainland and if any of them denied this certainty then their tongues

[1]Jamaica.

296

would be severed. "Each man is to suffer his tongue to be cut off every time he denies." So spake Columbus.

And then he sailed once more toward Cuba and dawdled among countless islands and turned due east at last, his back to the beckoning west, and thereupon he sank into a trance, a pestilential slumber that deprived him of all senses. He called it death, wherefore he could rise again, and his sailors hastened the ships to Hispaniola and Isabella and were awed of their admiral who babbled apocryphal prophecies as had St. John.

Upon arrival at the colony, he found that his brother Bartholomew had come out from Spain with ships and supplies and intelligence that the Crowns were vexed and grieved by affairs in the Indies. Therewith the malady tightened its seizure of Columbus and he, sadly aware that his brother Diego was not fitted for authority, did arbitrarily appoint Bartholomew governor of Hispaniola and this a flagrant assumption of royal prerogative.

This deed brought hue from all—the colonists, soldiers, gentlemen, and ecclesiastics, and anarchy threatened until Bartholomew struck with a bold hand, for he was not a vacillating dreamer like his elder brother or a mooning witling like his younger brother. Bartholomew Columbus forged a semblance of discipline and pulled from the fire the charred chestnuts of Don Christopher's caprice, and then came from Spain glad tidings that the Sovereigns still were firm in their faith in their admiral and viceroy.

The message revived Christopher Columbus and he shook off the seizure that had stricken him for five months and he and Bartholomew set forth resolutely to reorganize the colony and to teach the natives the theism of toil. The Indians fled and dogs were set upon them and many were taken into bondage and others were sent into the arms of their heathen gods from the branches of Hispaniola's trees.

A tax was levied upon the natives and when they shook their heads in agonizing bewilderment the Columbus brothers, Don Christopher and Bartholomew, ordered them to be beaten and branded while brother Diego told his Rosary and sickened for home and a quiet bishopric.

Mayhaps it was Bartholomew who convinced Don Christopher that gold is what yields gold or mayhaps the viceroy convinced his governor, but, be that as it may, the gold of Hispaniola was slavery and The Very Magnificent Lord began shipping fettered Indians to Spain on the pretense they were prizes of war and therefore subject to bondage.

Woe betide! The Sovereigns, forsooth, discerned the cunning. All Europe perceived the artifice, and the Church, and many were the clerics who shouted their protestations. The pious Isabel wept her mortification and Ferdinand turned his hind to the Augean stables of the Indies and squeezed his treasury and sent his army into Italy to struggle with France for domination of that exhausted land while a whole new world hung ripe for the plucking.

Quickly, and before the schism widened and the Pope himself could speak his displeasure, Isabel dispatched an emissary to Hispaniola with authority of inquiry and dictum to Columbus that he desist from slave trafficking. Now, as for myself, being a Moslem and a man of practical bent, I accept the institution of slavery as the proper status for lesser breeds, but the Queen naturally opposed bondage by others of vassals that belonged to her, for the Indies were possessions of Spain and the inhabitants thereof were subjects of the Sovereigns, they being the landlords, albeit the Indians were not liegemen as they had vowed neither homage nor fealty to the Crowns.

The arrival in Hispaniola of the Court's envoy constrained the viceroy into a bitter precipitancy and for months he wrangled over the meaning and shades of meaning of the inquisitor's credentials, harangued that delegate on the laws of contracts and defied his authority until the emissary wearied of the trickery and warned Columbus to accept inquiry or face the consequences at court.

This was an insufferable wound to the *soberbia* of The Very Magnificent Lord, and even the wisdom of Islam can not render the full meaning of *soberbia*, the hauteur, the pride, the entirety of a Spaniard within self. *Soberbia* is denied the Italian, the Frenchman and, naturally, the Briton.

He could not avoid the inquiry and it was adverse and Columbus assumed he would be humiliated at court and, thereupon, to appease his *soberbia* he humiliated himself and cowled his head in the humble hood of his Order of St. Francis and abased himself and was, therefore, beyond the insults and mockery of mere mortals.

His righteous mantle he pulled tight around himself, his shield and his buckler, and embarked for Spain and arrived in Cadiz in June of 1496 and journeyed to court in sackcloth and prostrated himself before his Sovereigns and wept his humiliation. Isabel rebuked him mildly and forgave him and he cast off his monastic garb and tarried at court, intriguing to restore himself to full favor and into command of another expedition.

The studdish Ferdinand, however, snorted his disgust for an admiral who came wailing in friar's cloth and gave his mind to his Italian campaign, and to his army that was melting away of a plague that had turned Naples into a charnal house.

This disease was the love scourge that now memorializes the legendary swineherd Syphilis, the youth who sang so woefully of the flame and ashes of his fervor; and this name only recently attached to the affliction and, remember, I now am an old man.

At first it was called the French disease by the Italians and the Italian disease by the French and no curse to compare ever has been visited upon mortal flesh. It swept Europe like a simoom from the desert, like a hurricane from the Indies whence it came.

I have informed myself on this cataclysm, partly at urge of my intellectual curiosity but mostly at behest of business, and I have found no acceptable evidence that the plague appeared in Europe prior to 1494 and the return of caravels from Hispaniola. In that year the armies began to move from Spain and France and into Italy.

But, heed! As I have recounted previously, one Ruy Diaz de Isla, physician, has writ that he treated the malady in Barcelona in 1493 and soon after our return from the First Voyage. Many of the sailors who accompanied Columbus home on the *Nina* went in his processional to Barcelona, although none from our *Pinta*. I heard naught of sores and sickness on the *Nina* and had Syphilis ravished the men I surely would have got bruit thereon.

I do know that, save the fevers and agues of our brave Pinzon, no man on our *Pinta* suffered ail or accident. Therefore, I am constrained to the judgment that the pestilence was not brought back from the First Voyage, and why, I know not. For we lay with many maids and now we know that most Indian shes were afflicted of the malady albeit their humors had accumulated specifics that held the blight in arrest among those people. Yet, and woe betide! when the virility of Spaniards pleasured the women it did awaken the sleeping Hecate and she took flight from the nethers and to the couches and bowers of Europe.

So I hold that, through the graces of the Fates, the Discovery Voyage did not fetch the demon to Europe, but that he rode the sails of the ships of the Second Voyage, those caravels that Columbus sent home in 1494, just as the armies were moving. Be that as it will, by the time the admiral himself returned in 1496 this plague had fastened itself upon the people and the lowly were dying in shrieking agony and the mighty in slobbering imbecility.

In France the dead were stacked like logs and grease was poured upon them and they were burned in ovens. Rome was a pesthouse, England a madhouse, and Spain was a pyre. The Poles, the Swiss, the Muscovites—and into Islam and India. No people escaped. The victims were herded into the countryside and none would feed them or give them alms. The soldiery dared not approach them and the people died in swarms.

Alchemists prescribed strong purgatives as a specific, and aloes became dearer than indulgences and a stream of gold flowed from Christendom into the treasury of Mudarra the Moor, the shunned one, the exile.

Then Europe came begging the services of Islam's anointers, for my people preserved their health through intelligent hygiene and diet and hospitals, and we had physicians while Europe practiced leechcraft and excoriated devils.

Islam's men of science dictated the mercury remedy, the restorative used for leprosy, and in this the sores were greased with mercury mixed with lard and the victim was secured in a box that was heated by a charcoal fire, and the poison was sweated from the humors.

The mercury dried the sores and removed all visible evidences, but the fires burned within and man knew not his lot when he lay with maid.

I dispatched agents into Spain and they invested heavily for me in the mercury mines of Almaden and the profits therefrom I rented to Genoese bankers, with instructions that, if the occasion presented itself, the gold should be advanced for the Science of Exploration.

I knew Christopher Columbus and I dangled the bait.

He still was at court, scheming for support for another voyage, but Isabel had no moment for his pleas as she and Ferdinand had scraped their treasury to manipulate nuptials between their son, the aesthetic Prince John of Castile, and Princess Margaret of Austria, and she a Hapsburg.

Now here I must tarry, and briefly, to refresh your memory on the events of Spain's royal amours, inasmuch as they affected Don Christopher, and what concerned him, concerned me.

It ever had been the policy of Isabel to ally Spain and Portugal through marriage and then into an Iberian empire that could control Africa and, aye, all of the Mediterranean and even holy Jerusalem—which, as you know, is as sacred to Moslems as to Christians and Jews because from that city Mohammed was ascended into heaven.

The first move in this contrivance to empire through wedlock was the union of Princess Isabel, the elder daughter of the Sovereigns, to Prince John of Portugal, and then the Prince died without heir.

The next liaison was the marriage of Princess Joanna to Philip, Archduke of the Holy Roman Empire, a German profligate of bestial instincts and Flemish arrogance. Joanna breached a son named Charles (aye, this was *the* Charles) and having performed this duty for State, she did madden into stark lunacy, and that, aroint! was that.

Then Spain delivered her heir, the sensitive Prince John, into the puissant embrace of Margaret of Austria, sister of Philip, and she did love her Iberian lord to death, clinging to him until she sapped his manhood and he wasted away and expired.

At this intermission in the drama, the only heir to Spain's crown was the boy Charles, son of a rake and a mad mother. This would never do, for Spain must not be delivered unto the Germans. Wherewith, Queen Isabel took her daughter, the widowed Princess Isabel, back to Portugal and there mated her with young King Manuel and to them was born a son and called Don Manuel, and this infant the incarnation of the hopes of an Iberian empire. His birth demanded his mother's life and this she gave that Spain and Portugal might have a joint heir, and then, sad hour, the prince died after a year and seven months of wizened life.

The Moerae often had jeered Spain, but now they had spat in her face, for the death of the boy was an incalculable tragedy. It dashed all dreams for an Iberian union and set the proud crown of Spain as a prize for German princes who loved Flanders more than Andalusia, the cold seas more than Mare Nostrum, fat horses more than ships, and pig grease more than olives. This will be the doom of Spain. Heed my prophecy.[2]

It was the enticement of expansion, the knowledge that Spain could not marry an empire and must create one, that provided Christopher Columbus the sortilege that opened the Queen's portals to him

---

[2]The narrator's hatred of Christopher Columbus leads him often to fanatical conclusions, but his perspicacity for things to come was remarkably acute.

again and alerted her ears to his honeyed words. Pope and Portugal were holding Spain from Africa, therefore Spain should build beyond the Ocean Sea. He boasted that, without loss of man or ship, he had possessed for her more than three hundred miles of Asia's mainland (Cuba) and that India's back door was opened for colonists and Cross.

To Isabel, empire was wheat fields and cattle and cities, but to Columbus it meant power to his family, for he held, in perpetuity, viceroyalty over all lands he discovered and accrual of ten per centum of profits therefrom. First, his appointment of Bartholomew as governor of Hispaniola must be approved by royal decree.

The Queen hesitated and then came news that a cargo of gold was in shipment from the island and when the ship arrived—the gold was slaves. Isabel was agitated into an infirmity and, adroitly, Columbus exonerated himself and his brother: himself because he was not in Hispaniola and Bartholomew because his authority there had not royal sanction.

Thereupon, Bartholomew Columbus was made governor of the island by royal appointment and was instructed to build a settlement on the south coast of Hispaniola and nigh the mines of Cibao, whence was trickling gold. Thus was founded the city of Santo Domingo[3] and the brothers Columbus were at the helm again.

Quickly Don Christopher pressed for appointment at court of his son Diego, legitimate, and his son Ferdinand, bastard.

It was done.

A bishopric for brother Diego.

Refused. That slothful cove was an alien, and Spain's bishops must be Spaniards.

The persuasion deftly was shifted from family to Spain. Hispaniola should be colonized by convicts bounded to four years of service and then rewarded with freedom and land.

Granted.

All goods moving to and from Hispaniola by order of the King, the Queen, and/or Christopher Columbus to be free of all duties.

Granted. But he no longer could have a monopoly on exploration to the west.

Columbus to have gold for a third expedition for discovery.

Refused. The treasury was empty.

[3]The oldest European city in the New World.

302

Now, Don Christopher, by astute manipulation, had accumulated considerable wealth (albeit impecunious by my standards, and ever mendicant) and this capital was with Genoese bankers to avoid Spanish taxes. But he elected not to risk his own money and turned to the Genoese bankers for loans secured by the Crowns and these were arranged, and for the first time The Very Magnificent Lord heard that Mudarra, the enterpriser of Tangier, was a lenient lender for causes scientific, particularly the Science of Exploration.

And so, on borrowed money and some of it mine, Columbus began equipping six caravels for his voyage and was harassed by delays because the Sovereigns insisted that the Ministry of Affairs of the Indies be kept informed of all details, and the liaison for this task was one Ximeno, converso.

Don Christopher, by the bonds of breed, had every reason to expect accord from Ximeno, but that civil servant forever was prying and carping, and eventually the admiral was seized of a temper and smote Ximeno with his fists and kicked him, and this in public view on the deck of an anchored ship.

Well might this effrontery to the Ministry have brought royal censure to the admiral and beached him, but then came intelligence from Hispaniola that stirred all to frightened endeavor.

Revolt had stricken the island and the rebels had pulled away from the colony and had founded their own command.

In Isabella and Santo Domingo, the colonists were making sport with Indians and matching them in bloody tournaments.

The colonists had seized the bride of a cacique and as ransom the chieftain had delivered five thousand laborers to the masters, and each laborer burdened with a sharpened stick with which to till the earth. The land was planted to cotton, and the cotton was tended by Indians bound to Spanish overlords by their own ruler.

And Syphilis was rampant. The Indians called it bubas.

Thus there was no moment for inquiry and correction in Spain, and on May 30, 1498, the Admiral of the Ocean Sea sailed his fleet westward on the Third Voyage; and this fateful event actually ten days after Vasco da Gama had taken the Portuguese standard around Africa and to Calicut, in India, and only a few days earlier a pilot nicknamed Llavrador led John Cabot and his English crew to a new land far to the north and west, and Cabot named it Labrador's Land.

The agents who fetched this bruit to Mita and me were rewarded most lavishly. To one we presented a Circassian slave and to another a Persian carpet and a bale of hemp and to all we served frozen cream, congealed by ice from the Atlas Mountains.

The fifteenth century was waning and Columbus was at sea again and I was a rich man in Tangier, but my soul yearned for the songs of comrades, for their clasps on my arm.

"Six ships he took, aye?" I asked. "What of these? What of the ships?"

"Caravels and naos, Mudarra. Creaking old jades."

"The *Nina*. Was she among them?"

"Nay. The *Nina* was sent ahead as a courier to Hispaniola. Also the *India*, a nao. The admiral sails *Santa Cruz*, nicknamed *El Correo*—The Mail."

"What of the *Pinta*? Any news of the *Pinta*?"

"That flying pig!" They all laughed. "We neglected to report that she is sunk. Somewhere off Italy, Mudarra. While serving the King's army in the campaign off Naples. Surely, it is of no consequence."

The *Nina* still sailing and the *Pinta* down. And then the agents were gone—back to their chores for me; and Mita and I were alone again.

# CHAPTER 22

*T*HE CHRISTIAN YEAR OF 1500, BEING 878 YEARS AFTER THE Hegira, came with ominous portents in Islam and in Europe, and holy men, both dervishes and hermits, prophesied that the Day of Judgment was nigh. Strange lights flamed the heavens, whirling plates and falling stars, and all Christendom was in a ferment of war and plague, and multitudes wandered from one principality to another and wailed for bread and salvation.

Calls for a holy war, the bloody jihad, were heard in Damascus and Mecca and yet Islam would not respond, for we were rent by feuds and were men of little faith, and The Messenger's apostolate was breaking into sects and divisions as the Christians soon must do.

We had no Saladin to unite us and they had no Urban II and the two great houses of God rotted behind their walls and clawed themselves in civil strife while the Kingdom of Christ was bled white and the empire of Mohammed was stagnant into prostration.

None of my Portuguese or Spanish agents came visiting that spring, for Islam had revived the ancient laws against Christians and compelled each to wear a bell around his neck and to sit his beast with his face to the rump, and I was without reliable news from Europe and, therefore, was restless and irritable.

Mita had become most intemperate of word and behavior because her barren womb had shamed her pride and had fastened a mania of jealousy upon her reason, and this affection ofttimes so violent that she beat with her hands any maidservant who dared look at me and railed publicly against the gentlewomen of Tangier who came to my shops for merchandise.

Some of the luster was gone from her eyes, albeit none of the flame from her lips or loins, and often she crawled onto my lap like a child and wept on my chest as I stared across the Strait toward Spain.

I sought solace in the piety of The Messenger and read the Koran thrice daily and she retreated into the sanctuary of her Judaism and although our beings were one in the unblessed wedlock of our choice, ne'ertheless our spirits were separated.

We gave without stint to the hospitals and to the poor, she to the Jews and I to the Moslems, and we traveled as far as Egypt and yet our leisure was a burden to us. She wove garments for my back, cloaks of silken and golden threads, and I studied the wisdom of Islam: the Particulars of Ibn Jinni, the Elucidation of Al Farisi, and the Examples and the Flowers of Speech. Sometimes, in our boredom, we played the ancient Persian game of chatrang[1] or strolled to the playing field to watch Arabian horsemen at the sport of mall.[2] But mostly we dallied in our patio and gardens and my waist was thickening into a hint of obesity while Mita remained as lithe as a reed.

Then the month of Jumada II was upon us and to celebrate the season I freed ten slaves in keeping with The Messenger's edict of brotherhood, for, as you know, under Islamic law the slave of today can be the master tomorrow and no man is born in bondage.

Most of the restrictions against Christians were lifted to stimulate almsgiving and to encourage trade, and therewith higher taxes, and my representatives began arriving from Portugal and Spain, and, by the Beard, the things that had happened.

The source of my fortune and the amount thereof was gossip in all the courts and I was accounted an amir of Islam, and this ridiculous, and a descendant of The Messenger himself, and this preposterous albeit a typical exercise of Christian ignorance, for, actually, I had no station whatsoever in Islam and this the penalty for my bastardy and my probity to a barren Jewess and the absence from my head of the colored turban of a pilgrimage.

A dog's spittle for Christian tattle, but to facts: Queen Isabel was grieving herself to death at loss of her children and the uncertain succession of the Crown of Spain.

Henry VII of England had, through craft and diplomacy, made himself the richest monarch of Europe and his kingdom was in a

[1]Chess.
[2]Polo.

flurry of expansion and building, and the King himself had contributed much to a chapel at Westminster which bears his name, and this edifice almost worthy of Andalusia.

And Don Christopher Columbus? Hold, and hear.

He had, for his Third Voyage, sailed not straightway to Hispaniola to restore order there, but had dropped far south and eventually had come upon an island which he named Trinidad, to honor the Trinity, and again he was near unto the truth: that my cry at San Salvador was the call to a new world and not to India at all.

For Trinidad is so nigh unto the Great South Continent that a single gesture to the Fates would have cast his ships into the mouth of the Orinoco River to touch for himself the mainland of the New World and to bestow upon it his name or any name he chose.

But Columbus dallied at anchorage off Trinidad and sought to entice the Indians to trade by compelling his gromets to beat upon brass chamber pots and to dance, and this behavior provoked the natives, as they took it to be a war dance and thereupon shot arrows at the fleet.

And the admiral set sail and moved north and thence through the gate that separates Trinidad from the continent and he was in the Gulf of Paria and saw the mainland in the distance and bethought it an island, and named it the Isle of Grace, and set not foot upon it.

Here it was that his men lowered buckets into the sea and the water was fresh and yet they were much distance offshore, and this surely evidence of a great river draining a mainland. This again was the time and this the place to follow his star and sail a few more leagues and discover the great river and know the truth; but the admiral refused to believe the obvious—that at last he had reached the mainland. Cuba was the mainland, and on that he stood and on that he fell.

Oh that Pinzon had been with him to urge him on. But, nay, Columbus complained of sleeplessness, of faltering sight, and bodily pains and secluded himself in his cabin and wrote his Queen a letter, to be delivered later, that he had discovered Paradise. First India, and now Paradise.

For posterity he writ: "The Scriptures say that in the earthly Paradise grows the Tree of Life and from it flows a spring which gives birth to four rivers." Three of these are the Tigris, the Ganges, the Nile—and he had found the fourth.

"No one can reach the earthly Paradise save by Divine Will. I be-

307

lieve that this water may come from there, even if it be far-away. The site is in conformity with the opinion of great theologians, and all facts also point that way, for I never heard or read that so much fresh water could mix with salt water and penetrate so far into it, and in this there is also some help from the soft temperature. And if this river does not flow from Paradise, the marvel is greater still, for I do not think there is known in the world a river so big and so deep."

This also was the place where, basing his opinions in part on scientific observations but mostly on superstition, he decided that the earth is not a sphere and so writ: "I always read that the earth was spherical. Now I observed so much divergence that I began to hold different views about the world and I found that it was not round, but pear-shaped, round except where it has a nipple, for there it is taller, or as if one had a round ball and, on one side, it should be like a woman's breast, and this nipple part is the highest and closest to heaven, and it is under the equinoctial line, in this Ocean Sea, at the end of the Orient. I call end of the Orient where all land and islands end."

Ptolemy was wrong. Salamanca was wrong. All philosophers were wrong. The earth is not a sphere. It wears a cap and from this cap sprouts a nipple that points to heaven. Mother of all! And this man called himself a scientist and a sailor.

He did observe, and rightly, that the waters of the sea move from east to west, and this a truth that Pinzon would have seized upon long ere this.

And now, having found Paradise, he sought trade with the Indians and sent men to shore and these, forsooth, the first Europeans to touch the mainland of the New World, albeit they believed it an island because their admiral so spake.

Columbus did not go ashore and his men fetched to him Indian corn and cobs thereof, and a brew made of this corn and it a potion most fiery, and very potent. Also they fetched guanin, a metal of gold, silver, and copper, but Columbus appraised not its value or its meaning and was suspicious of the natives inasmuch as they valued Spanish brass more than their own guanin, although this metal was more than fifty per centum of gold and twenty-five per centum of silver, and surely suggested a culture wholly different from the primitive existence on Hispaniola.

Confusion seize! For this was the Place of Pearls.

The sailors first noticed the pearls around the necks of the Indians and then found the oysters whence they came, and these oysters of such abundance that they piled upon the shore and drank the dew of heaven, and this dew impregnated the oysters and the pearls were their young.

A handful of these seeds to the court would have soared his star high over Spain and yet he dispatched none of the pearls to his Sovereigns, neither this intelligence, but charted the place and instructed the Indians to hoard bushels of the jewels for him, and that he would return.

Thereupon, he raised sail for Hispaniola after explaining to his men that he had supplies for the colony and must deliver them ere they rotted.

As you know, this behavior has borned the avouchment that Columbus schemed to keep for himself the secret of the pearls and to trick his monarchs. This I will not accept although the wormwood of my bitterness seeps into my humors and my contempt for Don Christopher Columbus floods my waking hours. He could not keep the Place of Pearls a secret and this he knew, for his captains and many of his sailors could sail dead-reckoned to the coast. Nay, it was the vanity of the self-anointed that he hold for himself for a while the knowledge that pearls in abundance were in *his* Indies, and the cunning of the charlatan that he withhold this knowledge from court until it could serve him best. His men could not return to Spain with the news until he sanctioned their return. Also, he was viceroy of all lands he discovered and no man could explore the Place of Pearls without his consent and if any man should, then ten per centum of all treasure found belonged to The Very Magnificent Lord by right of contract, the Capitulations of Santa Fe.

Thus, his body in pain and his mind in bliss, he hastened to Hispaniola and arrived there on August 31, 1498, and found the colony beset by revolt, plague, and sloth. Bartholomew Columbus was unable to cope with the situation.

Don Christopher strove to bring array out of confusion, and only increased confusion. He treated with the rebels rather than hang them and endeavored for peace with men who wanted no peace, but only slaves for their beck and women for their beds.

The people would not heed his commands and even the convicts he had settled upon the land became overlords and reviled him. They demanded enslavement of the Indians and this the court forbade and Columbus was trapped between the landowners who held for slavery and the Sovereigns who denied it.

Again he compromised and accepted the system of encomienda, through which workers were bound to the land by trust, and this heinous rule[3] remains in force at the time I write these words.

But this recedence did not satisfy the people who, having humbled their despised viceroy, were determined to pull him down and they did flash the dreaded steel and thrust it and proclaim publicly that which had been whispered for months: that the Columbus family were conversos.

Don Christopher reacted instinctively and protested it was a cabal to destroy him, and protested too much, and then writ a document that those who accused him were themselves conversos and enemies of the Crowns and of Christians. First he denied Israel and then flung at his enemies the same brand with which they had burned his brow.

The landowners turned upon him like hungry dogs and this time he was ensnared between the colonists of property and the rebels who owned naught, between order and anarchy, between the haves and the have-nots, the masters and the peasants, the autocrats and the democrats; and he capitulated abjectly to the rabble and gave their leader, one Francisco Roldan, an office in the colony and the title of Alcalde.

This surrender was certain to kindle repercussions in Spain and to pacify the Sovereigns and to shift their minds from his failures as viceroy he dispatched to them some of the pearls he had found, and charts to the Place of Pearls, and the letter that he had found Paradise.

Then in a trance of mysticism, he took himself to sea and communed with his saints and did write:

"I found myself in such extremity that, to fly from death, I left everything and went right out to sea, in a small caravel; then Our Lord came to my help, saying: 'Oh man of little faith, have no fear. It is I. Have courage; be not dismayed, and fear not. I shall see to all. The seven years' limit for gold is not over; and in that as in everything else I will set things aright for thee.' And so He dispersed

[3]A system of peonage that remained in force for centuries.

my enemies and showed me how to fulfill my offers. Oh unhappy sinner, I, who made everything depend on worldly hopes!"

And having heard the voice of God, he did dispatch a letter to his Sovereigns that they send him a learned man to administer justice on Hispaniola, and presumed to suggest that his own son, Don Diego, be sent forth—maybe as administrator, but surely with fitting privileges to assist his father. Brother Diego had failed. Brother Bartholomew had failed. Now the court should trust son Diego.

The letter of Paradise and the charts to the Place of Pearls arrived at the Ministry of Affairs of the Indies long before the letter asking that an administrator be sent out, and the Minister of Indian Affairs was Don Juan de Fonseca, whom Columbus had abused and whose man Columbus had smote down with his fists.

It was the Ministry that granted Alonso de Hojeda permission to explore beyond the Ocean Sea, after protecting itself with a ruling that the King himself, as far back as 1497, had canceled Columbus' monopoly on exploration and all this, I caution you, a legal enigma that has bewildered the best minds of Europe, as well as my own.

But be it legal or outlaw, Hojeda prepared an expedition and some of the money therefor was raised by Amerigo Vespucci, liar and braggart, albeit one of the best salesmen ever to swindle the unsuspecting, and the man whose coffers I had helped fill and who had helped fill mine.

Vespucci sailed with the fleet and they made the coast of the Great South Continent, and this in 1499, and found the Place of Pearls and named the land in those parts Venezuela, which is to say Little Venice, because the Indians' houses were on stilts.

Thence the fleet hied to Hispaniola and harassed both Columbus and the rebels unmercifully before returning to Spain with a cargo of slaves, and many pearls.

It was at this time, or thereabouts, that Vespucci wrote reports of his voyage and sent them to merchants throughout Spain and Portugal and claimed great achievements for himself, and signed these memoranda with his first name: Amerigo. Also, he prepared a map (or hired it drawn) and dated this map two years previously, to precede Columbus' Third Voyage to the same waters, and this a fraud of evil perpetration.

This map he also signed: Amerigo. And thus it came to be that

311

the New World was called Amerigo's Land by merchants and salesmen, and then simply—Americi.

That Vespucci. The sly one. Now there was an Italian, a Florentine, to match the cunning of Don Christopher. The pox for your brood, Amerigo Vespucci. I knew you well, you monger and clerk. You never pulled sail in your life. Would that you had lived long enough for me to crush you, as I would crush Columbus, for if the New World was not to bear the admiral's name, or Pinzon's name, then it should bear my name; I who saw it first.

But back to the business that confronts me. News of the Place of Pearls would not be contained within the court or the Ministry of Indian Affairs, and I tell you that it was pearls that launched the caravels of Spain. Not gold, or Cross or land, but pearls from oysters that drank the dew of heaven.

Peralanso Nino, who had piloted the *Nina* on the First Voyage, took to sea from Palos and fetched home a fortune in pearls. Vicente Pinzon, the head of the family since the death of my captain, made the most daring voyage of all and sailed straightway to the Great South Continent and there found brazilwood in plenty and a river of sweet water and great as a sea, and he named it Mar Dulce.[4]

Caravels were frothing the Ocean Sea from Asturias to Andalusia, fanning westward, for the age of exploration that we had borned was now of stride and all men knew a new world had been found, all save Christopher Columbus and he would believe not. It must be the Indies. God had spake to him.

But Benjamin Marino was right. A new world lay to the West and Spain remembered not the mild professor who had so spake, the bearded Jew who had sired my Mita.

(The turn of the century was nigh, the Christian year of 1500, and Ponce de Leon already had made one voyage to Hispaniola and was readying another; Ferdinand Magellan had given himself into the service of his Portuguese king; Hernando Cortes was a student at the University of Salamanca; Francisco Pizarro, the illiterate bastard of Estremadura, was tending swine, and in the same province an infant named Hernando De Soto was suckling his mother and concerning himself not a whit that Columbus' world had a tit that pointed toward heaven.)

[4]The Amazon, which, by volume, is the greatest river in the world.

Aye, pearls and brazilwood, and the dye therefrom, were enriching the royal treasury, but the only offerings from Hispaniola were reports of chaos and whines from the viceroy that his privileges had been ignored and that lawless adventurers were poaching in his Indies and stealing his wealth. The three Columbus brothers—Christopher, Bartholomew, and Diego—wielded the scepter in Hispaniola and used it one day as a club and the next as a jester's trinket and King Ferdinand himself eventually did sicken of the incompetence and bespake his wife:

"The man is a good admiral but a poor viceroy. He must be replaced."

And now Isabel did agree, and most sadly but with resolution, for Isabel, above all things, was a queen. There was an affinity between this lonely woman and Don Christopher, a maternal yearning in her heart that has been bantered by lewd fellows who cannot comprehend love without lust. She had pity and prayers for Columbus, but statecraft demanded his removal and she did not temporize with her emotions and steadfastly heeded her reason.

"Aye," she agreed. "He must be replaced."

Wherewith, Francisco de Bobadilla was ordered to Hispaniola with full powers as governor and magistrate and instructions to decide which gentlemen and other persons should be sent back to Spain, and to take any necessary action to establish order in the colony.

The first sight that greeted Bobadilla upon his arrival at Santo Domingo, which place had been made the capital of Hispaniola, was two Spanish bodies hanging for the vultures and a ship loading slaves, and some of these slaves were women with half-caste babies in their arms and their bellies again swollen with seed.

Salaried workers had not been paid and Spanish gentlemen were in chains, and Bobadilla did seek to have converse with Don Christopher and the viceroy shunned him and then openly defied him and his royal instructions. For a time Bobadilla was patient and Columbus harangued him on the laws of contracts and privileges, and proposed all manners of artifice to circumvent the magistrate's authority; and then came the monstrous rumors that Don Christopher had schemed with the Genoese to hand over the island to the city of his birthplace.

Now, this canard I will not believe, although many do.

Yet it is true that Columbus had made agreement with certain Indians that they should fall upon Santo Domingo at his instructions.

313

He and his brothers defied orders from the Sovereigns and, at last, Bobadilla was harassed into exasperation and commanded that The Very Magnificent Lord be fettered and returned to Spain for judgment.

No man of station would fasten the shackles on the admiral's feet or the iron bracelets upon his arms, and then his own servant, his cook, did volunteer gleefully for the task, and thus Christopher Columbus was fettered like a criminal and was imprisoned in his own gaol; he and his brothers Bartholomew and Diego.

And there he brooded his woe and talked with his God, and then came to him Alonso de Vallejo, a mariner of straightforward demeanor, a captain of many voyages, and he spake to Columbus: "Sire, you will come with me to my caravel."

The admiral's countenance was aggrieved and he asked: "Vallejo, where are you taking me?"

"Sire, Your Lordship is going to the ship, to embark for Spain."

"Vallejo, is it true?" The vehemence of his fear showed plainly on his face.

"By Your Lordship's life, it is true that you are going to embark. But, now hear this." The mariner drew himself erect in the pride of his calling. "Aboard my ship I am master, and I, the son of a Goth, will strike the fetters from my admiral's feet and from his arms, and this with my own hands."

"No, Vallejo." Don Christopher dragged his chains as he walked and winced the pain of his festering flesh. Then he held high the bracelets on his arms and spake his vow. "If I had stolen the Indies and given them to the Moors, I could not meet with more enmity in Spain. Therefore, and by St. Fernando, I shall wear these fetters until tears from the eyes of the Queen of Spain shall loosen this iron. To your caravel and to Spain, Alonso de Vallejo."

And he did depart Hispaniola on October 12, 1500, and this eight years from the morn when I sighted the New World and called out "Land!" and then, like a fool, had gloried in his promise of the Queen's pension and the velvet doublet.

He arrived in Cadiz on November 24 and walked ashore without aid, dragging his chains for all to see and debasing himself; he who was so cunning in the craft of humility, the mariner who would be a martyr.

The court was at Granada and Ferdinand and Isabel were appalled that Bobadilla had been compelled to shackle their admiral and they ordered the chains removed forthwith, and the Queen did weep and send to Columbus a purse of 2000 ducats; and her tears loosed the iron and strengthened his spirit, or, mayhaps, it was the ducats.

He and his brothers presented themselves to the Sovereigns, and Don Christopher sank to his knees and sobbed and the Queen herself touched his head and bade him arise and this he did and poured forth his laments and accounted his services to Spain, and beat his chest and swore fealty forever.

Brother Diego stared doltishly around the hall, ogling the rich trappings, and the monarchs dismissed him as the liripoop he was.

Brother Bartholomew, however, bent not his neck, but stepped boldly before Ferdinand and Isabel and spake: "I was asked by my brother to rise with him in honors and wealth and, to this end, I did pledge my services to Your Highnesses. I have given seven years of my life to Spain, only, at this hour, to be deprived of my honors and liberty. My salary has not been paid. I ask Your Highnesses to rectify this injustice. My services remain at your disposal if they are needed. Otherwise, I beseech dismissal as I am quite able to care for myself."

He was allowed to go in peace.

But Don Christopher was instructed to remain at court until adjustment of his case could be arranged. Meanwhile the Sovereigns were faced with more pressing matters of state. The Spanish Moors of Granada were threatening revolt and the Inquisition was dooming Judaizers in droves, and these ungrateful sheep were stirring a most unwholesome din by bleating the chants of old Israel as they were driven to slaughter. The kingdom was retching of blood.

It was then that a letter came from Hispaniola to Cardinal Cisneros, himself the Prime Minister at court and one determined to sanctify conversos by fire, and the letter did say: "For God's sake, since Your Reverence has been the occasion for freeing this land from the sway of King Pharaoh, see that neither he nor any of his nation ever come to these islands."

They were calling him Pharaoh, and Pharaoh meant Jew; and they were calling him *faraón*, and *faraón* was the vernacular for Jew.

Therefore, it appeared that the Cardinal, the tocsin of the Inquisition, had strove against Don Christopher and the suspicion was Jewry. The arrow that Mita and I had shot into the air from so far away and so long ago had at last fallen upon him, and he was pulled down from his exaltation.

The agents who brought us this news laughed most uncouthly at the broken fortunes of Christopher Columbus, but I felt no jubilation and a mask of pity was upon Mita's sweet countenance. "He remains in Granada?" she asked.

"Aye. He shuffles about the streets, for he is an old man, and the people jeer him."

"Is his mistress not with him?"

"Nay. She is in Cordova and lives on the Queen's pension that he awarded her. 'Tis not much, but it keeps her in food and raiment."

"Then he is alone?" Mita was sensitive to the affliction of loneliness. "There is none to comfort him?"

"Aye. A kinswoman of his mistress is with him. One Maraela Harana, and she tends his needs and remains at his beck both day and night."

Mita raised her eyes to mine and then quickly lowered them, for, over the years, I had told her scant fragments about Maraela and, womanlike, she had surmised much more and was jealous of a maid I had not seen since my boyhood, a woman who now was at thirty years and I had passed my thirty-first.

The agents departed us and Mita came and curled in my lap and sought to arouse me to vigor, and there was no vigor within me. I sat staring at my hands and they were scented of rose water and growing pudgy.

Mita flounced from my lap and scolded me and abused my manliness and I seized her wrist and pulled her to me and caressed her into serenity and then she did say to me: "Rodrigo, Christopher Columbus is fallen. My father's name shall never be vindicated and your vow of vengeance is empty, save you deign stand over a prostrate man and thrust for his heart."

Slowly I shook my head and looked upon the sea and beyond toward Spain, for the hour of my revenge soon must toll. "Nay, Mita. You, too, have ceded to the cunning of my enemy and hope mercy for a man who does not understand mercy. You pity the lion who has hidden his claws. You know not Christopher Columbus. His heart is of the century passed and his mind of the century to come. He is neither saint nor devil, neither feudal Christian nor a Jew of Job's ilk. He is a new breed, the genesis of a horde that will fasten purse and

Cross to their swords and trample the earth. The portents we have seen do not augur the end of the world, but the end of the world as we have known it. And Christopher Columbus is the sign, if we will but see it. He is the star-son of the Fates and they will raise him up again, for the Fates are jealous of their own. Even now, and this I wager, Don Christopher is scheming at court."

And so he was.

The Sovereigns wished he would accept a marquisate and retire from court and write his memoirs. But he held titles of admiral and viceroy in perpetuity, and this a source of much embarrassment to Isabel and of much vexation to Ferdinand for they could not easily strip him of his honors without exposing themselves to an indictment of duplicity, that they had suffered the seed of Israel to outwit them in the Capitulations of Santa Fe.

It was then that Christopher Columbus seized upon a stroke so bold that the populace gasped its astonishment and then cheered his resolve. He would go exploring again and fetch great wealth to the Crowns and this wealth should be used to liberate Jerusalem from the Moslems, for another crusade if need be. The spirit of crusade had been languishing for more than two centuries, but he quickened it and the people raised their pallid faces and bovine eyes to the dream of the Holy Sepulchre freed again. Like the demagogues of ancient Greece, he understood the obstinacy, the power of the masses, the inexorable pressure of bleating sheep.

He dared even propound a new doctrine and wrote: "I say that the Holy Ghost works in Christians, Jews, Moors, and all men of any other sect and not merely in the learned but in the ignorant."

Heresy. A maxim for revolution, and this years before the Reformation. Had he been less than The Very Magnificent Lord, the Inquisition would have charred his bones and damned his soul to eternal torment.

But he won. The court sent for him and promised another expedition provided he heeded these orders:

He must not bring back slaves.

He must not touch at Hispaniola on the outward voyage, although, homeward bound, he could tarry there long enough to take on wood and water. He was viceroy of the Indies no more, for the Crowns knew it was a new world and no man could be viceroy of a dominion of such magnitude.

317

And thus it came to pass that on May 9, 1502, the Admiral of the Ocean Sea took to his waters again in a fleet of four ships, and his star was low on the horizon, and blinking dimly. Bartholomew was with him. So was Ferdinand, his bastard son by Beatriz Harana.

Scarcely at sea, he did violate deliberately the orders of the court and sailed directly for Santo Domingo and there he was refused haven and was commanded to begone forever from Hispaniola.

He smelled a wind and sought a cove and then a storm fell upon the island with such ferocity that it sunk twenty ships at Santo Domingo and one of them loaded with gold, and the gold was lost as was Francisco de Bobadilla who had committed the admiral to chains.

Then Columbus sailed west and along the isthmus that, as we now know, connects the Great North Continent and the Great South Continent. He was seeking a strait to follow into the Indian Sea, for he still did believe that he had found the Orient.

Disasters of many kinds befell him, and vicissitudes, and he lost two of his ships and after a year of adversity he reached Santiago and there grounded his ships and marooned himself.

His ships were rotting under his feet, so he said. They no longer were worthy of sail or sea. This he put down in his journal. But there are those who say he marooned himself deliberately to be nigh Hispaniola, the accursed island that held him like a lodestone.

The wilderness of Santiago was the burial place of his last hopes. Many of his men mutinied and deserted him, and food was scarce, and the Indians were not in trust. There he surely would have perished had not the brave Diego Mendez, Andalusian, and Bartholomew Fieschi, Genoese, volunteered to dare the Ocean Sea in canoes and try for Hispaniola.

Thereupon, Columbus retired to the cabin of his beached ship and composed his long *Lettera Rarissima*, his wail to his Sovereigns.

For page after page he exonerated himself and castigated others and ended his epistle in a lament of despair:

"I have no hair upon me that is not white, and my body is infirm and exhausted.

"The restitution of my honor and losses, and the punishment of those who have inflicted them, of those who plundered me of my pearls, and who have disparaged my admiral's privileges, will redound to the honor of your royal dignity.

"I am ruined. Hitherto I have wept for others; now have pity upon me, Heaven, and weep for me, Earth!

"Of things material, I have not even a blanca to offer; in things spiritual, I have even ceased observing the forms here in the Indies. Isolated in this pain, infirm, daily expecting death, surrounded by a million savages full of cruelty and our enemies, and thus separated from the Holy Sacraments of Holy Church, how neglected will be this soul if here it part from the body!

"Weep for me, whoever has charity, truth, and justice! I did not come on this voyage to navigate for gain, honor, or wealth, that is certain; for then the hope of all such things was dead. I came to Your Highnesses with honest purpose and sincere zeal, and I do not lie.

"I humbly beg Your Highnesses that, if it please God to remove me hence, you will aid me to go to Rome and on other pilgrimages. May the Holy Trinity guard and increase Your lives and high estate."

Mendez and Fieschi launched two canoes and, with crews of Indians and Christians, did navigate from Santiago to Hispaniola and on June 28, 1504, Columbus was rescued and was landed in Spain on November 7 of that same year.

He asked first of the Queen, and the Queen was dying; and on November 26 she pulled her withered limbs under her covers lest the priests who came to shrive her see her bare feet and outrage her modesty, and then she gave up the ghost—and her last words were prayers for mercy and justice for her Indian vassals.

Her funeral was at Segovia and Columbus was at Seville and he longed to see her face once more, but he was stricken of a paroxysm in his joints and scarcely could walk.

However, after the proper mourning, he requested audience with King Ferdinand and a mule permit that he might journey thither and present his case, and Ferdinand acquiesced and received the tottering old man most graciously, albeit with bland urbanity.

Don Christopher requested that his title of Admiral of the Ocean Sea be passed, at his death, to his son, Diego, and with this the King agreed, for, in his own mind, he separated the title of admiral from the privileges of an admiralty. Therewith, Columbus spake willingness to submit his pecuniary claims against the Crown to arbitration.

The King held, however, that the fact of Columbus' admiralty and viceroyalty was arbitrable, and the old mariner shook his head.

No! He had been created admiral and viceroy, and these rights in perpetuity, for his heirs forever and forever, and he would surrender not one whit of his rights. If the Indies be a new world or the moon, he was viceroy thereof and this right to pass to his assigns; ten per centum of all profits in the New Lands and a Columbus forever viceroy.

The King tempted him with estates in Castile and all rents therefrom, but Columbus scorned the offer. He who had compromised so often now eschewed compromise. The Indies, or nothing. The New Lands, or let this realm stand adjudged of perfidy.

Ferdinand's jaw clamped his Aragonese obduracy and summarily Columbus was dismissed, for the King's patience was exhausted and he was wearied of this garrulous old man who prattled of laws and contracts and gold. The contracts patently were beyond enforcement. Therefore, aroint! And begone, Christopher Columbus.

Isabel was dead and Ferdinand had no time for converso sophistry, no temper for Franciscan piety. He must look to his kingdom, for his daughter was mad and he must claim the regency of Castile else that jewel pass to Philip of Hapsburg or to Prince Charles, the Flemish brat that his demented Joanna had foaled.

The court was moved to Valladolid and Columbus followed on his mule and took residence there and harangued all who would heed that Spain had stolen his youth and had deserted him in his old age. He loitered in the apothecary shops until the proprietors shunned him as a pest and a nuisance and when they sickened of his babblings they always sent word to his residence and always a young woman came for him, and led him home.

It was at this time that he remembered Amerigo Vespucci, and that scoundrel disporting himself in Lisbon and buttering the King of Portugal, and he, Don Christopher, did write Vespucci that he was planning another voyage and needed to borrow money against the wealth that would be his when his claims against Spain were settled.

He was not too infirm for a voyage—so he insisted; and, forsooth, his two sons would accompany him and they were stalwart of limb and sharp of intellect.

Vespucci showed the letter in Portugal and it furnished much amusement, but Vespucci answered most courteously and informed Columbus that he could not patronize such an expedition and pleaded penury.

However, Vespucci reminded the old admiral that Mudarra, the

Moorish enterpriser of Tangier, was a man so rich that he bathed in rose water and his harem in mares' milk, and that Mudarra was a lenient lender to all things scientific, particularly the Science of Exploration.

And thus it came to be that on April 12, 1506, I received a letter from The Very Magnificent Lord requesting Mudarra the Moor to wait upon him in Valladolid that we might discuss matters of mutual concern and profit; and assuring me security in Christian Spain.

By the black shadow of the Kaaba rock! And the beard of The Messenger who blessed it! Thirteen years I had waited. Now the hour of my vengeance was tolling. Let Christopher Columbus beware.

# CHAPTER 23

*F*OR AN EXPEDIENCY THAT WILL BE APPARENT TO ALL DISCERNING readers, I chose to return to Spain ostensibly as a Morisco, which is to say a Christian Moor, and this an astute stratagem and under no conceivable circumstance a denial of The Messenger. Hence, I must put away my burnoose, the customary habiliment of Islam albeit a cloak only of convenience and fashion and of no religious significance whatsoever.

But the turban I would wear because it is testimony to my submission and, therefore, inviolable and I must not expose my pate to Christian vision for cunning or security inasmuch as my mission was for self and not the Faith, and I would not forswear the tenets to consummate my oath of vengeance or for any other cause on this earth.

My beloved Mita, in pre-emption and presumption, took unto herself the task of readying my wardrobe and forbade the seamstresses of our household and enterprises even to touch the garments that would touch me, and excluded herself to her quarters for the devotion of garbing me as befits a wealthy Morisco on a visitation to Christian Spain.

I selected the most versatile mamluk of my possessed as my body-guard and servant for the journey, a fearless Turk whose homage I had purchased and whose usual assignment was the training of my horses, my falcons, and my messenger pigeons. His name was Nur and he wore the white burnoose, the blood-red girdle and slippers, and the two long knives of the Assassins of old, those disciples of Hassan who, in the days of the Crusades, was called the Old Man of the Mountain.

With Nur at my side for counsel, I betook myself to the horse market of Tangier and purchased an Arabian stallion and Nur swabbed his nostrils with cotton and tinted them with vermeil, the flaming red juice of the cochineal bug, which he mixed with mercury and sulphur. He personally saw to my saddle, to every stitch and thong that went into it, and I selected a bridle set with jewels and reins threaded with silver.

For himself Nur chose a Flemish palfrey of broad hind, for he had made the pilgrimage to Mecca four times and was adept in the wisdom of travel.

I gave myself to much study of a gift for Christopher Columbus and settled upon an inkhorn from an ox of Israel and studded with pearls, and a quill from a bird of Cathay; and the subtlety of this offering pleased me muchly and stimulated my humors into a delectable flow.

The manager of my enterprises in Malaga, an adventurous youth named Francisco de Coronado, bargained the services of a sole fisherman and instructed him in my wishes, that he should scour his craft with limewater and vinegar and have it at Tangier within two weeks and earn twenty gold ducats by delivering a personage safely in Cadiz.

Mita gave herself so industriously to her weaving and stitching that I saw her only for an hour each afternoon, when we took our customary quiescence together and talked or played chatrang, and at darkness when she came to my couch and always slept in my arms.

March passed into April and Mita's task was completed and she brought the garments for my approval, bouffant breeches of the finest cloth and embroidered with metallic threads both gold and silver, stockings of silk, and mantles of satin with rolling collars of silk.

And then, and to my tearful joy, she held up a velvet doublet.

Neither lavish jewels nor cruel gold embarrassed its simple dignity and it was as lustrous black as the eyes of my beloved, as luxuriant as my beard, in which not one strand of white marred its virility, albeit my hair, concealed by my turban, was thin on my pate and silver above my ears.

Mita kissed away my tears and helped me disrobe and this a chore usually performed by my body servant. She slipped the doublet over my head and tugged at the sleeves and the shoulders and adjusted it to her demands, and then she spake her say: "Rodrigo, my life, the threads of this garment entwine my heart. This doublet you have earned of my hands, and for a faithfulness and affection to me far

324

beyond my merits. You will wear it to face your enemies—the man you hate and the woman I fear."

"Maraela Harana?" I sneered my loathing of the name and held Mita's face between my palms and lowered her forehead and kissed it. "I only hope that she too is in Valladolid to see her kinsman pulled down and herself to writhe in the spleen of my vendetta."

My beloved raised her eyes to me and looked at me a long time, and turned from me and went to her quarters.

And when she was gone I stepped proudly to a long mirror to see myself and lo! the doublet did not fit and the disappointment lay heavy on my spirit. I jerked the sleeves and pulled the velvet tight over my belly, but it was without shape or grace. I removed it and examined it and in my hands it was a raiment of perfection. I slipped it on again and it was shapeless. Then it came to me that I did not fit the doublet, that this coveted prize, this trophy, was made for Lepe the sailor and that Mudarra did not befit its noble elegance.

Yet I must wear it lest her heart be hurt. I must wear it because she had made it.

Nur came to my apartment to discuss the horses and at sight of me his eyes glowed his pride and he called out: "Master, the garment is magnificent upon your shoulders and around your girth. Only Mudarra is worthy of such raiment and the good djinns themselves did see to the perfection of its relevancy, for it is as simple as your faith, as soft as your compassion, and fits your noble self as the turban fitted The Messenger."

Now this astonished me and I looked at myself again.

Mita returned with a chattering group of seamstresses and Nur backed away and the women shrilled their praises of the doublet and of my appearance, and then this came to me: Mita was blinded by love and the others really knew me not and could not see what I could see, although The Rabbit would have seen, and Arcos, and Pinzon.

I soon wearied of the laud and Mita sensed this and dismissed the women and Nur also left us, and when we were alone my beloved reached under her raiment and pulled forth a poniard and the sight of it burdened my heart with memories and this sufferance I concealed under a pretense of delight.

Its scabbard was bejeweled with topazes and amethysts and its hilt was inlaid with mother-of-pearl and on its blade of damascened steel was writ in Arabic: "Conquer, then forbear."

She fastened the belt around me and fingered the hilt of the knife and said, "This is the second poniard a woman has given you. Remember always that the first betrayed you."

"I will never forget." (I had, in the grip of my lust, revealed to her one night the story of Maraela's poniard.) "You are foolish to give thought to any other woman." And I sought to amuse her by quoting the Moslem proverb: "Women are an evil, but the greatest evil of all is that they are necessary."

She did not esteem my attempt at levity and tossed her head in annoyance. "So spake The Messenger and yet he had thirteen wives."

"And Solomon had a thousand." I, too, was irked. "And David a harem and the men of your people thank God in prayer that they are not women——"

"And the women of my people thank God we are as we are." The devils of her temper were in her eyes and I saw them there and took warning.

"Hold, Mita. Let us not quarrel on the eve of my leave-taking." I pulled her to me and kissed her mouth and her lips were cold, and then they were warm as I fondled her.

"Let us not," she said and seized my ear between her teeth and cooed. "But you will wear my poniard in Valladolid, and if you return not from Spain——"

"I shall return from Spain. If God so wills——"

"It is not God who will keep you in Spain."

"Aroint, woman!" She was vexing me into exasperation. "Your jealousy is a serpent. Did not Maraela Harana send my father into Quemadero's embrace? She is an evil djinn——"

"It is not Maraela Harana who troubles me." Quickly, adroitly, she maneuvered me to the defensive. "I can contest with any woman for your love. A fie for that Judaizing converso. It is no woman I fear, Rodrigo. It is the sea and Andalusia, for you are a Spaniard, and the turban never changes the heart of a Spaniard."

Then she gave me no moment for reply, but smothered my words with her lips and led me to my apartment and there we remained the day and the night, and when dawn came she did help me into the doublet again and fastened the poniard at my side and we summonsed our litter and were borne to the harbor. There my chartered fishing craft rode its anchor and the horses were forward, and secured, and the `crew of three awaited my commands while eying the two knives of Nur in obvious apprehension.

I instructed my mamluk to go forward and be near the horses and he cleansed himself and faced Mecca and prayed and then stepped timidly to the deck, for he feared the sea.

Mita clung to me and we exchanged vows again and troth to everlasting love and resolutely did I swing aboard and I was light of foot for the first time in years, and I commanded the crew to hoist the anchor and get her under-way.

We moved out and the mist rolled in from the Pillars of Hercules and Mita was hidden in the mist, and then the shore was hidden and I was bound for Spain once more.

I seldom spoke to the crew, as they needed no commands, but spent my time with the horses, for Nur was frightened into uselessness. He prepared my food in the Moslem manner, but ate nothing for himself and spent most of his time asking me the direction of Mecca and crying out:

"*Ash-hadu La ilada illa Allah, Mohammed rasul Allah.*"

We raised Cabo Trafalgar by moonlight and the next twilight brought us to the sandy spit on which Cadiz is built and we rounded the point and into the roadstead and it swarming with caravels for the New World, and the caravels with men at arms and sailors.

Several functionaries stared at us, at my turban and at Nur's crimson girdle, but they molested us not, for surely no enemy was so bold as to sail into the harbor as we had done and come to anchor under the bombards of Spain. Deliberately, and without haste, Nur led the horses ashore and then lifted our water cask to his shoulder and deposited it on a wharf and filled our bottles as no man of my station would drink the water of Cadiz because, as you know, it is the worst water in all the world. The city has only one spring, and it under the cathedral, and all other fresh water must be trapped in cisterns or fetched from the mainland.

I clapped my hands and Nur took a purse from under his burnoose and paid the fishermen and then he saddled our horses, and the Spaniards gasped their envy, for my stirrups were of gold.

"A potentate," one called to another in the tongue of my beloved Andalusia. "I'll wager he is to see the King."

"And I'll warrant that Ferdinand will steal those stirrups." The reply brought uncouth laughter.

327

"Do Moslems now sail into Cadiz as though we have not wrest this place from their infernal hands? Fetch me pork rind that I might toss it to them and thereby welcome them to Christendom."

I was glad that Nur understood no Spanish, lest a fight incur, and I was perturbed muchly that one of the fools might toss pork at us and therewith send my mamluk into murderous craze.

"Harass them not," a captain ordered. "One is a prince and a Morisco, for he wears a doublet and not the burnoose. The other is his slave. And princes travel where they choose to travel."

I pretended to understand none of the words and mounted and rode away toward the mainland and Nur did follow me, his head high and he deigning not a glance at the unclean infidels.

We stopped the night at a hostelry beyond Cadiz, and I was admitted because my appearance and bearing bespoke a Morisco and my purse bespoke power, and Nur did rent three rooms of the place that I might have my comforts and he a room in which to fire his brazier and prepare my food.

I supped alone and then, our bodies nourished, Nur came to me and recited the Creed for his own blessing and then instructed me to recite it, and this the privilege of a Moslem slave.

And he nodded his head as I spake:

"I believe in God.

"I believe in God's angels, in Gabriel, in Azrael, in Israfel, and in Michael.

"I believe in God's books—the Pentateuch of Moses, the Psalms of David, the Gospel of Jesus, and the Koran of Mohammed.

"I believe in God's prophets and the greatest of these are Adam, Noah, Abraham, Moses, Jesus, and Mohammed, and Jesus being the Sinless One and Mohammed being The Messenger.

"I believe in the resurrection of the body and in the last day.

"I believe in the predestination of good and evil."

Nur ended the recitation by quoting a sura and then said to me, " 'Tis well, master. Each day in this evil land we must recite the Creed. And now the blessings of Allah for the night."

He snuffed out the lamp and sat by me until I was asleep.

Thus we traveled north for Valladolid, riding fast, and sleeping only when fatigue was upon us and Nur could find rooms that satisfied his demands. My horse stirred the red dust of my Andalusia and I drank the dust with the air and I was strengthened, and my soul was uplifted at the sight of the red hills and the olive groves, the white sheep and the black cattle. This was my home, this soil my sinews, this sky my crown, and yet this I must deny myself.

I led the way through Marchena, purposely avoiding Seville else my memories lie too heavily upon me and distress me, and we crossed the Guadalquivir River and Nur wondered aloud why God blessed the infidel with so much water and the faithful with so little.

Into Estremadura we hastened and thence through Salamanca, and I in reverence of the great university and in remembrance of Benjamin Marino, and I blessed his name because he had sired my beloved.

It was in Salamanca, the last asylum of tolerance in all Spain, that a sentry challenged me and demanded my passport and quickly I motioned to Nur to sheathe his knives and then I loosed my scorn upon the soldier. "Fetch your captain, you pig of *putas*." I glared down at him. "Fetch your captain, you dolt, that he may know you have challenged Mudarra the merchant."

The sentry was frightened. "Whither, my lord? 'Tis only my duty. Therefore, whither?"

"To Valladolid, you fool. Is that not where King Ferdinand holds court?"

"Then pass, sire. And forgive me and report me not." He waved us on and was in a sweat, fearing his captain's wrath that he had dared stop a personage of such obvious merit.

Nur laughed at the incident and boasted of how his knives hungered for Christian trophies, but his boasts trailed into silence as we entered Old Castile and approached Valladolid, the roadway swarming soldiers and the city itself filled with nobles and ministers and all of them swaggering their pride. For this was the court of Ferdinand, the city in which he schemed to thwart the Hapsburgs, his own mad daughter and her Prince Charles, in which he contrived to hold in his own greedy hands the scepters of the dual monarchy and preserve Spain for Spaniards. He and Isabel had united Europe's first nation, had drawn people together by common interests and held them together by bigoted nationalism, and this dignified in the name of patriotism. But Isabel was gone. The brain and the heart of the realm was dead, and already Germanic aliens, the loathsome Hapsburgs, had their clumsy feet in the doorway to Spain's throne room.

Nur forgot his disdain and gawked like a provincial at the thin Toledo swords in the windows of the armorers' shops, at the plumes of the lords, and the uncovered faces of the ladies. We kept a tight rein on our horses and moved slowly through the city and by the church of Santa Maria la Antigua and the College of Santa Cruz and the university that had been moved to Valladolid from Palencia.

My mamluk found an acceptable residence near the church of San Pablo and gave a most generous purse that we occupy it immediately and that the owner move into a hostelry and, thereby, assure us privacy. Nur stabled our horses in a stall behind the residence and tended them before he tended me.

He asked me the direction of Mecca and then fashioned a kibla in my room and one for his own, and only then did he bathe me and trim my beard and dust the red earth of Spain from my velvet doublet.

The afternoon was half spent when I went forth to find the residence of Christopher Columbus and this was no task as all knew his abode and, for a blanca, a ribald led me to the place and begged from me an extra blanca, and this I gave as the sores of the plague already were upon his skin.

For an interval I looked at the house and it was shabby. My slaves lived in better quarters than this and I was filled with disgust, for Christopher Columbus was not a poor man even though he feigned indigence. The walk led into a patio and stalls were on both sides and a hogpen at the far end, and over the stalls were the apartments.

I held my nose and stepped gingerly as I passed the pigsty and found the steps near the rear of the patio and mounted them, and they creaked under my bulk.

The first door was awry and the first room was empty and littered with filth and I proceeded along the balcony until I came to a door that was latched. The shutters were drawn and about the place was the odor of human habitation, of grease and garlic and sweat. I tugged tight my doublet and felt my poniard and then I pounded on the door with the authority of one who demanded admittance.

Maraela herself answered the summons and only my determined imperturbability prevented an immediate revelation of my identity because, thank God, my face did not reflect the agitation within me. She was more beautiful than I had remembered her to be, lovelier than the gossamers of boyhood dreams; the woman I hated was more covetable than the girl I had loved.

Her hair still was primrose yellow and her eyes as blue as the noons

330

of Andalusia. She was taller than Mita, her loins more seductive, and her breasts swelling full within her bodice.

She glanced at me and instinctively a haunting dread darted into her eyes and then she peered at me and said, "Yes?"

"I have called to see The Very Magnificent Lord Don Christopher Columbus." My voice was much deeper than she could have remembered it and although my Spanish was fluent and proper I deliberately flavored it with Arabic accents. "He requested that I wait upon him."

"Then you are Mudarra." Again she looked at me and the dread had passed into perplexity.

"At your command." I bowed most gallantly and said, "And who speaks my name, if the privilege of query is mine?"

"I am Maraela Harana, the ward of Don Christopher." She did not curtsy, but continued to stare at me, full into my eyes and then at my turban and heavy beard. "You will follow me, if it pleases you. And you will forgive me that I bent not to your elegant bow, but it is the way of Christians never to bend to Moslems."

"It is the way of Moors always to bend to ladies." I stepped within the room.

She tossed her head at my jest and led me across the room and down a hallway and to a door, and this she opened and entered and left me standing in the hallway as though I were a ware-monger begging a sale and not the renowned Mudarra whose assistance her guardian sought. I took no offense, however, knowing my hour would come and waited patiently until she opened the door again and bade me enter.

Christopher Columbus was standing by his writing table and his hand upon the table and trembling. Merciful God! The toll the years can take. I had not seen him since the death of Pinzon, and could this specter be the Admiral of the Ocean Sea, he who had stood his quarter-deck the night of San Salvador?

His hair was as white as the snows of Thule and his body was contorted into the agony of gnomish affliction. His eyes were glazed by a film of opacity and almost sightless and his teeth were gone and his lips sunk to his withered gums.

Maraela presented me as Mudarra the Moor and Columbus nodded stiffly and said, "You will profit for answering my command that you wait upon me, although you are the first Moslem ever to cross my threshold."

331

I salaamed to The Very Magnificent Lord. "And you, sire, are the first admiral I ever have bothered to wait upon. Therefore, you should inform yourself and know that Mudarra is not a Moslem but a Morisco." It was a cunning of the lips and not a lie of the heart.

"By San Fernando!" His face testified his pleasure. "This, indeed, is welcome intelligence, for this is a Christian household. I go this very afternoon to the court and this truth will shame those who jeered me because I sought a business alliance with a Moslem." He rubbed his dry, bony hands together and cackled his jubilation. "You met my ward ——" He gestured toward Maraela.

"The pleasure all was mine," I said.

She smiled at my subtlety and some of the strain was gone from her face albeit her eyes remained full upon me, and then she excused herself and left us.

Columbus felt for his chair and sat down and waved me to a bench, but first I stepped close to him, and his breath was fetid, and presented my gifts. "The horn," I explained, "is from an ox of Israel."

"Spanish oxen are better." He lifted the horn close to his eyes and examined it, feeling the pearls and apparently not impressed at all that the trophy came from the land of Abraham, the land sacred to all Jews.

"The quill," I said, "is from a bird of Cathay."

That, too, he examined and put it aside. "I have seen the birds of the East, for, as you know, I discovered the Indies. But I have seen no birds of this plumage."

I subdued the pride that urged for expression and went to the bench and sat down and I was disappointed that my delicate ruse was lost upon his callous inherence. He twisted his head to one side like a spurless cockerel and reached out and felt my doublet and grunted. His own doublet was splotched with stains of soup and the grease of abominable pork and the grease was offensive to my eyes and nostrils.

"You must know——" The arrogance of the man, the vulgarism. "You must know that I will go this afternoon to court. I have arranged audience with personages of influence. Perhaps even the King will summons me. You are prepared to remain in Valladolid for some time, of course."

"As long as I consider necessary." My pride would not be stilled.

"That will be at least a week. You are prepared to talk business and terms?"

"If it profits me."

"I have no money." He put his hands to his head and whined the pharisaism. "I have been robbed by willful men. But only I have the key to the Indies and I will sail again, this time for the strait that connects the Ocean Sea to the Indian Sea."

"Your infirmities will not preclude a voyage?"

He glowered at me and his voice rose like the whinny of a frightened horse and cracked into a cackle. "My bones ache the suffering with which Spain has rewarded her admiral, but my will is indomitable. I will sail again, and with my sons—the stalwart Diego and the nimble Ferdinand. You may share in this enterprise."

"It is a matter for much discussion, sire. And I will await your return from court before revealing the terms you will meet. I am quite capable of patronizing an expedition and I will mandate a voyage if it pleases me."

He grumbled his displeasure of my firm pronouncement. "The court awaits me, and you will await my summons to converse." Then he pushed himself from his chair and scuttled across the floor like a sand crab and pounded on the door and called for Maraela.

She came to him and he spake like a master to a menial. "You will see to the wants of our guest. Food. Drink. His needs." Then he turned to me. "I regret I cannot offer you lodgings in this house, but forsooth, these mean walls are not worthy of one so affluent." He motioned for his cloak and Maraela put it around his shoulders, and most tenderly, and he limped along the balcony and to the steps, and then across the patio to the street; a fallen god who had lived too long.

Maraela watched him go and looked up at me. "He is a man of many infirmities, but you will not allow his decrepitude to influence your decisions. His sons are capable of any enterprise."

I returned to the bench and rested my hands on my knees and gave my mind to the problem at hand.

She stood before me, pondering my face. "I shall fetch food and wine, if it pleases you."

"The solicitude pleases me into artless reverie, but I already have dined and I take not wine as it languishes my humors and tends me to corpulence."

333

She sat in his chair and rested her arm on his table and toyed with the inkhorn I had fetched him, feeling the pearls as lovingly as he had done. "Do all Moors wear doublets as elegant as yours? And poniards so bejeweled?"

I was startled within myself at the precipitation of my hap, for she had opened the snare and had placed it around her neck. I gave myself an interlude to compose my eagerness and fingered the poniard. "A bauble for my attire. A gift from a lady of exquisite discernment and much wealth."

"Your wife?" There was a breathless urgency in her question.

"I am unwed and this poniard is not a troth." I raised my eyes from the blade and to hers and sweetened my tone into a longing and a loneliness. "But once I had a poniard as my troth. It was given to me by a maid and then her father took her away from me——"

"Rodrigo!" She sprang from the chair and stood trembling before me and I feared her to swoon and arose quickly and supported her shoulders with my arm. "I knew it! I knew it!" Her face twisted into a grimace of dismay. "Has the grave opened and sent forth its ghost to accuse me?"

"Accuse you?" I pretended bewilderment and cradled her chin in my hand. "Whyfor should I accuse you? Does a man wait his life and then travel from a far land to accuse his dream to be of unwholesome substance?"

My tone, my guile, loosed the panic from her, but apprehension and suspicion were in its stead and her Circean eyes clouded and then brightened and thus revealed to me the machinations of her wits. "You witnessed my Judaizing. My father compelled me to the heresy." Her mind was as nimble as Don Christopher's, as cunning. "I was pottage in my father's hands."

I drew away from her and sat on the bench and willed my impression into an image of subjection and accessibility. "Your loneliness has conceived a senseless fear. Have I journeyed so far only to see a mote in the sweet eyes that have warmed my dreams? Had I found you wedded or trothed I would have turned away, for I came to look again upon your beauty and not to wait upon your guardian at all. I came as Mudarra and as Mudarra I would have gone away."

All the apprehension went out of her demeanor, but the suspicion lingered and she pressed her hind to the table and leaned against it in a gesture most wanton. "You witnessed my Judaizing and did not report it. Therefore, you share my guilt."

"That is true, Maraela. It is the one thing I have been privileged to share with you, and the secret was locked in my heart many years gone and has long since evaporated into the memories of childhood. So, whyfor should I accuse you?"

"Mayhaps you think I fled Seville to be away from you. That, too, my father compelled." She hesitated and then dared flaunt a lie. "And your own father, Rodrigo. He entreated us to leave to spare you the burden of our transgression."

"My father is dead." I said it slowly and watched her face for a disclosure of her perfidy, but she unmasked no hint thereof. "The Inquisition judged him for selling sacrificial meats to the Jews. I know not the particulars because my shame was so heavy upon me that I renounced his name."

All the light was back in her eyes and even the cunning was hidden by her sudden confidence that my stratagem nourished. She walked toward me, her hips and shoulders flowing into a rhythm, and she sat by me on the bench and her voice came mournful and forlorn. "I am sad that you had to know. The Dominicans accused him and the Inquisition proved his guilt; both he and Mudarra——" She gasped and pressed her hands to her cheeks. "*Mudarra!* You assumed his name."

"Aye." The pattern was weaving as I had prayed it. "And his sonship that I might live in peace among the Moslems."

"But you have umbrage against Don Christopher. I know that you sailed with him and have heard that you did assume offense and did curse his name and that, in your impetuosity, you renounced this realm and even Christendom."

" 'Tis true." I locked my hands around my knee and rocked as though in meditation although I knew well my recitation. "A moment opens a wound, but time tends it and love heals it. I was the first to see the New Land, Maraela, but Don Christopher denied me the rewards and I was embittered. I had sought you and could not find you and in my mania I deserted this land, and to Tangier, where I prospered. I was accounted dead and truly Rodrigo of Triana was dead until I heard that you were with Don Christopher, and then life came back to my soul."

335

"You have forgiven my guardian?" She spake it softly, a sensuality in her inflection.

"Forgive? Could I hold hatred of one who has sheltered you? The promised reward was a velvet doublet and the Queen's pension." I smiled my amusement. "Why, Maraela, I pay menials more than the Queen's pension and my doublets are woven on the looms of Tuscany."

"It has troubled him," she said. "That he, an admiral, should deny a sailor a reward that would have taken naught from him and yet would have meant so much to one so worthy."

"Then whyfor?"

She looked down at my hands, at my brown flesh and a ring on every finger and my nails lacquered red, and then at her hands, white and without jewels, and her fingers long and tenuous. "Only those who know him can understand. It was a mania of manhood fain to be immortalized and now it is senile dementia. To him, the Indies are his, to have and to hold forever. He could not admit that another man first saw the land and, forsooth, he already had seen the Light of San Salvador." She privileged me to touch her hand and then withdrew it from my clasp and, bowing her head in demure prudery, she spake winsomely: "My father died soon after we left Seville and I was alone. I yearned to send for you and, yet, in my sin of Judaizing I forswore the longing lest I taint you and endanger you of the Inquisition. It was then I went to a kinswoman in Cordova, and she is Beatriz Harana and the mother of Don Christopher's son, of Ferdinand. I was loyal to my own and when Don Christopher needed one to tend him, to prepare his food else he be poisoned, it was I who sacrificed my youth to this service. He has been kind to me, Rodrigo. Therefore you have come not to harass him or degrade him. Say 'tis true. Grant my ears the welcomed assurance and my soul the tranquillity of your promise."

Again I took her hand and she suffered it to my fervid caress. "That a bosom so pure should lay upon it a tribulation so figmental. 'Tis a shame. Now, hear me: I had instructed my scribes to contain my regrets in an answer to Don Christopher's letter that I wait upon him. And then, and God be thankful, I heard that you attended him, and forthwith I hastened to this place."

"You will aid him?"

"And how?" I lifted out my hands in Islam's gesture of interrogation. "He is too old to take ships to voyage. He is too near the ghost."

336

She moved close to me and her thigh was against my thigh and she seized my hand and pressed it to her bosom. "That I know. But heed! The viceroyalty of the Indies is his by contract and a per centum of all profits therefrom. If he had a rich patron to press his claims——" She turned her face to mine and the glint of avarice sparkled her eyes and her lips were near and daring. "His heirs would be rich beyond all measure and I surely am an heir, and I could come to you as a great lady of this realm rather than an indigent ward."

I took her lips and fused my hatred into my lust and she responded to my caresses in tremulous ardor and then she placed her hands on my chest and pushed me from her. "Is this mean abode to be my bower? Is my master to take his slave with her shame covered only by coarse raiment? I dreamed of silk for your touch."

I said, "This abode is a palace because you are here. And your beauty transforms calicut into silk."

She stood and smiled at me and closed her eyes in a gesture of histrionic surrender. "My maidenly constraint cannot prevail against your threws."

And then she turned and walked toward her chamber and I went to Columbus' table and composed a message to Nur that he should trouble not about my absence, and thence to the patio where an urchin was cleaning a stable. I dispatched the message to my mamluk and returned to the admiral's room and removed my poniard and doublet and tossed them on his table.

And then I went to her chamber in anticipation of her divestment, but, nay, she was fully clothed and in silk and her garments I removed, yet all the time I was remembering a thing Mita had said: "A worthy love always uncovers herself and never in haste."

But Maraela compelled me even to unshod her feet and then I took my pleasure and the image of Mita was before me, taunting me that my fidelity had strangled itself in this sordid morass.

It was done. A man had consummated the ardor of which he had dreamed in his pubescence, and to all men who yearn to go back to the flowers they dared not debud in their youth, I say this: it is of no account, for the anticipation is of more delight than the act—a beautiful fancy that the fact makes ugly.

I could not, in my emptiness, bring myself to embrace Maraela and she looked at me in the infinite wisdom of her sex and then stood before me and, in dramatic grandeur, spake another lie. "The sacred ves-

337

sel is broken, my love. Vesta has fled her temple for the coming of Eos, and now I am a woman possessed of man."

I feigned credulity and bowed down to her else she read my thoughts and know that I was amused by her deception and then, in a lustful delirium, I lifted her and bore her into Don Christopher's room and there and upon his very table I occupied her again.

And, now, all that night I remained with her and the next day I listened for hours to her grandiose plans for both of us and to her scheme for Mudarra to sponsor Christopher Columbus in his claims against the Crown, and all the next night, and on the third day I gave her gold that she might purchase food for us and a silken shawl for herself.

She was bubbling gaiety when she came back with news that Don Christopher would return that afternoon; and then I did send a message to Nur that he prepare our baggage and saddle the horses and be ready to flee at twilight.

CHRISTOPHER COLUMBUS SHUFFLED INTO THE ROOM AND SLAMMED shut the door in the irascibility that was his nature and nodded abruptly to me and glanced at Maraela, then stared at her and quickly at me, and hobbled to his chair, mumbling a soliloquy while graveolent spittle drooled from the corners of his mouth.

Maraela was restless in obvious want that I address him immediately, but calmly I sat the bench and awaited his brunt, as I had learned in business and conflict that he who speaks first seldom speaks last.

Eventually, aware that I would give him no advantage in converse, he wiped his mouth on the sleeve of his doublet and spake, "The King did not grant me audience and I weary of the vicissitudes of court. Therefore, I will entertain a proposal that you mandate a voyage for me. My terms——"

I held up my hand and interrupted him. "I will speak the terms, Don Christopher." Maraela inhaled her surprise at the tone of my voice and a vestige of apprehension drooped her confidence. I gave my back to her and stood before Columbus and spake forthrightly: "Look closely at me, sire, and awaken your memory and tell me what you see."

He scowled and peered at me. "I see a gluttonous drake that is too fat for agility. Be seated, as I propose to discuss business and not your appearance."

That was a grievous blunder, for, as you surely have surmised, my obesity was my humiliation and this affront surged my humors into temper. I was welling a curse to pronounce upon his house when Maraela, agitated by the course that events were taking, interjected

339

herself into the matter. "Don Christopher," she pleaded. "Mercy upon me, my lord. He is not a Moor, but the amorist of my pubescence—one long lost to me who now has come for me. He is Rodrigo of Triana who sailed with you——"

"Mother of Mercy!" His mouth sagged and his chin quivered and, despite his infirmities, he sprang from the chair and stood before me, trembling as though of a palsy. "The sailor! The lookout on the *Pinta*——"

"The one who first saw land!" I loosed the initial shaft of my retaliation and then turned upon Maraela and commanded, "Stand at his side, vile harpy, that the vengeance of Mudarra may fall equally upon you."

"Apostate!" She shrieked the word at me. "I am betrayed!" She dart to his side for sustainment and jerked frantically at his arm. "He wooed me, sire, and spake a troth. He is a devil come to adjudge us both."

The minute was of sweet relish to me and my hand was on my poniard and my feet were braced wide. "Sacred vessel," I jeered. "An urn shaped by divers hands. And now that you have callously divulged your wanton submission, I tell you this: I return soon to the woman predestined for my life, a Jewess whose convictions are not temporized. And hold! If I am pressed, then all Christendom shall know that Mudarra, once a lowly sailor, has scorned the lust of an admiral's ward that he might bind himself forever to a Jewish waif in Tangier."

Columbus was stunned to muteness by the signification of my flaunt, but Maraela's face contorted her hatred and her tongue hissed its venom. "Gross Gog and spawn of Magog. If the seed within me stir to life, then your own image will curse your name and haunt you to the Day of Judgment."

I ridiculed her malisons and Columbus did bestir himself from his stupor. "This is the knave who publicly blasphemed both Church and State. Summons the King's soldiery, girl. Flee for succor and I will hold him here at the point of my admiral's sword." And thus saying, he withdrew his sword and brandished it.

I laughed my contempt of the bravado and the ludicrous gesture of an awkward blade in the withered hand of a dottering old man. "Aye, Maraela. Summons the King's butchers that they may seize you for Judaizing. That the Inquisition may know that Spain's admiral has shielded a Judaizer and taken her as ward. And this the consummate evidence that he himself is of Abraham's brood."

The admiral's sword drooped in his hand and clattered to the floor and he felt for his chair and slumped into it, and his misery was pitiable. "She was only a child in the transgression——"

"Child? She was old enough to plague my manliness with her swelling breasts and hungry loins. Old enough to contrive herself into your favor that she might scheme for an inheritance. Old enough to betray my father and the bones of her own father into the Inquisition's fire to achieve her disguise of a true believer. Old enough——"

"But you witnessed my malpractice," she shouted. "And reported it not. Therefore, you share my guilt."

"Then let Spain's King lay hand upon Mudarra the Moor and bring Islam's hordes swarming to the jihad. This I dare."

Her shrill bared her panic and she cowered to the bench and sank down and wailed her lamentations. Columbus clung to his table for support and called upon God to witness his misery and persecution and then, having spoken the name of God, he straightened from his debility and spake clearly his resolution. "Silence, Maraela! Silence I say, and by San Fernando! This rogue has want of us, or else he would not be here. He is a Moslem monger who puts trade before honor. We will treat with him." And upon saying, he faced me in vehement boldness. "What do you seek of us?"

"The truth. Only the truth and my just rewards."

"You shall have the truth." The words came as clear as his commands the night of Salvador. "You called me of Abraham's brood. That is falsehood. Wiser men than you have conspired in this calumny and to no avail. My life is my witness and a fie for the dastardly canards of ghouls. Therefore, you have one arraignment against this house—the dereliction of a child who now is a woman. One charge you have and one boon you will receive in bargain for your vow to silence."

"You feel for the shaft that is mine." I taunted him. "You would turn upon me my own lance. I will make the terms——"

"You will accept terms. You will vow to silence by the beard of your false prophet and by the Cross of the true Christ whom you have renounced. This woman has tended me in my infirmities and I will not forsake her save I be driven to desperation by your villainy, and then I will send both of you to the Inquisition and confess the sanctuary I gave her, and challenge all Christendom to judgment of my charity. So speak. One boon you have of me."

I believed him not. It was a stratagem to outwit me and I pondered his ultimatum while he held me fast in his contemplation, and Mara-ela was hushed and watched us. Should I die at Quemadero, Islam well might sound a holy war, for I had been pledged security by a lord of Spain's Christian realm. But of what service is a reprisal to a carcass? And martyrdom was not my inclination. One meed I was promised. Then mayhaps another I could inveigle.

This was the tide for me to shuffle off the fetters of my vanity and speak forth for Mita, to vindicate and immortalize the name of Benjamin Marino as the sage whose genius had shown Columbus the way —but, nay, I thought first of myself.

And so I put paper before Christopher Columbus and dipped his quill into ink and said, "You shall write."

"Whyfor?" he demanded. "And what?"

"The complement of the caravel *Pinta* on your first voyage across the Ocean Sea."

"The names have flown my fancy." He poised the quill above the paper. "The Pinzons I remember. And the Quintero brothers. A helmsman named Arcos and a rascal named Gomez Rascon. And you. But the others——"

"I remember them, sire. Thus you will write: Martin Alonso Pinzon, captain; Francisco Martin Pinzon, master——"

Wherewith he writ as I commanded and the names flowed in hallowed resonance from my reverie. Garcia Xalmiento. Juan de Umbria and Juan de Jerez. Francisco Garcia and Francisco Gallego. Juan Bermudez. And The Rabbit. Of course The Rabbit and the stalwart Arcos. My own name I spake proudly and in this manner: Rodrigo of Triana, of Lepe—the one who called out "Land!"

For only a moment did he hesitate, and then he inscribed for the ages:

Rodrigo de Triana, de Lepe (*el que canto "Tierra!"*).

I took the precious document and folded it into my sleeve and now I must speak for the perpetuation of Benjamin Marino's eminence that the name of Mita's father could take its place rightfully beside mine. But by the djinn of conjury, Christopher Columbus gave me no hap for speech, for he broke the quill between his fingers and cast it aside and addressed me in a placidity that muted my tongue:

"This I will tell you, and then you will begone—you did not see it first. I saw the Light of San Salvador and the light was land."

"Confusion seize, trickster! There was no light. A storm raged and we were thirty miles from shore."

"I saw the Light of San Salvador." There was an unearthly light in his own eyes and this did hold me as though in sorcery, and Maraela, also, for her face was uplifted to him and in the radiance of adoration.

By bent of my will I freed my tongue from the shackles of his conjuration and challenged him again. "A storm and night and thirty miles. Yet you saw. Then whyfor no other eyes save yours, the admiral who coveted all honors."

"Because you had no faith." His dispassion will haunt me beyond the portals of Paradise. Erect he was and stooped no more, and his eyes through me and beyond me and into the west. "Thirty miles or thirty leagues, of what matter is this? Is a miracle bound by time or space? The Pinzons looked to chart and compass, for they, even as you, were without faith and had pendency only in the frail instruments of man's own making. But I looked to the stars and put away the charts and trusted the promise of my God that all things are possible in faith, for if faith can move mountains it can open seas. And then the birds came and I followed the birds, and there the Light of San Salvador." He was smiling the remembrance, and I in the thrall of a great awe, and again he spake and without rancor. "Now begone, you who saw the land but were denied the Light. Leave us to our years—an old man to his memories and a woman to her regrets."

It was not within me to utter protest or to endeavor persuasion. My hands were stronger than his, yet his spirit had bested me. I glanced at his admiral's sword upon the floor, and the sweat of his hand and the salt of the sea had tarnished its hilt, and my malignity goaded me to press it underfoot and to spit upon it; but hear this: I stooped.

Rodrigo of Triana, Mudarra the Moor, bent his knee before Christopher Columbus and lifted the sword and placed it upon the table and regressed from their presence, and Maraela pulled her garb close to her feet else I touch it and foul it.

Out of the room, and the door I closed softly, and down the steps and across the patio and only then did the trance lift itself from me and I hastened to Nur and the horses were ready.

"Did you recite the Creed each day, master?" my mamluk said to me.

"I did. And now away from this accursed place."

We rode fast from Valladolid and I in a trepidation lest Columbus scheme a chicane to protect his ward and set the King's soldiery after me, and so I decided to return not by Salamanca and the way I had come, but straight for Portugal and the asylum of that kingdom. And in my anxiety we took the back trails of the gypsies and our journey was slow and laborious and we entered Portugal far to the north, thence down the border and avoiding the cities, and I nigh unto exhaustion when we reached the sea at Vila Real de Santo Antonio.

Andalusia was only a few strides away and Lepe an hour's ride and there I might learn the destiny of my Aunt Ronda, and then Palos and the fate of Arcos, and trod once more the sweet earth of my youth, but, nay, I dared not and knew that Spain was lost to me forever.

Only a pallet of filthy straw could Nur find for me in the village and no food acceptable to a Moslem save brinish olives, but he made me as comfortable as God had willed and went forth to charter a vessel and this a task of three days, and on June 6 we did depart that place and, bless the good winds, did reach Tangier in two days, and this at twilight.

My stallion was lame and I left him with Nur and took the palfrey and hastened to my house and darkness was about me before I reached its safety, and Mita was in the patio and a lamp near her head as she gazed toward the sea and Spain.

I called to her and my voice was choked and she ran to me and into my embrace, binding herself to me like a child long lost in the desert and at last found by one who loves it.

We said naught for a time, but each weeping our joy, and then she spake: "You saw him?"

"Aye. And he himself did write that 'twas I who first called 'Land,' and this treasure I have brought home."

"And the woman? What of Maraela Harana?"

"She was not in Valladolid. I saw her not." The lie came easy, for the addiction to mendacity is liken unto a leech which sucks the conscience into a torpor.

Mita looked at me and there was no accusation in her eyes, only a wonderment, and then she said, "And my father? Did Columbus admit that he followed my father's maps and charts?"

"I know now that he did not follow the maps of Benjamin Marino." This lie did not come easy. "They were in his possession as I have told you, but he followed them not. Of this he convinced me." I could not look into her face for fear my own eyes would betray my craven duplicity.

She took my hand and led me to a table in the patio and lifted the lamp and studied my face, then dampened the tip of her shawl on her tongue and removed some of the dirt from my face and kissed my cheek. "Forsooth, he did not use my father's maps. I should have known as much the many years hence when I accused him falsely."

"Oh? And what is this you say?" A suspicion gnawed my caution and a dread was upon me.

"The truth came to me after your departure and in my solitude as I watched the sea and awaited your return. Did my father's maps not show new land to be beyond the Ocean Sea?"

"Aye. *Terra incognita.*"

"Then had Columbus followed my father's maps to land he would have believed my father, and would have known it was a new land and not the Indies."

Her induction was beyond refutation, and my deception had been without meaning or avail and this bitter knowledge greatened my remorse, albeit I did not confess my transgression to her but determined to resign the judgment to the mercy of God.

" 'Tis true," I said and watched her face in the light of the lamp. "Your logic exalts your wisdom. I should have so reasoned from the first. I should have known."

She came close to me and found strength in my propinquity and my arm was around her shoulder and she shuddered. "The steel of this irony strikes deep into my heart, Rodrigo. The truth was in his hands, for my father gave him the truth. But, wherefore he had faith in no man save himself, he knew not that he had discovered a new world and died in ignorance of his true attainment, verily of his own greatness."

My thoughts were confined to my useless turpitude and then her words nettled my abstraction and awakened my wits. "Dead! Is Columbus dead?"

"Aye." She was perplexed by my surprise. "You did not know?"

"When?" I seized her arm and peered into her eyes. "He was enfeebled when I saw him, but death was not nigh."

"He died on May 20. I assumed you knew——"

"Three days after my departure." I almost whispered it. "He died three days after I left him, Mita. And I heard naught because I

345

escaped into Portugal and thence to the sea through the back country." I shook my head to arouse my reason and dispel my exhaustion. "The admiral dead? Whence came this intelligence to you?"

She left me and soon was returned with a communication from Di Negro and Spinola, an informatory document that they sent at intervals to all houses of trade in Spain, in Portugal, and in Italy. "It came three days past," she said. "From your agent in Cadiz."

I unrolled the scroll on the table and pulled close the lamp and did read these bruits, perusing rapidly the entries to reach the news I sought:

In London, Prince Henry, who will be England's eighth king of that name if he survives his father, has betrothed himself to the widowed Catherine of Aragon, whose father, King Ferdinand of Spain, has refused to sanction the troth and perchance will appeal its validity to Mother Church.

In Santo Domingo, Vasco Nunez de Balboa, enterpriser, pleads penury to his debtors and, to re-establish himself, seeks an expedition westward to find a strait between the Ocean Sea and the sea beyond.

In Rome, Seigneur de Bayard, the plume of France's chivalry, has declined papal service to continue his fealty to his king.

In Valladolid, The Very Magnificent Lord Don Christopher Columbus, Admiral of the Ocean Sea, died on May 20, and this the Day of the Ascension; and shriven by Franciscans ere the ghost departed the body; and attended by his sons, Don Diego and Don Ferdinand, and his ward, Maraela Harana. His will attests Don Diego as heir to his property and privileges, and commends to his benevolence the care of his family, especially the ward, Maraela Harana, and the mistress, Beatriz Harana of Cordova.

The testament enjoins Don Diego to increase the entail, to press the family's claims against the Crown and that the family serve the realm and Christendom.

Further, and in the scription of The Admiral: "Don Diego shall watch over the welfare of Beatriz Harana, Don Ferdinand's mother, and see that she is in a position to live as befits a person who is so much on my conscience; and let this be done as a relief to my conscience for it weighs much on my soul, and the reason of it, it is not licit for me to write here. And Don Diego, after having inherited and obtaining possession of this entail, shall sign my signature which I now use, which is an X with an S above, and an M with a Roman A above, and above it an S, and then a Greek Y with an S above it, with their strokes as I do now. And he will sign nothing but The Admiral, even though the King might give him, or he might win, other titles."

The testament was signed thusly:          .S.

.S.A.S.

X M Y

*Requiescat in pace.*

In Paris, King Louis XII . . .

I loosed the scroll and looked up at Mita and there was an empti-
ness within me for I felt that an age had passed, an era into dust.
Then I stared at his signature. "The S for Senor, the Admiral," I said.
"The S.A.S. for Su Alta Senoria, the Viceroy; and X M Y for Excellent,
Magnificent, Illustrious."

"Nay." Mita's face was saddened and her eyes flooded tears. "Signa-
tures do not give titles in the third person. Heed the strange pattern,
Rodrigo. 'Tis the Cabala and in it I see the shield of David."

"Aye? Think you that he came back to his people in the end? That
his soul was Christian, but his heart of Israel?"

She touched her shawl to her eyes and dried them. "He was no Jew,
Rodrigo. Nor Gentile. Neither Spaniard, nor Portuguese or Genoese.
He was of the sea, of the New World he found."

"The judgment is writ," I said. "Now God will weigh his evil."

"And man his greatness," she said. "For none save a great man
could have been hated so bitterly by some people and loved so much
by others."

"Greatness?" I was baffled by her behavior. "Is greatness in duplicity? Is honor in chicanery? 'Twas he who tricked me and but for him
I would be this night in Andalusia."

She rested her head on my chest and her sweet hair was upon my
neck. "Does it matter? For when Abraham mourned his dead he
spake to the sons of Heth and said, 'I am a stranger and a sojourner
with you: give me a possession of a burying-place with you, that I may
bury my dead out of my sight.' Can we say less, Rodrigo?"

I spake not, but held her bound to me and she said, "He was the
span between yesterday and tomorrow, the bridge to a glory he could
not believe. He was named aright. St. Christopher bore the Child
across the stream, but Don Christopher bore the hopes of men across
the Unknown Sea."

She lifted her head from my chest and I prayed her eyes to be
wondrous bright, but they were sad. "Come, Rodrigo. I will prepare
your couch and fetch you sup. And your burnoose. You must back to

your burnoose now, Rodrigo, because the doublet fits neither your valiant shoulders nor your triumphant merit. The garment is shapeless from the stress of your pilgrimage and now is without form or dignity."

There was compassion in her voice and this pity surely for the enemy I had helped pull down—and yet I upbraided her not, but followed her across the patio and in no thought of remonstrance as I was weary of the long journey and grateful that I was with Mita again.

And now, good readers, may the blessings of God attend you, for here I part from you and close this journal and again I am weary; and now of years.

CHAPTER 25

*T*HE LAST TESTAMENT OF MUDARRA OF TANGIER, AND THIS
BEING AN APPENDAGE TO HIS JOURNAL:

> *In the name of God, the Compassionate, the Merciful!*
> *Say: He is God alone:*
> *God the eternal,*
> *He begetteth not, and He is not begotten,*
> *And there is none like unto Him.*

I, Mudarra of Tangier, have ordered that alms be given to the indigent of this city in evidence of my gratitude that I have been spared to finish my journal, and this journal I entrust to the Caliph of Damascus with this admonition: Suffer it not into hands of the Christians lest they destroy it, as they have many documents of Christopher Columbus, or vary it for their own aggrandizement, as they have divers journals and histories.

And now, firstly, I attest these observations as no man has witnessed such an age as I have and none ever shall, for, in my seventy years, I have seen the mysteries of this earth revealed to mankind:

The world is circumnavigated, and this to the glory of Spain, which sent forth Ferdinand Magellan, naturalized from Portugal:

Charles V reigns in Spain, he being the Flemish and Hapsburg heir of our mad Joanna, and the sun sets never on his empire:

Mexico is ours, and Peru, and the Great South Sea between the New World, called Americi, and Asia. Florida is Spanish land and Hernando De Soto is mandated to explore the Great North Continent. Tangier and mostly all of North Africa are Spain's and the conquerors never molest me, for the record of my blasphemy is long forgot in the archives of Seville and even the Andalusians who hold here know not that I am the son of a Goth:

Only Portugal in Africa and India, and France in the Great North Continent test with Spain for empire, albeit England is seeking routes to the Spice Islands and evidences scant concern with the New World:

The Great Schism has rent Christendom and the German states are succumbing to the apostasy of Martin Luther. France is restless under the Mother Church and England is in revolt and the dissenters are demanding separation from a papacy that gave its tiara to a Borgia and a torch to Savonarola:

The Pinzons of Palos have entered suit against the heirs of Christopher Columbus and this a tangle of judicial mesh that is exceeded only by the contests of Columbus' heirs against the Crown of Spain.

And now, secondly, and in dismal bereavement: My Mita is dead and this cruel hap of five years past and before I began my journal:

She died without issue, the Shema on her lips, for truly she took upon herself the Jewish yoke of the Kingdom of Heaven and the yoke of The Law, and, in her last agony, begged my forgiveness that she gave me no son, neither any image of myself, no flesh to immortalize my name.

And now, thirdly, I assign the Caliph of Damascus to execute my will and charge him to dispose my possessions thusly:

One third thereof to the *hebrot* of Milan for the migration of Jews to the Kingdom of the Turks, for they have been banished from all of western Europe and the Turks offer refuge; and this I do in commemoration of my beloved:

One third thereof to the Caliph of Jerusalem for the Mosque of Omar:

One third thereof to the College of Seville and in the name of Juan Ruiz de Medina, and the money to be used to gather data and documents on the First Voyage of Christopher Columbus, and with these records ever shall remain the complement of the caravel *Pinta* as writ by the admiral himself and my own name thereon:

Rodrigo de Triana, de Lepe (*el que canto "Tierra!"*).

And now I say this: Three pilgrimages have I made to Mecca and each of these upon a beast, but on the morrow I set forth again on the hadj, and this time I will ride only to Cairo and then afoot to The Messenger's city, albeit my feet now swell in pain with the weight of my bulk and my jowls hang to my neck and my girth is an abominable encumbrance.

And this I say also: It is a grievous punishment that conscience forbids me to bequeath one blanca on my fortune to the son borne me by Maraela Harana. Neither he nor the world must know that I am his father, for he serves valorously the Spanish cause in the New World. Only one message have I received from his mother, and that many years gone and it a plea that I claim never my son as she had been taken to bride by an excellent hidalgo who accepted my son as his own and bestowed upon him a name of honor.

Of this Mita knew naught, and for this I thank God; and thus I speak for my beloved and for the son I shall never see:

*When the Sun shall be folded up, and when the stars shall fall.*
*And when the wild beasts shall be gathered together,*
*When souls shall be paired with their bodies . . .*

*And when the leaves of the Book shall be unrolled.*
*And when Hell shall be made to blaze, and when*
*Paradise shall be brought near—*
*Every soul shall know what it hath produced.*

*And by the Night when it cometh darkening on,*
*And by the Dawn when it brighteneth . . .*
*Whither then are ye going?*

*Verily this is no other than a warning to all creatures:*
*To him among you who willeth to walk in a straight path.*

*Tangier*                                                     *Mudarra*
*October 15, 1539*